Welcome To The Divide…

.S.P. Daley

...

. . . I . . .

. . . "We" . . .

...

101.01 ...SEE THROUGH PERCEPTIONS DIVISIONS...

...Staring into the oblivion that masquerades as the world around us, we see nothing... Eyes gaze out of a window, into the vacant fields in front of the facility... Everything is cloaked under the cover of overcast night and thick layers of snow... The earth is a blank slate of white, and the sky is an infinite black void... Hanging in the surface of the window before us, our reflection stares back at us, with our shadow cast over it... Reticent and stagnant as the scene we're in; our mind focuses not on the images of blurred/cloaked simulacra, but pierces deeper through the surfaces in view... Our eyes are of little use to us in this view... Under our vacant stare, we contemplate the very nature of our perceptions... Gazing into the abysmal depths of this world as it is reflected back to us, with our own image and shadow impressed upon it; we wonder... How is it we've come to see this way?

Pondering these notions, we seem lost to our-selves... Eventually we might consider the paradigms that may have contributed to our dissociated state, but right now it seems we've become far too accustomed to this depersonalization... Recently, we have begun to note the strangeness of such colloquial norms... Collectively, we have been urged so strongly to consider the views of others as more important than our own... Everyone in general and no one in particular seem to always be urging us; to walk a mile in some other

...

entity's shoes, to be more understanding of others, to remember we are all in this together, &c, &c, &c... Perhaps this has led us away from our-selves, and into some state of imagining our-selves reflected in every other entity's perspective state... This practice of imagining our-selves displaced in others, and others displaced within our-selves can become confusing very quickly... In effect, we project our-selves into others, and imagine observing our-selves through their eyes; as if what we imagine them to imagine of us is what we are... Our own identity ends up being reduced to some sort of composite, of all the entities we imagine seeing in our reflecting-selves... Notions of our own identity are confused with some collective-impressions of what we are as a whole... Somewhere in this collage of confused simulacra we must still exist with some form of identity, separate from this collectivized perspective...

Doesn't there have to be a way to cut our-selves out from this haze of collective-confinement? It seems there must be some way to separate our-selves from the totality of this collective-entity and its intrusive impressions... Visualizing how we might see our-selves in the midst of all this, we imagine blacking out all of the things we are not, so they can't project/reflect any images upon us... Inside this blacked-out world, we see nothing at all... Separated from the truth of our own reflections, we gaze into this darkness... Imposing our shadow upon the surface of every blank snow-covered figure and every reflective-plane, we try to see our-selves in this world... Oblivious as to how we might find our-selves in this darkness, we wonder why we are so compelled to find our-selves at all... Nothing appears to us as if it is everything, and everything seems to be nothing to us now... Seeing anything at all must require some new insight that we have yet to discover... What might there possibly be for us to see? We wonder...

101.02 A FIGURE APPROACHES...

A figure approaches the control-room of the facility, as we stand transfixed in gazing upon these reflections before us... As the figure comes closer, we find it easier to separate it from the background... The figure begins to take shape with more perceptive clarity... It begins to appear as an entity with separate features... These features appear as separate properties, comprised in a way that creates this larger entity... The properties are projected in a unique manner, allowing us to differentiate this figure from others... Each feature is a division of order, and the sum of them cuts through the oblivion of infinite possibilities... After enough division, we can discern the name that precedes the entity of this figure...

It should be noted that at the facility, we are not allowed to identify anyone according to our own perceptions, methods, &c, &c, &c... Instead, each entity must pass through the facility's standardized identification-process... The facility's standardized identification-process consists of several criteria... It is the duty of the security-drone in the control-room to ensure this process is adhered to with strict compliance...

In the event of any deviation from this process, the subject not in compliance is to be denied entry, and such deviations are to be immediately reported to our immediate-supervisor... For more serious cases, we may also be required to notify the director of facility

...

operations (Ronald P. Vincent PhD MD)... Should the process be completed according to the standards outlined in the security-drone manual, no such notifications are to be required... These standards may be altered by authorized-personnel in special-circumstances... Standards for determining such authorities/circumstances are included in the security-drone manual... If a drone is uncertain in any instance, they may contact their superiors...

The first standardized-criteria for authorized-entry to the facility, is the scanning of an entity's proper facility identification-badge... A badge is to be scanned with individualized information pre-coded into it for the entity to which it has been issued... When a badge is scanned, an image associated with the badge-holder is displayed on a screen, along with that entity's name, date of birth, height, weight, &c, &c, &c...

It is the security-drone's responsibility to ensure this descriptive information matches that of the entity attempting to gain entry to the facility... Although it does state in the security-drone manual that drones are not to identify anyone according to perceptions/methods of their own, it also states that they must visually confirm each badge matches the description of the entity that possesses it... This is not officially recognized as a contradictory-precept...

After scanning the appropriate badge in accordance with the facility's requirements, several other actions are to be completed... These include retinal scans, finger-print scanning, a DNA test, dental-imprint matching, voice authentication, &c, &c, &c... If all of the procedures are in compliance with the proper guidelines, access may be granted to the facility... As the security-drone on duty, we are to oversee this entire process... No exceptions are to be allowed at any time, or under any unspecified circumstances according to the security-drone manual...

Successful completion of the authorization-process is followed by the security-drone's procedural response... This response consists of pressing the green button labeled, *authorized*... Due to the facility's computerized-safeguards, the green button will not function until all criteria are met successfully...

Almost all drones are capable of administering this process with acceptable levels of competency... Tasks of this nature are primarily administered by what might be classified as a, *nobody*... A nobody is typically defined as someone associated with administering tasks of this nature... We seem to have become classified as such a non-entity...

Non-entities (or nobodies) such as our-selves, are often associated with a set of generalized features... These indefinite features make it difficult for others to distinguish us as individually-definable entities... Predominantly, there is a visual similarity in nobodies that makes them appear rather indistinct... Defining what is so commonly indistinct in nobodies is actually rather difficult...

It would seem that even nobodies exhibit some degree of variation, but without projecting any uniqueness in their characteristics, overall appearance, presence, &c, &c, &c... Instead, nobodies exist in a sort of undefined manner... Without such distinct deviations, we remain in oblivion, divided from the world of distinction, each other, perhaps even our very selves, etc, etc, etc... How is it that such indistinct similarities seem to divide us so entirely from everything? We wondered...

As the approaching figure arrives in the immediate vicinity of the control-room we occupy, discernment becomes possible... After the figure has completed the facility's I.D. process, proper confirmation reveals this figure to be Ronald P. Vincent PhD MD... He passes through the barrier, without any acknowledgment of our presence, as we press the green button... Despite his lack of acknowledgment, we offer the normal greeting gestures commensurate with the passing of entities in relative proximity...

Although this process has officially identified Ronald, we wonder who he really is... What is it that distinguishes Ronald P. Vincent PhD MD from the rest of the entities and non-entities at the facility? Isn't there more to someone's identity than such synonymous associations as their names, titles, figures, &c, &c, &c? We wondered...

Once Ronald had completed his entry of the facility, the vicinity of the control-room became quite devoid of activity for some time… The vacancy of the scene drew our attention back to its previous orientation… We commenced to stare inquiringly into the oblivion beyond us…

The reflections of our own image seemed more like that of some foreign creature than a projection of our-self… It had become difficult for us to relate to any of our own images… This apparition within our gaze was indeed what we had come to associate as our own image… With all of our depth compressed into this flat image, it appeared as if any true part of us had become diminished, detached, &c, &c, &c… Whatever depth might be within us could not be seen…

Our shadow is cast upon this image of our-selves reflecting… The shadow seems to merge with this image, but in a way that it remains separately discernable… It appears as if the shadow is cast upon this reflection, that this reflection is impressed upon this shadow, that both are integrated, &c, &c, &c…

There simply must be something more, beyond our shadowy reflection, the black and white surfaces of the outside world, &c, &c, &c… Some substance of clarity must remain undiluted by the spaces of emptiness; undistorted by the chaos of the colliding visual wavelengths from every entity's projections, reflections, deflections, shadows, &c, &c, &c… What must we do in order to see it? We wondered…

As we continue standing, staring, and dreaming of all these notions, a knock is heard on the door behind us… This is the door that allows entry/exit to the control-room from within the facility… There are only certain individuals authorized entry into this room, to include; security-drones, specified management personnel, &c, &c, &c…

As we view a monitor displaying a visual feed from a camera pointed outside the immediate vicinity of this door, we see Ronald P. Vincent PhD MD… He is one of those authorized-entities according to our security-drone manual… We are able to open this door when we visually confirm the requested entry is authorized... Ronald P. Vincent PhD MD appears to be feigning patience with us as we open the door...

"Where is your immediate sssupervisssor?"

Ronald asks, as we open the door... We attempt to acquire this information by contacting Our Sssupervisssor over the radio... Our Sssupervisssor only informs us of his location after insisting we explain why we are requesting this information... Once we inform him that Ronald has requested the information, his tone of voice becomes less perturbed, and more apologetic...

It should perhaps be mentioned, that Our Sssupervisssor's voice was tainted by a speech-impediment... Ronald was attempting to conceal his inherent disdain for the unpleasantness of this slurred-speech... We were also attempting to refrain from demonstrating any personal disparagement, although Ronald would likely have found such honesty to be quite welcome...

After Ronald acquired the requested information, he informed us to relay a message for our supervisor to remain at this communicated location... This request was completed promptly, but Our Sssupervisssor would not confirm receiving this information... Several attempts to make confirmation were made before Ronald turned to leave, and advised us to cease any further attempts... Again we were left alone in the control-room, with our reflections, responsibilities, etc, etc, etc...

101.03 SAUL/PAUL/RAUL(Y)/ &C, &C, &C…

Another figure approaches the facility control-room, as we remain lost inside this vacancy… Upon reaching this location, the figure bangs obnoxiously on the outer surface of the door… Then in an exaggerated tone of mocking amusement, the figure's voice exclaims…

"Open thisss door now, you ssstupid drone!"

The voice associated with this declaration, is of another of the facility's security-drones… His name changes from time-to-time, drone-to-drone, &c, &c, &c… Some of us know him as Saul, others as Paul, or Raul, or Rauly, &c, &c, &c.

This entity has become known by so many names in order to remain anonymous… Anonymity allows this entity to engage in a variety of actions, without being identified in connection to these acts… Being unidentifiable has allowed this character to get away with a litany of mischief, mayhem, &c, &c, &c…

Predominantly, this anonymity-loving character is enthralled in causing Our Ssupervisssor distress… It seems this has been his primary objective, since first arriving at the facility some time ago… Since then, things have managed to escalate consistently…

…

Due to several naturally-occurring circumstances, Our Sssupervisssor has been unfortunate in these matters... Unfortunately, Our Sssupervisssor has a speech-impediment that makes him slur his *s's*... Saul (as he is *officially* named) disliked Our Sssupervisssor due to his authoritarian-demeanor, speech-impediment, &c, &c, &c... Soon after this disdain developed, Saul began referring to him-self as Paul... His explanation for this name-change was that he...

"...didn't want that sssuck-asssss, mouth-molesting his good name..."

After a few confused confrontations between the two, Paul started adopting other names, further perpetuating the resulting confusion... Primarily, Paul used names of other drones at the facility... The facility already had several other drones with names like Paul, Saul, &c, &c, &c...

Then Paul began making up new nicknames/names for these other drones, &c, &c, &c... One drone named Raul began to accept Paul's nickname *Rauly*, in place of his real-name... This amused the others, and they subsequently began to adopt the nicknames Paul used for them...

These nicknames allowed Paul to further confuse the identities of all the drones within the facility... Not content with the results of this, Paul also started making some of the drones call him Rauly... Then other nicknames were reassigned to him-self, the others, &c, &c, &c...

Saul's job had been to create/assign badges for the personnel authorized entry to the facility... Taking advantage of this situation, Saul began making extra badges, issuing them, swapping them around, &c, &c, &c... In order to access the facility, it was necessary to go along with Saul's ruses... Our identities were tied to these badges, and Saul had dominion over them...

As a result of all this, the members of the facility were no longer able to function according to any certain identity... Anyone could be identified as any/every-one else, no one, &c, &c, &c... Who we were depended on Saul's determinations at any moment...

It became part of each drones best interest to keep up this facade... Failure to cooperate could lead to being identified as part of this whole conspiracy... Being identified in this way would mean termination, reprimands, &c, &c, &c... No one could admit to anyone else who they really were... This became every bit as confusing as it might sound...

Our Sssupervisssor had not been on positive terms with any of the other drones at the facility... Actually, he had never even attempted to get to know any of the security-drones... Some of the drones found this to be incredibly insulting... His rapport with others had never been of any esteem...

In the non-security-drone sections of the facility, he was disliked due to his speech-deficits, lower-class mannerisms, authoritarian-demeanor, &c, &c, &c... His behavior seemed to be motivated by a desire to lash-out at others in some authorized way... Our Sssupervisssor was able to lash-out by strictly enforcing the rules, procedures, guidelines, standards, &c, &c, &c... He even had a tendency to interpret the use of his authority in a manner that was extensively desperate, irrational, unfounded, &c, &c, &c...

Our Sssupervisssor was also quite sensitive of his speech-impediment, and often became irate as a result... He was hypercritical of every *s* sound pronounced in his presence... Even in cases where there were no intentions of mocking, Our Sssupervisssor would perceive an *s* sound as an insult... There was nothing in the security-drone handbook regarding speech impediments, or impressions of such... Despite this fact, Our Sssupervisssor considered any perceived mocking to be a form of insubordination, and a verbal *aessault* as well...

Such aessaults would be met with attempts to punish the drone considered responsible for them... All such attempts had been negated/dismissed by H.R.... Soon this trend was made known to those that were not involved in the accusations of such aessaults on Our Sssupervisssor...

After being continually accosted by Our Sssupervisssor's failed attempts to punish them, the other drones became increasingly and openly disdainful towards Our Sssupervisssor... Soon they learned that slurred mocking of Our Sssupervisssor was permissible, provided it wasn't done in the presence of non-security-drones... These acts of retaliation became more and more prevalent...

Our Sssupervisssor became the target of other retaliations as well... Paul managed to alter Our Sssupervisssor's badge, so that his job-title read, *Sssupervisssor*... This was noticed by many of the others inside the facility before Our Sssupervisssor became aware of it... It was due to this that he became known as, *Our Sssupervisssor*...

These open insults upon Our Sssupervisssor cut to the core of his insecurities... Although we personally tried to abstain from such aessaults, it was often quite difficult to refrain... We found it strange how Our Sssupervisssor's insecurities led him to such preemptive hostilities, and how this inevitably resulted in aessaults upon his insecurities... How could such a perpetual-cycle ever end? We wondered...

Due to Our Sssupervisssor's inability to identify the drones in the facility, voluntary-compliance was necessary for him to attempt any recourse... Once Saul had demonstrated non-compliance, the other drones immediately took note... Saul would insult Our Sssupervisssor with slurs, leave the room, then feign obliviousness, &c, &c, &c ... Our Sssupervisssor would then attempt to reprimand Saul anyway... Then Saul would protest this initiative, feigning that he was truly innocent, outraged, &c, &c, &c...

This made it nearly impossible for Our Sssupervisssor to punish Saul... Soon the other drones began to mimic this type of behavior... This further escalated things, and soon everyone was involved with greater and greater negligence...

Unfortunately, we were left with the choice of joining-in, or putting our-selves at risk of being singled-out... To be singled-out would make us the target of the other drones... Being the target of the other drones would have allowed them to make us the target of Our Sssupervisssor... The result of this was our resigned cooperation against Our Sssupervisssor, in favor of Saul's antagonism...

We were all to blame for Our Sssupervisssor's loss of control, and yet it was impossible to place any of the blame on anyone in particular... Total chaos was the result of this... This total chaos somehow seemed to be typified with banality...

For a great length of time this became the normal functioning of the security-drones at the facility... Our Sssupervisssor never quite understood what was going on with the whole thing... He seemed unwilling to admit the extent of this dilemma, his loss of control, or any possible wrong-doing of his own, &c, &c, &c... Some confession on his part would have been necessary in order to even possibly resolve this conflict, but no such effort seemed at all likely...

Admitting negligence would only be appraised as incompetence, and likely result in the termination of employment at the facility... Refusing to make such admissions meant the perpetual continuation towards some terrible end... Under the threat of certain shame or uncertain horror, the uncertain was deemed preferable... We would all rather face the darkness than an unfortunate truth it seems...

It is also of note, that there was little effort to prevent this fiasco from escalating or being curtailed... Our Sssupervisssor never tried to be more affable towards the other drones, did not attempt any form of appeasement, truce, &c, &c, &c... He never even engaged in any casual conversation with any of the drones...

Instead, he denied the extent of the problem, and diluted him-self with notions that he would somehow manage to punish those responsible... Slowly he began to unravel, as each attempt to address the situation failed... Each effort was attempted in a predictable manner that Paul was easily able to anticipate, negate, &c, &c, &c...

In one attempt to thwart this identity problem, all facility personnel were to be assigned new badges... Our new badges were to have a letter-prefix based on our job-classification, followed by numbers based on our official service-numbers, our facility enlistment-dates, &c, &c, &c... This did not solve anything, but instead resulted in new complications...

Due to the fact that every official job-classification at the facility began with an *s*, all of the letter prefixes became *S*... Many of the subsequent numbers ended up as duplications as well... These numbers with letter-prefixes were intended to function in place of our names, so that we wouldn't be able to alter them with such ease... However, it was difficult to identify anyone by a number, especially given that these numbers were not unique... Furthermore, now the problem of identity was no longer limited to security-drones, but had spread throughout the facility...

As a result of this mishap, Saul began amusing him-self by calling everyone *S*... This was also done in reference to something that had been done when we were first hired as a security-drone at the facility... As an initiation ritual, other security-drones used to refer to newly hired drones as *S*, until they could learn to remember our name(s)...

Personally, we had somehow never managed to become known to anyone in the facility as anything other than *S*, or one of Saul's inventions... Our identity became further diluted as a result of all this mischief... We became no more than part of this collective of drones that were all referred to as *S*... Was it our own lack of distinctions that had become shared, or the collective's lack of distinctions that became ours? We wondered...

Returning to the present moment of our concern, Saul is continuing to bang incessantly upon the door of the control-room... As we allow him to enter the control-room, he informs us that he will assume our duties... This will allow us to complete a walking-patrol, take our scheduled-break, &c, &c, &c... We follow protocol, notifying Our Sssupervisssor by radio that our post is secured, that we've been properly-relieved, &c, &c, &c...

Confirmation/authorization is given, and we proceed to exit the control-room...

The standard walking-patrol route of the facility is oriented with the commons-area/break-room positioned at its midpoint... After completing the first half of our patrol, we are to take our scheduled-break, and then complete the remaining portion of our route, &c, &c, &c... Under circumstances that require our presence during our break-interval, we may be required to respond directly, and forfeit the remainder of our scheduled break-interval, &c, &c, &c... This is intended to increase the productivity of the facility's available resources... (We are also sometimes referred to as resources, personnel, &c, &c, &c...)

Exiting the control-room, we begin our walking-patrol of the facility, proceeding towards the commons-area... Every stride takes us deeper and deeper into the center of the facility's sprawling expanse... As we walk past a series of doors with names printed upon them, we are expected to ensure that each of the rooms is vacant, secured, &c, &c, &c... All of the science-drones are supposed to be gone in the evening hours, except for those expressly authorized by Ronald P. Vincent PhD MD... There are approximately 10-15 of these drones on any given night... On this particular evening there are only 5, including Ronald P. Vincent PhD MD...

None of the science-drones present this evening have their names printed upon any of the doors in this sector of the facility... Even though Ronald's office door is in this sector, his name is not displayed on it... This lack of identification upon the office doors of the facility's elite is deliberate... A certain degree of deniability is to be preserved in case of certain unknown circumstances...

Many of the facility's elite, are not even to be identified by the security-drones... Instead, they are to be escorted into the facility by Ronald P. Vincent PhD MD him-self, in order to pass through entry-control... According to the special instructions issued by Ronald P. Vincent PhD MD, these entities are to be issued gold-plated badges that have the engraving, *Don't Ask* on the front surface... This golden insignia also serves as an official policy concerning the activities of the entities assigned to wear it...

As we stroll serenely through the empty silence of the facility, we find a sense of calm... We have often noticed how these solitary moments bring a unique sense of comfort... For some reason, our mind feels most affirmed during these moments of solitary rapture... Alone, we find our focus intensifies, our resolve increases, our esteem swells, &c, &c, &c...

The paradigm notion impressed upon us, that being alone is synonymous with a certain feeling of emptiness, is strange to us... It seems absurd that our mind should feel empty on its own, when it is so full of thoughts, wonder, etc, etc, etc... Contrarily, we have often found emptiness in the presence of others within this shared oblivion... How strange are these notions of wonder, fullness, emptiness, &c, &c, &c? We wondered...

These are among the variety of things we often contemplate in our solitary walks through the facility... On this evening, we are absorbed in the allegorical notions of the scene we described at the very beginning of this tale... Why are we so fixated on the allegorical notions of such a scene? Where might these thoughts lead? What are we in this sense of things? Inside our mind, these thoughts wander along the lineaments of perception, entity, identity, &c, &c, &c... As we wonder/wander, we find only closed doors, echoes of footsteps, empty spaces, &c, &c, &c...

Nearing the immediate vicinity of the commons-area, we hear voices... Entering the commons, we are careful not to disturb the science-drones discussion, cause any awareness of our presence, &c, &c, &c... We stealthily deposit our-selves into a chair in the opposite end of the break-room without any audible disturbance... Then without disruption, we remove from our pockets a small paperback novel, a notepad, a pen, and a sealed ration of food, &c, &c, &c... Opening these objects in order to consume and digest the cognitive and nutritional contents is done with sonic-invisibility...

Despite our cloak of silence, one of the golden-badge drones is somehow disturbed by our presence, and stares at us with disdain projecting through his gaze... The conversation of the others continues, as if only this drone is in any way aware of our presence... Seated in the furthest possible position from the group, we are careful not to make any impressions upon the others, and hope the disturbed-drone will become disinterested in our presence...

In agitation, this drone appears to be progressing in his mind towards some breaking-point... Ronald P. Vincent PhD MD enters the break-room moments after our initial arrival, and observes this scene with casual astuteness... His passing glance over our faces appears to inform him of all that is occurring in this scene... He even seems to catch the title of the book we hold in our hands...

The other drones cease their conversation as he enters, and the tension rises within these drones... We are well aware of this tension, but we hardly experience it from within our-selves... For us, it seems we are not present enough in this world to warrant any concern for circumstances such as these, &c, &c, &c...

Ronald's visual observations are accompanied by swift sweeping strides... The strides carry him toward the congregation of drones seated around the circular tables in the far corner of the commons-area... He proceeds to lean against a wall just on the outer edge of the group's vicinity...

It's difficult to gauge the group's awareness of the subliminal message present in Ronald's positioning... His presence is both physically and figuratively positioned; above them, watching over them, &c, &c, &c... Some might call this a projection of superiority, but there is more to it than that... Superiority may often be accompanied by some form of responsible devotion... As the operations-manager at the facility, Ronald has been appointed over them, but he is also responsible for them here... Is this what is truly being projected in this scene? We wondered...

Though quite aware of this scene, we remain more focused on the book within our hands... Our concurrent awareness and duplicitous focus sparks a burning curiosity in Ronald... When we see Ronald's eyes begin to focus on us, we somehow know our anonymity is already lost... In our mind, this moment marked the end of our existence as a non-entity inside the facility...

"Would you care to join us?"

Ronald imposes this as less of an invitation and more of an order... We respond with coyness, not wanting to impose upon the group... Our initial attempt to evade this urging, is based on our involvement with the book in our hands... In response Ronald dismisses this claim's validity...

"You can read that old-thing any time. This conversation is only happening now. Come on, what do you say?"

We try to imply that our participation will only be a hindrance on the others... This is of course an insufficient excuse... After Ronald again urges us to join the group, we notify him that our break will end soon... With laughter Ronald walks over to us, informs us that he needs to check something, and grasps the radio from our uniform...

"This is Ronald P. Vincent. Someone advise the sssecurity sssupervisssor, that I require the employee currently on break to remain in my presence until further notice."

Our Sssupervisssor acknowledged this, and no objections were presented... The expectation for us to join the group had essentially been mandated... In response, we taped the table as if it were a chess timepiece, and announced with amusement...

"Check-mate..."

Our response seems to stoke the coals of Ronald's already burning curiosity towards us...

"Before we begin..."

Ronald cuts in…

"…What is a security-drone doing reading something like that?"

The inquiry is an attempt to acquire some sort of background information on us… We are supposed to answer in a personal/informative manner, addressing the nature of interests in some illuminating manner… This is not what we did…

"What can be intended by reading anything? Perhaps it's more interesting to wonder what might have been intended in the writing of something like this, &c, &c, &c…"

Our reply elicits feigned eye-rolling from several of the other drones in the group… Ronald's curiosity however, is further intensified… He exhibits signs of difficulty in concealing this curiosity it from being overtly displayed…

"So what is your opinion of it so far then? How far along are you?"

As he asked these questions, he reached out, taking hold of the book to see the page number to which our book was opened…

"Page 301… Only 20 pages or so left to read. Have you read this one before?"

Before we can offer any reply, Ronald continues to amuse him-self with questions and statements that were meant to provoke some kind of response other than a simple reply…

"You'll have to tell me what you think when you're done. Have you read any of this author's other books?"

We nodded our head at this inquiry in the affirmative, and Ronald began to list other book titles… All of the titles he named were met with the same limited response of an affirmative gesture…

"Have you read this one before?"

Ronald asked us this question in reference to the book he was still holding, as he anticipated our response...

"The last 20 pages aren't part of the story's text..."

Examining the pages again, Ronald noticed that this content had indeed been accompanied with an extensive *afterward* section... Then he asked us for our impressions of the author's overall messages...

"Life being what it is, one dreams of revenge-"

Our reply was a segmented quote from the French post-impressionist P. Gauguin... Before completing this quote, we made a nod towards an adjacent wall of the commons-area... A reproduction of this artist's famous, *"Where do we come from? What are we? Where are we going?"* was displayed on this surface...

Ronald became openly enthused at our reply... He pulled out a chair as his enamored grin was transposed into a smirk... Then he commanded with affable ease...

"Join us."

It was seemingly impossible to decline or escape at this point... As we obliged, the words we had just spoke echoed back to us in our silent inner thoughts... *"Life being what it is, one dreams of revenge-"* The rest of this quotation seemed to resonate within our thoughts... *"...and has to content oneself with dreaming..."* What dreams were we to content our-selves with now? We wondered...

Over the course of the conversation, we seemed to make a strange impression on those gathered in the commons-area... Mostly we tried to listen quietly, hoping to avoid becoming more extensively known to the group... Occasionally, Ronald would expressly ask for us to provide our thoughts on something... Every response we gave seemed to produce a general surprise and intrigue...

The group seemed to be in apparent disbelief that a security-drone could be offering these responses... There was a novelty in the fact that a *nobody* possessed the ability to respond intelligibly in such conversations... This was simply not the paradigm...

All the while, we hoped that our novelty would ware off, and we could get away... We were being deprived of our time alone... In a certain sense, we were even being deprived of our-selves... Amidst all these others, we were desperately missing our-selves...

Our intense desire to remain alone preceded our own memory... For us, becoming known to others was something rather esoteric... We felt that we had not yet become known in any real sense to our-self... Without knowing what we were, it seemed that becoming known to the outside world would compromise our ability to discover what we truly were...

It seemed to us that the world would project its own notions of us onto ourselves... Our own true reflections would then become distorted with these projections, and we might never discover what we were within the oblivion of the world around us, &c, &c, &c...

Eventually, we became relieved as the meeting was finally disbanded... Despite our effort to slink-out amidst the others, and return to the unknown ranks of security-drones, we were obstructed by Ronald's presence... He had blocked the exit by initiating an impromptu conversation with one of the other drones, standing directly and deliberately within the space of the exit...

After concluding this conversation, Ronald instructed us to visit him in his office before leaving the facility... This request of our presence was seemingly contingent upon our ability to be identified... Could we remain hidden in the oblivion of drones without distinction? Would Ronald be able to differentiate us from among the others? All throughout our walk back to the control-room, our mind was filled with these questions... What were we to do? We wondered...

Wandering towards the control-room, the facility seemed to be constricting around us... All the walls were closing in, the ceiling was lowering, and the emptiness of the surrounding space seemed to vanish... Although the dimensions were unchanged, it was as if the facility was collapsing into a cage... The whole thing was collapsing without crumbling... As we maneuvered the constricting spaces in wonder, we began to feel trapped...

101.04 WHAT A WASTE...

Upon returning to the control-room, we found Paul and Our Sssupervisssor in the middle of some conflict... Our Sssupervisssor was stammering, stuttering, and slurring more than usual... He was even physically wobbling, as if his balance had become as impaired as his speech... As he was screaming at Paul, a very potent bouquet of alcoholic scents flooded the control-room... It was clear that Our Sssupervisssor was intoxicated, angry with Paul, and on the edge of some great disaster... Though we had a clear understanding of what was happening; we desperately would have preferred to stay out of it... (Life being what it is...)

Paul was cracking-up in Our Sssupervisssor's face, as allegations came slurring out of his alcohol-scented meatus...

"It'sss been you all thisss time. I know it'sss been you. You're an identity-thief, and a fraud, and you're fired for insssubordinationsss!"

Laughing in syllables, Paul continued to antagonize Our Sssupervisssor...

"Sssay insssubordinationsss again, pleasssse! Ssshow me how itsss ssssuposssssed to ssssound!"

...

Our Sssupervisssor became even more irate, and his blood-shot eyes nearly burst out of his crimson glowing face…

"Get out of here now! Your asssss isss sssusssspended indefinitely!!!"

Without any concern for this empty threat, Paul sliced right back…

"Sssusssspended? Who'ssss sssusssspended? Cccertainly not any of usss. Isss it?"

The exaggerated pantomime motions/expressions Paul made were meant to be an over-the-top impression of Our Sssupervisssor's flailing, but were actually rather accurate…

Our Sssupervisssor pointed his finger in what was likely the direction he believed to be towards Paul… It was actually closer to our own position, and as he screamed in the same direction, the scented slurs wafted forth again…

"Thisss isssn't a cassse for the facccility. Thisss isss a policcce matter. I'm calling the copsss on your asssss!"

Breaking-out in an eruption of laughter, Paul's echo could be heard throughout the facility…

"What are you going to tell the copersssssssssssssss?"

As Paul slurred the last syllable, he sent saliva sputtering towards Our Sssupervisssor… This was unnoticed, as Our Sssupervisssor stumbled toward the phone… As he picked it up, he was careful to block it from view… He pretended to call the police, but no call had been made… It was clear that this was the case, but Our Sssupervisssor tried to keep his bluff…

"I've already got them on the line. I'll have them dissssposssing of your asssss in no time. Your asssss isss headed to the ssslammer. I'll help them throw you out of here myssself!"

Still placating Our Sssupervisssor, Paul cut-in again…

"Have they really anssswered yet? What'sss their ressponsse time?"

Our Sssupervisssor pretended to cover the phone so Paul couldn't be heard by the imaginary-dispatcher... Then he pretended to tell the imaginary-entity to send a patrol, and paused before thanking them in advance... This scene was quite poorly acted-out, and even considering the state of Our Sssupervisssor's intoxication, it still seemed quite pathetic...

"They'll be here sssoon, asssss-hole! We'll sssee what you have to sssay when they do get here. Your asssss isss going to sssuffer for thisss!"

"What are the chargesss?"

Paul spit back sharply, with his feigned slur...

"Fraudulencccce! Fraunulenccce isss the charge. They'll aressst you, and sssentenccce your asssss for thisss. You'll be sssentenccced to the greatessst extent of the lawsss!"

"Fraudulenccce isss a pretty big accusssation. How isss any of thisss fraudulencccce?"

Paul managed to project another sliver of slurred-spit on Our Sssupervisssor's forehead with these words, but this went unnoticed yet again...

"You've been making fakesss. Fakesss of everything... Fake I.D.sss, Fake namessss... You're a fake your-ssself! You're a fake and a fraud!!!"

As Our Sssupervisssor said these words, he flailed and lost his balance... He looked down as he stumbled, and when he looked back up it was in our direction... It appeared that he could not separate which of us was which... Paul noticed this development and decided to exploit it...

"What do you have to sssay for your-ssself, and your fake-asssss?"

Paul slurred these words at us, but without the split, as a small courtesy... We didn't say anything, hoping to avoid becoming further involved in this scene... If we could just remain quiet, maybe the moment would pass over us without drawing us in...

Our Sssupervisssor's eyes were scanning back and forth at both of us... He was completely unable to tell us apart... It was only then that he realized we were both in the room with him...

"You're out of here too, you double-asssss-holesss! All of you are gonna' be out on your asssssesss now!! I'm ssstarting from ssscratch. You can't jussst ssstand-by asss everything goesss to ssshit. You all played the sssame part in thisss ssshithead'sss gamesss. You won't get away with thessse sssschemesss! I'm sssusssspending you all for insssubordinationsss!! You're all sssusssspended indefinitely!!!"

Now Paul was in hysterics... After cracking-up so hard that he nearly lost his breath, and turned an unnatural shade of red, he slurred back...

"Indefinitely; asss in maybe we are not sssusssspended, or asss in sssusssspended until further noticcce? Aren't you going to be ssssusssspended too?"

"What would I be sssusssspended for assss-clown?"

Our Sssupervisssor's voice cracked at the end of this statement, in the way puberty often affects the voices of adolescents...

"Incompetenccce, Ssshit-asssss!!!"

Paul's voice seemed to nearly shatter the glass surfaces inside the control-room, and his eyes shifted into a piercing glare... His whole demeanor was no longer amused, but combative, as he seemed to be staring-down Our Sssupervisssor...

"Get out now!!! You're all ssshit-canned! You ssstupid asssssholesss! You're all sssscammersss, and accccessssssoriesss of sssscammersss!"

There had still been no police, or HR representatives for that matter, and we all knew Our Sssupervisssor didn't have the authority to enforce such commands... Having become irritated with the situation, Paul began to take full advantage of Our Sssupervisssor's broken state...

"Sssuck it, ssstupid-asssss!"

Paul's last slurred-syllable shot a thick mist of saliva into Our Sssupervisssor's face... Then Paul paused for a moment, before spitting directly into Our Sssupervisssor's right eye... Our Sssupervisssor's limited capacity for restraint broke-down...

Our Sssupervisssor lunged toward Paul in an apparent attempt to tackle him... He missed Paul completely, and slammed into a desk behind Paul... We tried to pacify Our Sssupervisssor at this point, but he shot back to his feet, and immediately started swinging his fists blindly... As he lurched back towards Paul swinging, we restrained him by clasping our hands around his torso... Holding onto him from his back, he continued to flail around furiously like some child mimicking a propeller... After eventually realizing he couldn't strike Paul as long as we impeded his attempts, Our Sssupervisssor relented... Assuming a passive demeanor, he feigned composure ...

"...sssorry, sssory."

This apology was accompanied by Our Sssupervisssor's hands becoming passively raised, with his palms relaxed and facing away from him...

"I didn't want any of thisss. Sssorry. I'm done with thisss. I'm finissshed."

His posture became quite flaccid in this moment, and he began to shuffle away from Paul, with his head drooping down in shame...

Then, he suddenly reversed course... With a sudden twist of his uncoordinated body, he launched not towards Paul, but in our direction... As he flopped forward, he swung a wide, sweeping right-hook intending to hit us in the face...

Having trained extensively in the martial-arts, our reflexes had been conditioned to take over in an instance such as this... That is exactly what happened... We instinctually wove out of the path of the sloppy hook, and in a state of ataxia, countered with a quick right-cross... Our Sssupervisssor's chin met the punch, as he continued forward... His body went limp, and slammed to the floor... His eyes rolled-over white, as they turned toward the black darkness within his skull...

As he'd crashed to the ground, a glass bottle shattered in his front pants-pocket... Shards of glass cut into his legs, as the contents remaining in the bottle flowed out... His pants were wet with the alcohol, and blood began to stain through as well... Then another liquid began to flow from a nearby area, as he lost control of his bladder... The smell of booze and piss filled the control-room... Paul picked up the phone to call HR...

HR arrived just as Our Sssupervisssor was regaining consciousness... Once we were able to revive him, he began screaming that he was going to have his revenge... We were then instructed to escort Our Sssupervisssor outside, wait to transfer him into the authorities' custody, &c, &c, &c... When the authorities had assumed custody, we were to meet with HR outside of Ronald's office...

Our Sssupervisssor was predominantly compliant, as we escorted him out... Most likely this was due to the fact that he was barely able to walk in his drunken stupor, and there was now glass lodged in his leg... His only real resistance was made as we tried to get him to his feet in the control-room...

Unable to resist mocking Our Sssupervisssor, Paul amused him-self... Before we exited the control-room, Paul pointed to the sign on the door that read, *control-room*, saying...

"-mind the door, pleassse."

Our Sssupervisssor buckled his legs at this joke, and said we'd have to carry him out if it was going to be like this... Soon this resistance was surrendered, and he assisted us in carrying him out...

Paul helped us carry Our Sssupervisssor out of the facility and to the outer-perimeter where the authorities were to meet us... This time in transit was used by Paul to further incite his victim... Paul kept making cracks about Our Sssupervisssor's lack of control over bodily-functions, composure, alcohol consumption, &c, &c, &c...

Our Sssupervisssor responded with empty threats, attempted insults, indecipherable slurs, &c, &c, &c... All of this banter was quite juvenile, but Paul seemed to be in amusement/command throughout these exchanges...

The strangeness of Paul's control over this whole fiasco made a definite impression on us... His use of confusion resulted in such dominance over this place and everyone in it... He hadn't merely managed to cause Our Sssupervisssor to break-down, but had gained influence over a great deal of the facility as a whole... All that Paul had managed to do here was the result of confusion... It wasn't just Paul that had demonstrated the effects of confusion, but it was as a result of Paul's deceptions that we began to understand it... What was it about confusion that could hold so much control over everything? We wondered...

When we reached the outer perimeter, another security-drone opened the perimeter-gate so we could exit, and wait for the authorities... There was another gate beyond this, and we carried Our Sssupervisssor there, before insisting that he stand on his own...

Outside of the facility's perimeter, there were some sanitation-personnel departing along the controlled access-road... They usually arrived in this approximate time-frame each morning, and would acquire the facility's waste for transfer... Our Sssupervisssor saw them as they drove away, and screamed at them...

"I've got a pile of ssshit for them to dissspossse of right here"...

He collapsed to the ground as he screamed... Then we noticed the smell of excrement joining the piss and booze scents emanating off of him...

We were relieved to see the authorities when they finally approached the perimeter of the facility... When they did arrive, they initially refused to accept custody of Our Sssupervisssor due to his unbearable stench... Paul informed them of the sanitation-personnel that had just passed... The authorities decided to try and make contact with the sanitation-personnel...

Some time went by as we awaited their return, and Paul continued to prod his victim... Returning with the sanitation-personnel, the authorities instructed us to deposit Our Sssupervisssor into the back of the garbage-truck... They insisted we apply restraints to Our Sssupervisssor after we loaded him into the garbage-truck...

During this time, our former supervisor kept bursting with obscenities, and incoherent statements... Before we had even loaded him into the garbage-truck, it was as if his humanity had been previously disposed... As the truck pulled away, we could hear our former supervisor's voice fading in slurred curses... Saul looked pleased as he watched them disappear... Once they were gone he turned to us, saying with amusement...

"What a waste."

We shook our head... He'd stated the words we were thinking... Did he mean them in the same way we'd imaged them? We wondered...

101.05 HR INTERVIEW...

We returned to the control-room of the facility, having disposed of our former supervisor... The HR Manager had left to attend to some other concerns, but left instructions for us to remain here... He didn't recognize us when he returned to the control-room, and asked us if we had seen the two drones involved in *the scuffle*... We informed him that we were the drones in question...

Saul nudged us in our rib cage with his elbow... He was directed to remain in the control-room with the HR Manager... Our instructions were to proceed to the HR Manager's office, and await further instructions... In full compliance, we went to wait in the HR Manager's office... Saul remained in the control-room, where he was to give statements to HR regarding the incident...

The HR Manager's office was actually a desk in the lobby area outside of Ronald's office... We decided to be seated on a couch that could have been understood to be part of either the HR Manager's office or the lobby area... For some reason it seemed improper to wait in a closer proximity to the HR Manager's personal office area...

It was only a short few minutes before the HR Manager came to speak with us... The HR Manager came into the lobby/office area, and we followed him to his desk... He motioned for us to be seated, and settled into his chair opposite us...

...

Then he produced a folder from a file-cabinet next to his desk... He opened it, and asked for our name and ID number... We felt it necessary to ask him what name and number he was asking for, since they had been changed so many times... Not only had they been changed since we began to work in the facility, but we had been required to be issued new names/numbers on many other occasions... This was the start of the HR Manager's distress, and annoyance with us...

We tried to explain that we had never been interviewed for hire at the facility... Instead we had been transferred from another site to supplement the facility's security-staff... It was initially intended for us to remain at the facility on only a part-time basis... For reasons unknown to us, we ended up permanently assigned to the facility... The HR Manager scoffed at us as we explained all of this... Then he asked us to give an account of our previous employment... Our summary of this information seemed satisfactory and uninteresting to the HR Manager...

Following this, the HR Manager asked for our account of *the scuffle* that had occurred earlier... We began our account of what had transpired, but found it difficult to convey how it all occurred... The difficulty was due to the whole Paul/Saul/Raul/Rauly...-dilemma... Although we had tried to avoid mentioning this whole identity problem that had developed here at the facility, it became imperative after the HR Manager began to question us further... Under the circumstances, we felt it unavoidable to surrender, and gave the HR Manager a quick briefing on the dilemma...

After we explained the whole Paul/Saul/Raul/Rauly...-dilemma to him, he became completely lost... Instead of offering any response, he just stared at us, while occasionally fidgeting... We were about to go back over the whole debacle in greater detail, but he began inquiring of us again...

"So what is the name that you started going by when you first arrived here?"

He asked, clearly fearing he would regret it...

31

"At first everyone just used S to refer to us... We all went by that initially, and once the other drones became familiar, some other name would be adopted... No one ever needed to differentiate us though... All security issues could be dealt with by any of us... In our case, none of the other drones seemed to ever become too familiar with us at all... Speculatively, we might assume that this was due to the fact that we worked solitary postings exclusively... That, and the absence of any eccentric quarks, other than the lack of them, our reticent nature, &c, &c, &c..."

This seemed upsetting to him...

"You mean to tell me, you didn't have a name when you started working here?"

"Yes..."

"What did you call your-self after you began working here?"

"It varied..."

"It varied?"

"Yes..."

"How did your name vary?"

"Well, there was the whole thing with Saul/Paul/Raul-"

The HR Manager cut in...

"-I know all of that already, or I've heard as much anyway. Didn't you have an actual name for your-self?"

"Yes, in a way..."

"Well?"

"After reading the DSM-IV, there was a term in there that seemed fitting... It seemed fitting for us according to the criteria, so we started thinking of our-self as a *schizoid*..."

"So... your name is Schizoid?"

"No, not exactly... The criteria fits, and we could be referred to as a schizoid in terms of its definition, &c, &c, &c... Honestly though, it hasn't been something others use to refer to us, and the term is no longer in use under the subsequent edition of the DSM..."

The HR Manager appeared to be on edge with us...

"Just who are you then?"

We couldn't answer that one... Just who is anyone? We wondered...

"Why can't you tell us who you are? Everyone is someone. I'm the HR Manager here... You must understand that I have a job to do... To do that job, I need you to tell me who you are..."

Looking straight at him, we said nothing, but our expression demonstrated that we were contemplating how to answer him... Then after a while, we thought of some way to try to explain it to him... Some background information might help him understand...

"When we were young, they took us to a live-in school... There, we were mixed-in with somewhere around 500 others in each class of pupils, and we were told there were at least 500 classes in the school... They gave us numbers instead of names to identify us on account of the high-population... The number assigned to us was some kind of code, but somehow not all of us ended up with a unique number... Only the staff ever had us use these numbers, and usually only on assignments, or tests... Unfortunately, we can no longer remember what our number might have been..."

"So you were brought up in this live-in school, and no one ever knew you except by number? Is that what you want me to believe?"

"Not exactly... Other names were sometimes used for us, but they were used for others as well... Sometimes the angry-characters would call us by names like *Ayss-Hoal, Dyck-Hedd, Smairt-Ayss*, &c, &c, &c... We never knew any of them our-selves though, and they rarely interacted with us either..."

"You didn't have any friends or enemies there?"

"No, not really... We've always been rather solitary, and kept mostly to our-selves..."

"So would you say you are rather solitary now?"

"Right now, we are speaking with you, but in general, yes... In fact, probably more so..."

"What about after your schooling? Did you have a name then?"

"After schooling, we were assigned to vocations based on our performance records... Our numbers became mixed up as a result of some mischief, similar to what has recently taken place here... No one knew anything about our records, so they opted to randomly assign us vocations, &c, &c, &c... That is how we became a security-drone... Before we worked here at the facility, there was never any inquiry as to our identity... A number or name would be assigned in some way, or sometimes we were just identified by proximity, pronouns, &c, &c, &c... The name most often used for us would probably be, *you*, as some gesture would be employed to distinguish us... Once we came here, things have been as we've explained them already..."

The HR Manager was not pleased with this, as the brow of his face became folded, as if his skin were collapsing into the center of his visage...

"Everyone has some identity they are given at some point in their life. We are all given a name. What is your name? Just, tell me, what your name is. Don't explain how your names have been changed, or anything about this whole, Saul/Paul... *scheme*. Tell me, in simple terms. What is your name?"

There was no way we could explain our-selves... Life being what it is, we still had to try...

"After being transferred into this facility, we were all subjected to a meeting with an HR Representative and a qualified psychologist..."

Showing irritation, but restraining him-self from interrupting, the HR Manager glared in our direction...

"During that meeting, we were assessed according to some criteria... When this took place, the psychologist asked us... *'What are you?'* This was the first question asked of us, and may have been misspoken on the psychologist's part... Perhaps what was intended to be asked was, *'Who are you?'*... In any case, we answered the question presented to us... Intending to be affable and informative, we responded with the qualifying term *schizoid*... Unfortunately as it turns out, the psychologist had only recently graduated, and was unfamiliar with this term... The HR Representative was likely unaware of how to spell this, and didn't want to be embarrassed by asking us... On the paperwork we were required to sign following this meeting, there was a block labeled *name*... In that block, the HR Representative had entered the letter *S*... All of our records, that haven't been mired in this whole Saul/Paul/Raul/Rauly...-debacle, have used the letter *S* in place of our name... So, perhaps that is what our name is..."

The HR Manager began sifting through some of the papers in one of the file-cabinets... He squinted at one page, then another, and another... Eventually he stopped scanning his papers, and muttered some obscenities under his breath... Then he looked back at us...

"You can't just be *S*. A letter is not a name. I don't know how this paperwork has managed to be neglected for so long, but you can't be named *S*. This isn't the kind of fictional place where something like this can go on."

When we asked him how the paperwork could manage to be neglected until now, and how that constituted our own negligence, he became sullen... Then he mumbled something about having thought the paperwork had just been incomplete, or that it wasn't supposed to have any name on it, or that he'd never seen the tiny *S's* there before, &c, &c, &c... It wasn't intended that we hear all of these comments, but it wasn't as if we weren't to hear them either...

Our response to his inquiry proved to be both insufficient, and beyond the extent of rational frustrations... The HR Manager seemed personally insulted over the matter... After some considerations, the HR Manager spoke again...

"I've had enough of this fiasco. What I'm going to do now, is create an identity for you. As long as you are here at this facility, which may not be for very long at all sir, you will use the name I give you. Do you understand this?"

"So what is the name we are to assume now? It isn't *sir* or *you* is it? We have previously been referred to by those names as well..."

"No! It isn't going to be either of those. Perhaps you should tell me what you want to be called from here on-out. What would you like to be called?"

We thought for a moment...

"Either *Schizoid* or *S* would be fine, as far as we are concerned..."

Beside him-self, the HR Manager shook his head...

"You can't go by *S*! *S* is just a letter. We've already been over this."

"It's been used just the same as a name for some time already now... *S* is versatile... Even if we change what we are quite drastically, it would still likely be fitting to call us *S*... We could just imagine *S* to be an abbreviation for anything comparable... *Schizoid*, *security-drone*, &c, &c, &c..."

The HR Manager cut-in...

"Alright, how's this then? Your name will be recorded here as *Schizoid*, but you can still use *S* as a sort of abbreviation or nickname in unofficial matters."

"That could become confusing, but it sounds acceptable to us..."

"Fine then. You sir, are now officially, *Schizoid*."

Then the H.R. Manager began to complete some forms, and our identity as *Schizoid* was created... He handed the papers over for us to sign... This was the first full-signature of our own... After signing the papers, he took them back from us, and examined them... Once he had looked them over, he asked for us to stay put, and went to process the papers through some official-channels, so we would have a documented-identity...

When he returned, we were handed a laminated badge with our name, a new number to identify us, and an image of our face, that had been used for the last ID badge Saul had made for us only two days prior... Upon receipt of this badge, we asked if we needed it for anything in particular... After he scoffed at our question, he told us to hang on to it...

Following our identity-assignment, the H.R. Manager took his seat again... As he sat down, he began asking us to tell him what had just happened with regards to Our Sssupervisssor (again)... We gave him a brief account of the incident, as he took notes and recorded the conversation... After we had finished, he asked some more questions about the whole Saul/Paul/Raul/Rauly...-dilemma... Once this was apparently cleared up, he asked us to confirm a few things...

One confirmation was that we had hit Our Sssupervisssor, or former supervisor, as the HR Manager corrected him-self... Confirming this fact, the HR Manager asked us if we were aware of the facility's zero-tolerance policy on violence... This policy was in the security-drone manual that we were required to read, understand, and carry with us on duty… Having informed him of this and the fact that we were aware of the policy, he asked us if we knew what that meant…

"It means that you may terminate our employment in such a case as this, and that we may have to face assault charges."

Saying these words seemed to please the HR Manager… With a smile on his otherwise blank face, he began to exhibit a superior demeanor towards us…

"So you understand what is going on quite well now. Good. Now, tell me why we should refrain from terminating you or pressing assault charges."

"That is completely up to you to figure-out… You have all the facts, and there is nothing else to the situation that can warrant any consideration… How you chose to interpret the facts according to the rules/laws is entirely up to you…"

This seemed to deprive him of some satisfaction… He became irate…

"So you have no defense for your actions! Not only that, but you seem to think that it's your place to define my role in this matter. You seem to think you can go around punching anyone you want, if they so much as look at you wrong, and then talk-down to your superiors when they ask you to explain your-self. What the hell is the matter with you? Don't you have any tact, or anything to say for your-self?"

Our composure and posture remained unchanged…

"The facts of the matter have been conveyed to you… You know what happened… It has been explained in detail, and our reasons have been given for all of our actions… What else could we add? What superior have we talked down to in this matter by the way? If we've seemed to talk down to someone, it hasn't been done intentionally…"

The HR Manager didn't answer... We imagine he had felt as though we might have talked-down to him, and that he'd considered him-self our superior... He must have then become aware of the fact that HR was a separate division from security, and he was not officially our superior, but an outside neutral-party... After some intense scowling in our direction, he decided to speak again...

"I'm going to tell Ronald that there was an altercation with you and this already disposed of, former supervisor of yours... When I tell him this, he will ask for my recommendation... I will recommend that you be terminated, but that no charges are pressed, since you could probably get away with self-defense... What do you have to say about that?"

"What is there to say?"

The HR Manager started walking towards Ronald's door... Then we thought of something that might have been important to mention to him...

"Oh, perhaps there is something you should know... Earlier this evening Ronald requested that we have a conversation with him before our departure... It might not concern you, but you might mention this to Ronald before you discuss *the scuffle*, &c, &c, &c... It might be necessary in order for him to decide if that conversation is still desired, when he would like to have it, &c, &c, &c..."

Saying these words made the H.R. Manager became completely unnerved... His face shook violently, and turned molten-red, as if a tectonic-plate had shifted beneath its surface, and a volcanic-eruption was about to occur... Then his voice burst, with words like igneous-soot...

"No! Not you! NO, NO; No, No, No!!! You can't be the one he wanted me to make sure didn't leave here before he met with you! It can't be you. NO!!! I don't know what kind of game this is, but you won't get away with it... I won't let you... Don't you move... I'm going to get Ronald right now... Don't you move!"

We remained still, as the HR Manager went to Ronald's door and knocked respectfully... A moment later Ronald announced for the HR Manager to enter... He went in without us, and spent a few moments with the door closed behind him... Then he came back out, and told us to come inside... Entering Ronald's office began another strange scene at the facility...

101.06 RONALD'S OFFICE...

There was an odd look on the HR Manager's face as he opened Ronald's door... His expression held the glare of his disdain, but it appeared less openly projected... This burning contempt had become like a hot-ember in a fire that had been poorly-doused... Although it was now dormant, all he needed was the smallest amount of dry-tinder to reignite the fire, and burn away at us... We could see his eyes searching desperately for an opportunity to revive this fire, and satisfy the desire to scorch us...

Over his shoulder came Ronald's voice...

"Send him in, send him in!"

As we came to the entryway, the HR Manager stood blocking the door for a moment before letting us past him... His inability to provoke us in this manner made his eyes appear to flash with hatred... As the HR Manager closed the door behind us, we took note of the door's construction...

The door was composed of a very heavy and thick wood, with a dense coating of high-gloss lacquer... It likely muffled a great amount of sound... We thought that this was probably useful in times like this, when the HR Manager had just commenced to scream in the area just outside of Ronald's office...

...

Even given the secrecy of the facility, it still seemed odd that Ronald's name was not posted upon his door... Other offices had customarily displayed the name of the occupant in some manner... Typically the more elaborate or expensive the sign, the more prestigious the occupant's position...

Inside the office were 4 identical chairs of fine construction, a luxurious couch, some office-plants, &c, &c, &c... Behind his desk was a lithograph of a figure holding an impossible-cube and staring at it... It may very well have been an original by a famous etching artist... When we were seated across from Ronald with the HR Manager on our left, we noted the expression on Ronald's face... It appeared to be quite similar to the face on the lithograph as he gazed at us...

Ronald was already seated when we entered, and began speaking just after we were seated...

"So I've just been told by the HR Manager here that there was a bit of a... *scuffle*, if we could call it that. Were you in fact involved in this *scuffle*? Did you hit your former *sssupervissson*?"

He was in fact slurring the *S's* in a mocking fashion when he spoke, and his face showed a guilty child-like amusement, as if he knew he shouldn't be doing it, but would none-the-less be able to get away with it... At the same time, his eyes maintained the curiosity resembling the etched-figure behind him, as he stared at our hands...

"Yes..."

"With which hand?"

" This is the hand..."

Ronald was leaning forward trying to get a better view of our hands...

"Right then. I see it must have been a clean strike. You don't appear to need any medical attention. Let me take a look at your hand for a moment, just in case. Have you seen any doctors for your hand yet?"

Ronald extended his body further across his desk to view our hand, as we held it up for him... We indicated that we had not seen any doctors thus far, and that we didn't have any intentions of doing so... He asked us a few subsequent questions...

"Have you had to use your hands much? I mean in this sort of manner. Have you any history with physical altercations?"

As we gave our response he prodded around various areas of our hand...

"Yes... We have had to defend our-selves in this sort of way before, &c, &c, &c..."

"How so?"

"Well, we were stationed in what became the Over-Runs for a while... Before they became the Over-Runs of course... That's where we started being trained in combatives, boxing, jiu-jitsu, &c, &c, &c... On occasion we were required to demonstrate this training, although only in simulations... Since then, we've only maintained some of this training as a habit, hobby, &c, &c, &c..."

"You keep saying, '*etcetera, etcetera, etcetera*', as if it has some special sort of esoteric meaning for you. What is it you're trying to convey with this expression? Why is it you keep saying it this way? Can you tell me?"

We began to answer, as Ronald continued to prod away at our hand...

"It seems to us that there are three omissions that are neglected with great regularity... Using this manner of speaking is intended to acknowledge what might be left out... There's always a great deal that is omitted in any thought, etc, etc, etc..."

43

"What are these three omissions that you find are so often neglected?"

"First, there is usually something that is purposely omitted as unessential... This is either due to an insufficient amount of relevance, or a perceived irrelevance... Other things are left out due to oversight, where they are known in some way to exist, but are not taken into consideration... These things may or not have any relevance, despite not being taken into consideration... Then there are things left out due to complete obliviousness, etc, etc, etc..."

"So in essence, what one considers, fails to consider, and is oblivious to, would qualify as the three omissions conveyed by this expression..."

"Those three things are only the first omission..."

"How do you figure?"

"These things merely constitute a sum of what potentially exists..."

"What are the other omissions then?"

"The second omission is the functioning of tetralemma-logic with regard to the first omission... It is the infinite, meta-computational iterations of how everything is related to everything, and how that relates to its-self, etc, etc, etc..."

"So the second omission indicates how the first function results in larger implications/possibilities in contexts, and how this effects subsequent logical considerations. Is this what you mean by this? Does that sound right? Am I close?"

"Yes, that all sounds correct..."

"What about the third?"

"That is unknown..."

"So whatever can't be determined to be known or unknown is the third."

"No… That would be involved in the second omission… The third omission is just unknown…"

"So the third omission is a declaration of what cannot be declared?"

"Yes, but not only in the sense that it is declared, but also in how it is not declared, &c, &c, &c…"

"Doesn't mentioning this *etc, etc, etc* in any manner, only act as a way of disclaiming your claims?"

Ronald's question wasn't spoken as words, but as a trap intended to cage our thinking… Such a cage couldn't confine us, &c, &c, &c…

"Perhaps… Although it could also be a way of claiming any disclaimers, disclaiming any disclaimers, &c, &c, &c…"

This statement was made out of pure amusement, and Ronald understood it this way… We continued to speak, but with a more serious intent…

"Every time anything is said, it leaves everything else out in the process… It seems some indication of our omissions should be somehow *observed*… If only because of the way everything appears to be affected by the way it is all projected, reflected, absorbed, deflected, &c, &c, &c…"

Ronald seemed to have some understanding of our rather quixotic and abstract notions behind the use of this expression…

"In any case, just because we say it or omit it, doesn't mean it is or isn't there…"

We grinned approvingly at this response Ronald offered laughingly…

.S.P. Daley

(*Note*: It was for this same reason, that ellipses have been used instead of standard punctuation in many instances of this text... These ellipses may be interpreted as an abbreviated form of *etc, etc, etc*...)

After a moment, Ronald began to compare our left hand to our right, as he pressed on both of them... He also had us perform a series of movements to evaluate our hand's functional condition... Then he gave us his assessment...

"Your metacarpo-phalangeal joint appears to have some minor swelling. It doesn't appear as if there are any fractures, or serious damages to the joint-capsule, or sagittal-fibers, but I would recommend that you rest, elevate, and apply ice to the dorsal-surface of your metacarpo-phalangeal joints on your affected hand."

"Obviously it would be advisable to refrain from boxing or other similar activities until inflammation has ceased, &c, &c, &c..."

"Yes. Obviously, you should take a break from training for a little while. Besides, the training seemed to be effective enough in this case."

We shrugged our shoulders in a manner indicative of general espousal in response to Ronald's assertions... Following this gesture, Ronald tilted his head slightly to one side, and continued to observe us with the same etchings of curiosity... He then commenced to ask us more questions about our training...

"What is the draw or compulsion of this training habit/hobby of yours?"

"There's an interesting process involved in it... On some basic level, it's a process of elimination... Over time, the process has a way of separating the things that aren't an essential part of us, and leaving the remainder of us in truer form, &c, &c, &c... For us, it's mostly a way of getting to the core of our-selves... At least that's what we would like to believe about it, &c, &c, &c..."

"That's an interesting way of looking at it."

Ronald tilted his head slightly to one side, and then continued speaking...

"Although your perspective is of particular interest to me, there are some more pressing matters to discus. Perhaps we can discuss these other things further at another time. For now, we had best concentrate on the matters at hand."

Ronald was a bit mused at his statement, and was pleased to observe the slightest smirk we gave in acknowledgment of his pun... (The HR Manager didn't seem to find any amusement...)

"So fact is; there is a zero tolerance policy here at the facility. Therefore, you will be terminated from your vocation as a security-drone here. There is a small issue to resolve on that note though, and it will also have something to do with the next matter that I wish to discuss."

When Ronald spoke of our termination, the HR Manager fidgeted in his chair, straightening his posture to a proud orientation, appearing to be quite arrogantly pleased, &c, &c, &c... Then his expression quickly faded to a more attentive one, with the undertones of his arrogance still present, as Ronald paused before continuing...

"It seems apparent, that there are some very serious issues concerning the identities of the entire security-drone staff here. This issue is a bit convoluted to say the least. In fact, it's actually extremely convoluted. It's even down-right preposterous how convoluted it is. At any rate, here is what will be done in response to this matter."

Looking straight at the HR Manager, he paused to allow him to take note of his next words...

"First, we will need to replace the entire drone-staff in the security-department. Transfer them all to another site somewhere, and import the necessary replacements. Make sure this is done immediately. Be sure that all the current badges issued-out in the facility are disabled after tonight. New badges are only to be assigned to essential-personnel. Because of this problem, there's a possibility that there has been some security-breech already. No such breech can be allowed to be made possible in the future. Did you get all that?"

Ronald watched for the HR Manager's affirmative nod... Then he continued to address the HR Manager directly in an authoritarian tone...

"This issue involves some very serious mismanagement. It is mostly on the part of the former security-*sssupervissor*, but I should be clear about this issue with you right now. You were the one that hired him, and you delegated the ID tasking for him to oversee. Those are your responsibilities. In the future, you will be held accountable for ensuring that everyone maintains positive identities. Should you delegate that task to someone else, it will still be up to you to ensure that it is properly managed. I will personally be checking in on this process to ensure your work is being done in accordance with our standards. Is this clear? I need you to tell me now if it is not clear. If it isn't clear you should say so now. Is it clear to you now?"

The HR Manager's face became lifelessly pale at that moment... His words didn't seem to be any part of the hollow exhalation of his breath... They seemed to escape from an emptiness beyond him...

"Yes, it is clear to me now."

"Good. Now, as to this one here. I understand that no known identity had been assigned for this character up until moments ago. Is this correct? Effectively, is this correct? Is it?"

Ronald looked at each of us, moving his eyes from one to the other as he asked... We both gave an affirmative nod to confirm it was correct...

"Well, if that isn't something... OK, let me think for a moment."

Ronald began rocking back and forth in his chair, with all of his fingers interlocked; except the pointer-fingers that were extended, and rested against his upper-lip... His eyes shifted their contemplative curiosity to the empty space in line with his shiny reflective desk-top, as he rocked away in his chair... Then he turned his head to one side, and looked up, as if to try and catch a glimpse of a thought inside of his mind... There was an interested smirk that accompanied this movement. Following that, with his hands still clasped, he lowered them to his desk top, and aimed his two extended pointer-fingers in our direction...

"You've never really had any identity impressed upon you that you've ever identified with, have you? Is this predominantly true? Is it?"

We had to consider Ronald's question for some time... After a quick scan of our life's memory, we were fairly certain his statement was accurate, but there was something further that we became aware of as well...

"It doesn't seem as though we've ever really been identified by this world at all... Nor does it seem as though we've ever identified our-selves, this world, &c, &c, &c..."

Ronald was elated to hear us say this... He sprang from his chair, and turned away, facing the etching behind his desk...

"Hmmm... That is truly remarkable. Hmmm... Well then..."

His mind must have been overloaded a bit, as he took a long moment to collect his silent/inaudible thoughts...

"Well, seeing how you didn't have an identity for the time of the incident involving your former *sssupervisssor,* here is what will be done."

He looked over to the HR Manager...

"Initiate the *lightning-bolt* protocol. Strike any name of any of the drones from the records. It shouldn't really be necessary, but it would be best to take precaution in any case. Make sure the addresses are vacant too. More than likely, since this former *sssupervisssor* was drunk, incompetent, and violent, there won't be anything more to this case. Just to be sure though, make the arrangements. If any inquiring is to occur, declare that the entity involved was terminated. Whoever might investigate should only be able to search for someone that doesn't exist, amidst a group of unknown entities, so that it is useless for them to pursue this case."

Ronald paused for a moment to see if the HR Manager had caught everything so far...

"None of that will be an issue. I will see to it that everything is taken care of immediately."

"Should they find reason to investigate our records, tell them that storage of our paperwork has been outsourced. If they inquire further, they may be referred to me. Do you understand all of this as well?"

"Of course. If anyone tries to pursue this case; we do not give out our records, and they are not kept on site. Should there be any further inquiries regarding the issue, they are to be referred directly to you."

The HR Manager began to regain his composed confidence, as Ronald gave him an approving nod...

"That should be all we need for anything outstanding on this issue. Now then, as to the other thing. We will be hiring this individual for the new position. I spoke to you about this after the meeting in the commons-area I believe."

Shuffling through some papers, the HR Manager produced a template, and showed it to Ronald...

"Yes, the *separate-services* position. Let's start the orientation."

The HR Manager looked over at us with resolved disbelief, as Ronald indicated we were to be given this new position...

"What was the new name we assigned this character? The one you came up with, or this character came up with, or... whatever. What was the name? What's the name we will be using now?"

The HR Manager spoke with repressed sarcasm...

"I believe it was *Schizoid*. Was that it?"

He looked over to us disdainfully...

"Yes... *Schizoid* is the name you asked us to come up with..."

Ronald was interested in this name...

"Schizoid, Schizoid, OK... Schizoid then. So that's the name you'll be using. It's quite fitting, actually. Do you know what it means? Do you know where it came from? You know, don't you? Do you?"

As he paused, we let him know that we knew of it from an outdated manual for disorders...

"Yes, yes that's it, indeed! There are some interesting things related to that though. Its etymology is interesting. The meaning of that word is something like, *'of the divide'*. So you've claimed that you don't have an identity, and then taken the name of a disorder to refer to your-self as, *'of the divide'*. That's quite interesting. Do you understand how odd and delightful that is for someone like me? Do you? You don't. Do you? Never mind. It doesn't matter. Where was I?..."

As he paused, we thought of what he might find so incredible or incredulous about our choice of name... There were a few things that indeed could be strange about it, but as he had said, they didn't so much matter...

"You were just making arrangements for Schizoid's new position here I believe."

The HR Manager posited...

"Right. Of course I was. Thank you. Now Schizoid, you will be accepting this proposal in order to keep us from having to turn you lose on your own without a vocation. This position comes without any actual title, or job description, or any actual records that will be kept. Essentially your name will be added to our payroll, and the rest will be unknown to anyone that should try to inquire. No one will be inquiring though, in any case."

"So, our identity is to be the sole property of the facility..."

"Well, that's not how I'd put it. Your identity will be yours, but no one outside of the facility or to some extent even inside the facility will have any knowledge of it. Is there any problem with putting it this way?"

"Perhaps there is, but it sounds acceptable..."

"Alright then, moving forward. You will be employed here to help us with some of the projects we are currently working on. These projects are of a very secretive nature. None of the projects you are to work on will be mentioned in any way to anyone outside of this facility, and only those directly involved in these projects are to be given any information regarding them. Is this understood?"

"Yes..."

"These projects seem to require someone with a special sort of perspective to help us complete them. You fit the non-existent criteria of what I think is needed in a person to complete this work. Although I have been able to bring in any expert that might be of use, we are now in need of something else. What I need is divergent thinking. Expertise of existing knowledge has taken us as far as we've come, but in order to continue towards our goals, we need new ideas. Because it appears to me that you do not think according to restrictive paradigms, I want you to offer your perspective to us. Your job will be to give us your own thoughts on things, your own ideas of what might be done; *etc, etc, etc*... -as you might say. How does this sound?"

"Acceptable..."

"Very well. What we are going to start you off doing, is reporting to this facility at a given time, and studying things I believe will be necessary for you to communicate with the others working on these projects. This studying may be challenging, and you may want to challenge the content of the studying as well. You will be learning from my-self and some of the other staff members here. They will be instructed to allow you to refute anything they are educating you on. Even during this phase of study, you are to give your own thoughts as feedback. Do you follow me so far? Do you understand what I expect of you? Is this all clear to you?"

"Yes, it is clear..."

We knew before Ronald even began explaining this job, that there was no point in trying to get out of this new vocation... Although we were not compelled, excited, or pleased to accept the position, there simply wasn't anything we could think of doing instead... Ronald however, was very excited at our acceptance of his proposal... He handed us a paper from his desk top, and continued...

"Here is a copy of an itinerary I've started preparing. Take that with you tonight as you leave. I will give you a completed copy when you return here. The start time and place will be the same. That much is official. Anything else is subject to change, but you will report here at the time listed on that document. When you arrive, we will issue you a lab-coat, and all the other necessary items you'll need. We will have an office prepared for you with a locker, shower, wardrobe, *etc, etc, etc*... Oh, before you leave here, see that we have The Taylor take his measurements."

He spoke the last comment in the direction of the HR Manager... The HR Manager confirmed this would be taken care of before we left... Ronald nodded in response to this acknowledgment, and went on...

"Now, on that point. I suppose you can wear whatever you wish when you come to work. The only dress-code is that you wear your badge visibly, and that you have your lab-coat with you. When you are in one of the labs, it will need to be worn, but otherwise it is optional whether you wear it or carry it. Everything else can be discussed when you return."

Ronald rose to his feet and walked to his door, indicating that we should follow him out... He shook our hand as we reached the door, and addressed us, continuing to shake our hand, &c, &c, &c...

"Be sure to be on time. There is no time to waste now. We will be working hard to make full use of you now. I'm very excited to see what you can offer. This is a great opportunity. For all of us, I mean."

He stopped shaking our hand, and we exited his office... As we left, it seemed as though Ronald had become quite attached to us... We even thought he might have felt more comfortable locking us in a cell somewhere in the facility, with restraints fastened to us... As we walked out of the lobby, Ronald announced to us...

"Goodbye until tomorrow... Until the next hello, goodbye... Get some rest. You'll need it. Goodbye."

In this parting, we suddenly realized that Ronald had been deliberately attempting to repeat things in *threes* when speaking to us... We exhaled in scoffing-amusement, and began to smirk... The HR Manager was displeased by this unexplained gesture and change in our demeanor...

The Taylor was in the nearby hallway outside his office, having just arrived for a day of work... The HR Manager had escorted us directly to this juncture from Ronald's office... We knew quite well where this office was located in the facility, since we had passed it on each of our evening rounds for some time... However, the HR Manager didn't want to take any chances that anything might go wrong after the meeting with Ronald... He'd mentioned as much as we walked along the hallways of the facility toward The Taylor's office, &c, &c, &c...

Our measurements were taken inside the Taylor's office... The whole process took only a short time... Once our measurements were all assessed, we were escorted by the HR Manager to an empty office that was to become our own...

This was the location we were to meet with Ronald when we returned to the facility... It was a fairly large office; with all the normal furnishings of a live-in-office ... The items Ronald had mentioned were already in place for the most part... There was even a fold-out bed concealed in one of the walls... We didn't see any restraints however, or at least not yet...

Above the door outside was the facility's room number... After we went back out of the office, we noticed this number... Oddly enough, it was room #301.20... That was the same number as the coded indexing-number used in the DSM to denote *schizoid personalities*... Of course it was, of course...

From our new office, the HR Manager took us to have a new badge made... He didn't want to risk that anything should go wrong with this process, even considering the short time that had transpired since he had created an identity for us, &c, &c, &c... After the badge had been completed, we were required to test it... Once this was satisfactory, the HR Manager disabled the system, so no one else could use it to issue any new badges without his ID, password, &c, &c, &c... Then he took our badge away, and said he would return it when he thought it appropriate...

Before we were allowed to exit, another of the security-drones pulled us aside... The drone had been instructed to ensure that everyone leaving the facility sign a form before their departure... It was a confidentiality-agreement...

This form stated that no information involving the facility, or anyone present in the facility, or any action associated with the facility, be disclosed to any entity outside of officially-authorized facility-personnel, &c, &c, &c... Any claims or disclosures with regard to the facility would be denied, and we may face penalties in any event such claims were made... Such actions could result in prosecution up-to and including treason, and subsequent penalties to include summary-execution…

Henceforth, it stated, that we were not to divulge our identities to anyone outside of the facility without consulting HR… In effect, the facility was to be considered as if it did not exist outside of it-self… Everyone attached to the facility was to exist apart from it, unless they were officially engaged as an authorized part of it… By signing this form, we would become legally sworn liars, and were obligated as such, &c, &c, &c…

Unable to leave the facility as it existed currently without singing this form; we complied by inscribing it with the letter *S*… The HR Manager didn't make any notice or objections to our signature. In fact, we had looked in his direction before signing our *S* on the paper, intending to clarify what name to use …

Most of our reasoning was due to the nature of our new identity… If we'd signed this paper as *Schizoid*, we thought that we might have to sign another confidentiality-form, or even be forced to come up with a new identity as a result, &c, &c, &c… Since the HR Manager still held our ID, we figured it wasn't ours as of yet… We thought this might be his way of informing us what to sign, and that by turning away from us, he had wanted to keep us from discussing the topic in the company of the security-drone, &c, &c, &c… No one else seemed concerned with our identity, or what any of this might have actually meant, &c, &c, &c…

As we handed the form over to the security-drone, he checked to see that there was ink in the signature-block… Then he put the form in a folder marked *signed*, and authorized our departure, &c, &c, &c… The HR Manager tossed our ID to us, and bounded back into the facility…

Leaving the now *officially* non-existent facility, we wondered if it would still be here when we returned, or if it would be something else… According to the form, we weren't to consider it as if it existed, unless we were inside of it… In our mind, we were leaving a place we vaguely knew, in order to return to a place we wouldn't know at all... Wandering away from the non-existent facility, we began to wonder about our-self... What might we be or become when we returned to the non-existent facility? Who were we now? We wondered...

101.07 HOME, DRONE CYCLE OF OPERATIONS, MEDIA-VIEWER…

Departing the facility, we trundled toward our living-compartment, through the blinding glare of the returning sun… It was easier for us to see in the dark… During the diurnal phases, it was an arduous endeavor to see through the solar-glare… Due to the reflective-snow, this glare was intensified on our journey… After years of practice, we had developed an impression of this commute that guided us, despite our hindered sight…

We had gradually become accustomed to this trip… We'd look for signs of change/motion, rather than the figures of objects, shapes, entities, &c, &c, &c… By forming an impression of the things around us, we could anticipate what might be present, in spite of our inability to see what was truly there, &c, &c, &c…

On this particular transit, there was a large wooden sculpture carved out of a tree-stump that appeared to have been hit in an earlier accident… Based on the impressions left in the snow, it had apparently been cleared away earlier, but had fallen over again… It had now rolled back into the street… Stopping short of colliding with it, we got out of our transport, and rolled it out of our path…

The sculpture was of these faces that were overlapping each other… Each face held half of another, and they formed this *circle* around the

…

tree-stump... What was interesting about it, was that if you looked at it another way, it seemed as if the overlapping faces were also faces inside of larger faces, &c, &c, &c... None of them actually had much resemblance to actual faces, either on their own or collectively... Engraved at the bottom of the stump were the words, *Totem's Toll*... Only as we moved the stump out of the way, did we observe this engraving, and the fact that it had been hollowed-out...

With the *Totem's Toll* removed from our path, we continued toward our living-compartment... On this occasion, we opted-out of our usual routine, and neglected to frequent the gym prior to returning to our living-compartment... Arriving at our compartment's parking area; we exited our transport, and walked around the structure of the building...

Then we descended some broken steps to our doorway, unlocked the access-door, posited our-self inside, and activated the media-viewer... As the media-viewer projected the colloquial news-cast, we absorbed it with absent-mindedness... Most of our energy and vitality had already been expelled at the facility, &c, &c, &c...

The ability to focus on anything with interest or attention was a difficult tasking inside our living-compartment... This is what we had learned to expect to feel when we were *at home*... Our life's energy was spent gazing into monitors, watching faces pass us by, staring into the rising sun, &c, &c, &c... Home was not a place we wanted to spend our time... Even using the term *home* seemed somehow inappropriate, unpleasant, &c, &c, &c...

For us, home was just an enclosure that offered us rest devoid of reprieve... Our compartment was a sub-dwelling, located in the basement, underneath the foundation of the structure upon which the other compartments were constructed... Numbers had been placed above most of the front-doors to each living-compartment in order to differentiate them...

After we had lived in this structure for some time, an Official Inspector came to review the structure's adherence to ordinances, codes, &c, &c, &c... Following this visit, the building was required to add a suffix to each living-compartment … Compartments above ground level used numeric suffixes, preceded with a dash… All subterranean compartments were required to precede this suffix with a decimal… Our door was located 2 levels below the main level… Incorporating the suffix, our living-compartment was identified as building 301, level .2, compartment 0… This was usually abbreviated as *301.20*… Of course it was…

While at home, we might occasionally become involved in some desired action, but only with whatever vitality remained in us after the time spent at the facility… What remained of our food-rations were usually reheated for consumption at this time… Our life it seems was always being reheated with our evening-meal…

Whatever was left of the news flowed from our media-viewer… We broke-down in the chair facing the media-viewer, with our heated leftovers to consume… Soon we would have to see about completing the *drone cycle of operations*, but this was our interval of *reprieve*…

Perhaps we should give some form of explanation as to what all is entailed in this drone cycle of operations…

Drone Cycle Of Operations…

The first operation in this cycle is to awaken… Predominantly, this is achieved by programming an external sound-emitter to initiate an irritating alarm at the prescribed time… This alarm acts directly on the drone's resting brain, startling the drone out of slumber and into alert consciousness… After the shock of being startled into consciousness wares-off, the drone may begin the next step in the drone cycle of operations, &c, &c, &c…

Once awake, the drone must begin daily maintenance procedures on their bodily-equipment… Any remainder of non-essential body-mass is to be expelled as urine, excrement, &c, &c, &c… This mass is deposited into the plumbing-system of the drone's residence in most cases… In the unlikely event that this evacuation of unnecessary-mass occurs during the hours of rest, the drone must dispose of or isolate any effected linens, clothing, &c, &c, &c… Some items may be cleaned or washed, but others may need to be discarded as a result of such a case...

After proper disposal of bodily-waste, the drone must attend to cleansing their flesh... Using proper washing-techniques, the drone will cleanse their skin and hair... Primarily, this is accomplished in their personal-shower... If the drone is cohabiting, this process may require some delays due to the availability of necessary resources...

In addition to cleansing the outer layers of skin, it is appropriate to ensure that the drone takes proper care of their teeth... Brushing and flossing are recommended to be completed at the beginning and end of each daily cycle... Drones may also opt to use a mouth-rinsing fluid as part of the proper care of their oral components... Fluid-rinsing is not considered to be imperative for most drones, and may be considered optional...

Drones are typically expected to conform to an appearance policy that mandates the removal facial-hair... Male drones might characterize this mandate as, *castrating their visage of masculinity*, or something to such an effect... Although they may object to this mandate, compliance with such policies is ultimately of their own volition...

Some drones may use an electrically-operated device for this task, but that is sometimes considered a substandard practice... Most drones will use a blade or a set of blades, along with a lubricating-gel/cream to cut their hair at a level close to the surface of the underlying epidermis... Often times this will result in accidental abrasions that may bleed for some time...

In the event of a serious injury, it is recommended that the drone apply direct pressure to the damaged area, and if necessary contact a qualified emergency health-professional... For other more minor cases, it is advised that bits of toilet-tissue be applied to soak up the agglomerating blood... Once this is completed successfully, the drone will want to cleanse its face, and remove any bits of tissue/blood... An after shave balm, lotion, or scent may also be applied at this time according to preferences, &c. &c. &c...

If the drone has any length of accumulated hair upon their head, or if there is an allowance for facial-hair, it is often recommended that it be groomed and styled... This can be done in a variety of ways, and may require any number of products, depending on the desired specifications... Typically this is achieved using combs, brushes, sprays, gels, &c, &c, &c... For more information on this process, it may be necessary to consult a beautician, cosmetologist, &c, &c, &c...

With the drone's body properly cleansed in compliance to standards, the next objective is to meet the standards of dress... Most drones are expected to adhere to a very specific dress code... According to the security-drone handbook, there are several standards of dress to be complied with...

For instance, security-drones are only to wear items issued to them... The clothing items issued as complete uniforms, are to be cleaned and pressed prior to each shift... This full uniform is to include the slacks, shirt, hat, under-garments, socks, boots, belt, &c, &c, &c... All issued patches are to be worn in their designated positions, and no loose-threads are allowed in view... Boots are to be highly shined prior to each shift as well, &c, &c, &c...

Completing these tasks according to specifications results in what is considered to be a *presentable/ professional* appearance... It is considered an imperative for drones to demonstrate this professional appearance... Once the drone is able to demonstrate a professional appearance, subsequent steps in the drone cycle of operations can be accomplished...

Although these steps may be completed in various orders, most drones follow this model quite habitually, and with little deviation... Any deviation from these steps; or any other normative-paradigm for that matter, would require the drone to take full responsibility for any resultant consequences, &c, &c, &c... Drones seem to be inherently apprehensive of any such personal-responsibilities...

Having made the drone's appearance compliant with expectations, the drone can attend to the issue of proper nutrient-intake... It is advised that drones consume substances that meet their daily caloric/nutritional needs, without exceeding the amounts required... Most drones consume 3 meals in each drone cycle of operations...

The first meal is typically consumed prior to departure of the drone's living-compartment... In the event that the drone should be operating on a time restriction, this meal may be differed until a later time... Unless these time restrictions or other concerns negate the process of consumption, the drone will prepare a portion of food at this time...

After consumption, the drone may want to clean the area used in the process of preparing the portion...Cleaning of any objects used in this process may be necessary as well... Dishes and cooking utensils may be washed by hand, placed in a dishwashing-device or left for later, depending on the situation... There are some drones that may be able to designate others to deal with such tasks as cooking, cleaning, &c, &c, &c...

The next task in the drone cycle of operations is to commute from the drone's residence to their place of employment... This may be done by implementing personal or publicly operated transports, manually operated bicycles, physically walking, &c, &c, &c... Some drones may live inside their place of employment, and will not be required to complete this step in the cycle of operations... It is recommended that drones that are required to complete this task, allow extra time to complete this process due to external variables that can affect their journey...

As the drone arrives at the place of employment, they are expected to promptly begin engaging in the endeavors of their vocation... Drones are typically expected to notify some entity of their arrival, or verify their presence by some other means... Vocational requirements may vary greatly from one assignment to another...

Predominantly, drones are expected to work 8-12 hours per weekday, for a total of 40-60 hours each work-week, but there can be great variance in this paradigm.... At the end of the shift, drones are typically expected to checkout or clock-out with some authority...

After this is completed, the drone may exit their place of employment, and proceed to their next destination...

Drones may either proceed from their work site to their residence, or any number of other locations... Many will journey to places that sell items they desire to purchase for their sustenance, enjoyment, &c, &c, &c... Any tasks that require the drone's presence in order to complete are most often included in this time between the cessation of work and initiation of a sleeping-interval...

With the multitude of things drones might do in this time, there are some things that are more prevalent... Media-viewing from a drone's place of residence is the most prevalent activity of this kind... This act of media-viewing allows the drone to engage in vicarious-imaginings based on the programming... It is possible for the drone to imagine not only real things while viewing media-programming, but they might even imagine being engaged in activities that are unreal, surreal, &c, &c, &c...

Indulgence in these media-viewed fantasies is considered to be a necessary coping-mechanism... This is believed to be due to the dissatisfaction most drones experience in the world they inhabit, the stress associated with the drone cycle of operations, &c, &c, &c... It has also been reported, that drones are born with a predisposition that limits their ability to accept the real world on its own...

After a reprieve or attendance to matters deemed necessary, the drone may choose to make final preparations for the following day.... Once the drone feels confident that they are prepared, they may find it possible to initiate a sleeping-interval... Some drones may prefer to leave preparations for a later time, rather than accomplish them prior to their sleeping-interval...

In either case, alarms are typically set to initiate the next drone cycle of operations prior to sleep-initiation... There are some drones that may require the supplementation of medication(s) to aid them in initiating sleeping-intervals... Some drones may still find difficulties in initiating or completing proper sleeping-intervals, even with these medicinal-aids, &c, &c, &c...

Those that do manage to sleep successfully may experience dreams… Dreams may or may not be remembered upon waking… Drones might also experience nightmares… Occasionally, it might even be difficult for a drone to distinguish a dream from a nightmare… Often times it is difficult for a drone to separate their desires in dreaming, from their yearnings in wakefulness… Another difficulty sited by many drones, is a difficulty differentiating their nightmares from their actual lives, &c, &c, &c…

This drone cycle of operations is actually quite extensive, and this account is very abridged… Many drones are unwilling/unable to even acknowledge that this process is so elaborate/extensive… Although almost all drones are quite aware of this process's consumptive effects upon them, they mostly prefer not to think about it… Continuing to complete this cycle has become the dominant portion of our very lives…

Admittedly, this description of the process may seem tedious, tiresome, &c, &c, &c… There are other activities and interests that drones pursue, but the amount of time they are involved in such things seems miniscule in comparison… We feel that attempting to convey a brief account of this cycle will help illuminate the nature of its preponderance, pervasiveness, &c, &c, &c …

We had become quite accustomed to this cycle of operations in our own respects… This was in essence, the religious-ritual of which we had all been commanded and conditioned to partake… So long as we observed this sacrament, we would be looked upon with favor… Our existence would be sustained with provisions for food, water, shelter, &c, &c, &c …

Somehow despite our obedience towards this sacrament, we felt not sustained, but desperate, hopeless, hollow, &c, &c, &c… Our own faith in this world to which we prayed seemed to be diminished as a result of this… In our servitude, we wondered what it was we might be serving, what the use might be in this effort… Another question emerged from within us… What did any of this service do to define our-selves? We wondered…

Having never having managed to discover our own identity as a result of this cycle, we were led to believe that this process was a hindrance to our efforts... This *liefstyle* didn't permit experiences of living vitality, and therefore couldn't be considered a lifestyle in our mind... Such a liefstyle was only a prolonging of death...

Dying wasn't our ultimate concern... Becoming lost in this oblivion, having never truly known our-selves, would have been something far more terrible than any death... It was our desire to live; to live in the understanding of what we truly were, to separate our selves from this vapid prolonging of death, to break-free from this oblivion, etc, etc, etc... Despite our desperate yearnings, we perpetuated this cycle like everyone else... How could we possibly deviate from this cycle? We wondered...

Enough has been said on this subject, and perhaps it should have been omitted... Especially when considering all that might be done in life, all that might be written, etc, etc, etc... It does seem better not to allow the things that perturb us to eat away at our thoughts, our time, our lives, &c, &c, &c ... How is it that we find it so necessary to dwell on such matters? We wondered...

Media-Viewer (Virtuous Drones)...

Having already prepared for the next working shift at the facility, we were relaxed enough to focus on the media-viewer... The first complete segment we viewed was an editorialized perspective piece entitled, *"The Backbone of Our Collective-Virtues"*... It was quite common for news programming to present things like this, &c, &c, &c...

Over time, drones ceased to recognize the difference between objective-reporting, and subjective-editorials, &c, &c, &c... Media-viewer projections of what was called, *The News*, had come to consist primarily of subjective-commentaries, human interest-pieces, other agenda driven content, &c, &c, &c... News programming was steadily streamed around the clock, and on multiple signal frequencies... Most news programming held a common centralized theme, though the commentary/content used to perpetuate this message was variable, contradictory, &c, &c, &c...

In this particular media-viewer program, drones were shown in quick, cutting clips of rapid succession... A voice-over rhetoric was read by a respected reporter-drone, conveying the verbal-content of the piece... Observing the separate visual and auditory information simultaneously was intended to create a combined-effect... The complementing and contrasting of the two sensory-projections had an almost hypnotic effect on most viewing-drones, &c, &c, &c...

Each visual-clip had images of drones that appeared to be struggling in some manner... Some drones appeared to be street-dwellers... They would watch ambulating-drones pass them by... Occasionally, an ambulating-drone was shown depositing a small sum of credits into a container extended by a less-fortunate drone... After this donation, the face of the street-dwelling drone was shown fading/overlapping the mutually esteemed face of the generous-drone... This was accompanied by orations declaring the virtues of shared-struggle, esteem, &c, &c, &c...

Another sequence showed seemingly exhausted-drones engaged in manual-labor... Then another set of drones came to relieve these drones, taking charge of their tasks, &c, &c, &c... An entire series of scenes flashed with a similar theme in this presentation... The voice-over perpetuated declarations of the sentimental-zeitgeist... Stating over and over again...

"We're all in this together."...

Voice-over statements incessantly expounded on this point... This rhetoric created as sort of philosophical-scaffolding that seemed intent on building some kind of collective/social-structure... The content of this piece was related to recent assertions that our guvorning and echonomical structures were on the verge of complete collapse... In earlier reports, this was said by some to be inevitable... Other accounts dismissed these claims as sensational exaggerations of minor problems, &c, &c, &c...

This point and counterpoint style of interpretive-insight, would be used to polarize drone reactions... Presenting things in this dialectic/black-and-white manner reduced the populous into two apocopated groups... Once nearly everyone was relegated to these opposing groups, they would then be abridged according to some *common-ground*... Then they were led with greater ease in a more singular direction, &c, &c, &c...

Though this was quite clear to many of the drones, there was little resistance or effort coordinated to negate its effects... Most of these efforts were scattered, disorganized, small, &c, &c, &c... There was also a great deal of uncertainty as to what forces or entities were responsible for this coercion, manipulation, &c, &c, &c...

Additionally, these directions were guided with great subtlety, implemented gradually, &c, &c, &c... There was also a considerable amount of misdirection incorporated as well... It was extremely difficult to observe the actual trajectories or destinations as a result of this, &c, &c, &c...

The overarching theme of all drones being *connected* or all being in *it* together was almost omnipresent... All of the notions/paradigms of seemingly every social-concept were built around this precept... Any drone that might try to deviate from the collective was unanimously admonished as deplorably-selfish, inconsiderate, evil, &c, &c, &c...

Most laws and punishments were understood to be in place to protect the collective from such *self-centered* drones that might deviate from them... Deviations were detested by the drone-collective... Even drones that didn't violate any laws, or intrude on any other drones in any perceivable manner, could be despised/discredited for any *self-minded* actions, &c, &c, &c... Professing any self-minded thoughts or aspirations was unofficially-prohibited... From our earliest memories, we can recall this as the predominant essence of colloquial-thinking, &c, &c, &c ...

Many of the supporting-structures of this collective-conception were used in the media-viewing we were observing... There was the mention; as if fact, that whatever status or vocation of a drone, it was their duty to fulfill their social-obligations towards each-other... This would foster a sense of unity between drones of all varieties...

The continuum of drones was to aspire towards being universally equivalent to each-other... Drones that did not possess high-value skill-sets, didn't receive large payment-sums, and weren't as revered as others... This was to be considered an inequity, even though they were given lower expectations, demands, &c, &c, &c...

These drones of lower-repute were also considered to be more vital to the functioning of the collective, and were considered the *backbone* of its structure... Highly-esteemed drones would fit inverted criteria in a generalized-sense... Generalized-senses were the colloquial-senses...

For all drones to become equal, they would have to become more selfless in service to the collective... A drone could only achieve self-esteem as a result of some self-sacrifice... This was reported as the only form of true-happiness... Everything else was some selfish form of destruction, perpetrated against the good of the collective, etc, etc, etc...

For a drone to sacrifice something for the greater-good was considered honorable... All that was sacrificed by the individual-drones that made up the collective would inevitably benefit the whole collective ... If enough could be sacrificed in this manner, the collective could attain its most valued goal of *absolute-unity*...

It was strange for us to imagine how sacrifice could be construed as a means of production... To us, it seemed that these *honorable* acts were contrary to their intent... If everyone had less, than it seemed impossible for anyone; let alone everyone, to have more...

Such a paradox was portrayed as socially-inevitable, despite its mathematical impossibility... Contradictions were not welcomed in our-society, and those of this nature were treated as if they didn't exist as such... We were to keep these notions submerged within our-selves, or be drowned-out with them in the tides of this present age...

The *facts* in this media-viewing were concerned with recent legislative measures... Due to a recent trend of *selfish* actions in the drone-community, the leaders of our-collective were addressing legislature on the matter... They had reportedly come to the conclusion that legislative policies had not been designed in accordance with the greater collective-good...

To correct the problem of *selfishness* and all the subsequent negatives attached to this, they enacted a resolution... Drones would no longer receive higher pay-rates for working hours past their standard schedules... Scheduled standards were increased as well in most vocations, as it was reported that there was a great deal of work to be done...

Those drones paid on an hourly-rate would be taxed at an increased rate, and all the proceeds would be applied to a community-fund... This community-fund would of course be implemented by the leaders of the collective, and applied towards the greater collective-good...

Minimum pay-rates were to be raised, in order to lessen the burden on less-fortunate drones... All higher rates of pay were to be fixed, until it was determined by the guvornmints that any subsequent changes were warranted... No exceptions were to be permitted without special-approval from a newly appointed guvornmint-committee...

Along with these initiatives, the resolution reclassified all private-property as collective-property... Although there were no intentions at this time to cease any property, it was decided that drones shouldn't consider property to be owned, but shared... Also in the resolution was an order that drones limit their use of resources to include non-publicly operated transports, fuel, food-rations, &c, &c, &c...

At the close of the program, we were again reminded that we were *all in this together*... Then they advised us that in order to prevail, we would have to do it together... If we all pulled-together, then according to the media-viewer messages, we would all pull-through...

We had heard all of this before, and had come to expect these perpetual reiterations... For some reason, we had never fully realized how detestable these concepts were... The truth was completely separate from these abominations...

These were the kind of lies that diluted the truth... They did this in a way that made the truth appear to dissolve within the murky sludge of these filthy lies... This resulted in a perspective where the *truth* was merely a part of the same smut as all these lies... What could be more despicable? We wondered...

That day, we slept in another kind of darkness... We experienced no dreams, but managed to remain asleep throughout our entire sleeping-interval... Many of our previous sleeping-intervals were hindered by restlessness, disturbances, frustrations, &c, &c, &c...

When we woke to the disturbance of our alarm, we felt something only vaguely resembling what might be considered *rested*... In our mind, we believed what we felt was something more along the lineaments of *resigned*... What were we resigned to upon our waking? We wondered...

101.08 UNDER THE TUTELAGE OF RONALD P. VINCENT PHD MD...

The inaugural shift at the facility under our new title and identity was rather uneventful... We arrived in our office promptly; to await Ronald's presence, and commence with our orientation... Throughout the evening, we received various briefings, lectures, explanations, &c, &c, &c... Throughout this evening, we were advised of the facility's expectations, objectives, &c, &c, &c... After this mundane shift, we were instructed to return to the facility according to a schedule Ronald had assigned to us... This schedule was of course subject to change, &c, &c, &c...

Subsequent evenings quickly took on a repetitive nature... Ronald, or one of his designated instructors would give us some text, begin a lecture, a discussion, &c, &c, &c... Our role of absorbing the information was carried out in accordance with expectations... In terms of our progress, Ronald seemed to be pleasantly surprised at our rate of learning...

Various facility-drones often performed demonstrations of the practical applications of the content we were studying... Once we had developed a more functional understanding, these drones would occasionally ask us for input on matters related to their work... Many of them seemed strangely intrigued by our input... Whenever Ronald

...

was present, he would accent this intrigue by commenting that he had, *told them so*... What exactly had he told them? We wondered...

There were quite a few projects being developed at the facility during this time... Many of them had something to do with nano-technologies... The potential of nano-technologies was astounding... Robots built from single-atoms could be made to replicate themselves, be introduced into the blood-stream, operate as a network, &c, &c, &c...

Depending on the programming, these *nano-probes* could be put into human-drones, locate damaged or cancerous cells, repair these cells, clear blood and neuro-pathways, &c, &c, &c... These nano-probes were intended to be implemented in ways that could perfect the physical functioning of their hosts... Health defects would be solved almost entirely... Mental abilities could potentially be improved beyond any intelligence levels ever known... This was something that could have been difficult to believe for most drones, and there was a possibility that it could be used in terrible ways as well, &c, &c, &c... For this reason, progress on this technology was kept extremely secret within the facility...

Most of the other projects were somehow related to this pursuit, and our educational-focus was structured appropriately... We were educated in the fields of physics, psychology, neuroscience, biochemistry, &c, &c, &c... Ronald took interest in the supplemental subject-matter we thought of as relative to this pursuit... In our mind, we would need to study semiotics, linguistics, &c, &c, &c...

Our view was that everything the mind perceived could be associated with some divide... It is by dividing away from everything else that something becomes an entity... Entities are given names in order to keep track of their characteristic divides...

Some entities may be combined into larger entities, reduced into smaller components, given new names, &c, &c, &c... All of this is really just varying orders of division... In our view, everything is comprised of these infinite orders of divisions, &c, &c, &c...

Understanding the relationship between language and math seemed imperative under this pretense... Language was influenced by mathematical predispositions, and mathematics was influenced by predispositions of language in our conception... We considered mathematics to be a language of division, and language was a characterization of the mathematical principles of such divisions, etc, etc, etc...

After explaining this to Ronald, he encouraged us to formalize these ideas into an organized-theory... Unbeknownst to Ronald, we had already initiated this process, and had expanded upon this conception throughout our lifetime... Somehow, we felt it best to pursue this project in private, without presenting it openly, disclosing our progress, &c, &c, &c...

We eventually began to privately refer to this project as, *Schizm Theory*... Our ambitions for this theory became quite grandiose... *Schizm Theory* had the potential to be an explanation of the entire universe, everything in it, etc, etc, etc... It was to be a true theory of everything...

The primary equations within this theory were quite simple, but difficult to utilize in any practical sense... For instance the equation, $\{(f) \div\} = \infty$... Although in words this might be translated as *the function of division is infinite*, in existing mathematics there was little use for this... Extended techniques or functions of the elements of *Schizm Theory* were more malleable, and useful towards projects under development at the facility...

Most of what we called *Schizm Theory* was kept in a single notebook inside of our living-compartment (away from the facility)... Some of the notions of our theory were presented, but never as part of our larger theory... They were only offered in direct utility towards a project...

Each disclosure of this kind made us feel as if our mind were not our sole possession, but property of the facility under our *rheostat*... Over time, we began to feel as if we were losing our mind to this process... Why did we feel this way? We wondered...

74

Years went by as our studies continued... Ronald even sent out for various professors to be brought into the facility, so we would receive the highest form of education possible... By the time we had completed our indoctrination of this educational process, we could have held a number of degrees in a variety of disciplines... This fact alone was something Ronald took great pride in having contributed towards...

Our interest had been held in this process for the most part, but we were not concerned with our level of achievement in the scholastic sense... We wanted something else... To know what had already become known was of little consequence to us... There were plenty of science-drones at the facility with equal or greater knowledge of the contents we had studied... None of this knowledge had led to any real progress on the projects in development, &c, &c, &c...

In order to be successful, we would have to go beyond the realm of current knowledge... For us, this was the true objective in everything... What we wanted was to break-through every existing barrier... It was our desire to shatter the reflecting-glass of the snow-globe-world we had been displaced in, and see the real world from which we'd been divided ... How could this be done? If it could be done, what would we come to see? We wondered...

A certain routine had become part of our studious years... This routine was not unlike our drone cycle of operations... There were some differences, including certain privileges we were granted... These privileges though appreciated, did not serve to separate us from the same abysmal feelings associated with the world of obedient oblivion...

We had been permitted more time to our-selves, due to shorter scheduled service-hours... Although much of this time was intended to be used in development of ideas useful to the facility, it also allowed us to engage in various solitary refinements... This solitude seemed to restore our daily expenditures of vitality, energy, &c, &c, &c... The restoration of our daily energy-expenditures did allow us to be more productive at the facility... Although, by the time we departed the facility, we were still as exhaustively spent as ever...

Every morning after our duties, we would depart the facility, and arrive at the gym to engage in training sessions... Despite our exhaustive state, we still felt it necessary to endure this routine...Our time inside the gym was instrumental in refining our emerging perspective, &c, &c, &c...

Training held some semblances to the *religious sacraments* for us... The gym was like a *church* or a *temple* where drones would enter to make *atonal-sacrifices, confessions*, &c, &c, &c... Then they could emerge feeling *absolved, redeemed*, &c, &c, &c...

Entering the *sacred synagogue of sweat* exposed the auditory senses to a *choir* of *chaos*... Every sound was *intoned* as a living *testament* of this *congregation*... Inside these *testaments* were the *scriptures* of eternal conflict, virtuous ascension, &c, &c, &c... *Hymnals* were *chanted* in the *strange-tongues* of grunts, gasps, &c, &c, &c... Voices of fists' percussive syllables were pounded into bags, pads, sparing partners, &c, &c, &c... Each sound was *praising* its purpose, *decrying* its *nemeses*, pronouncing its *divine* presence, *confessing* its weaknesses, *praying* for its redemption, &c, &c, &c... All of existence seemed to be compressed into this cacophony of sonic-collisions... Inside of each individual sound were its own *apocalypse*, its own *revelation*, its own *genesis*, &c, &c, &c...

Everything was grinding away inside this *furnace* of furry... Sweat poured from the skin, and was flung from its surface in every pounding concussion... Heat radiated off of the *congregation*, as if they were *exorcising demons* that transformed the whole area into a massive *inferno*... Everyone seemed to be on the verge of combustion... Inside every eye, was the *fire* they were projecting, the *fire* reflected, and the affirmed resolve to survive this *holy-battle* despite this exhaustive *inferno*...

The violent forces in the room were responding to their own great *tribulations*... With every *orthodox* strike, the friction of the clashing surfaces was like an *iconoclastic* dispute ... Entities *condemned* their *graven-images, renounced* their body-fat, &c, &c, &c...

All this violence tore muscles to shreds, dividing them into broken strands... Only the very core of what things were could withstand the intensity of this room's intensity... Everything was dissolved to its *spiritual* essence... Could this process strip us down to the absolute depth of what we were? We wondered...

Following this *sacrament,* we would feel the need to be *baptismally* cleansed, so we might become fully *absolved* of our sweat... There was a locker-room with benches, lockers, showers, &c, &c, &c... We would deposit our *possessions* into our assigned locker (# 301), before utilizing the showers... As the water poured-out onto our outer epidermis, we felt the sweat being dissolved away from us, further distilling us into a more concentrated form of our being... After we had been fully cleansed, we would return to our locker, dress in clean garments, &c, &c, &c...

Upon completing our daily training-interval, and subsequent cleansing process, we would return to our living-compartment with a feeling of *deliverance*... Since we had accepted our new position at the facility, we had been transferred to a new living-compartment... This compartment was larger in size, of greater elevation, &c, &c, &c...

It was located on one of the upper floors of a prestigious structure, where other facility-drones were sometimes lodged... There were 5 levels that this structure consisted of, including a rooftop/penthouse, basement storage level, &c, &c, &c... In this building, the basement was considered floor 0, the main was the 1st, the rooftop/penthouse was considered the 4th, &c, &c, &c... Our compartment was behind the first door on the left, on the third floor... Above our door was the room number, *301*... Of course...

Each floor had approximately 20 living-compartments, for a total of 80, plus the rooftop/penthouse... We never discovered what entity was supposed to occupy the level above the one we inhabited, and we weren't even aware as to whether or not any entity lived up there at all... Who might occupy such a place? We wondered...

This structure of our living-compartment was located along the same route we had traveled between the facility and our previous address... Each commute to our new residence would take us to the place where *Totem's Toll* was located... Every time we passed this location, we would find the object in our way, and would have to remove it... No matter what we did to ensure it would not end up in our way again, it always managed to end up obstructing our journey... How could this *Totem's Toll,* always manage to get in our way? We wondered...

Inside the structure of our living-compartment, we would typically activate our media-viewer, prepare a ration of food, and begin settling into the rest of our routine... Every broadcast alluded to the inevitable collapse of social-order, if some greater efforts were not made on the part of every drone within the collective...

Our attention's periphery would absorb these so-called reports with passive acknowledgment, disinterest, &c, &c, &c... None of this social instability, or potential collapse seemed to warrant any real concern... What use was there in any such concern? We wondered...

As the media-viewer droned-on in our periphery, we engaged in other pursuits... Predominantly, we focused our mind on the development of *Schizm Theory*... Working on this theory proved highly beneficial to the pursuits of the facility... Elements we discovered in the development of this theory became directly assimilated into the facility's projects as we offered them... This theory was still incomplete, but even in this developmental stage it proved useful, insightful, &c, &c, &c...

This theory was originally intended to be used in defining things for our-selves... Our ultimate motivation behind this pursuit was to truly define our-self... We still didn't feel as if we had any real identity, despite our new name, occupation, living-compartment, routine, &c, &c, &c... How could any of this be considered what we were? We wondered...

It seemed to us, that if we could comprehend how things truly became understood as entities, then we could understand our-selves as entities... Developing *Schizm Theory* continued to offer us insights into this problem of obliviousness, but it had yet to explain anything in full... Could this theory ever define us according to whatever we might truly be? We wondered...

When the hours fell upon the vicinity of our routine sleeping-interval, we would try to conclude our current series of thoughts... Then we would prepare for the next drone cycle of operations, and initiate our sleeping-interval... Even though we felt our-selves progressing toward something wondrous, it was strange to observe how little this sentiment affected us... Our general affectivity remained predominantly flattened, dysthymic, &c, &c, &c... Why didn't our sense of wonder have a greater effect on us? We wondered...

In many ways, our disposition seemed to result from the uncertainties still prevalent in our perspective... We were perpetually aware of the fact that we hadn't truly defined our-selves in this world of oblivion... In our development, we had begun to see our-selves as separate from the rest of the world around us, but without any definite clarity... It was the absence of our own self-awareness that seemed to tarnish everything around us...

We began to explore our own inner-conflict in the development of *Schizm Theory*... It had seemed to us that conflict was the result of opposing entities/forces... We theorized that there were three methods of conflict... These methods of conflict were defined as opposition, deflection, or embrace... Everything that appeared in the form of conflict would inevitably result in one of these three actions... Each of these forms of conflict could also be associated with a certain tense...

Oppositional forms of conflict are associated with the present tense... In opposing conflicts, it is intended to resolve the conflict by way of immediate action(s)... The act of opposing a conflict is always concentrated in the present tense...

Deflection as a method of conflict, attempts to displace the conflict into some future tense... This deflection could eventually exceed the lifetime of one or more of the opposing entities, &c, &c, &c... The ideal result of deflection is to eternally delay confrontation, into or beyond the future...

Embracing a conflict is only possible if the resolution underpins the conflict it-self... This method is focused on the past tense, for it considers the resolution to be in precession of the conflict... Conflict is very rarely encountered in this manner, and it often seems this method is impossible to even consider...

What kind of inner-conflict were we going through? How were we to approach the conflicting elements of the outside world? We wondered...

101.09 PROGRESS AND PERFECTION...

Following the completion of our educational process, there was a period of exponential progress at the facility... Many of the projects moved quickly to the verge of completion, became completed, &c, &c, &c... Several outside consultants were brought into the facility to verify/test the projects that reached completion...

These consultants were primarily used as *neutral 3rd party verification experts*... They were to evaluate all of the projects in the final testing phase with extreme skepticism... As far as all of the science-drones were concerned, all of these consultants might as well have been the same person... According to their tasking, they were to remain as objective as possible, refrain from any subjectivity, and ensure that their assessments were as thorough as possible, &c, &c, &c...

We began to form an impression of these neutral, impartial, evaluative entities... It seemed as if they could indeed be thought of as a singular/collective-entity... The Skeptic became the name we used for whatever consulting-drone was present in the facility...

Ronald would periodically organize select gatherings in the commons-area of the facility... During these gatherings, none of the projects were to be discussed openly, by name, in actual substance, &c, &c, &c... No one was to disclose any specific information as to what they were working on, or who might be working on a particular

...

project... These were intended to be broad range discussions of theoretical issues, conducted in general/hypothetical terms...

Ronald P. Vincent PhD MD was always present during these discussions to ensure no breach of protocol would occur... He also guided the discussions, and prohibited them from taking place in his absence... The intention behind these meetings was to generate inspiration, while developing a generalized perspective on the nature of the future we were working to create...

We were required to attend all of these discussions without any exceptions... No work was to be conducted during these conferences without Ronald's express permission... Many drones looked forward to these discussions, but others found them to be of little benefit... One of the drones that seemed to enjoy these meetings most, was Thomas H. Traubert PhD MD...

Thomas H. Traubert PhD MD was a descendant of a prestigious line of renowned physicists, writers, psychologists, politicians, &c, &c, &c... The *Traubert* name was synonymous with intellectual excellence and prestige... Ronald personally considered Thomas to be the most well rounded and well informed member of the facility's staff... He held more degrees, in more fields, than anyone else in the facility... His title at the facility was, *Vice-Director of Operations*... There was very little that went on in the facility that was not a direct result of Ronald and Thomas's initiatives...

We had learned many interesting/important things under Thomas's instruction... During our time with Thomas, he had come to see us as strangely talented, unique, mysterious, &c, &c, &c... In his estimates, we were very useful, but he wasn't quite sure as to our commitment, trustworthiness, &c, &c, &c...

Our own assessment of Thomas's position was that he was very astute and often quite correct in his thinking... At some point we became overtly aware of each-others thoughts on such matters... Both of us appreciated this open honesty between us... Working together became quite productive as a result of our mutual understanding, &c, &c, &c...

Our work with Thomas had allowed the facility's projects to progress exponentially... Over the years we made great progress towards the facility's ultimate objective... The ultimate objective was to create the technologies that would be merged to create an event referred to in advance as the, *technological singularity*... This *singularity* would be the last and greatest achievement of humanity... It would bring about an intelligent self-programming entity, capable of autonomy, advanced computational operations, &c, &c, &c...

The work had ceased to progress according to projections before we began assisting Thomas... We were instructed by Thomas as to what the difficulties had been, and what attempts had been made to solve them... Our assessment was that the language of the programming had to be developed differently... In our view, it was imperative that the new entity understand the concept of *entity* with much greater comprehension than humans...

If this singular-entity were to understand it-self as the higher-functioning of comprising-entities, it could inversely consider the world as part of its own identity... If this was done, the entity would not perceive other entities as potential threats, but as functional components of its-self... Without this premise, there was the possibility that this singular entity might eliminate humans as being potentially threatening... Considering these entities extreme capabilities, there would be little recourse for humanity in such a scenario...

Eventually, we convinced Thomas to allow us to develop programming that would make this premise possible... We modified the pattern-recognition parameters to function as continued-iterations... Instead of reaching determinations and terminating computations, it would reach recognition, continue functioning, and modify its own recognition parameters, &c, &c, &c... This required an immense amount of computational power, and the hardware to run such functional programming had not been developed...

After consulting some specialized producers to develop such hardware, there was one interested response that showed potential... A fabrication company that had started building powerful quantum-computers sent a consultant to the facility upon request... This consultant had devised a new form of quantum computer that had the potential to operate with unlimited computational capacity... If it could be built, it would allow us to make great progress on several facility projects...

When we met with The Consultant, there were a lot of questions that concerned the way this device was supposed to work... Thomas led the inquisition, and conducted a very thorough review of the information provided by The Consultant... After a great deal of consideration, the decision to proceed was made... The Consultant was to build this device under the facility's control, and was required to be escorted by a liaison at all times... Anything necessary for constructing the device was to be requested through the proper facility channels, progress reports were to be completed periodically, &c, &c, &c...

All of the support necessary to develop this device was promptly given, and the progress was rapid... In only a few short months, the device was ready for testing... Testing was extensive, reviewed skeptically, and took longer to complete than the device it-self... Following this phase of intensive testing, the device was approved for use... With the proper tools in place, we could now begin programming this device in order to begin realizing the results towards which we had all worked so hard...

The nights that followed were long and arduous... We worked away at the programming codes, finding progress, dead ends, &c, &c, &c... There were times when everything seemed to work perfectly, and other times when nothing worked at all... All of time seemed to flow into it-self, diluting its own passing into a stagnant pool... Overall progress was good, but it all seemed as if it would somehow end up nowhere, even if it all came together... After a while, our *divisional-orders, entity-recognition, recursive-structuring,* and *iteration-awareness* programs proved to be effective...

With all the components completed, the next objective was to make them work together... This meant altering the operations systems, tweaking the programming, &c, &c, &c... It was as extensive as the preceding process, and followed a similar paradigm... Over time, it eventually came together, and the next phase was to be ready to be approached... The next phase was to get it all to work within the framework of specific applications...

This phase of the process was the most extensive, elaborate, &c, &c, &c... We worked countless hours developing this process... Some elements of our theory became necessary to explain, in order to continue to make steady progress... These disclosures were somewhat conflicting for us, but after what seemed like ages, our work began drawing close to its completion...

One of these countless nights, we were attempting to finalize some work involving the basic operating systems for the *nano-probes* ... There was supposed to be one of the scheduled discussions on this particular night... Moments before our scheduled departure for this discussion, it seemed as if we were on the verge of a break-through...

Just as we were about to depart the laboratory to join the others in the commons-area, we had a sudden epiphany... A few lines of code could be altered in the programming we were using, and our work on this phase of development could be completed... We asked Thomas to assist us, and allow us to delay our departure... Thomas knew that this phase of our work was essential to making progress on almost all of the remaining projects at the facility...

Thomas listened to our explanation, and allotted us five minutes to implement our plan of action... As he viewed the application feedback on a monitor mounted outside of the containment-room, we altered the code, activated the test probes, and implemented the new programming... Seconds later, Thomas stood transfixed in viewing the results of our efforts... It was only at the end of the five allotted minutes that he informed us of our success...

We quickly started bounding towards the commons-area, racing to be the first to announce our success to Ronald... Our strides soon turned into a slower, walking pace... We'd each felt suddenly compelled to observe this moment in quiet contemplation... Thomas halted in front of us, and looked at us with an expression of detached wonder...

"*This*, will all be over soon. When it is..."

Thomas never completed this statement, and he never explained what he meant by it... Did he even know what he meant by this? We wondered...

Arriving in the commons-area first, Thomas pulled Ronald aside before the discussions began... When they joined the group, it was announced that our discussion was to revolve around the concept of perfection... Ronald and Thomas both had almost transcendent expressions on their faces... The Skeptic displayed a very different expression in response to the announced topic of discussion...

What ensued had been in the process of being revealed for some time... The very nature of our existence leading up to this event was a part of this scene... Everyone in the room had some notion of everything that would be said... We had all contemplated these notions in some way prior to this event...

In time, these oratory events became known as Thom Traubert's *Perfection Imperative*, and *The Skeptic's Indictment of the Universe*... Within each of these contrary presentations, we observed some of our own concepts being used towards their respective ends... How did they manage to use the very same words/concepts that we had hidden away from the facility in their speeches? We wondered...

101.10 PERFECTION IMPERATIVE...

Ronald allowed the group to converse for a moment after announcing the topic of discussion, and then called the room back to attention... He announced that there had been some recent developments, and that it was no longer necessary to abide by the rules of strict secrecy... Then he advised that we still adhere to the policy of anonymity...

We would be allowed to speak of our actions, our thoughts, our work, &c, &c, &c... However, we were not allowed to speak of ourselves, or our colleagues, or use any names &c, &c, &c... Following these introductory announcements, the floor was yielded to Thomas, who was now standing tall before the group... Moving over to his usual spot along the wall, Ronald remained standing, as Thomas began to address the group...

"Tonight we are on the very verge of achieving a state of perfection, and it is only natural that this should be the case. It is only natural that we achieve perfection, and that we speak of it now. Even if you don't yet believe this claim to be true, it will soon make sense as to why perfection is in fact inevitable and imperative."

Members of the crowd furrowed their brows, fidgeted, perked up their ears, &c, &c, &c... Ronald was in a state of apparent transcendence that made him seem detached from everyone else...

...

As Thomas continued, we observed that The Skeptic seemed annoyed, and had started to take notes…

"First, I would like to focus on why perfection is inevitable. It seems as though the nature of infinity, the law of large numbers, the evolutionary imperatives, and everything that governs this universe, has ordained this to become true. Let's continue without dwelling on any notions or beliefs that pertain to the existence/non-existence of some gawd or gawds, if we may. Such matters are actually irrelevant in this case. Whether it is by gawd, gawds, nature, *my green candle*, or whatever other causality, perfection is an inevitability that can be explained separately."

The Skeptic muffled a scoffing-exhalation at this statement… Some of the drones folded their arms in protest of omitting gawd(s) from this topic, but remained silently attentive… Thomas seemed to notice this, but was unaffected for the most part… He only paused for a slight moment before he continued…

"On an infinite time-line, all probabilities will become actualities. According to this fact on its own, it becomes inevitable that perfection be achieved. Even if this fact is not an absolute truth, we can still calculate the probability of when perfection might be achieved. Considering even highly conservative perspectives, it is all too likely that perfection is actually near. After what we have discovered tonight, it is perhaps even here already, and we have just yet to perceive it."

Aside from The Skeptic, everyone became very attentive to Thomas… The Skeptic made another note, and fidgeted in silent agitation… Ronald was apparently aware of what was happening, but only as if watching from a distant pinnacle…

"Soon we will be integrating the things we have been developing here at the facility. When we do, the world will no longer be in turmoil. There will be no reason for any imperfection. We have perfected the technologies necessary to perfect humanity, and thus the world. Our nano-probes will be able to prevent and treat every ailment capable of hindering our biology. No diseases, viruses, bacterial infections, or even improper nutrient balances will exist soon."

These pronouncements had largely been understood as part of the objectives attached to the facility's projects... In stating these things as if they had practically been accomplished, the majority of the group was still compelled to demonstrate a sense of optimistic awe...

"The human brain will be perfected by these nano-probes. Neuro-pathways will be cleared, organized, maintained, and formatted in a way that allows perfect cognitive functioning. Intelligence levels will become vastly greater than any ever observed before. Everyone will have this technology available to them, and will benefit from it in the very same way. We will all have super-intelligent, perfect minds."

The Skeptic seemed pleased to have discovered something in Thomas's speech as he was writing his notes... Thomas paused to observe the crowd as they seemed to be dreaming with him... Ronald was still in his own dream, though he now appeared more in sync with the rest of the crowd...

"All of this has been inevitable all along. Through evolution, humanity has developed into the most dominant being on this planet. Now humanity is about to move into the next phase of development, beyond our current stage of evolution. Over the course of our evolution, we developed biologically at first, and then cognitively. We will soon begin evolving technologically as beings, in order to be perfected."

The Skeptic seemed to be in mocking disbelief of these statements... He marked down a few more notes, as Thomas began to pace around the commons-area... We had begun to pay closer attention to The Skeptic during this last segment, since most of what Thomas was saying fit the mold of things we had heard from him before...

"If you consider the processes of evolution, the dominant trend humanity has followed has been exponential-growth. Humanity evolved faster than other species, developing things like our advanced brains, thumbs, and upright posture. Using tools further advanced us in our ascension of this world where our physical evolution left off. Then our technological advancements carried us onward from our primitive-tools. All of our developments have been according to exponential-growth."

At this point Thomas went into the time-line of progressions in evolutionary phases… He demonstrated how the rate of evolutionary traits had developed with increasing speed between innovations, mutations, &c, &c, &c… We had seen this presentation before, from an inventor that was renowned for his ability to project future trends, &c, &c, &c…

Under this perspective, humanity had already evolved to its full mental/physical potential… Humanity was now integrating with technology, and evolving through the advancements of integrated-technologies… Now, this integration was being perfected, and the term, *trans-humanity*, had been invented to characterize this integral-process…

"In merging with our technology, we will all have instant access to information via nano-probes… These devices will connect all of us together in remarkable ways. Instead of referencing information over the web, it will be seamlessly referenced and integrated into our thoughts as if it were already known to us. Combined with our enhanced intelligence, we will have created the minds we've always wanted."

The entire group seemed to be in a state of glorious rapture, as they imagined the kind of mind they might attain from this… Only The Skeptic remained anchored to the current scene…

"We will not only be able to access information instantly, and have the intelligence to apply this knowledge in ways currently unimaginable to us. It will also be possible for us to have complete rational awareness of our emotions. This will allow us to modify our emotional states, in order to avoid becoming casualties of our strongest impulses. What we will be as a result of all this is beyond our current capacity to even imagine. The only real word to describe something like this is, *perfect*."

The group was now eager to attain this dream... What would they be willing to do in order to achieve it? We wondered...

"With perfect minds, we will actually be capable of creating and sustaining world peace. We will also be able to use our technologies for other miraculous feats... Imagine a world where we can control the weather, end world hunger, end poverty, and never be required to work another day in our lives. Then imagine that our lives may be extended indefinitely as well."

As unimaginable as this might seem, everyone tried to imagine it... Even The Skeptic seemed to be contemplating these notions...

"There won't be any need to perform any form of labor. Machines will be designed by technological-entities to more efficiently and venerably perform every function of any necessity. All that will be left for humanity to do is enjoy their existence. Any functions that we do engage in, will be made easily enjoyable, and our abilities in these actions will quickly be perfected. Our world will become an expression of our own perfection. Even heaven would be jealous of the earth if it wasn't a part of it!"

These words seemed to turn the room into a still-life... It seemed as if every breath in the room was being held... The Skeptic continued to make notes with a subtlety that appeared rather blatant amidst the contrasting discreetness of the room... All else froze... Then Thomas cut through the frozen tension...

"According to one of our colleges, there is a tendency for all things to collapse into their essence, as a result of their cause. I believe there was actually a similar quote from another *self-reliant* fellow, but I forget how that one goes. There are a few interesting ideas related to this concept."

This idea seemed like a complete departure from the rest of what Thomas had presented... Everyone seemed to be a bit confused at this sudden diversion... Thomas paused for a moment to reference a manuscript of some kind, and then continued...

"From the very core of something's essence, it projects what can most closely be associated with its- *self*. All that is projected from its core becomes diluted in the expansive realm beyond it, amidst other projections, emptiness, &c, &c, &c. Such projections remain attached to their cores, as they expand farther and farther away. At a certain threshold, these expanding projections collapse. The result is a return of something's *self* to the core of its essence."

These words seemed very similar to certain sections we had written in our *Schizm Theory*... It had been some time since we had made any progress on *Schizm Theory*... After hearing these words, we suddenly wondered if this notebook might still be resting between the R.W. Emerson and F. Dostoyevsky texts where we had kept it... As we pondered this, we noticed Ronald's expression changing out of our periphery... Ronald had apparently come out of his trance, and appeared to be in a state of apprehension...

"Perhaps I have not explained this idea very well, but it does pertain to something. What I mean to convey in all of this, is that we all try to project some perfect image of our-selves. If the reason we do this is because at our core, we exist as our perfect our-selves, then at some point it would be inevitable that we would collapse back into the core of our own perfection."

This idea seemed to be a bit too abstract and esoteric for the group to grasp in the manner it was presented... In our own explanations of this concept in *Schizm Theory*, it required a great amount of elaboration, and explanation to organize the idea in a coherent manner... If this was indeed intended to be the same idea in principle, the way Thomas explained it contained a lot of similarity to our own words. Why might this be? We wondered...

"To summarize my formative point here, while briefly reiterating it, perfection *is* inevitable."

The Skeptic grimaced at these words, as if to passively scream...

"Moving on to my second point, perfection is also, *imperative*. There is only one potential problem with the laws of large numbers and perfection. If we come into non-existence before we reach perfection, there will be no means of achieving it. It is our responsibility to our own existence, to ensure we follow through in achieving our own perfection. Unless we accomplish this task, we may fall into the other possibility."

At this, The Skeptic ceased to write... He began to watch Thomas as if he were waiting for him to conclude his speech... Thomas shifted his tone in a way that sounded more foreboding ...

"This other possibility is annihilation. As some of you may be aware, there are other exponentially evolving forms of life that are maligned to our own. Viruses and bacteria for instance, are ever evolving as well, and they do so at an even faster pace than humanity. Without continual technological break-throughs, these things would almost certainly overwhelm humanity. With our new potential, we may actually be able to move beyond their reach."

At this, the room became paralyzed... The recent media-viewer reports of mysterious outbreaks of unidentified viruses flashed in our mind... Thomas continued with his perfection imperative...

"Another imperative aspect to our success is that of life-extension. In the primary phase, our nano-probes will perfect our organic bodies. They will maintain our health by monitoring, modifying, and protecting all of our cells. Once this is initiated, these probes will begin to learn ways of further perfecting our biology. Our goal is to eventually evolve past our dependence on our mortal and biological bodies. If this is successful; and it is likely that it will be, then we could eventually live indefinitely. Unless this occurs though, we will be forced to fend for our survival; against these ever evolving microbial threats, changing environmental conditions, &c, &c, &c..."

Having used our redundant qualifying phrase, Thomas looked in our direction, and winked with his left eye... We nodded in return without any definite expression on our face... Whatever this gesture was intended to communicate to us was unknown... Thomas then began to conclude this line of thinking...

"Should we fail to achieve perfection soon, it could very possibly mean our end. Many of you have some privileged information concerning the dilemmas that we are facing now. Even without this privileged information, it isn't difficult to understand that things are unstable. Media-viewer reports are unable to avoid mentioning the impending potential of a complete collapse of every institutional entity we rely upon. The result of this potential collapse depends on us. We can either collapse along with everything else, prevent this collapse by achieving perfection, or prepare for what might ensue as a result of this collapse. Perhaps we should ask our-selves..."

Thomas looked at us with another wink, and then cast an eye upon the painting we had referenced on the first occasion we became included in this group...

"...Where do we come from? What are we? Where are we going?"

He took note of each member present in the room... His gaze upon The Skeptic was almost a challenge... The Skeptic projected the look of a confident combatant... After quickly dismissing such glances, Thomas completed his closing argument...

"Perhaps there is no answer for us to give at all. For us, perfection might not be imperative, or inevitable. Perfection could very well be imminent."

Except for Ronald and The Skeptic, everyone appeared considerably optimistic at this juncture... Ronald seemed conflicted towards Thomas, as if he were abiding some indiscretion... The Skeptic seemed mostly dismissive... Thomas took a seat next to The Skeptic after his conclusion... Then, The Skeptic placed his hand on Thomas's shoulder, and used that bond to steady him-self onto his feet... No one seemed to notice this, including Thomas...

The Skeptic was just about to begin speaking, when Ronald moved to the front of the group... Ronald whispered into The Skeptic's ear, and then addressed all the others gathered... As he spoke, The Skeptic seemed mildly perturbed by the situation, &c, &c, &c...

"It seems as though we are a bit short on time tonight. We'll reconvene on this topic later."

Everyone rose to their feet, and began to leave the commons-area... The Skeptic watched them all leave, without moving... As we were moving towards the exit of the commons-area, Ronald pulled us aside... With only The Skeptic, Thomas, Ronald, and our-selves in the room, the two operations-managers looked pointedly in The Skeptic's direction...

The Skeptic looked up to see this gaze, and began to move toward the exit, glancing back as if through time, at the spot where the group had been gathered... There seemed to be something unseen that was pushing The Skeptic away, and something in the past The Skeptic kept searching for, that restrained and impeded every attempted motion... What might have been behind these unseen forces? We wondered...

101.11 THE EXTORTIONIST...

Once The Skeptic had departed, Ronald brought us back to the area everyone had been seated... Then he listened for a moment to ensure no one was nearby... As we were seated, he went back to the entry-way to visually inspect the area, ensuring we were truly secluded...

"You might have noticed, that some of the words Thomas used tonight sounded a bit familiar. I would like to address this issue, but there is something you should be informed of first. Please pay close attention to all I have to say. This information is not to leave this room. Once you leave here tonight, there will be no mention of these things at any point in the future. Do you understand this? Will you agree to this? Is this clear?"

We were quite confused by Ronald's overall demeanor at this time... In our confusion, we were compelled to agree with his conditions so we might not remain so perplexed...

"Understood, agreed, clear..."

"Good. OK, now... Well, where does one begin? Thomas, what should I begin with?"

Thomas looked back at Ronald...

...

"I've always believed that we begin with what first comes to mind."

Ronald shook his head affirmatively and exaggeratedly...

"Yes, yes, of course, yes. So let me think."

Thomas chimed in...

"Do you want me to start?"

"No. No, that won't be necessary. I've got it now. Thank you, though, Thomas. Thank you. OK. So... There are several things that are happening right now, and that are going to happen soon. These things have been touched on by the media-viewer reports in some ways, but there are some things that they are not reporting. All of these things are very serious, and very real. What they have to do with our work here at the facility is hard to explain, but it concerns us all."

We were waiting for him to get to the point, and Ronald seemed to observe this... Most of what he told us was already clear to us... Our ability to understand the media-viewer reports for what they didn't report on was on par with what Thomas had alluded to already...

"The entire system is going to collapse. It was always doomed to fall from the very beginning. Mathematically this has become inevitable, imminent, &c, &c, &c. We have been planning for this eventuality for some time. That has been our entire purpose in this facility. Our projects are designed to rescue the present from the future it is headed into, or create the possibility of a new future... It was with this purpose that we approached all of our work."

Ronald's face turned red, and he looked quite upset...

"Thomas is right when he says that perfection is imperative. If we should fail to complete our work before this collapse, it will mean the end. The phynancial system cannot be salvaged in any way now. There will be efforts to convince the populous that something will work to save it, but it is impossible. Because of this, the guvornmints of this world are going to cease to function or even pretend to function. Food-supplies will not be able to sustain current populations according to the last assessments conducted. Weapons will be used by various groups to acquire resources in order to survive. The world will be full of disorder, death, destruction, &c, &c, &c. Anyone that survives this will likely be infected by biological weapons, radioactive affects, or some other horrors of what is likely to follow."

A number of scenarios were described by Ronald where the guvornmints would take various actions to minimize the threats likely to become present, and what the results would be... His depictions all ended up very bleak, and humanity came to an end in each testament he made... We were all doomed...

"The work we have nearly completed now, that you are involved with, is the only way that there can be a lasting future. If we can perfect the nano-probes, there will be a chance for us. These probes could save us from everything. Using these probes, we could appeal to the rational mind of everyone, preserve our resources, and prevent much of this impending doom. All of our hope is in this project. Failure to complete this project means damnation. Do you understand this? Do you?"

We looked Ronald as firmly in the eyes as we could, although he was unsteady in his imploring state...

"Everything you've said makes perfect sense... We will do everything possible to complete these projects... Thomas might have updated you on the progress we have made this evening... If all goes well, these projects will be completed soon... Now, why were Thomas's words so familiar?"

Ronald was comforted by our assurances, but he quickly became distressed at our inquiry...

"I was hoping you wouldn't ask me about that after everything else I told you. You did ask me though, and I did say that I would explain my-self on that matter. As a man of my word, I will hold to what I said. First, I want you to understand that all of the things I told you are true. Not only that, but it is my sole responsibility to prepare for whatever may happen because of it all. Because of this, I had to do everything possible, even beyond the point of my own moral comforts. Do you understand this?"

It wasn't our intention of forcing Ronald into an apology or explanation... However, we also knew Ronald had the kind of character consistent with that of a Dostoyevsky novel... He had once told us that he would rather be punished for a crime he didn't commit, than get away with one that he did...

"Of course we understand... What is it you have to tell us?"

"Someone came to me. They never identified them-self. I was sitting in a café having my usual, and they sat next to me. Then they handed me a binder. This binder had copies of pages from a notebook. As I looked them over, they informed me that these pages had been stolen from a notebook belonging to one of my special-drones. After that, they demanded a small sum of money for the copy they had presented me. If I refused to pay, they would burn the copies and the original. They also told me that they would consider disposing of the notebook's source, and framing me for it if I didn't pay. On the other hand, if I did pay, they would let me know where they had acquired the notebook. I paid them, and they left a slip with your address on it. Oddly, they wouldn't give me your name. Then they got up to leave, and used the extortion-money to pay my café-bill, and tip the barista! The whole thing was incredulous."

"Did you recognize this extortionist?"

We asked knowing the answer...

"No. I couldn't see their face because they wore a hat that concealed it from view. Their voice was strange too, like they were imitating someone else. There was nothing about them that I could identify. I don't even know if they were male or female."

"So they left you alone with the copy of a notebook… How did you connect the address to me, and how did Thomas end up with my words?"

"Later that evening, I began to actually read the contents. I didn't even need the address to know this was your work. No one else could have written it. The ideas were too closely related to the morsels of perspective you sometimes offered us. As I continued to read through the contents, I understood the progress this could lead to at the facility. Considering how you have always been such a private creature, I figured you'd have preferred to keep this notebook private. My mind wouldn't let me loose of this conflict. Thomas walked into my office as I was deciding what to do."

Thomas broke in, offering an explanation…

"When I saw Ronald he was pale. I asked him what was the matter. He explained everything. Then I explained the responsibility we had here at the facility. My position was that you had been given the education that made it possible for you to write this, and that it was your responsibility to provide us with the kind of intelligence contained in the contents of this notebook. Had you come forward with this information, there would never have been any conflict."

Thomas looked at us as if he was disappointed in our non-disclosure of this notebook… We tried to trim things down a bit…

"So you took the copy from Ronald, and studied it… Why didn't you tell us about this whole thing? What about the person that *sold* this copy? Did it occur to you that this person could be dangerous, either to our work functionally or us personally? Shouldn't this information have come to our attention?"

We looked at both Ronald and Thomas… Thomas cut in…

"It was considered irrelevant. You were aware of the contents of that notebook since you created it. The notebook was taken from your address, so it was your responsibility to notice if it went missing. As to the dangers, it seemed that putting anyone on alert might only make things more dangerous. Criminals such as this one are known to be most dangerous when they are exposed. Not to mention the fact that you had kept this notebook secret. We can hardly be obligated to give full disclosures, without reciprocity."

Thomas was extremely indignant with us... It was clear that he was trying to cast us as a negligent figure... So we broke the mold...

"Perhaps we should offer our own perspective... Some unknown person intruded on our privacy, stole something from us, and went to you... When they presented you with this property in the manner that they did you paid them off... Not only did you give them what they wanted in order to dissolve the situation, but you decided to take a look at the contents... Before you made this decision, you were well aware of the fact that these contents had been stolen... By looking into that copy, you knew that you were also taking part in that theft... At some point you even understood who was being violated with such theft... After this, you shared the plunder with Thomas... You didn't know what the contents was until you stole a glance at it... So to claim that it had to do with the best interests of the facility, or the world, is simply not true... It was your own curiosity to steal a glance that led you to do so... You were surely aware that it could have simply been returned to the address you were given... Does this sound accurate?"

Ronald shook his head... His skin-tone faded, and looked like that of a corpse...

"Yes. Indeed it is all quite correct."

We put our hand on Ronald's shoulder to try and console him... It wasn't our intention to break him down... Then we turned to address the other party involved...

"Thomas, it seems you are alleging that we were obligated to disclose the contents of this notebook as part of our involvement with this facility... By withholding these contents from the facility at our own residence, we assumed responsibility for their safekeeping... We are therefore negligent for the theft of these contents from our residence… Furthermore, you seem to imply that by failing to disclose these contents, we were essentially stealing them ourselves… In effect, we were the thief, and these contents were actually returned by this *extortionist* for a small fee… Is this what you are implying?"

"You were taught quite extensively in this facility under the tutelage of Ronald, my-self, and a host of others. You were given this invaluable education so that you could contribute towards the projects and objectives of this facility. It was your duty to do everything possible to contribute to our progress, and you knew this full well. I wouldn't like to use the term *thief* in this matter, but perhaps that is the correct term. Your ideas aren't your own. They belong to this facility. My responsibilities warrant that I make full use of every available resource. Ronald's responsibility to provide us with useful resources obligated him to bring these ideas to our attention. It isn't our intention to place any blame at this point, but if it were…"

Thomas gave us a condescending look instead of completing his speech verbally… We responded with a cutting tone…

"First of all, we have applied our lessons from this facility to the projects within it… The contents of that notebook however, are not a result of the teaching we received here… All of the contents of this notebook exist outside of everything we learned here altogether… The ideas came to us not as a result of our teachings, but despite them… Furthermore, the contents have not been kept away from the facility… Whatever contents have been relevant to the projects we've worked on have been provided to the facility for consideration… That notebook is not only a personal-project, but it isn't even finished…"

Thomas seemed to be building up heat and pressure, and trying to refrain from releasing it all at once… We ignored his tension…

"That notebook doesn't contain mere facts, figures, or diagrams… It contains personal expressions of discovery… Every mark in that notebook is personal… Those marks are the result of our own mind's creation… When we made those marks, we did so alone…

No one else made them, and no one else could have... There is a much more personal depth beneath those diagrams, equations, &c, &c, &c... The projected essence of our very being is imprinted on those pages... Does that belong to the facility?"

Thomas voice burst under the heat and pressure he'd built up within him-self... His words were like a sharp blade, pulled from a bed of hot coals, and swung violently as if to slice right through us...

"Of course it doses! You belong to this facility! Everything belongs to us! We are all in this together!!! You would be nothing without us. Before Ronald pulled you aside, you were nothing. Look at you now. What do you think you would be without us? Just who do you think you are?"

We paused to consider our response, and allow Thomas to decompress, cool down, &c, &c, &c...

"All of our life, we have been trying to understand our-self... *Who are we?* That is the very question that led to everything we have ever discovered... Everything in that notebook is a result of our search to separate our-selves from the whole of oblivion... What we were exploring in that notebook is the process of individuation, or how things become individual things... For something to become an entity, it must be understood as separate form everything else... Each entity we perceive is separated from every other entity... All of existence is really just division... Until something can be separated, it remains unknown, outside of understanding, etc, etc, etc... Who do we think we are? You ask... What if we don't know? What if we haven't been able to separate our-selves out yet?"

Our questions reignited Thomas's fury... He sharply snapped back...

"You know damned well that I wasn't really asking you that."

"The problem with everything is somehow involved in these questions though... We have considered our-selves part of this facility, but that hasn't enabled us to define who we are... Instead, it has created this split-perspective of our-selves... We are split between trying to be a part of this facility, and knowing that at least part of us is something else… In our search to understand what else we might be, we still found it possible to be of use to the facility… Inversely, as part of the facility, we had been able to pursue whatever else we might be…"

Thomas managed to regain a more resolved composure, and added some constructive input at this point…

"Let's forget about anything that's already done for a while. As to the nature of this notebook… Are you trying to say that, without having truly discovered your-self or your own identity, you have been working to discover some way of doing so? Is this notebook then, the process and result of that search?"

Reaching to recover the manuscript he had referenced earlier, Thomas held it in front of us so we could see it was a copy of our notebook…

"Yes… That is essentially what it is…"

"You also said that both the aims of the facility and the aims of your own individuation were never in conflict previously. In fact, they were perhaps complementary, up until this evening. Is this correct as well?"

"Yes…"

"Now, there does appear to be a conflict of sorts here. Would you characterize this conflict as a *schism* of how the facility defines you, and how you seek to define your-self? Would that be an accurate assessment?"

"That could very well be the case…"

"As to this conflict, I would like to make the point that I made earlier. Although, I would like to put it into the context of this topic. We are on the verge of a complete collapse of everything. Should we not complete our work here, there will be nothing for you to discover, and you may not even exist in order to discover it. Therefore, it is in your own best interest that the facility takes every possible action to prevail over this collapse. Do you understand this?"

"Absolutely... Your role requires you to do everything in your power to accomplish the objectives of the facility... That is not being discounted... However, we feel it necessary to establish that we are not mere property of the facility... We exist as an entity of our own... As such an entity we also possess things, such as the ideas inside this notebook that belong to us alone, and not as property of the facility... What was stolen isn't from our-selves, but of our-selves. Does that make sense?"

Rolling his eyes at us, Thomas groaned with annoyance... Ronald hardly seemed present in the room at all... His mind seemed to be elsewhere, and the rest of him had just been left behind ...

"I suppose that is clear enough. In the future we will be more *considerate* of your personal privacies. As for this content here..."

He waved the copy again...

"...Perhaps our acquisition of this material was less than commendable. Now that it has become known to us though, we will need to make full use of it. Surely, you'd have to agree with this?"

"Putting these ideas to use has never been an issue... If this content is to be put into full use, it will obviously need to be distributed... Perhaps the content could be converted into a less personal format before distributing it... Then you could turn that copy over to us... If our notebook is still missing, and wasn't just copied, we would be glad to have something in place of it..."

"That won't be possible. Other copies have already been made, and are being distributed. You will receive a copy of your own before you leave. When our work here is finally done, you will be greatly responsible for our success. That should be a point of pride."

"There is still something very bothersome about all of this that hasn't been mentioned... How could this extortionist have known of our involvement at this facility? Why did our specific living-compartment become invaded? How could this have been done with no signs of intrusion? Why did this extortionist bring the copy to Ronald? What is it that could have allowed all of this to happen in such a way as it did?"

We waited for some reply that never came... Ronald held a genuine look of uncertainty, obliviousness, &c, &c, &c... Thomas seemed indifferent, as if none of this was of any concern ... So we asked...

"Should we start taking any other steps to ensure our work at the facility isn't further compromised or threatened?"

Thomas looked at Ronald as if he wanted permission to answer first... Then without any response from Ronald, he cut in...

"We've already taken steps to ensure our interests are protected. It would be ill-advised to explain these actions due to the vulnerability they might impose upon our efforts. You might want to consider paying closer attention to your surroundings, and review your living-compartment for any evidence that might exist. If you do observe anything that could have implications on the facility, be sure to let us know immediately. In fact, we should be contacted prior to notifying any of the authorities, due to the facility's special circumstances. Is this clear?"

Our head nodded affirmatively without any consideration, deliberation, &c, &c, &c... We had become conditioned to accept anything imposed on us by an authority-figure... In this moment, we became aware of this for the first time... We began to understand something about our own lack of discernible identity, through this selfless obedience to authority... Without being officially dismissed, we turned to leave...

As we left the room, we felt lost... Thomas studied the copy of our work, and Ronald stood next to him as if he weren't even there...

We walked to our transport, and made our way to our living-compartment... Even as we arrived inside our living-compartment, we felt lost... Was it even possible for us to define our-selves in this world? We wondered...

Media-Viewer (Drones Pull Together)...

Inside our living-compartment, we stared into the media-viewer... We watched with vapid absorption, as the usual *news* was projected into our view... There were serious concerns being reported, such as a possible phynancial collapse of the global-*baneking* system, a guvornmints funding issue that could unravel, an erosion of social-order, &c, &c, &c...

A special-presentation on selfishness was projected... According to the narration of the news drone, there had been too much selfishness in drones... Statistics were displayed to support this claim, although there was no direct correlation of these statistics to selfishness, and they were likely based on faux-data... Productivity had dropped despite the increased working-hours... Expenses had increased despite the new taxing, community-funding, &c, &c, &c... Inflation was also rampant, although no mention of a cause was given, such as the recent wage adjustments, increased quantities of currency put into circulation, &c, &c, &c...

More initiatives were announced in the scroll of text that ran like a conveyor belt along the bottom of the projection... Drones were now to pay an increased tax percentage... New taxes were put on non-issued food-rations... Residential costs were to be fixed at the rates currently in place... No evictions were to be allowed without authorization from the guvornmints...

A curfew was put into place for all drones not commuting to or from their place of official-duties... Even charitable actions during such hours were not to be permitted without special-authorizations...

Criminals found guilty of violent crimes could now be tried under the death-penalty... Other crimes were to be tried under greater penalties as well...

Following these announcements, an interest-piece was projected, focusing on one particular drone... This drone was donating all of its personal-time and resources to help others... It had cut its sleeping-intervals to only 3 hours per 36 hours... All of its income was used to provide for other drones' basic living-expenses... The drone was welcoming other drones to live within its living-compartment free-of-charge... In the hours not committed to official-duties, the drone helped to repair living-compartments, volunteered for serving needful-drones in food-lines, &c, &c, &c... According to the drone, it was important that other drones start doing likewise... A quote from the drone concluded this segment...

"We are all in this together, and we are nothing without each-other."

Then the media-viewer advised drones of ways they could volunteer their time... They advised that each drone could do something to help the collective... In a dignified tone, the narrator-drone reiterated the colloquial-narratives...

"We are indeed, all in this together, and together, we can make it through anything."

This projected facade was contrary to everything we considered true... We'd had enough of this incessant indoctrination... There was no desire to view any more of these hapless-lies, collective-imperatives, &c, &c, &c... It was now impossible not to despise this drivel, considering everything we had seen, all we had learned, &c, &c, &c...

We turned the media-viewer off, and immediately felt an improvement in our perspective... Then we thought of leaving... We thought of leaving the world of media-projections, the facility, the collective, &c, &c, &c... What if we just left? Could anyone just leave? Was it even possible?

As we prepared for the next iteration of our cycle of operations, we wondered... Soon, we were ready to initiate our next sleeping-interval... Even as we were nearly adrift in sleep, these thoughts ran through us... What if we did just leave? We wondered...

During our sleeping-interval, we experienced a strange occurrence... It was unknown to us if we were asleep or not for this occurrence... We felt our-selves drifting in total darkness... There was no light at all, and we couldn't move or even attempt to see our-selves... This darkness made it seem as if there was nothing at all... Even our own presence seemed to be a part of this darkness... At first, we thought this great darkness was just a part of our living-compartment... After a while, we figured we must be in a strange dream... Whatever the case may have been, at some point we drifted into a dark sleep...

When we woke some time later, we found our living-compartment to be quite dark, but not in the complete form it was during the occurrence... In waking, we felt as if the experience had separated us from everything around us... It had even seemed to separate us from our-selves... Then, in waking, we felt a strange form of relief... For some reason, it felt as though we had returned to *our-selves*... What had transpired in this strange occurrence? We wondered...

101.12 IT BEGINS TO BE SEEN…

On our way back to the facility, we passed the area where the *Totem's Toll* stump was located… We realized that it had not obstructed our previous commute from the facility… It had been in the way of our travel towards our residence on every other occasion, since we had become aware of it… Now it obstructed our journey in the other direction…

Getting out of our transport to remove it, we noticed that it had been split across one of its several *faces*… It hadn't come apart, but it was barely held together… What had happened to it since our last encounter with it? We wondered…

As we arrived at the facility, Thomas had been awaiting us with enthusiasm… Apparently, he had even tried to reach us during our sleeping-interval… There had been some new developments in our absence… We completed the identification-procedures, went into the facility, and walked to our office with Thomas… Once we set foot inside our office, he began to inform us what had happened…

"The nano-probes have begun to divide them-selves into orders. They're separated according to operational purposes. Not only are they evolving into ordered functions, but they're doing more than just replicating. Instead, they're creating specialized nano-probes.

…

Each iteration also seems to become more efficient... The nano-probes that are less efficient are either upgraded or integrated into newer iterations. It's as if these things are deliberately evolving free of intervention! We may have already finished everything short of releasing this marvel into the world!"

None of this was a surprise to us... Our programming was designed to establish this outcome... These nano-probes were created with the first generation of what would become known as extra-computational mechanics... The abbreviation ECM was to be used for this technology... In addition to the nano-probes, there were projects designed to create other mechanisms using this ECM technology... Once these projects were completed, the perfection described by Thomas would actually have become feasible...

Thomas explained some specific details on these developments, and escorted us to one of the facility's laboratories... Inside the laboratory, a drone had been isolated inside a containment chamber... Nano-probes had been introduced into the drone's biology... This drone had exhibited certain health defects prior to the introduction of nano-probes...

Following introduction of the nano-probes, these defects were eliminated... Prior to the introduction; skin cancer cells had been spreading, cholesterol levels were unbalanced, lipid content had exceeded functional-levels, &c, &c, &c... After a period of only 6 hours, the drone now appeared to be in perfect health... Biological monitoring systems showed his statistical functioning to be at optimal-levels... What had been an ailing-drone, was now a specimen of perfect health... Was physical perfection this easy now? We wondered...

Touring the facility laboratories with Thomas, we found that this was only the beginning of what was being done... Ronald joined us after a while, and seemed to be dreaming next to us... The next site we visited was a laboratory containing a drone that had been transported from a local penitentiary...

This drone was a notorious criminal that had been making media-viewer headlines for some time... The drone had committed over 300 murders, multiple assaults, thefts, &c, &c, &c... According to the current manual for classifying disorders of cognition, this drone had a severe *social-integration disorder, reverse-empathy derangement, violence addiction*, &c, &c, &c... No existing treatments had been developed for use on such drones with any real success...

Nano-probes had been covertly introduced into the drone 12 hours prior to our observations... The drone's brain had been physically altered by the nano-probes... These nano-probes restructured the drone's neural-connectome, balanced neuro-chemical processes, modified genetic-properties, &c, &c, &c... Some demonstrative testing was to commence, in order to test the results of the nano-probes' effect on the drone...

The Notorious Drone had a history of cruelty towards animals... In an interview, the drone had expressed that every time it saw a cat, it would feel a need to kill it... This compulsion was overwhelming, and the drone felt as if it would die if it did not act on it... While confined to the penitentiary, the drone had become known for this cruelty... Some feline-specimens were brought into the penitentiary to combat a vermillion-infestation problem ... Many of the incarcerated-drones developed positive sentiments towards these feline-specimens ... Despite the others' sentiments; the Notorious Drone would kill the cats on every possible occasion...

In order to test the effects of the nano-probes, a kitten was brought to the laboratory where the Notorious Drone was being held... Then the drone was left in the room with the kitten... No other entity was to remain present... If the drone had been placed in such a scenario prior to this, it would have undoubtedly attempted to kill the kitten...

According to the observations of this experiment, the drone did not attempt such an act... Instead, the drone had approached the kitten passively, lain down next to it, and begun to pet its face calmly, &c, &c, &c... Once this had been observed, the security-drones were sent to separate the kitten from the Notorious Drone... The drone carefully handed the kitten over to the security-drones, and asked that they take good care of it...

These security-drones were instructed to be harsh with the Notorious Drone... In accordance with instructions, they had forcefully pushed the Notorious Drone against the wall... Instead of retaliation, the Notorious Drone apologized for the inconvenience it had caused the security-drones...

Then the drone began to request an opportunity to apologize to all of the drones it had wronged in its life... Soon the drone began to weep openly... As the security-drones exited the laboratory, the drone requested once more, that they be kind to the kitten... This scene was beyond astonishing... What was to be done with concern to this drone now? We wondered...

There were other applications that had been in testing at the facility as well... Thomas escorted us through the containment-areas in order to show us the results of our work... As he showed us around, we began to feel a strange sense of detachment... Everything seemed unreal to us... It was as if the whole world had been exchanged for some bizarre counterfeit version of it-self... We felt a distance between this world and our-selves, and a distance between us and our very selves, etc, etc, etc...

Everything we witnessed was according to facility designs, plans, objectives, &c, &c, &c... Despite these intentions, it was perplexing to see it in front of our eyes... Another project, designed to optimize lung-functioning was viewed... A subject was submerged in a tank of water, with respiratory monitoring displayed on a screen... This subject had been suffering from emphysema prior to nano-probe introduction... When we arrived, the subject had been holding its breath for over 3 hours without any difficulties... All vital signs were strong, healthy, functional, &c, &c, &c... With a wide grin on the subject's face, they gave us a *thumbs up* as we'd entered, and exited...

Continuing our tour of the facility, we arrived in the testing-area for other radical applications... This area was host to multiple demonstrations... On a treadmill, a subject was running a marathon at an Olympic sprinter's record pace, and had almost completed this feat... Another subject demonstrated a variety of physical abilities... The subject demonstrated a vertical leap that exceeded any ever measured, performed hand-stand pushups with only two fingertips secured to the ground, punched a hole through a ¼ inch steel panel, &c, &c, &c...

As this was being demonstrated, another subject read volumes of books, while also reciting separate passages upon request... The subject had also proved the Riemann hypothesis, created and solved a *rubrics-hypercube*, &c, &c, &c... This subject had been born with a learning disability, and had never attempted any artistic designs prior to introduction of nano-probes... Before we left, the subject sketched a depiction of the facility's exterior from memory... Later, it would be compared to the actual facility's exterior, and proven to be accurate to scale in every detail portrayed in the sketch...

Everywhere we looked there were equally miraculous sights to be seen... The nano-probes could transform human dysfunction into savant-like-powers, transcendent-abilities, &c, &c, &c... Each subject had been transformed as a result of the nano-probes... They were no longer afflicted in any way... The facility had succeeded...

Days later, Ronald organized a gathering on the facility's rooftop... This was to demonstrate the weather-alteration technologies that had become theoretically functional... Ronald input a command to initiate a thunderstorm in the vicinity of the facility... Within mere minutes, the storm had gathered, displacing the clear blue sky, &c, &c, &c... Upon input command, torrential-rains fell all around the facility... Not one drop came down upon the rooftop though... After a moment of this rain, Ronald input the command to end the storm... Seconds later, the sky was clear-blue again...

Having witnessed all of these things, we almost couldn't even imagine what kind of future would result from these marvels... As we were walking back into the facility, we heard Thomas speaking to Ronald... His voice softly said the words...

"This is only what begins to be seen."

For this to be a mere beginning was somewhat contrary to our stated objectives... Our understanding was that once these things were proven to be effective, our work would be complete... Hearing these words, we began to think of the implications of such a statement... An ominous feeling began to set into our mind... If this was only what had begun to be seen, what was next? We wondered...

101.13 CELEBRATORY-ACTS...

Following the weather display, Thomas and Ronald held private conversations in Ronald's office for several hours... Someone had mentioned on the rooftop that all of this progress merited some celebration... After their private discussions, Ronald and Thomas went to inform various members of the facility that certain accommodations were being made to celebrate our successes... We were informed to meet in the commons-area at a specific time for more details...

As everyone gathered in the commons-area, we observed the sentiments each of the drones projected as they arrived... Everyone seemed to be in anticipation of what celebratory news might be imparted to us... Despite all that had occurred in the facility over the past few days, it was the celebration that intrigued everyone...

The drones all speculated where the celebration would be, what they would drink, how much they would drink, what amatory-adventures they hoped to engage in, &c, &c, &c... We observed them with a disturbed curiosity... Were these the things we should be concerned with? Should we have felt more like them? We wondered...

Ronald and Thomas entered the commons-area, and everyone cheered in response to their entry... They acknowledged the cheers,

...

and Ronald called for order... Thomas took a seat, and the others all followed his lead...

Then Ronald announced that we were to depart the facility, and gather at another specified location... Everyone was to make arrangements for transportation before departing, and determine how those that might become inebriated were to be transported afterwards... Once this was determined, we all departed for the destination of our celebration...

We had been selected to transport most of the drones in a large transport that one of the other drones owned... Our selection for this task was determined by the fact that we did not consume inebriating substances. Those that were not transported in this vehicle, departed the facility in personal-transports, and made separate plans for their departure from the celebratory-site...

Along the way to the celebratory-destination, the drones became quite enthusiastic about the substances they intended to consume... Arrangements were made to determine what purchases would be made as a group, what activities they would try to initiate in conjunction with this consumption, &c, &c, &c... They were enthralled with all the minutia involved in these inebriated-activities... These activities represented their ideals of a good time... What was this ideal? We wondered...

Arriving at the predetermined celebratory-destination, the passengers ecstatically burst into nonsensical vociferating, jouncing, &c, &c, &c... Before the transport even came to a stop, they had opened the doors, evacuated the transport, and were bounding towards the entrance... They rushed to the front door, attempting to gain some hierarchical prestige or precedence... As they arrived at the door, they had to form an organized line in accordance with the establishment's entry-procedures...

Inside the establishment, there was a loud droning of earsplitting sound-waves being emitted from a series of loudspeakers... Intense lights of greatly varying color were projected in rapidly shifting patterns, as strobe-lights pulsated in bursts of blinding brightness,

&c, &c, &c… It was difficult to see or hear anything coherently…
Our senses were overloaded, as if being bombarded with sensory-
munitions, severing any communicative capabilities, &c, &c, &c…
What was it about this sensory-encumbrance that others found so
exhilarating? We wondered…

Throughout the night, the drones consumed massive quantities of
alcoholic beverages… The alcoholic content of these beverages was
produced as a result of the bio-processes of yeast… Yeast consume
the carbohydrates within the substance of these beverages, and then
excrete alcohol and carbon dioxide as a result… This alcohol
excrement is primarily of the ethanol variety, as opposed propyl,
isopropyl, methyl, &c, &c, &c…

Yeasts have also been used to generate electricity in microbial fuel
cells, and in production of many biofuels… One of the projects we
had worked on at the facility, involved the possible methods that
nano-probes could process alcohol, and its subsequently metabolized
toxins… The nano-probes could actually convert these disruptive
substances into fuels to power them-selves, and expel them as
functional forms of carbon, hydrogen, oxygen, &c, &c, &c…

On this occasion, alcohol was being used to fuel the drones in their
celebratory-acts… Some of the most esteemed minds of the entire
collective-populous became indistinguishable from any common-
drone in this alcohol fueled frenzy…The primary reason for this
blurring of distinguishable cognitive prowess, has to do with the way
alcohol interacts with neural-activity…

Alcohol interferes with the brain's neural-processing, and can disrupt
cognition extensively… These disruptions can change mood,
behavior, coordination, rational abilities, &c, &c, &c… In some
cases, this can cause an elated state, though the opposite effect is also
observed… As alcohol consumption increases, there are a series of
behaviors/effects that may be observed… On this evening we
witnessed most of them…

Thomas displayed a great number of these effects… Upon entering
the establishment, he promptly ordered several rounds of shots for

all the drones from the facility... Soon after this, Thomas displayed features of diminished inhibition, euphoria, &c, &c, &c... With uninhibited impulsivity, he implored various drones to dance, consume more alcoholic beverages, &c, &c, &c... His dancing became erratic; his equilibrium, destabilized; his speech, impaired; &c, &c, &c...

More consumption of the inebriating liquids ensued... Thomas and some of the other facility drones began to show signs of emotive dysregulation... Their reasoning was impaired, and incidental actions were perceived with malicious intentionality... When a group of non-facility drones accidentally stumbled into Thomas as he was holding a shot, the liquid spilled onto the floor, depriving Thomas of its consumption... He immediately accused these drones of deliberately doing this, and threatened to respond with violence...

The non-facility drones made amends with Thomas by buying him a drink... Following this, they were welcomed into his company with exuberant esteem... Together they continued to consume massive quantities of alcoholic beverages... These drones were from another scientific institution in a nearby area, and Thomas was delighted to learn this... Throughout the evening they toasted every prominent scientific discovery, excluding those that occurred recently at the facility... Quantitatively speaking, it would be difficult to even estimate the amount of alcohol imbibed throughout the evening...

Eventually, Thomas reached his tolerance-threshold as a result of all of this alcoholic consumption... He had just finished a toast to *Archimedes of Syracuse*... In his toast, he quoted Archimedes in Latin (yelling over the background noise), as he raised a cylindrical-glass containing a sphere of ice...

"Transire suum pectus mundoque potiri!"

This quote was actually inscribed on Thomas's Fields Medal that he had shown to us at one point... In translating this phrase into English, it can be expressed as, "*rise above oneself and grasp the world*"... Following this toast, Thomas vaulted him-self onto a table, extended his arms towards the ceiling, and then collapsed...

His body caused the table to collapse along with him, and the representative of the establishment came rushing over in response... Some of the drones helped us revive Thomas, and escort him to a nearby booth... We were advised by the establishment representative to get control of Thomas in order to avoid being thrown out... Payment for the broken table was also demanded in exchange for our continued occupancy... The drones all pitched in currency to settle the dispute over the table, and Thomas was allowed to remain, as long as he *behaved*...

Thomas remained in this booth for the remainder of our time in this establishment... Other drones continued to drink heavily, behave erratically, speak in impaired-tongues, &c, &c, &c... We kept watch of them, in order to ensure that they could all be transported out of this establishment safely, and without any major disturbances... Why had we agreed to this implicit set of responsibilities as the sober member of the group? What interest did we actually have in any of this? We wondered...

When the establishment's clock struck the hour of its mandatory closing time, the drones were finally forced to leave... We went around the establishment trying to corral the disorganized herd of drones for departure... With great effort, we finally managed to gather the herd into the parking-lot... From there, it was some time later that we actually managed to crowd them into the transport in order to depart the establishment...

As we drove each of the drones to their respective living-compartments, we found our own tolerance-levels approaching threshold... While we attempted to acquire directions, they sang songs, engaged in incoherent shouting, nodded off, &c, &c, &c... What they didn't do, was attentively provide us with the information necessary to reach their living-compartments... Somehow, we eventually managed to drop them all off ... Later; it would become known to us that some of them had inadvertently mistaken their residence for some other location... By the time we had departed with the last of them, we were quite exhausted...

Having completed the distribution of drones, we returned the large transport to the facility, entered our own transport, and proceeded towards our own living-compartment... As we drove-on, it seemed as if we had become completely detached from everything... Despite our familiar surroundings, we were uncertain as to where we were... Questions of our non-geographical positioning passed through us... Where did we come from? Where were we? Where were we going? We wondered...

Finally, our transport pulled into the parking-lot of our residence, and our disorientations faded... We entered our living-compartment, as we began to think of the nature of this celebration... The reason for this evening's celebration was supposed to have been the achievements of our minds... Our minds had created the means for a new future after applying such immense diligence, focus, innovation, &c, &c, &c...

In the practice of celebrating our minds' achievements, it was somehow supposed to be appropriate to impair the mind's ability to function... After creating something so profoundly useful, we were to destroy the very thing that enabled us to do so... How could this be considered such a fitting conclusion? Why was it that everything seemed to lead to some break-down? We wondered...

101.14 THE SKEPTIC'S INDICTMENT OF THE UNIVERSE...

After the celebrations, we were unable to complete a proper sleeping-interval before returning to the facility... Most of the drones were quite impaired due to lingering effects of alcoholic consumption... This had little effect on most of the work being done at this point... The Skeptic had not partaken in the celebrations, and was now busy reviewing our results... Throughout this phase of the facility's projects, most of us were only present in order to answer The Skeptic's inquiries...

Eventually, the time came for us to gather into the commons-area for another scheduled discussion... On our last meeting, The Skeptic had been unable to speak due to time-constraints... This evening was quite different... Likely due to the lethargic effects of the other drones' consumption, none of them felt much like speaking... Even before the meeting began, the room seemed to be a crypt filled with lethargic undead-entities, &c, &c, &c...

Ronald was last to arrive, and asked if there was anything the group wished to discuss... He looked physically ill as he posed this question... No one so much as stirred in response... Most of the drones were staring at the floor... Then The Skeptic spoke-up...

...

"Perhaps we should resume our previous discussion on the nature of perfection."

There was no response for or against this motion, so Ronald invited The Skeptic to lead us in the discussion… The Skeptic approached the front of the group as he reached into his pocket to reference his notes… Once he had skimmed over his notes, he returned them to his pocket, and leaned against one of the pillars of the facility before he began his speaking…

"Life being what it is…"

He spoke as he looked around the room to see the reaction…

"…we never really know anything, rarely know well enough, and all end up dreaming of revenge."

As The Skeptic spoke these words, it appeared that a few of the drones strained to focus on his speech…

"Without any means of knowing anything in life, we cannot truly comprehend anything, let alone the concept of perfection. Perfection is an impossible conception. In fact, it isn't even a conception. A conception is contrary to what the conception of perfection would have to be. Actually, the nature of any conception is a misconception. This is the first conception that we must articulate, and of course it is impossible to do so. Despite this, some explanation might make it possible to convey this *misconception*. Ha, ha."

The Skeptic appeared to have the limited attentive capacity of every drone in the room, although they still appeared quite out of sorts… This first premise was presented in a light jovial manner as if it were almost a joke…

"Let me begin by articulating something about the nature as to why we can never really know anything. First of all, there is the proven physical notion that we call the *uncertainty principle*. According to this principle, we can never measure an object's position without altering its velocity, and we cannot measure an object's velocity without altering its position. As a result, everything in the physical world is subject to uncertainty."

This uncertainty principle had been held true to the drones in the facility since primary-school, and they were all following The Skeptic's logic easily enough thus far…

"In addition to this uncertainty, there is another problem that relates to it. This uncertainty is built into the atomic matter all things are comprised of. As larger entities are observed, their uncertainties also become greater in proportion. Uncertainty is projected and reflected from/onto every atom that exists. The larger an entity, the more uncertainty exists within it."

None of the drones seemed to be thrown off at this point, although some disinterest was slowly developing…

"As if the physical uncertainties of the entities we observe aren't enough of a problem, there is another issue that arises. Everything we observe is disconnected from us. We cannot observe anything as it is, but only as some simulation of it. When we perceive an entity in sight, we do not see the entity. What we see is mere simulacra. Photons are projected from the object, as others are projected unto it, and reflected off of it. Then these photons reach our eyes… An image is then projected back, with all the other photons focusing in, and our mind alters the image in a way that it finds useful. That is not to even mention, that this is a two dimensional compression of at least a three-dimensional object. Only the face of the object on a plain that can directly reach our view is seen. All we see as a result is a conception of these simulacra. In all this dilution, it is impossible to know anything as it truly exists. Life being what it is, we can never really know anything."

Some of the drones began to develop a more alert focus at this point, but others began to become dismissive… The Skeptic started to exhibit greater confidence as he went on…

"Since we can't know anything really, we are forced to make the most of whatever it is that we are capable of, short of real knowledge. We essentially construct some notions of probabilities based on experiences or equations, make some assessment of this, and consider it truth until proven otherwise. As a result, we discover that we rarely know anything well enough."

The Skeptic paused to drink some water from a bottle that had been set on a counter top nearby before this meeting began... One of the drones asked how The Skeptic could know if it had actually drunk any of the water... A smirk appeared on The Skeptic's face, but no answer was given... Instead The Skeptic continued to develop its premise...

"Instead of knowledge we substitute conceptions. Conceptions are the result of taking our uncertain *simulacral* perceptions, comparing them to other perceptions, and translating them into some form of language. Language affects mental-imagery in a way that precludes its conceptions. It is as if the uncertainties are cycled back into them-selves, in a way that increases their presence, projecting them onto a greater portion of them-selves and their source."

The Skeptic seemed to be conceptualizing the *precession of simulacra*... This *concept* had been explained to us in translation and interpretation from a text entitled, *"Simulacra and Simulations"*... This *concept* is not too difficult to comprehend...

If a man is used as a reference for a statue and that man is to disappear... The statue will continue to exist and be seen despite the lack of his presence... As people that had both known and never known the man observe the statue, it becomes their *conception* of the man... In the event that this man should reappear some great length of time later, even if he had remained miraculously unchanged, he would be compared to the statues likeness, and the statue would not be compared to his likeness... Because of this, it is as if the man becomes distorted by his own likeness, as the simulation (statue) becomes a precession of its basis (the man)... A great deal more can be explained from this, but essentially this is what The Skeptic was likely alluding to...

"Not only are conceptions mired in their derivations, but there is another problem with them. This problem has only recently come to my attention. Just a short time ago, we were all given a copy of this material."

The Skeptic was holding a copy of our notebook that had been produced from the copy Thomas had acquired from Ronald, &c, &c, &c…

"The anonymous author refers to this problem as, *the comparative truth dilemma*. If I may read an excerpt from this copy of the text, it will perhaps prove relevant, but then, how could we know?!"

It didn't seem as if The Skeptic were actually reading our words, but as if they were being translated into some strange language… Due to this, we are unable to present The Skeptic's reading of our words in the form of dialog… Instead, we have decided to provide a copy of the words that were present in the copy that had been given to us at the facility… (Neither the original notebook, nor The Skeptic's copy of the notebook were available to us for use when this section of our text was prepared…)

Comparative Truth Dilemma…

"There is an inherent problem that results from comparisons… This problem is easily characterized in terms of the conceptions of truth… When comparing things in terms of their level of truth, we observe this comparative truth dilemma…"

"In order to establish what is most true, or the ultimate truth, we must compare the truth of everything… Without establishing an ultimate truth, there is no conception of truth as an ultimate… If there is no ultimate truth, then there is no true definition of it… In order to have a true definition, there must be some exemplary manifestation… Because of the infinite nature of things, of change, and the continuum of possibilities that result, no ultimates are possible… On an infinite continuum, there is always some possibility of exceeding any claim of an established ultimate… Instead of establishing a true definition of truth, we substitute some precession of what is believed to be ultimate truth, based on our truest conception of this truth…"

Inside of our notebook we had written a great deal more on this, *comparative truth dilemma*, the elements involved, the definitions of terms that preceded it, &c, &c, &c... The Skeptic had no use for this other material at this time... Some of the drones continued to read through their own copies of our work, others tried to follow The Skeptic's lead, while some were lost in gazing into the oblivion before them, &c, &c, &c...

"Logically enough, we can establish from this that the conception of truth is a misconception. Not only that, but everything then is a misconception. We have to substitute something in place of any real truth. So we use an unknown-variable in place of truth, and try to solve the equations for this variable. The problem is that every part of our equations consist of such variables. All of our numbers, operations, functions, and everything else are merely unknown-variables!"

The Skeptic had not apparently read all of the contents of our notebook... Our notebook had presented a great deal of progression away from this dilemma, and into a new conception of its components, implications, translations, &c, &c, &c... As the impressionist painter's quote has already been simulated with redundancy, *Life being what it is*...

"With these broken-equations of unknowns, we live without really knowing anything, but trying to learn to live well enough. Due to the uncertainty principle that is projected into everything, and our comparative truth dilemma, and everything else that precludes us from *true* knowledge; we are only rarely even capable of achieving this *well enough* standard. Just look back at the course of history. How often does it seem that even basic *infallible truths* turn out to be the cause of some atrocity? History is really just the study of human ignorance over time! Why should I even bother to site any particular events, or developments? Getting things wrong under the greatest assurances of certainty is apparently the defining feature of what humanity calls truth."

Many of the drones displayed some signs of emotive acquiescence in contemplative stares, subtle nods, &c, &c, &c... This seemed to empower The Skeptic's voice, as the character ceased to lean against the walls of the facility for the first time in this speech... The Skeptic's next words were often used by other drones in the facility during times of discouragement...

"Our failures and successes are all irrelevant. We don't even seem to know the difference at times. Even though they are irrelevant, we hardly even know that. Only when we come up with some use to make things into a success or a failure, do we decide which it is to be. When we want to circle the earth, it becomes round. When we want to plunder or destroy a people, it's gawd's will! Faith is always in precession of truth, and desire precedes faith!"

The religious-drones communicated their disdain with silent scowls...

"What is it we want? Animals show a desire to live. Everything they do is in order to attempt to stay alive. We are nothing more than clever animals, and all animals are ignorant. Even our most esteemed cognitive mighty can't objectively prove or disprove anything without debating the existence of some form of gawd or gawds. They debate this issue in order to preserve one tradition against another. In the end, one side (usually the side that is struggling the most to keep up with the other) plays the *unknowable card of faith*. This *card* is used to negate everything; exclaiming that no one can prove anything, and all there is to any idea or belief is faith. If they believe there is a gawd, or no gawd, or a dead gawd, or some abstraction of such, it is irrelevant. They all have only their faith that their reasoning is true. No one can prove there is any truth, and therefore no one knows what the truth of anything might be."

Despite the uncanny resemblance the argument being made had to what had just been called the *unknowable card of faith*, The Skeptic had managed to offend those of almost all *faiths*... As The Skeptic continued to develop these thoughts, the room seemed to become physically hotter in temperature... Some of the drones in the room began to turn red and sweat as a result of their anger, the heat, &c, &c, &c...

"Two problems result from this gawd-dilemma. One problem is the riddle of Epicurus. This problem was recorded by Lactantius:"

The Skeptic pulled out its notepad to read some notations...

"Gawd either wants to eliminate bad things and cannot, or can but does not want to, or neither wishes to nor can, or both wants to and can. If he wants to and cannot, then he is weak – and this does not apply to gawd. If he can but does not want to, then he is spiteful – which is equally foreign to gawd's nature. If he neither wants to nor can, he is both weak and spiteful, and so not a gawd. If he wants to and can, which is the only thing fitting for a gawd, where then do bad things come from? Or why does he not eliminate them?"

This old riddle had a way of offending faithful believers for ages... Some of the drones in the room tried to interject, but The Skeptic rose in tone as it went on...

"By this riddle, it seems there can be no such thing as a good-gawd, let alone a perfect-gawd. So either the notions associated with gawd are wrong, or the very notion of gawd is a fallacy. If the notions of gawd are incorrect, then our notions of perfection are flawed. Supposing instead that our notions of perfection are incorrect as they relate to the notions of gawd, then we are unable to conceive of a perfect-gawd. How can there be a gawd that we can't conceive of? Furthermore, how is it we would think to conceive of a gawd we can't conceive of? This implies that gawd cannot exist, and also must exist concurrently. This simply cannot be. If our perfect-gawd is not perfect, then our gawd/perfection is an imposture."

Thomas broke in at this point, as The Skeptic was drawing a breath in order to continue...

"What difference does it make if gawd exists or not in terms of perfection? If gawd exists, and is perfect, but our notions are skewed, then it is only our notions that are imperfect. Assuming this is true, then *gawd-willing*, our notions can be perfected. If gawd exists imperfectly however, then this riddle shows that we understand everything perfectly. If gawd doesn't exist, then it doesn't matter, because gawd doesn't exist to matter, and perfection exists on its own."

"That all makes sense, in its own sense. Another question can perhaps mire all of that into absurdity. What can be perfect, if not gawd? Most a-theists, in fact all of them that I have encountered, claim that in the absence of gawd, it is man that must act in place of the divine. If any man has ever made a serious claim that they are perfect, it can only be received as an absurdity of the highest order. Every religious entity I have encountered uses gawd as their basis for perfection. That is why the gawd-dilemma epitomizes the problem of perfection. With or without gawd, there is no perfection, or at least none that has been comprehended by humanity to date."

Thomas was seemingly impressed with The Skeptic's reply, but was unshaken all the same... He tore right back into The Skeptic with his own affirmations...

"Who knows? You may be correct to the point we have reached thus far in the evolution of humanity's capacity for knowledge. However, in light of our new technological discoveries, and the paradigm shift in the cognitive capacity that results from this, perfection seems inevitable. It's even preposterous to me, to even suggest that this technology will be unable to lead to perfection. When we integrate this technology into our lives, it will either be perfection, or bring it greatly closer to us. What reasoning can there be to suggest that this isn't true? Even if there may be some reasons to suggest that perfection can't be attained, it's all beside the point really. This technology will improve our lives. Things will be better as a result, and therefore, we will be closer to perfection, or whatever exists in place of it."

"This isn't about the dialectics as to the notions of the technologies being good or bad. What we are trying to discuss, is the notion of perfection. Although, if we can't know what is best or worst, then how can we even determine good or bad? Without a compass bearing true north, how can you reach the North Pole, travel *north*, or navigate to any destination on this earth? Do we have to stumble through this world unaware of everything in it, and unaware of the very world these things comprise?"

We suddenly began to realize something about The Skeptic's perspective... All The Skeptic could do was reflect on the distorted views that everyone else projected... Because of this, The Skeptic could never come to project anything as its own... Instead, The Skeptic became trapped inside its own mind, held hostage by the thoughts of others, and unable to see either its-self, or beyond it... Unable to see otherwise, The Skeptic could only assume this was the nature of thought... We could see the desperation this caused for The Skeptic...

While yearning for some glimpse of light through blindfolded eyes, The Skeptic wandered in the darkness of the world... It wasn't possible for The Skeptic to believe in blindness, or that it was blindfolded... Instead, The Skeptic chose not to see, claiming that there was no such thing as sight, or that sight could never be understood, or that even if they could see, there was no way to prove that seeing was sight, &c, &c, &c...

"In the end..."

The Skeptic continued...

"...we all end up dreaming of revenge. What kind of vengeance we seek to dream of varies. Some might not even feel a vengeful wrath of sorts, but there is another kind of vengeance. Revenge is defined as an act to retaliate or gain satisfaction. This other vengeance is one that yearns for some wisdom, or clarity, or a means of some sort that can be used in order to right the wrongs. Vengeance of this kind is a sorrowful wanting. We wish we could fix everything, anything, something, but all we do is dream. Dreams of this kind, aspire towards perfection. Perfection in this dreaming sense is perhaps the oldest dream there is."

Just as The Skeptic was about to continue its closing statements, it was cut-off. An alarm was sounded over the facility's emergency systems... The alarm that sounded had been designated for security-breaches... It was to be sounded if an unauthorized-person gained entry to the facility... None of the drones in the commons-area recognized this alarm... Having once been a security-drone, we were able to remember this alarm's distinctiveness, and notified the others what it was to signify...

According to protocol, all non-security-drones were to remain in their current areas, and the security-drones were to lock down, sweep, and clear the facility... A security-drone arrived in the vicinity of the commons-area in mere moments of the alarm's initial sounding... We were all informed that the Notorious Drone that had been brought in for tests had escaped... Ronald went out of the commons-area in order to control the situation...

As the rest of us were restricted from leaving, under Ronald's orders, The Skeptic folded into a chair with a dissociative demeanor... The Skeptic was breathing some words repeatedly for no other ears to hear... We were eventually able to make out what The Skeptic was saying, despite the alarm's incessant reverberations...

"...There's always something in the way... There's always something in the way..."

Eventually we were exposed to more information about the escape of the Notorious Drone... Having been treated with nano-probes, and achieving *perfect* cognition, the Notorious Drone was apparently able to discover some means of escape... A note had been left before the Notorious Drone left the facility... This is the content of that note...

To those concerned,

Having recently come to understand the nature of our life previous to now, we must now consider what we are, and where we are to be going. Due to the damage that has been done, there must be some atonement. Know that there is no desire within us to commit any senseless acts of violence or other senselessness. Though we were in your captivity, it isn't in accordance with any reasonable notions that we should remain so confined. Our life is our own, and all that we do or have done is ours alone. As to the effects of our own life that have imposed on others, it is impossible to undo. This is not to say however, that something can't be done to make some amends. Even if amends could not be made, it would be best to attempt them. In leaving this facility, it is our intent to make whatever amends are possible for us to attempt. Though we may never succeed, there can be no success without attempting to do so. Some may wish to punish us as a means of amends. That is to be determined according to those that have been affected, and according to the affect that has been caused. If we should meet our end in our undoing of what we've done, it can only be considered just. Should any harm befall us, it is not for us to seek retribution, for our past precludes us from any such claim. When you read this, we will be far from your sight, but close at heart. May your work succeed in others, as it has with us. Our thanks go out to you, even if you should despise it.

Regards,

(Name Omitted)

This note was only brought to our eyes sometime after it had been discovered... When we read this note, we found it odd that the particular language it used was not noted by the others that had already read it... Many things were puzzling to us about this note...

What perhaps intrigued us the most was the omission of any name, and the use of the article *we*... Although it was common among drones to communicate in such a way, we wondered why the Notorious Drone might use such language... Could the Notorious Drone have made use of this linguistic style in order to communicate something beyond its own declarations? What could be the nature of this *we*, if not the Notorious Drone its-self? We wondered...

101.15 PROCESSION OF PROGRESS…

We were only allowed to exit the facility with armed-escorts… This was only allowed after the facility was given several full-sweeps, no signs of the Notorious Drone were discovered, &c, &c, &c… Our transports were also searched before we could depart the facility…

All of us were advised prior to leaving that if we should become taken hostage, we were to use the duress word *denouement* as means of communicating this fact… The idea in using this duress word was to inform the guard without overtly informing the fugitive in the process… It was to be assumed that this would ensure greater personal-safety as a result… Despite all that was done to locate the Notorious Drone, no trace could be found… This was an incredible disappearance…

For some time after this disappearance, the drones of the facility felt anxious about the possibility that they could be vulnerable, or targeted, or threatened in some way… Most would admit however, that their fears were unfounded… It was unlikely that the Notorious Drone had any interest in them, less likely that the drone still had any hostile tendencies, &c, &c, &c…

None of the members of the facility had even been made known to the Notorious Drone; aside from Ronald, Thomas, and four other drones, including us… Two of these other drones were on the

…

security-detail that escorted the Notorious Drone into the facility... The other was a janitorial-drone that cleaned the area where the drone had stayed... All of us were questioned extensively on our interaction with the drone... None of us had any information that was considered to be of any use...

Eventually, the novelty of this event evaporated... Then the event not only became seemingly forgotten, but as if it had never happened... In discussions, it didn't just cease to be mentioned, but no one seemed to know what had happened on the rare occasion that it was alluded to in some way...

Activities in the facility went along quite normally thereafter... All of our work was evaluated by The Skeptic, and our progress was carefully monitored... Every evaluation of our progress came back positively... The Skeptic could find no justifiable cause to doubt our success... It was the personal position of The Skeptic, that there had to be something wrong with everything... What might have been wrong with anything The Skeptic evaluated was never made clear, so our progress continued...

Even The Skeptic's evaluations of our work at the facility were eventually completed... The new technologies that had been created were to be distributed among various institutions, before being put into actual applications... We were not informed of what would become of our success... Until our work was put into actual use, we would have no way of knowing what was being done with it...

Without knowing the fate of our efforts, we began to feel as if our work had been torn away from us... Considering the amount of ourselves that had been invested in this work, it seemed as if part of ourselves had been torn away with it... As increasing amounts of time transpired without any evidence of our work's implementation, it began to appear as if it had become lost...

This sense of what was lost expanded, and we began to drift farther and further away from everything... Whatever wasn't ripped away from us, seemed to repel us... We were developing an aversion to everything, as it all seemed to be tearing away at us...

We started noticing our repulsion in the break-room… All of the drones' discussions seemed to be no more than colloquial ruminations of media-viewer indoctrination slogans, briefings on the personal inebriated-exploits, erotic-escapades, &c, &c, &c… None of it had either interested or bothered us in the past… Now this chatter was so repulsive, we couldn't stand to be anywhere near it…

Perhaps we should mention that we had lived according to a certain set of our own principles, standards, &c, &c, &c… We never consumed the alcoholic beverages, used *controlled* substances, engaged in recreational-coitus, &c, &c, &c… There were a plethora of normative-exploits that we had never attempted, had no compulsion towards, no interest in, &c, &c, &c…

Some drones refrained from such things as an adherence to some religious doctrine, but this wasn't characteristic of our motivation… In our considerations, it seemed that these activities were destructive in nature… We thought of our lack of engagement in these activities as *anti-accomplishments*… A certain esteem came to us as a result of our ability to deny the urgings of others, and rely on our own principles of reasoning…

This virtuous solipsism was something that most drones seemed unable or unwilling to even attempt… They all seemed to be compelled to follow others, and perpetuate this reciprocating tendency in others… Despite the perpetual attempts of others to suede us, we continually sought our own approval… In some undefinable way, we felt this was essential for us… What made us feel so strongly about acting according to our own reasoning was quite elusive… Why should we be so resolute in defying everything apart from our own principles? We wondered …

Our lack of conformity had always seemed to make others prefer our presence to be kept distant… This distance was only reduced during efforts to assimilate us, or when our abilities were desired to be put to some use of their own… Due to the lack of any projects that required our unique perspective, the distance between the other drones and us increased… We found that the greater this distance grew, the more splendor we experienced…

We spent ever increasing amounts of our time in isolation ... By closing our-selves inside of our office; we could avoid becoming involved with others throughout most of our time in the facility... We even started to take our meal-break inside of our office in order to avoid using the commons-area... It was unfortunate for us that there wasn't a private-restroom attached to our office... If there were, we would have had almost no incidental interactions with others...

When departing the facility, we would travel straight to our living-compartment... All of our time in isolation was spent inside of our own mind... This almost made it seem as if we existed apart from the outside world... Why did this ubiquitous-isolation only seem so apparent within our own confines? We wondered...

When we did direct our focus on the world around us, it was mostly by some sudden draw into the media-viewer... It often seemed strange that we should be drawn into it by the content that captured our focus... Mostly, it was the usual subject matter...

Banks were going to collapse, if drones didn't cooperate with the guvornmints' initiatives... Then the guvornmints would collapse, and all of their institutions, &c, &c, &c... New viruses with fatal effects were spreading in certain areas... Due to increased populations and lack of housing provisions, there was a rampant rise in the number of street-dwelling-drones... Criminal activity had become more prevalent, &c, &c, &c... As the media-viewer continued its incessant projections, we watched in complete detachment...

Then one day, an advertisement of all things, caught our interest with great intensity... We had even doubted it had been a real experience after the first several instances that we had seen it... Only after it had been aired on our media-viewer several subsequent times did we believe it was real...

The advertisement was for a new medically-licensed, fully-approved, specialty-establishment... Its name, purpose, product, and slogan could all be expressed by the words that initially captured our attention...

"Create the mind you've always wanted!"

As these words came blasting into our ears, we felt our blood-pressure drop, our vision become narrow, and our balance become unsteady... The advertisement explained how *science* had now made it possible to perfect the human mind... Before we confirmed the advertisement was real, our mind seemed lost. Is this what had become of our work at the facility? We wondered...

We had seen this advertisement on the first day it had been projected on the media-viewer programmings... Others at the facility had seen it too, and we couldn't avoid overhearing their reactions... Some made comment as to how it was high-time they should be able to make use of the technology they had helped create... Others claimed they should be granted this service for free, or at a discount... Most seemed only mildly interested in the whole thing, &c, &c, &c...

Ronald came to our office early in that shift to see if we had seen the advertisement... He confirmed that the very project we had developed was being marketed as this *C.T.M.Y.A.W.* concept... Somehow it had already become popular, and had become known under the abbreviation that was pronounced, "*See-Tee-My-Awe*"... It seemed to be a burden for Ronald to have to tell us this fact...

We had thought that our work would have been put into some greater use, although we hadn't considered what that might actually be... Somehow we also understood that Ronald was trying not to say something while he was informing us on the matter... Soon we realized what might be entailed in Ronald's implicit omissions... In horror of the thoughts that had occurred to us, we tried not to let Ronald see that we had picked up on what he wouldn't say...

After Ronald left our office, we began to think things over... Did Ronald have any notion of our awareness to what might be going on outside of this place? Who else might already know? Should we tell anyone? Could we be right about what we thought was going to happen now? What should we do? We wondered...

101.16 BREAK-ROOM...

After Ronald's visit, we wandered around the facility in a strange state... We were both completely lost in our own thoughts, and hypersensitive to everything around us in the facility... Everything seemed to be both far away and directly in front of us... All the world seemed to be right in view, but out of reach...

None of the drones had any notions as to what could be derived from the recent advertisements... All of them were in complete oblivion... As we passed right by them, it was as if they were in no proximity to us, but in some other realm altogether... Somehow we knew there was no reaching them, but we felt some urge to try... How could we reach them? We wondered...

When it was finally time to travel to our living-compartment, we felt relieved to be leaving the facility... Once we were at our residence, we still felt as if we needed to get away... It seemed that everywhere we went was a place we needed to leave...

Inside our living-compartment, we began to feel constricted... The walls felt as if they were collapsing... Actually, everything felt as if it were collapsing now... This constriction seemed as if it were some manifestation of the total collapse that had been impending for so long... In fact, the collapse seemed to have already begun, but it had yet to be seen...

...

It began to seem as if *home* no longer existed... This place we were occupying was not our home, not anymore, perhaps not ever... Upon further thinking, we realized that indeed *home* was something that had never existed for us... All our life, we had been occupants of some foreign oblivion... We began to wonder what *home* even was...

New thoughts began to follow in rapid succession... Everything was pressing in on us so tightly, constricting tighter, and tighter... The tension that constricted around our-selves seemed to be squeezing our thoughts right out of us...

A sudden epiphany burst out of our mind... We had seen this world as an oblivion, masquerading around us... Within this view, we had tried to consider our-selves to be a part of that oblivion... This had confined our thoughts of our-selves to the realm of oblivion... Our attempts to compare whatever we might be, to the oblivion of the world around us had precluded us from seeing our-selves at all... What could we consider our-selves to be, if we considered our-selves to be a part of what we were not? We wondered...

In search of something, in a world that appeared to us as nothing, we focused instead on the depths within our own mind... All we could see was our own reflections in the same oblivion... We had been looking within our-selves in the same way we had been unable to see beyond us...

Under the impression that we were a part of this world, we had made our impressions of this vapid world into a part of us... This resulted in a reflective property; where our relation to the world of oblivion, became our relation to our own impressions of our-selves... We had been rendered completely oblivious as a result of this...

Why had we only realized this now? Why did the entire world have to collapse in order for us to think of this? We wondered...

Our existential oblivion prevented us from initiating our routine sleeping-interval... Due to the effects this disturbance had on us, we notified Ronald to expect our absence... He asked if we were alright, and we told him we might be...

Then he asked what was wrong... There were several things we thought of mentioning, but we restricted our comments to our sleep-disturbances... This was somehow a relief to Ronald, and he advised us to get some rest... He also advised us to notify him if we required any subsequent absences... Before our conversation concluded, Ronald advised us that he could send someone if we needed anything... What might we have needed? We wondered...

Feeling displaced and constricted inside our living-compartment, we thought we might be able to sleep better in another location... It seemed that we would be able to relate to a foreign place as what it was, and that we might be able to relax enough to sleep as a result of this... This idea was resilient, and perpetuated into compulsion...

We acquired a few essential-items, and left our living-compartment... After entering our transport, we drove without any intended destination... Our direction of haphazard travel took us by the *Totem's Toll*, and we had to move it from our path... Then we continued traveling, until we eventually selected a nondescript lodging-establishment...

After checking in, we felt a calm without relief... Inside the room, we stretched out on the bed, staring straight above us... There was a ceiling fan circulating air around the room... It was going around in circles, the way we had been going around our whole life... It wasn't breathing any new air, merely propelling the same perpetual air around it...

Eventually we were able to complete a proper sleeping-interval, and return to the facility... When we did, the facility seemed vastly strange to us... Like all the world, it had always seemed strange to us, but now it was prominently evident... What was so evident about the facility's strangeness could not be identified by us...

A security-drone in the entry control-room advised us that Ronald had requested we report directly to his office ... We acknowledged this message as we proceeded inside the facility... This request was very suspicious to us, although we couldn't explain why... What could Ronald want us to meet him in his office for? We wondered...

Instead of proceeding directly to Ronald's office, we went to the door with our number printed on it... This was the most familiar thing we would see all day, and yet it was somehow strangely distant to us... Inside our office, we found the same detachment of our-self from our environment...

We picked up the receiver to contact Ronald... Ronald answered, and immediately asked us if we had been advised to come to his office... Instead of answering simply, we asked if there was a reason that necessitated our physical presence... He told us there was, but refused to provide any explanation... We attempted to suggest that Ronald might come to our office instead... In response, Ronald directed us to proceed to his office without delay... Hanging up the receiver, we considered what we might do... Should we trust Ronald's insistence? We wondered...

Since Ronald knew where we had contacted him from, he could send for us, if we didn't report directly to his office... We had become so suspicious of Ronald's recent actions that we didn't want to have any direct encounters with him... After apprehensive consideration, we decided to leave our office... From there, we went to the break-room...

Inside the commons-area, we found the usual discussions under way... This wasn't an organized discussion... Without any activities that demanded their presence, the facility's drones had taken to malingering in the commons-area... Thomas, The Skeptic, and Ronald were all present as we arrived... Ronald's face turned into an unexpected hue of red at the sight of us...

At that point, we were certain that he wasn't to be trusted... Something sinister had to be going on under the surface of things... Ronald seemed to be unable to speak to us, as we entered the room... We felt a sense of caution, as well as confidence, resolve, &c, &c, &c...

Ronald regained composure, and quickly excused him-self... As he did so, he requested that we accompany him on his departure... We began to follow him out, but halted after taking a few strides down the hallways of the facility... We had intentionally left our bucket-hat in the break-room... Our bucket-hat was almost never removed from our head, and we were a bit surprised that Ronald had not noticed anything before we had left the commons-area...

We told Ronald that we needed to retrieve it before we went on to his office... Then we assured him that we would proceed directly to his office after we'd retrieved our *cover*... He insisted that we make haste to do so, and consented to reconvene in his office... As Ronald proceeded to his station, we departed for the break-room in order to retrieve our cover...

When we returned to the break-room, we recovered our cover, and noticed that the others had shifted topics... These drones were now venting fears into each other, whilst trying to dissect them in order to ascertain the root-cause of such woes... They voiced concerns on the most recent media-viewer reports of the impending collapse of our phynancial institutions, guvornmints, &c, &c, &c...

There were two perspectives on the impending collapse that had polarized the drones in the commons-area... One perspective was that everyone was doomed to this collapse, even though the collective deserved better... The other position was that salvation was still possible, if everyone would just stop being so selfish and collectively work together...

Before we had vacated the commons-area, one of the drones asked us for our opinion... After a moment's pause to consider the ramifications of conveying our current perspective, we wondered... Why not?

With our idiosyncratic hat in our right hand, we pressed it to the left side of our chest... Under our breath, we mouthed the words inaudibly, "*life being what it is...*" We seemed to be speaking as if we were dreaming aloud... Our words were all we had left to content our-selves with in this moment... Using the only voice within our-selves, we declared our existential-disposition...

"There's one question that it doesn't seem anyone has asked... Why shouldn't it collapse?"

One of the anonymous drones asked us what we meant by this question... Where do we even begin to explain our-selves? We wondered...

"Everything is divided... The first division may be conveyed as the *schizm* of infinity from oblivion... In the *byble's* opening depiction of *kreation*, this schizm is articulated as the separation of the light from the darkness... Prior to this initial-schizm, gawd's kreation of all the *hevuns* and the *eurth* was formless, empty, immersed in darkness, &c, &c, &c... If we were unable to perceive this division of existence from non-existence, we would be left in a state of formless, empty, darkened *thoughtlessness*... This division of existence from non-existence is the first order of division that we perceive..."

Most of the drones gathered in the commons-area were no longer concerned with what had preceded our comments... They had only been waiting for something to distract them from their anxieties of the world around them... Whatever words we might say were welcomed as a result of this...

The Skeptic appeared to be morbidly infatuated with some element of this idea we'd stated... It wasn't clear to us what The Skeptic might have found so infatuating, but we didn't pause to wonder... Our attentions were divided among other things...

"There is something that must be pointed out in this division of light and dark, or existence from non-existence... Light or existence can only be defined to exist as it deviates from the darkness or non-existence, and darkness can only be defined as a contrast to light..."

This compelled The Skeptic to interject some of the principles of disbelief that were such an integral-part of this character's essence...

"In other words, all that exists, exists in the context of non-existence. So without non-existence, nothing can exist. If anything exists, then non-existence must exist as a precondition. However, if there is only non-existence, then there is no precondition that there be any existence. Essentially, non-existence can be more certain, than existence!"

The Skeptic was basking in the delightful notion that nothing existed... It was almost a shame to respond... The shame wasn't to be ours though...

"A duplicitous-edge cuts through these things... Only according to their deviation can either darkness or light exist in separation... Non-existence paradoxically, cannot exist without the division from existence, as it is defined as such... Without existence, non-existence would be all that didn't exist... In this respect, it wouldn't *exist* as non-existence, since it would no longer be definable in the way that it is defined... Referring to this lack of existence/non-existence would require the use of another term, such as *un-existence*..."

The Skeptic broke in, with the intention of shattering our proposed notion...

"How would it be possible to define this *un-existence* then?"

"It is the context that defines everything... Each context is a separate division... We define things based on what they are not... In this case, *un-existence* would be what is not existence/non-existence... Another way of expressing this would be that, *un-existence* is to non-existence, as non-existence is to existence..."

Some of the drones in the commons-area appeared to have lost interest, and others appeared to be on the verge of a mental break-down, a few actually managed to laugh, &c, &c, &c... The Skeptic seemed to be struggling to swallow something, while searching for something lost before its discovery...

"Perhaps we should get back to the subject of our initial intention... To reiterate, everything is divided... Perception is the organization of these divisions..."

Thomas offered a cutting-remark...

"Division, division, division… What is of substance in all this division?"

"Everything is the result of these divisions, including what would be called, *substance*… The first order of division we observe is that of existence/non-existence… This order of division separates everything into vapid non-existence, or the *substance* of existence… After dividing things into existence, they must be further divided in order to be perceived of as entities… The more these things are divided, the more features are subdivided, &c, &c &c… Any level of this division, is the process of separating what is, from what is not…"

Thomas slashed back again…

"If everything is divided, then at what level does this division end? Isn't there an inherent eventuality, where things become indivisible?"

"At the most finite-level, there may be an emergent property of indivisibility… Each unique particle at the indivisible level would be infinitely divided from everything… To exist indivisibly would require them to remain infinitely divided… Otherwise, they would become divisible…"

The Skeptic broke in…

"How would they preserve this infinite division?"

"They wouldn't need to preserve it actually… If they exhibited some pattern of division or synchronicity, that would just be a different characteristic order of division… The indivisible particles would still be infinitely divided… These less-finite orders of division that exhibit some pattern of synchronicity are what we perceive as entities, movement, etc, etc, etc…"

Thomas placed his hand on The Skeptic, and asked to cut in before continuing to play the inquisitor's role…

"Perhaps you can give some example to illustrate how this *synchronization of division* can create the *projection of entity*."

"Of course... A bridge was designed to sway in order to withstand high-winds without breaking... On this bridge's opening-day, a race was scheduled to be held... Runners gathered, and the race began quite normally... Soon after this initial start though, the runners noticed that the bridge was moving back and forth under their feet... This motion of the bridge forced the runners to alter their strides in synchronization with the bridge's motion... Unless the runners' strides were synchronized to the bridge's motion, they would lose balance, and fall down... Rather the runners fell down, or became synchronized; they were all subjected to the bridges movements..."

Thomas hacked in with a question...

"How does this explain your premise?"

"When the runners began to move, the force of their motions were applied to the bridge... Each runner exerted its own pattern of force onto the bridge by their individual strides... The bridge's motion was not a result of its own motion, or any of the individual runner's motions, but as an emergent property... All of the projected motions formed a new order of division that created the property of the *bridge's* motion... Then, all of the individuals on the bridge became synchronized according to this pattern of motion... In effect, these runners became a collective-entity... If you were to look at them from afar, they would appear as if one giant-worm, or a swaying-bridge... This apparent entity of the swaying-bridge composed of runners, is an example of an entity made apparent as a result of the properties of synchronized-division..."

Thomas and The Skeptic had seemed to grasp the concept, but were now wondering how this might relate to the original question we had posed... After a moment, Thomas imposed our question upon us...

"So what does that have to do with your premise? You had asked why things shouldn't collapse. Perhaps you can tell us."

"This analogy can be applied to our currently impending collapse... The apparent entity of the moving-bridge can be equated with any of the social-institutions impending collapse... Just as the bridge moves according to the dominant actions of the runners, and the runners synchronize to this motion, the same is true for us... Our institutions are the projected-entities that result from our actions, and we synchronize according to the way they are imposed back onto us..."

One of the selfless drones broke out in exaltations...

"So if we all just quit being selfish, and work together, there shouldn't be any collapse!"

"The opposite is true... Using the allegory of the bridge, selfishness is what caused the emergence of the entity of the moving-bridge... Ceasing to be selfish would be the equivalent of ceasing to move, so that the bridge's motion could guide everything... Without the runners self-generated motions, the bridge will cease to move... The bridge's motion will then collapse, leaving the immobile-runners, and the stagnant-bridge... Since the movement of the bridge is what made it an entity, without this movement, that entity will have collapsed into no longer existing... To quote the author of *Self-Reliance*... '*All things are dissolved to their center by their cause, and, in the universal miracle, petty and particular miracles disappear.*' So..."

The selfless drone cut us off short...

"-What if instead of ceasing to move, the runners just kept the pace imposed on them by the movement of the bridge? Then they could all keep the same pace. That would be more of what selflessness is in this allegory."

"If the runners try to run at any stride other than their own pace, it defeats the runner... Over time such a foreign pace becomes too much to keep up with, or too slow to tolerate... Runners drop-out, and the bridge stops moving... That is how selflessness destroys not only the selfless, but all that they impose their selflessness upon..."

Again the selfless drone cut in abruptly...

"But if the runners were all selfish, then none of them could continue to move according to any of their own paces. They would have to adopt the pace imposed on them collectively in order to continue running. Wouldn't they try to adopt the selfless pace of the whole?"

A sinister smile appeared on the selfless drone's face... Underneath this smile, we could see just a hint of sorrow, guilt, &c, &c, &c... Very little joy/contentment managed to be projected from this expression...

"Once the runners lose their own pace, it is only in order to try to regain their own pace, or reach their end, that they continue running... So long as they remain on the bridge, its motion will be imposed on them... They will inevitably either tire of this imposition and cease to run, or abandon the bridge altogether... If the runners reach their own finish-line, they will have no use for the bridge... In any case, the bridge will lose its ability to move over time, and inevitably collapse..."

To our surprise, no one broke in after we'd made this point...

"Additionally, those sedentary runners that remain on the bridge will impose their stillness on the bridge... In order for the diminishing number of runners to keep the bridge in motion, they will have to exert a greater amount of force... This will eventually surpass the threshold of each runner's ability, and they will be forced to relent their efforts... Again, the bridge will eventually stop moving, and its essence will have collapsed..."

The selfless drone appeared to be recoiling into some acceptance of an unpleasant truth... Thomas seemed to be in denial of this same kind of sentiment, and wanted to project this denial...

"As soon as there is any runner on the bridge, it will begin to move. Even with only a single runner, the bridge's movement will be imposed on that runner. With every subsequent presence on the bridge, there would be a subsequent resultant effect. So every occupied bridge will impose upon its occupants accordingly. Without the collective-pace, what is there?"

It appeared as if Thomas was now searching us in order to determine if he had drawn any blood with these cutting-remarks...

"This is the essence of the dilemma... Everything affects everything... Essentially, it is the degree of variance within the runners that leads to their imposition... The runners could perhaps be divided into groups of less variance, over multiple bridges, &c, &c, &c... Of course this would only diminish the effects of what would be imposed upon them, and would not prevent the inevitable..."

Thomas cut in with another slashing-remark...

"How could the runners be organized according to such groupings?"

"That would essentially be for each runner to determine on their own... If they were able to choose a bridge that moved closest to their own manner, they would be less imposed upon, and less imposing to others..."

Now Thomas was intent on shattering our asserted projections...

"None of this is at all practical, or even feasible. You still haven't explained how it could be done."

"It is already done... This division of order is constant... Those that have the greatest impact on the bridge will have the least amount of variance imposed on them... Each and every runner must adapt to whatever is imposed upon them in their own way... Given the option of a more accommodating bridge, the runners would split-up in order to run at a pace closer to their own stride..."

In a cracking voice, Thomas broke in again...

"What in the non-allegorical sense are you implying we should do in terms of our current dilemmas? Is there any practical application to this diatribe of yours?"

The answers seemed so obvious to us, but no one else seemed to be able to see through everything that was imposed upon them…

"Here at this facility, we have managed to create the most impressive variety of tools, technologies, &c, &c, &c… Instead of fussing over the impending collapse of our phynancial systems or guvornmints, we could be setting a new pace, building new bridges, &c, &c, &c… We could set-up any number of bridges, at any range of cadences, using any number of methods, resulting in exceedingly greater satisfaction for each and every individual, &c, &c, &c…"

Thomas seemed alarmed at our statement… He wasn't surprised by any of the statements, but seemingly haunted by the fact that they were stated… His eyes flashed as they deflected the reactions of the other drones in the room, and seemed poised to pierce right through us…

"So we should just overthrow everything in exchange for some, undefined system of systems, in order to fit the individuals? What makes you believe this could, or even should be done?"

"It doesn't matter anymore… All of you must decide what to do on your own… In that sense, nothing has changed… As you look around you, or look back, or imagine moving forward, it all comes down to the same thing… However you respond to this world is entirely up to you… None of this concerns us any longer…"

Our feet moved toward the exit at our own pace, as we turned away from the others… Thomas swung his arm out in front of us, to cut-off our departure… We side-stepped his obstruction, and then he tried to impose on us…

"What do you think you're doing? We aren't finished with this discussion. You're still a part of this."

With our back now facing Thomas and the others, we continued towards the exit, and secured our cover upon our head… We turned to face them with one last declaration, before we broke-away from them…

"I'm not a part of this, and I won't let it break me!"

The break-room began to echo with the drones' chatter, as I walked away... Their voices gradually grew fainter, until they were no longer audible... At the facility's exit, I was advised by the security-drone that Ronald had demanded to be contacted before anyone could leave... I told the drone I would contact Ronald on my own... The drone had already reached Ronald's phone, and handed me the receiver to speak with him... As soon as Ronald answered, I informed him that I was leaving the facility for good, and that I wished him the best...

Ronald tried to persuade me to say... He tried to suggest that we could remake the world in any way we wanted... I refused his urgings, appeals, pleas, &c, &c, &c... My resolve was made quite clear to Ronald, and he finally accepted my decision... Then, he asked me a question I had been considering for some time...

"Why do you feel you have to leave?"

In response to this question, a detailed explanation was given... Essentially, I had determined that I was unable to define my-self within the oblivion of this collectivized-world... I would only be able to realize any true identity that might exist for me, by separating my-self from everything that was imposed on me...

Ronald took a moment before saying anything in response to all of what I'd said...

"If I can't convince you to stay with us, is there anything else that I can do?"

"Only for your-self..."

There was no response...

I said farewell, and hung up the receiver... As the security-drone gaped at me in confusion, I ordered him to expedite my exit of the facility... The security-drone's vacant stare seemed to follow my departure of the facility... I walked to my transport, and drove through the exits... With the facility vanishing into oblivion behind me, I made my way through this world, looking only forward...

...II...

..."I"...

...

201.01 EXODUS FROM US...

Leaving the facility was easy... Trying to make it *home* was quite a challenge... *Home* never seemed to have existed before, but now it seemed to exist somewhere unknown... Driving towards the living-compartment, I knew that home would not be there when I arrived... Somehow despite this notion, I still felt as if I were finally on my way...

Along the way, I came across the stump that seemed to always be in my way... Getting out of the transport, my shadow was cast onto the stump... Looking at *Totem's Toll* as I lifted it onto my shoulders, I saw something that was no longer there... I saw my face inside all those others, as if it had always been there... Seeing it was repulsive, and forced me to close my eyes, so I wouldn't see it... Refusing to look at the surface of that dead-stump didn't seem to remove my imagined-image from it...

With a shrug of my shoulders, I launched that stump through the emptiness of the night... A harsh cracking sound came as *Totem's Toll* collapsed upon the surface of the earth, splitting into fragments... All the faces were shattered in this smashing collision, exploding into splintered-shrapnel...

...

I felt more than the weight of the stump released from my shoulders... It wasn't just the fragments of this splintered-stump that seemed to have been severed... What else had been separated? I thought...

Getting back into my transport, I saw my reflection on the transport's surface as an undefined-figure of my own... As I returned to my seat, it was as if I were settling into something more than this ambulatory-object... As I began to drive away, it felt like I was extracting my-self from that broken-stump, evacuating the void, escaping the confinement of condite-forms, &c, &c, &c...

Parking outside of my living-compartment was not the usual arrival... Although, nothing had changed in sight, everything appeared to be different, further away, &c, &c, &c... What had changed in this view was not in sight, but in seeing... I had changed, and it was my mind that was now so far away from it all...

As I moved through this distant space, strides carried my feet to the front door of my living-compartment... Passing through the entry way was like invading some eerie place... It didn't seem as if I was inside this place at all, but as if it was a part of someone else's dream, that I was beginning to wake from...

My fingers reached to activate the media-viewer and turn on the lights, as if by someone else's instincts... Sitting in the chair facing the media-viewer, I tried not to make an impression on the cushion... Somehow it seemed an imposition to disturb the chair, the room, the world, etc, etc, etc... I watched the media-viewer with increasing detachment, as it projected its images, sounds, messages, &c, &c, &c

Inside my mind, there was a strange repetition of words, as if a voice were bypassing my auditory senses... It was repeating two phrases in succession... The first phrase consisted of the words...

"Get out..."

Each time it was repeated inside my mind, the intensity became greater... Following each iteration of this phrase was the question...

"Where are you going?"

The *voice* seemed foreign to me at first, but with each repetition of its messages, it became more and more my own... Could this *voice* really be my own? I thought...

Continuing to stare into the media-viewer screen, its images existed only as a deception of this world... Its images bombarded my eyes, until I saw less than nothing... My vision shifted inward, searching through my memory to find somewhere to depart to, something to pursue, anything to lead me out of here... Lost in this gaze, I began to move around the room blindly...

My hands reached for a backpack, a duffel bag... My feet paced the living-compartment as the bags were stuffed with various items... My movements of ataxia packed clothing, hygiene supplies, containers of food... My bags became stuffed with things that might be useful if I abandoned this living-compartment... There were plastic-bags, metal coat-hangers, &c, &c, &c... In the middle of this activity, I suddenly became aware of the fact that I had already decided to leave...

My mind came into focus, and I continued to make preparations for my departure with undetached focus... Then there was a sudden knock at the front-door... I froze in immobile-stealth, and stared at the door in auditory-invisibility... The entity on the other side of the door knocked with increasing intensity... Who could it be? I thought...

An eternity elapsed within the next few moments of my silent-paralysis... The entity eventually stopped pounding on the surface of the door... After another extensive-pause, there was the sound of something being deposited next to the front-door... Then footsteps could be heard moving away from the vicinity... I stood still for some time before I dared to move again...

Eventually I crept to the front-door with vigilant-stealth... Reaching the front-door, I took a peek out of the peephole, and then softly pressed my ear to the door... After being unable to directly view any presence, I slowly turned the doorknob with meticulous-caution... Then I opened the door a mere smidgeon to peer out...

Confirming again that no one had remained in the vicinity, I opened the door the rest of the way, and reached out to gather the package... This whole process was done in utter silence as well... Then the locks and latches were replaced, securing me from whatever might be outside...

I placed the package on the floor, and seated my-self in front of it... The package it-self was black, and was marked with a red-to-blue color-shifting script with a letter *S*... For quite some time I deliberated as to whether or not I should open it...

Eventually the curiosity to open the package prevailed, and I reached into one of the bags I'd just packed to obtain a knife... After cutting an opening in the package, I removed its contents one item at a time, and arranged all the items in front of me... Once the package was empty, I gently tossed it aside, and began to inspect each of the items...

Most of the contents were divided into separate envelopes, except for two items in small boxes... The first item observed was inside an envelope marked, *Read This First*... It was a letter written with the same color-shifting script on black paper... I was uncertain as to what to make of the letter's contents... Here are the contents of the letter...

Please accept these items as a token of gratitude. They have been sent to you in the interest of serving your own interests (whatever such interests might be), etc, etc, etc. The path you choose shall be opened unto you. You now hold all the keys you may require, to unlock the doors to whatever future you may pursue, etc, etc, etc...

Best Intentions,

(No Signature)

After first reading this letter, I found the content to be rather quizzical... Rather than focus on what might be entailed in the letter, I decided to inspect the other items... The next item was inside a red envelope, marked with a blue-to-black script with the words, *What's Next...*

Inside of this envelope were media-clippings, all post-dated for the near to distant future... These clippings were arranged in ascending chronological order... They described a series of events, including the collapse of guvornmints, phynancial systems, &c, &c, &c... There were also accounts of *peaceful demonstrations of violence, depopulation incidents, conversions of arboreal regions into infernos,* &c, &c, &c...

There were also a series of advertisement clippings, inserted along with these shards of journalistic-exploits... One was for the recently created business, *Create the Mind You've Always Wanted* (or *CTMYAW* for short)... A more comprehensive account of the project was included in the advertisement, and they were claiming to have been responsible for *the future that was yet to be seen...*

The next item I opened was a black box marked in blue-to-red script with the words, *Careful...* Inside this box was a folding-knife along with a short note... This note explained that the blade on the knife was engineered using nano-technologies... It also explained that the materials of this knife were of superlative hardness and sharpness, due to new technologies... According to the note, this blade could cut through virtually anything, and would never become dull as a result...

Unfolding the blade, revealed an inscription along the broad face of it... I read the words with an ominous feeling that they were somehow acquired from my own un-uttered thoughts... As my eyes were drawn over the etchings, I mouthed the words aloud...

"Welcome to the Divide..."

Using this special blade, I next opened the green envelope, labeled with black-to-red script, *When and Where*... Inside this envelope, was a map that had several markings scrawled onto it... GPS grid-coordinates were circled, and marked with scripts colored gold, silver, red, blue, black, green... Inside the *legend* section was a color-coded explanation of this system of notation... On the reverse side of this attachment was a list of addresses with a heading marked, *Beware*... At the very top of the map, was an inscription in glittering silver script reading, *The stars can only guide those that know now to read them*... For some reason, I burst into laughter when I read this line...

Next, I opened the gold envelope, labeled with silver-to-black script reading, *Means to Your Ends*... The contents of this envelope consisted of various phynancial papers... Another note was attached to these, explaining how there would be only one bank remaining after the phynancial collapse... It did not yet exist, but when it did, there would be an account in my name...

According to the note, these papers that were enclosed would provide me with access to unlimited funding... Also in the note, was a mention that soon after this phynancial institution became operational, funding would no longer be a concern for any living being... None of this made much sense to me, and I was beginning to wonder if this package were some kind of practical joke...

Two items remained unopened in front of me... I decided to open the dark gray box, with gold lightning-bolts embossed onto each of its surfaces... The box jingled as I moved it, and opening it revealed a set of keys...

This was not any ordinary set of keys that came tumbling out of the box... It appeared to be a set of novelty-keys, that Ronald had been given as a gift to commemorate the completion of the facility's weather-manipulation project... There was a small touch-pad dangling along with the keys, with the inscription, *Zeus's Keychain*... On the back of this touch-pad, was an emblem of a faceless Zeus, leaning over the edge of a cloud, with a lightning-bolt raised as if to thrust it downward, &c, &c, &c... The distinctness of this emblem left little uncertainty that this had formerly been Ronald's keychain...

If this had truly been Ronald's key chain, then it must have either been stolen from him, or given away by him... I couldn't see the contents of this package as being in line with Ronald's character... Although, for someone to steal this item in order to forward it to me made even less sense...

What was I to do with this thing? Giving it back to Ronald, would be difficult, and possibly insulting/implicating under the circumstances... If he was responsible for the package, he obviously would find it offensive to have it returned to him... If instead it had been stolen, and I was to return it to him, he might accuse me of having stolen it... Ultimately, I didn't want to go back to the facility under any pretense, and so I decided to hang on to it until it could be returned to Ronald anonymously...

Only one item remained unopened before me now... As I looked at this large blue envelope with red-black ink labeled, *Lost and Found*, I wondered if I should even bother opening it... Thus far, everything that I had opened, had only managed to cause me increasing levels of perplexity... Curiosity is a most persistent force though...

When I conceded to opening the envelope, I became flabbergasted at the sight of what was inside... From the first partial glimpse of this item, I knew it was the notebook containing *Schizm Theory*... Now that it had returned to my view, I stared at it, reflecting on all that had occurred since I'd last seen it... Somehow, I no longer felt the same detached sense of being lost in this moment... All the world still seemed as if it were a foreign land, but my sense of being at a loss had departed...

With the exception of the notebook, I placed each of the items back into their respective envelopes or boxes... Then I resumed my efforts to determine what items were to be packed or left behind... Soon, I had completed this effort, and felt properly prepared to vacate the premises of my soon-to-be former living-compartment... I picked up all the bags I had packed, walked to the door, and turned to take one last look at my former residence... Stepping outside felt like a leap beyond the point of turning back...

After loading all the bags into my transport, I settled into the driver's seat... Where was I going? I thought...

I decided to stop-off at a megastore in order to obtain supplies... Initially, I'd had no intentions of making any stops on this *journey to nowhere*... As I was driving, I thought of the potential collapse of phynances, the information in the package I'd received, &c, &c, &c... Then I decided there was no reason not to spend all of my currency on provisions for my *exit-us*...

At the megastore, I loaded a cart with an absurd amount of canned food-rations... Then I loaded several large plastic water-jugs into my cart, considering them to be of greatest importance... An assortment of other items that seemed useful were loaded into the cart, as I perused the megastore... When I reached the pay-booth, I had added some rope, various tools, fecal-paper, &c, &c, &c...

I also decided to purchase a series of items that almost seemed unsuited for my journey... Among these items were an assortment of periodicals, books, a laser-pointer, &c, &c, &c... The most impractical item that I decided to purchase was a musical instrument... It was being advertised as an, *indestructible instrument*, made of, *revolutionary new materials*... This instrument was sold as an, *acrousticgrittare*... Why did I feel like I had to have this thing? I wondered...

All the items I purchased were loaded into my transport, except the acrousticgrittare, which I tied to the roof of my transport... Then, I set off for another location that suddenly seemed to have become necessary... It was an antiquated supply-store that I had seen advertised on my media-viewer the previous night... The store sold antiquated camping-equipment, fishing-paraphernalia, &c, &c, &c...

Before I went inside the store, I decided to put some of the items I'd just purchased, and a few food-rations into my primary backpack... I also started untying the rope that secured my acrousticgrittare... My intention was to secure the acrousticgrittare inside my transport's personal-seating area, as I went to make more purchases... When I returned, I would be able to tie any additional items to the roof, along with the instrument, &c, &c, &c...

As I was almost through untying the rope, a street-dwelling drone approached, in order to ask me for charitable-donations... I told the drone that I was no longer a compartment-dweller my-self, and that I may require every scrap of provisions I possessed... The drone seemed appalled, when I refused to offer him some sacrificial-toll for his unfortunate despairs...

An alternative-notion came to me, and I asked the drone if some form of a mutual-exchange would be of interest... If the drone agreed to monitor my transport until I returned from the antiquated supply-store, I offered to pay for this service with all the canned-goods the drone could carry in one load... The drone agreed to this proposal... After shaking hands on the deal, I went into the antiquated supply-store...

Inside the store, I found the inventory to be an interesting variety of both extreme utility, and complete uselessness... Because they didn't have any 1-person tents, I picked out a 2-person tent... I also purchased some fishing-paraphernalia, water-sanitizing kits, a sleeping-roll, and some assorted items of peculiar interest that would likely prove useless, &c, &c, &c...

At the clerk's post stood a drone of Asian-heritage... She asked me a series of questions about my intentions for the items I was purchasing... Telling her of my intentions, elicited a mocking grin... Her grin widened, and she advised me to buy a few more items for what she called, "*good- many-blessings*"... Initially I declined any interest in purchasing a *feather-stick* thing... With an ire of amusement the clerk made an appeal to me...

"This is much better than phynances! What good will your phynances be where you're going? You'll be glad you bought this. It will give you *good-many-blessings*."

In amusement over this appeal, I consented to buy the *feather-stick* thing... Before I made my exit, the clerk at the register smiled widely, rubbed her hands together, and looked up at the clock on the wall above the exit...Then she bid me farewell with an interesting expression...

"*Katchin katchin!* Time is money! *Katchin katchin!*"

After all of these items were loaded into my transport, the street-dwelling drone was given the provisions agreed upon... As I was about to leave, the weaponry-dealership across the parking-lot caught my eye... It seemed like a good idea to at least have a look at their inventory... There was still a large sum of phynances that I had yet to spend, and the idea of depleting all of this currency appealed to me...

The street-dwelling drone was still nearby... I offered to make the same deal again, if the drone would keep watch as I went into the weaponry-dealership... Again the drone consented, and I walked towards the entrance...

A clerk-drone came bounding over to me as I entered the doorway... The clerk-drone recommended several items of lethality that might best suit me... I arranged to purchase a .38 snub-nose, a shotgun, two rifles, and an assortment of munitions for each item of lethality... In order to keep these items organized and protected, I also bought carrying-cases, cleaning-kits, &c, &c, &c...

As I was leaving, I saw that there were other items of interest to me... With the aid of the clerk-drone, I picked out a bow, a crossbow, some arrows, some tip-attachments, &c, &c, &c... The clerk-drone agreed to waive the standard-regulations normally required in the purchase of these items, in exchange for extra phynances... I went back to my transport with my newly acquired items of lethality...

The street-dwelling drone helped me load most of the items onto the roof of my transport when I returned... As I was helping him load his arms with provisions, another drone came rushing over to us... This drone was holding a .50 caliber pistol, and pointing it at my face as it made declarations... Demanding that I step away from my transport, and keep my mouth shut, the drone entered my transport with the gun still pointed at me, and proceeded to steal my transport...

Two shots were fired as this all happened, and I went prone on the asphalt, frantically low-crawling towards a parking-curb for cover... As the armed-robber-drone sped around the corner, some of my possessions came flying off of the transport's roof... Some of the items included my primary backpack, acrousticgrittare, weapons of lethality, &c, &c, &c...

The street-dwelling drone assisting me appeared to have been punctured by one of the shots... When I tried to approach the wounded-drone, it bolted to its feet screaming...

"MERDRE!!!"

Without a moment's pause, the street-dwelling drone went sprinting after my former transport... The drone continued running over the distant horizon, and I heard the poor-drone exclaim again and again as it continued to pursue my former transport...

"MERDRE! MERDRE!! MERDRE!!!"

As the drone's voice died-out, I calmly walked to gather my things... Using the rope, I managed to organize these remaining items in a way I could carry... The weight of all these things caused me a bit of concern for the effect they might have on my spine...

There was a sturdy looking stick in the gutter nearby... I cropped the stick in order to utilize it as a walking-stick, using the knife I had received in the package... Then in a moment of bemusement, I also carved the last word I expected to hear another's voice exclaim...

Having studied 'pataphysics at the facility, I knew that this wasn't actually a word... It was actually a variation of a French word, *merde*... Even at a time like this, I couldn't help but laugh as I examined the etched image... (*MERDRE*)...

Steadying my-self with my new *merdre-stick*, I continued my journey away from all of this... With each step, I felt more aware of how lost I had been... Oddly enough, the items that had just been stolen from me didn't cause the slightest sense of loss... In fact, I actually felt a bit relieved... What had I really been robbed of? I thought...

As I wandered along, I began to understand something about my approach to this departure... I had instinctively tried to acquire a vast assortment of attachments, so I wouldn't become exposed to this world alone... Without these attachments, I would be forced to rely on my own abilities, my own mind, my own virtues, &c, &c, &c...

My reason for this whole journey was to face the world alone... I had figured that this would be the most plausible way of discovering what I truly was... As I continued striding along this way, I almost pitched everything attached to me into the gutters... Why didn't I leave it all behind me? I thought...

201.02 THE PRESERVATION SITE...

The entire sum of my possessions was now strapped to my back, or held within my hands... Every other attachment was now in a past, that each of my steps left farther and further away... My steps reached towards the oblivion of the ever-retreating horizon, the unknown future it held, &c, &c, &c...

I began to think of the roads as vast, vascular-systems, within the bodily-structure of civilization... They pumped traffic in the same way drones pumped blood... Everything within them was to flow according to a pulse... Remaining within these arterial-pathways confined me as a part of the system I was attempting to separate my-self from... The very arteries that carried me away from the failing heart of civilization, could only lead me back, along its indeterminate-veins...

Wandering the open-roads, my mind wondered... Where was I going? My thoughts drifted around this question like a caravan of travelers around a navigator... This question kept leading me onward... Only the increasing sum of distance was of any real concern... There was no destination, no destiny, no direction, &c, &c, &c... It wasn't my intention to arrive at any place... For now, it was only the departure that I could content my-self with...

Where was I? Where had all of this led me? I thought...

...

I'd always been nowhere it seemed… This was just an annexed-region of the same nowhere that was everywhere for me… I wanted to find somewhere far from this endless nowhere, and all its synonymous nothing… If I was going anywhere, it was some-where in this sense… Was there any *where* such as this? Had I left anywhere in my pursuit of this abstract notion? If I had, where was I now? I thought…

The sun set behind me, and cast shadows all around… My feet trampled over the darkness cast by the figures of the earth, as the sun's light was projected elsewhere… As the moon's reflections of the sun's light were cast down through vacant skies, I perpetuated my incessant wandering… It didn't matter how dark it might have been, there was nothing in sight under any light for me… Everything was just the darkness reflected, &c, &c, &c…

Every step I took was its own victory, and its own defeat… Each step was further from what I'd left behind me… That was the victory… These steps never landed anywhere closer to any perceivable destination though… This was their defeat… A battle of footsteps raged on like this for days, without any reprieve… I could not stop leaving until I felt I had actually left this vast nowhere, or arrived at some *where*… With relentless determination, I wandered…

After experiencing this delirium in what seemed like an eternity, a sight appeared in the distance… There was a rough-path that led away from the road beneath me… It was overgrown with foliage, and littered with whatever the wind/time had lost to it… My slumped posture straightened… Then the drudging cadence of my dragging feet was bolstered into an advancing march…

I stumbled valiantly along this desolate trail, trudging brazenly through the overgrown bushes, fallen tree-limbs, garbage, &c, &c, &c… The path became obstructed by a 12foot fence; with c-wire atop its height, and vines interwoven into its chain-link facade, &c, &c, &c… There appeared to have once been a gate over the pathway that was now chained to stay shut… A post nearby held a sign, half-dangling, with faded words that could still be read…

NATIONAL WILDLIFE PRESERVATION SITE FOR
ENDANGERED POLE-CATS, STINK-BADGERS, AND
SKUNKS

After reading these words, we noticed another sign resting on the
ground beneath this one... Its shape appeared to have left its
impression upon the face of the other sign... In red letters this sign
read...

CLOSED INDEFINATELY
NO TRESPASSING
KEEP OUT

A series of images and segmented-factoids flashed in my mind from
various media-viewer reports... Due to the threat of extinction, a
preservation site had been dedicated to the survival of these various
stink-spraying creatures... Once they had been relocated to this
preservation site, they began to breed prodigiously... They quickly
integrated with their relatives, and new sub-species were created...
Then the sub-species began to breed exponentially, and migrated
beyond the perimeter of this preservation site...

These creatures reproduced at such a rapid pace, that they soon
began occupying urban areas far beyond their site of origin... They
initially occupied urban areas with the least amount of human
presence, but continued to spread into the hearts of the larger
cities... This caused quite a conflict...

Whenever the possibility of a threat was presented to these *skunk-
badgers* they would project an odoriferous-mass in the general
direction of the perceived-threat... The odor these creatures
produced was much more potent and appalling than that of their
predecessors... This odor caused involuntary reactions to those
exposed including, burning and watering of the eyes, nausea, violent
coughing or choking, dizziness, &c, &c, &c... Another deviation of
these skunk-badgers from their relatives was that they could spray
much larger amounts of this atrocious spray... They also never
seemed to run out of this dreadful scent...

Encounters with these creatures became increasingly common... Urban guvornmints received an influx of complaints on the matter... Unfortunately, there was little that could be done... Resources necessary to address the problem were scarce in the midst of all the phynancial crises...

Even if the resources could be allocated, there were other concerns that made this problem more of a quandary... These creatures were an emerging-species according to legal definitions... Therefore, terminating any of these creatures was a punishable offense...

Another difficulty was the fact that, the preservation site where they had originated, had been forced to shut down due to funding issues... Of course, this site was also overly populated with other variants of this species as well... Even if these creatures could be captured, there was nowhere for them to be relocated... Capturing these creatures was not advisable either... They tended to spray aggressively in captivity, and had developed very sharp claws that allowed them to cut through some cages, traps, &c, &c, &c...

Of all the rotten-stinking things in the world, none were met with such hatred as these skunk-badgers... Even imagining the scent of these things seemed to bring me right back to the very place I had hoped to abandon... The remnants of their scent had become an integral part of the smell of the city it-self... How is it that the past manages to haunt all that deviates from its demise? I thought...

Somehow this scent was not as strong in this preservation site, as it had been in my memory of the place I had abandoned... In recognizing this, I had seemed to begin thinking of that place as existing elsewhere... I had finally managed to depart from that past place... Now it was relegated into the remnants of memories that would be associated with it... Would even its memories fade away like a diluted scent? I thought...

As bizarre as it might seem, this place was exactly what I needed... This place existed outside of the rest of the world... Not only was it disconnected from everything outside of it, but it represented what all of those other places were not... There was nothing that could appeal to the desires of any colloquial-drone here... A place like this didn't offer any social-cooperation, collective-benefit, &c, &c, &c... Inside this place was nothing... Only two potential offerings resided on the other side of this fence; preservation and isolation...

If I was going to survive on my own, this was the place to do it... The very threat of its inhabitants' scents would likely keep any other rational person far away... Living in this place would isolate me from everything I had left... There was the potential threat of coyotes, wolves, bears, &c, &c, &c...

Despite the potential threats, nothing I expected to encounter posed any threat to my autonomy... Could I really expect to survive in a place like this? Was this the way I wanted to live apart from everything? I thought...

Soon, I decided to enter the preservation site... If I changed my mind, I could always just leave... I took out my new knife, and set everything else next to the post... Then I climbed up the vine-laced fence, and reached the c-wire... Using the knife, I cut the c-wire carefully, and let it fall off to both sides of the incision...

I climbed back down to retrieve my possessions, and transported them through the opening in the c-wire... Once everything was inside the preservation site, I climbed over my-self... Before continuing further inside the preservation site, I very carefully took the two detached ends of c-wire, and twisted them back together... Observing the result of this effort, I was certain that no one would be able to tell that I had done any of this... Was my past fully obscured and divided from this place? I thought...

As I gathered my things, two of the site's residents came into view... These creatures became aware of my presence moments after I had spotted them... They elevated and fluffed up their tails, as an apparent warning for me not to intrude on them... After a moment of remaining still, the two quadrupeds began to scamper away... This was my first encounter with such creatures, and I was uncertain what varietal of *skunkoid* creature these might have been... What were these things? I thought...

With my possessions loaded back onto my shoulders, I followed the remnants of a path into the preservation site... This led me to the ruins of a *visitor's-area*... In this former *visitor's-area* was a *surveying-stand*, an *information-center*, and other small structures that had all begun to deteriorate, &c, &c, &c...

Inside the former information-center were a series of pamphlets on the site's various inhabitants, its geography, &c, &c, &c... Most of these inhabitants were described as having crepuscular tendencies... Since it was now getting close to sunset, I decided to utilize the surveying-stand for a sleeping-interval...

Approaching the surveying-stand, I could see a large number of the local inhabitants roaming around the vicinity of these structures... I managed to get into the top of the surveying-stand without incident, but the threat of such an unwanted occurrence seemed inevitable...

Inside the stand, I was able to see much of the preservation site by peering over the edges... Although the structure was rotting away, there was a large enough area in the flooring that seemed capable of supporting my weight... It became immediately clear that this structure was only to be used temporarily... I would have to venture further out in order to acquire a more appropriate dwelling, but I could rest here well enough for now...

I took my packs, and spread them over the portions of the floor that I wasn't intending on occupying for my sleeping-interval... It soon dawned on me that I had no bedding... In order to stay warm as the night became colder, I used the other clothing items in my baggage... This was not a viable substitute for a proper blanket or sleeping-bag, and I had a great difficulty in my efforts to sleep...

Eventually, I awoke in a way that seemed as if it were not from a state of slumber, but less conscious exhaustion... My eyes had great difficulty adjusting to the daylight... I had lived nocturnally throughout most of my life, and had become more accustomed to the darkness than the light... Most of the time I had spent during the diurnal hours was done under the shade and shadows of the facility, or other metropolitan structures that surrounded everything...

What my eyes would see after some adjusting was quite a sight... There were several skunkoid-carcasses near the area I was positioned... Along with the skunkoid remnants was a creature that might have been a form of coyote... The 'yote had a slash-wound over its throat, and was nearly deceased... From my position in the stand, I could see the state of these things with clarity...

I took the bow and an arrow from my possessions... Then I aimed at the 'yote, hoping to be able to end its suffering... My first attempt to do this, missed short by about 3 feet of the 'yote... On my next attempt, the result was a frightening form of peace... The suffering creature ceased to struggle... Somehow I felt as if its struggle had become my own... What was this struggle? Why did it seem to become my own? I Thought...

Climbing down from the stand, I began to focus on the concerns of the day... Having been too discombobulated to have eaten for some time, I retrieved a ration of food from my possessions... In order to access the contents of the packaging, I cut into the metal cylinder with the knife that had already proven to be of such great use... Consuming the essential nourishment, I then set to work on the next task...

Surprisingly, the skunkoid remains were unencumbered with the notorious-scents they were known to project... Except for their bones and fur-covered skins, there was very little left of the former-skunkoids... Carefully cutting away any potentially stink-riddled areas and fleshy-bits, I isolated the pelts from the rest of the remnants... After I had managed to collect about a dozen of these pelts, I piled them all together...

Then I went to retrieve the merciful arrows, and removed the fur from the former-'yote... According to a map inside one of the pamphlets from the former information-center, there was a creek near this area... I proceeded in the direction of the stream with my bow, arrows, pelts, &c, &c, &c...

I soon reached the creek, stripped down, and used the water to rinse the pelts very rigorously... Once I was satisfied that they were as clean as possible, I piled them next to the creek... Then I commenced to fully immerse my-self in the creek's waters... The water was extremely cold, but I needed to cleanse my flesh of all the unwanted particles that had been displaced onto it...

As I got out of the water, the cold was even more intense... I put on my clothes, grabbed the pelts and the rest of my items, before returning to the visitor's-center... Some of the skunkoids were in the vicinity of my path, and delayed my return... By the time I did return to the visitor's-center, it was getting close to dusk...

I spread the pelts over the roof of the visitor's-center... There was a nasty, dust-covered tarp strewn under a heap of rubbish inside the visitor's-center... Desperate to stay warm over night, I considered using it as a blanket... After rummaging around the area, I eventually found a cellar-door behind the visitor's-center... Opening the cellar-door was a bit of a struggle, since it was constructed out of a hefty ¼ inch iron sheet...

Inside the cellar there was a shelf lined with water-jugs... Another shelf was lined with lighter-fluid, charcoal, flashlights, &c, &c, &c... Ignoring the generator and gasoline cans on the floor, I hoisted one of the water-jugs onto my shoulder, and carried it out... Then I took a big, long, sloppy drink from it... Following the elation of quenching my incredible thirst, I went to drag out the dirty-tarp, and rinse it off a bit... The tarp was hardly clean when I was done, but it would suffice for a night's sleeping-interval...

I left most of my possessions down in the visitor's-center, except for my primary bag, tarp, acrousticgrittare, &c, &c, &c... Before I attempted to initiate a sleeping-interval, I decided to experiment with the acrousticgrittare... Although the sounds that I made with the acrousticgrittare didn't make any muzikal-sense, I enjoyed the process of experimenting...

There were almost certainly no ears within auditory range capable of hearing these sounds intelligibly... This was perhaps the first time in my life that I had made any sound that truly seemed to be my own... After setting the instrument aside for the night, my sleeping-interval was initiated... Drifting easily to sleep, the last thoughts my mind held before slumber were not of any words or questions, but of sounds...

In the subsequent days of waking, I tried not to waste a single moment... There was a lot of work to be done in order to turn the ruins and wilderness of this preservation site into a habitable-area... None of the structures remaining in this area would serve me very well for long... If anyone else were to wander into this area, I would find my-self exposed to them... In order to survive alone, I would have to find a more secluded and secure location...

A litany of concerns occupied my thoughts, my time, my focus, &c, &c, &c... What would I do for food? What should I do to in order to survive the inevitable winter? How should I manage the resources I'd acquired already? I thought...

201.03 ALONE IN THE DARK...

Despite the challenges of the preservation site, I became quite
contented with things... Using my knife to sharpen the end of a tree-
limb, I made a balanced wood-spear... This allowed me to remove
fishoids from the streams in the area... Fishoids were in abundance,
and became my primary source of nourishment... Birds could be
brought down with my bow after I became more skilled, but they
occasionally distressed my digestive-system... I found a cherry tree
too, but it was too small to consider as anything more than an
occasional indulgence... There were also some apple trees scattered
about the site, as well as other horticultural prospects, &c, &c, &c...

After a while, there was no thought of food in terms of flavor...
Food was a necessary thing to consume in order to stay alive...
Eating was still quite satisfying, but the pleasure was derived from
aspects that preceded consumption...

I took pride in my abilities to single out a fishoid, focus in on it, and
spear it with a single coordinated effort... Every time I speared a
fishoid, I felt a rush of personal esteem... Everything I did became
an essential part of the process of living, staying alive, &c, &c, &c...

With extensive efforts, I managed to build a new dwelling to shelter
my slumbering-self... I constructed my *nest* in the elevation of a
mighty tree... Building this nest was quite an undertaking...

...

I had found a sharp piece of sheet-metal on a previous occasion... With a bit of innovative thinking, I managed to form this sheet of metal into a set of saw-toothed strips... By strapping these sharp strips to a bowed tree-limb, I could use this item as a *hand-sahw*... Before constructing this *pseudo-saw*, I had managed to make a series of *hatchaetes* out of rocks and tree-branches... My hatchaetes kept breaking as I chopped away at the tree-trunks, but there were plenty of rocks and tree-limbs to replace them... These items were poor substitutes for proper tools, but with a great deal of work, they did allow me to cut-out enough pieces to build what I would come to call my *sky-shanty*...

Building my sky-shanty was of no small cost... It consumed a great deal of time, and fall was closing-in when it was completed... My hands became blistered, cut, calloused, mangled, &c, &c, &c... Due to the amount of blood I had leaked into the materials, I thought of my sky-shanty as being made out of an *artificial-red-wood-composite*... My hands had become so course, it was hard to tell if the flesh had healed or died...

My sky-shanty kept me above the dangers of the ground at night, and stored my possessions quite effectively... Most of the items that I had arrived with had quickly become expended, or discarded... Only the package and its contents, my primary backpack, acrousticgrittare, and items of lethality were still of any apparent utility...

I had used the knife from the package to cut slivers of metal, and used the slivers as needles... Then I used strands of loose thread to mend my clothing items... I also attached the pelts from animals together, and completed a number of other related projects, &c, &c, &c...

Food, shelter, clothing, and the other base-level concerns of the *Massloathian hierarchy* had all become satisfied in a minimalistic fashion... In fact, certain higher-levels of concerns were also satisfied... According to the *Massloathian hierarchy*, I lacked the social-functioning components, but I had deliberately omitted these components preceding my arrival...

When I set off on my journey to nowhere, it had led me here... In contemplating my progress, other questions were formed... Where was I now? What was I doing here now? Was I accomplishing my objectives? Had I found my self? I thought...

During the diurnal hours, my life consisted of obligatory actions... In the night, under the distant glimmers of dead or dying stars, I would ponder, wonder, dream, &c, &c, &c... I would have my acrousticgrittare in hand... My own thoughts were serenaded to the sound of my own creations... Alone in this darkness, I learned how to make my own light, sound, &c, &c, &c...

I managed to stay warm through what turned out to be a fairly mild winter... By burning the firewood I had piled-up over the summer, it was also possible to keep the skunkoids at a distance... Sometimes, I would sit by my fire, and look at the sky above... I would think of the light that reached down from so far away... The stars that projected their light, most probably had collapsed long ago... Only the haunt of light still remained, as if it were the ghosts of those radiant immensities...

In the midst of so many other thoughts, I kept thinking about these ghosts... What if those stars were all gone? What if their light ceased to haunt this earth? On those nights that were overcast enough to imagine a sky turned black, I would wonder... Even if that light didn't reach the earth, it would have to be projected somewhere... What if there were nowhere left for that light to reach? How would it keep going? I thought...

Lost inside these thoughts, I would find my-self almost obliviously involved in other activities... My acrousticgrittare was most commonly discovered in moments like these, positioned in my hands as I projected sound from it... Over time, my ability to project more comprehensible sounds with this instrument improved... I would find my-self engaged in the projection of my own sonic creations, with almost no regard for anything beyond them...

As time went on, I engaged in an increasing number of projects, and my presence in the preservation site increased as well... By the next summer, I had explored the entire site... I had come to consider the entire area my own... There was one question that kept propelling me forward... What else could I do? I thought...

I modified the preservation site to fit my own intentions... The skunkoids were primarily concentrated where their *kricketoid* food sources were in abundance... In order to limit my encounters with the skunkoids, I studied the kricketoids... The kricketoids were discovered to feed mainly on decaying-plants, occupy warm areas, chirp more frequently in areas with higher temperatures, &c, &c, &c...

After acquiring these insights, I turned various areas into kricketoid feeding-grounds... I piled up big heaps of plant-fodder on top of some of the rocky areas... My thinking was that the rocky areas tended to be warmer, and the plant-fodder would allow the kricketoids plenty of nutrients... Then I started populating these areas with kricketoids...

The kricketoids became extremely prominent in these areas... They could be heard on the warm summer nights chirping away in colossal choirs of kricketoid cacophony... This sound succeeded in attracting the skunkoid populations into its vicinity...

Having managed to concentrate the populations of these creatures, I was now able to navigate the preservation site with greater ease... I'd roam about the area thinking of things to build, develop, alter, &c, &c, &c... The whole site became host to the myriad of projects I chose to indulge...

With all of this space to my-self, I had set about doing something without even realizing it ... Essentially; I was doing what everyone else had been doing everywhere else in the world... All I was doing was projecting my-self out into the world...

It soon became clear to me that the only thing I had changed in coming here was the context... Here I was alone, and everything I projected was unaffected by the impressions of others... Was there any real difference in how I related to this place, compared to any other entity? I thought...

201.04 THE SHRINE…

I began to engage in deep introspections concerning the truth of my-self in this place… One night, under a heavy curtain of clouds, there was no visible starlight, and the moon's reflections were lost… From one darkness to another, my mind slipped into an abysmal sleep… Within the darkness of this slumber, something else began…

It began in the manner that dreams do, with no true beginning… Initially, there was nothing in this dream… By nothing, I mean that there was only a black void where nothing existed… Even I didn't seem to exist in the void of this dream… I only seemed to become present within the dream in a most detached sense…

In the ethereal sense that dreams are allowed to make, I seem to find my-self in the darkness of this dream… My-self is not something I can sense in any real manner… A sense of being drawn *inwards* propels me… I begin to drift inside of the dreaming void… The dream makes it known to me that I am drifting towards my *self*…

The greatest sense of detachment is prevalent throughout this darkened dream… My self exists apart from my dreaming-mind, and the void exists beyond these dissociations, etc, etc, etc… It's as if there isn't any such thing as space/time …

…

Despite the darkness and surreal detachment, I drift without motion towards this sense of my self... Somehow, I begin to sense that I am drifting closer to my self in this void... Then I begin to *see* the darkness as obscuring my ability to perceive my self...

In this *non-sense* of dreaming, I see that my self is not only obscured by darkness, but also by a collage of forms... The forms them-selves are also dark, and only appear as less darkened mass... None of the forms can be seen clearly enough to be identified as anything in particular... Everything remains obscured from me...

As I observe the forms, they seem to be attaching them-selves to what my dreaming-mind associates with my self... The forms seem to appear out of nowhere in the void, and drift towards the area around my unseen self... They appear to be forming some sort of formless shrine... This shrine is to my self, and precedes its presence...

Formless figures affix them-selves to the shrine, and immediately begin to degrade... Fragments of the black shapeless forms crumble away from the shrine, and become evaporated in the nothingness of the void... As this is happening, the remnants of the shapeless forms seem to dissolve into each-other... These dissolving forms are diluted into the whole of them, and *form* the shapeless structure of the shrine... Nothing holds any form in this dream, not even the shrine...

A terrifying sense begins to possess my dreaming-mind in this darkened dream... Suddenly, I begin to fear that my self might become dissolved into the formlessness of the shrine... My drifting *presence* becomes forcefully propelled by a desire to break through the formlessness of the shrine... I plunge through the formless-forms, and submerge my dreaming-presence beneath them... Another vacant void exists between the penetrated shrine and my unseen self...

I am still unable to perceive my self in this void of voids... The shrine disappears into the outer void, as I drift deeper and deeper towards my sensed self...

Within this dream, I begin to wonder... What will happen if I find my self? What would become of me, if I were to discover my self? Would I become diluted into my self, or would my self become diluted into me? How would I be able to merge with my self, or avoid such a merger? What am I to do? Terror grips my dreaming-mind, as I continue to drift through this void of voids...

I become detached from even the very act of drifting... At this point, I no longer have any intentions of drifting towards the core of my self... Instead, it is as if I continue drifting in spite of my dreaming-presence... Wondering what there might be within this void and beyond it, I continue to drift...

With a maddening subtlety, my dreaming fades into my obliviousness of waking... As I transition into waking, the dreamscape's darkness becomes the blackened night... My drifting through the dream's void of voids fades into a sense of falling... Instead of colliding with my self in the dream, I collapse onto the earthly surface beneath me...

Another kind of darkness follows this for what can't be measured in increments of time... When I wake from this darkness, I realize that I have fallen from my resting place... I look up to see the damaged floor of my sky-shanty, directly above me... Then I realize that I might have been knocked unconscious by the fall... If this assertion is true, I might also have acquired a concussion... My memory reminds me, it is not advisable to sleep with a concussion... Obliged to remain awake, my mind seems to be in bad shape from the fall, the dream, &c, &c, &c...

My mind continues to consider the many aspects of the dream... Painfully awake, I think of the dream, my life, my self, &c, &c, &c... Even after the sun rises fully above me, my thoughts continue as if they are still in this dark dream... Was it the dream or the fall that had brought me down to this? I thought...

201.05 MOVING BENEATH...

After the fall, I thought it would be best to stay closer to the ground... I began to search the area of the preservation site in order to find an alternative shelter... Considering where the concentrated populations of kricketoids and skunkoids were, I focused my search on specific areas...

One day, I came across something unusually fitting for my sheltering project... While attempting to stalk a *gavagai*, I noticed a very interesting tree... This tree had grown on a hillside that had become washed-out in a flood... This tree's roots formed a pseudo-skeleton... A space large enough to use as a shelter was contained within this hollow *root-structure*...

The gavagai I had been following hopped inside the hollow region of the root-structure... Instead of slaughtering the gavagai, I chased it out of the area I intended to occupy... Inspecting the area inside the root-structure, my decision to occupy this space became resolved...

I had to contain my-self in all the subsequent excitement of finding a suitable shelter... As I turned to leave the root-structure, I was startled to see the gavagai reposed at the edge of the entrance... At that point, I realized my need for something to eat was still a necessity... Using my well-practiced bow and a whittled-arrow, I drew aim at the gavagai... For a moment, I held my aim on target, in

...

spontaneous hesitation... In this delay, I suddenly thought of the human overpopulation stories on the media-viewer from my nearly forgotten urban inhabitance...

They used to insert quick, cutting images of *rabbitoids* whenever they projected a program addressing excessive populations... Recalling this also made me remember other pseudo-subliminal images they would project in other media-viewer programing... This led me to a strange sentiment... It began as something of a resignation, and then took the form of displaced animosity...

The moment seemed to last longer than the miniscule slice of time in which it occurred... As the sentiment seemed to possess me in this moment, I released the tension from my bow, my-self, &c, &c, &c... When I retrieved the dinner-rabbit, my mind began to wonder... How is it that things can become so possessed with these associations of meaning? What is it about something that gives it any meaning at all? Is meaning just a conditioned effect of repetitive absorptions of *Pravlavian* projections? I thought...

Due to the diurnal cycle's waning hours, I decided to trek back to my sky-shanty for the night... Moving into the root-structure would require more time than there was remaining before the crepuscular skunkoid commute... Carrying the dinner-rabbit with my possessions, I made haste to avoid an encounter with the projectile-stink-anuses of the olfactory-aggressors... Along the way, I continued to think of the nature of relative-meanings, the process of naming things, the affected-perspective that results, &c, &c, &c...

Amidst the quiet of the preservation site, I became suddenly aware of what sounded like distant humanoid voices... I had almost reached my sky-shanty when these sounds were first heard... As I encroached on the area surrounding my sky-shanty, the voices became more audible... In order to avoid a potential confrontation, I halted my advance, and tried to listen closely to the source of these vocalizations...

Although it was apparent that the voices were in all probability human, very little of their speech could be made out coherently...

There were at least 5 voices that could be heard distinctively... These voices all seemed to be coming from the immediate vicinity of my sky-shanty... They seemed to be debating as to whether or not to enter the structure... After a while, they began to split-up, and were probably searching the area around my shelter... I didn't waste time thinking what they might have been searching for...

I decided to evacuate the area, and return to the root-structure... As I began to retreat in silence, I suddenly heard barking consistent with my impressions of canines... The barking continued, and began to move in my general direction... In order to avoid the *barkoid* creature, I left my dinner-rabbit behind me... With the dinner-rabbit placed between my direction of withdrawal and the advancing barkoid, I expedited my hasty evacuation of the area...

As I fled the area of the abandoned dinner-rabbit, I started to hear the voices again... They were closing in on the vicinity of the abandoned dinner-rabbit... There was a hill nearby, where I might have a line-of -sight to that area... Swiftly and stealthily, I made my way up the far side of the hill, attempting to remain out of the potential view of the voices...

From this vantage point, I could see seven figures gathered around the barkoid and the dinner-rabbit... They were laughing at the barkoid as it ripped into the dinner-rabbit's flesh... I was initially relieved to see this, but my relief quickly faded ...

My relief had been from the notion that the arrow's puncture mark had been erased by the barkoid... This prevented the figures from becoming overtly aware of my nearby presence... I'd quickly realized that these figures were almost certainly intent on staying inside this preservation site... Inevitably, I would either become exposed to them, or be forced to evacuate the preservation site... Neither of these options was welcomed at this time...

Watching the figures from my vantage point, I noticed a few things about them... They were all dressed in military-style clothing... None of them were dressed according to regulatory standards, but they were wearing authentic-looking uniforms... Attached to each of their left arms, were tan brassards, bearing an emblem that was indiscernible from my vantage point... Each of them was also equipped with some form of weaponry attached to them... Although they didn't use any hand-and-arm communications, and were not in any standard-formation, they still seemed to have some bearing of military-mannerisms... It appeared as if they were all formerly attached to some military unit, but had discharged out for some reason...

This notion was very discomforting to me... If this notion was correct, they might not have been discharged honorably... The possibility of this meant that any formal introductions would be ill-advised... It also supported my initial notion that I might have to leave the preservation site in order to evade them... In addition to this, I would have to become extremely cautious if I did remain here amidst these figures... What was I to do now? I thought...

Observing the group for some time, it appeared that one of them functioned as their commanding figure... All of the others repeatedly looked in this figure's direction, addressed the figure directly, acted in response to the figure's directions, &c, &c, &c... This figure seemed to have the most upright posture and confidence of those within the group... The other figures held their posture with varying degrees of slouching, head drooping, &c, &c, &c... After observing this, I began to focus more closely on this particular figure...

The *Commanding-figure* was pacing the area surrounding the dinner-rabbit, looking carefully at the ground... If they were trying to find foot-prints, it was unlikely that they would succeed... The ground was rather rocky, and I was careful to avoid leaving any obvious traces in my evacuation of this area... As they continued to scrutinize the area, the others meandered around a pseudo-perimeter without any apparent vigilance... Eventually, the Commanding-figure made a declaration to the other figures that I could hear from my position...

"Let's move out before it gets dark."

One of the other figures cut in...

"Do you still think there's anybody out here?"

"I don't see any reason not to. You saw the shelter. It couldn't be more than a few years old, and there was a fire pit nearby. This might not have been a *baited-bunny*, but that still doesn't change the rest."

Another one of the figures broke in with a question...

"What do you think they might be doing out here?"

The Commanding-figure shrugged its shoulders, and looked at the ground, sagging out of posture...

"What the hell is anyone doing these days? You answer me that in any way that makes sense, and I'll be piss-pleased. My guess is that they'd have to be doing the same thing anybody else is trying to do out here now."

Yet another of the figures broke into the conversation...

"Are you sayin' what we're doin' doesn't make any sense or somethin'?"

"I might as well. Anybody here know how to make sense of anything anymore?"

None of the other figures took a crack at the Commanding-figure's question... Then the Commanding-figure went on...

"Pay attention. If I'm right, they've been out here longer than we have. They probably have some idea of the lay of the land here. I'd say it would be best to consider that they even know we're here. In light of that, we're gonna have to stay on our toes a bit. When we get back to camp, we're gonna have to pay close attention on watch tonight. I don't want to risk having anyone form an invasion on us. Now, is everyone clear on that?"

The figures responded in unison...

"Who-Ra!"

Then the Commanding-figure led them away, at an azimuth divergent from those that would lead back to my sky-shanty or the root-structure... I watched and listened carefully to ensure they had cleared the area before I moved from my vantage point... As I patiently confirmed their departure, my mind mused it-self with an eccentric notion...

This utterance of *Who-Ra* had been present in my period of military assignment... This utterance had been derived from several various origins, most of which were disputable... Of these reputed and disputed origins, it had been used to mean dive, farewell, forward, strike, &, &c, &c... Later, these utterances metamorphosed into *backronyms*... Eventually, these backronyms would be combined into the singular term *Who-Ra*... *Who-Ra* evolved into a term that was used to mean anything other than no... As a strict rule, the word no was not acceptable in most circumstances within military environments...

The utterance seemed to exist as a declarative statement, but sounded as if it could be the words of a question... This apparent question would have been grammatically improper... However, the sound of this utterance could be articulated as, *Who Ra?* If this were modified to be grammatically correct, it could be denoted as, *Who's Ra?* or, *Who is Ra?*...

Interestingly enough, *Ra* was the name of the *Agyptian soalair-gawd*... Over the course of Agyptian mythology, Ra was merged with the concepts of other gawds, including the gawd *Horeus*... When merged with Horeus, Ra's name could be interpreted as *Ra, the Horeus (gawd) of both horizons*... Effectively, Ra was considered to rule over everything in a way that didn't allow any exception or *no* as a result...

In my mind, there was a strange correlation to the nature of this all-encompassing gawd's etymology, and the derivations of the utterance's colloquial meaning(s)... Both the gawd and the utterance had etymologized from disputed origins, merged with other conceptions, and become synonymous with everything other than their negations (which were considered pejorative)...

I mused my-self with further thoughts on this matter, as I monitored the figures' departure... If *Who-Ra* signified everything except for its refusal, wouldn't *Ra* be signified in this militarized-utterance? If so, wouldn't that imply that Ra couldn't negate this utterance? How could this utterance signify Ra, if Ra couldn't deny it? Could this make the utterance into a negation of Ra? For this utterance to negate a component of its meaning, would that not contradict its meaning as well? I thought...

Then I wondered; if this utterance could signify everything except for its negation, then could any part of it not negate any other part of it... Wouldn't that preclude the possibility of negations altogether? Was *Who-Ra* a negation of its own negation? These things offered a puzzling form of amusement in the time that it took for the figures to finally vacate the area...

When the area was finally vacated, I set my-self in motion back towards my sky-shanty... My intention was to gather my possessions from inside, and abandon the sky-shanty for good... This meant I would have to travel in the midst of the crepuscular skunkoids, the figures, &c, &c, &c... Was the risk of continuing without my possessions greater than the risk of retrieving them? I thought...

I was very cautious not to startle or stumble upon any of the skunkoids along the way... My movements were kept slow, deliberate, &c, &c, &c... As I arrived, the sun had settled beneath the horizon, and the visibility of the preservation site was limited to twilight...

With limited visibility, I crept up to the entrance of the sky-shanty, using superlative stealth and caution... When I reached the threshold of the sky-shanty, I thought I could hear subtle movements inside... I halted for a frozen moment, and tried to listen even more carefully...

No subsequent sounds were heard, and I peeped into the opening of the sky-shanty... My eyes caught a quick glimpse of a figure inside, before I pulled my-self away from being exposed... The figure was slumped over, and appeared to be sleeping in a seated position... Even in the limits of twilight, I could see that the figure was in the uniformed military-clothing...

I considered how I would respond to this observation... My possessions were still positioned by the opening of the sky-shanty... It seemed possible for me to reach them without alarming the slumbering-figure... As I contemplated the thought of extracting my possessions, I moved into the concealment of the brush nearby...

Before I could conclude what to do, two developments occurred... The first was a skunkoid's arrival within the vicinity of the sky-shanty... The second development was that the figure had dismounted the sky-shanty, having apparently awakened... I saw the figure position it-self by a tree, as sounds of urination followed...

The resultant geography placed me between the skunkoid and the figure... I was facing either becoming exposed to the figure, or alarming the skunkoid... The longer I hesitated, the less likely I would be able to negotiate the situation... If the skunkoid sprayed, I might also become exposed to the figure as a result... Alternately, if I became exposed to the figure the skunkoid could become startled in the process...

I quickly decided to creep back into the sky-shanty while the figure's back was still turned to me... When I reached the sky-shanty, I reached inside my possessions to obtain my pistol... It had not been disturbed in my absence... As I grasped hold of it, I ensured it was loaded... Then I pointed it towards the opening of the sky-shanty, anticipating the figure's return...

My plan was to either quietly inform the figure that I had just come to retrieve my possessions before leaving, or terminate the figure... If I could keep things quiet and compliant, I would have then tried to tie the figure to the sky-shanty... Then I would have fled the preservation site immediately... Should I find my hand forced to terminate the figure, I would have absconded the preservation site with frantic ardor...

As I reeled in anticipatory angst, I began to hear something moving beneath me... It was the sound of the figure as the skunkoid's presence became known... The skunkoid became startled just as I peeped my head out of the sky-shanty... It sprayed directly into the figure's eyes, and scampered off into the night...

I heard the figure swearing on the ground, as I bolted away with my possessions... The figure was blinded as a result of this spraying incident, and was unable to hear over its own screaming... Due to these circumstances, I was able to clear the area without being directly exposed to the figure... Unfortunately, the smell was still potent enough in proximity to me that I absorbed some of it in the process of my escape... How much more intense must the figure's exposure have been? I thought...

My eyes watered, and I became nauseous while I continued my evacuation... As I adjusted to the scent, my mind began to focus on other pressing concerns... Although I had managed to retrieve my possessions without being seen directly, the figure would be able to discover the absence of my possessions... When that happened, it would confirm my presence inside the preservation site... Then the group of figures would consider the events surrounding the extraction of my possessions, and form some kind of response... How might they react to all of this? I thought...

If they sent their accompanying barkoid in search of me, I would surely become exposed... The smell of the skunkoid-spray could easily be traced to me, even by a human with a marginal sense of smell... There was very little I could do to prevent this from happening... What could I do?

I bounded frantically towards the nearest stream in the area... It wasn't far, and I arrived in almost no time at all... I tried hastily to soak, scrub, and rinse-off my body, clothes, possessions, &c, &c, &c... The water was approximately 8-10 feet deep at the point that I entered the stream... After plunging in, I began to drift down-stream with the current, while making attempts to remove as much of the scent as possible...

Drifting down-stream, I suddenly heard a great deal of commotion, as I rounded a bend... I crouched down near the bank to conceal my-self from view... From the area of the commotion, I could see some tents, a fire, and the movement of figures... The figures were all heading in the direction of my sky-shanty... My nose alerted me to the presence of the skunkoid scent, coming from the same area as the figures...

It was likely that the figure that had been sprayed came here directly, after discovering my possessions had gone missing... The figure might also be soon to approach this very stream in order to deal with the skunkoid scent... I managed to slip past the figures' site, while still observing them... They had all left the area, and even the skunkoid affected figure had followed after the others...

Realizing this left their site abandoned, I had an idea... I went into their site, and used a stick to leave a message in the dirt... My message was placed where they would surely be able to find it when they returned... To ensure this, I posted some large tree-limbs in the ground surrounding my message... The message read, *Please keep to your-selves*...

I left my message, and sprinted away from the area... Throughout the night I kept moving without rest... If the figures returned to their site, they might cease their search for the night... Assuming they had seen my message, they would either consent to avoid pursuing involvement out of reciprocity, or from fear that I had gained a present advantage over them... It was still possible that they would continue their search for me, so I remained mobile, restless, &c, &c, &c...

I finally decided to return to the root-structure, after the sun had started to set again on the following day... Although it was relatively close to the area the figures might be searching, I figured that I could mitigate the risks associated with the circumstances easily enough...

My sudden resolve to stay in the preservation site despite everything that had happened or could happen was quite out of character for me... Perhaps that was why I was so determined to do to it... The challenges involved in surviving in the midst of these figures were also strangely appealing... What was I doing this for? Where could it lead? I thought...

201.06 ROOT-STRUCTURE...

I figured there were a few things I should do before occupying the root-structure... My primary concern was to conceal the structure from the other figures' view before they discovered it... If I couldn't conceal the root-structure before the figures happened upon it, they would be able to see through whatever concealment I used... Should they discover the true form of the root-structure before I occupied its space, there would be no way for me to avoid being exposed...

As I made my way towards the root-structure, I happened upon the figures in the vicinity of the abandoned sky-shanty... All of their attachments were now located around the abandoned sky-shanty... They were all gathered around a fire, and seemed to be discussing their next organized action when I crept into the vicinity...

The Commanding-figure appeared to be struggling to project a confident composure, while restraining a strong sense of blind resentfulness... Some of the figures referred to me as a *'specter*... None of them wanted to actively engage in attempting to locate me... Eventually, the Commanding-figure declared that they would have to stay vigilant in case this *'specter* was still in the area... They were to pay close attention on watch, report anything unusual immediately, not to go anywhere alone, &c, &c, &c...

...

The information I gathered on this reconnaissance was invaluable to me... I decided to slip away, as the figures discussed specific details about their other activities... As I approached the root-structure, I carefully examined the area for any trace of evidence that the figures had been present... No traces were discovered, and I decided to move forward with my plan...

I began to cover the open areas of the root-structure with the tarp I had kept from the visitors-center... The tarp was large enough that I could wrap its ends around the farthest roots left exposed from erosion... Then I secured the tarp in place, using some strips of *rowpe* I'd made from stripped wood-bark... Next, I began retrieving dirt from inside the structure, and packing it on top of the tarp... After applying a good layer of dirt, I emptied out a container of water from my pack to get the dirt muddy... In order to get all of the dirt wet enough, I had to retrieve more water...

In order to conceal the root-structure, I considered attempting to retrieve a water-jug that I had previously abandoned... It had been abandoned because it seemed to be slowly leaking from an area near the top... I was reluctant to retrieve this jug due to the possibility of the leak creating a trace the figures might possibly follow... However, it seemed unlikely that the figures would actually be able to follow such a trail... Retrieving the jug was necessary to allow me to avoid making multiple trips to a water source in the process of concealing the root-structure...

Having considered my options, I set off to retrieve the abandoned water-jug... It was found to be precisely as I had left it, and I looked around to see if anything in its vicinity had been altered... Nothing appeared to have been trodden upon, so I recovered the item, and continued to the nearest stream...

At the stream, I filled the jug with water, watching and listening carefully for the presence of figures... As I was placing the cap on the water-jug, suddenly something came darting out of the brush on the other side of the stream... Although, my initial assumption was that it was one of the figures, it turned out to be some kind of wild *catoid* creature… The beast had plunged into the stream after a *birdoid* creature that had been resting in the middle of the shallow stream…

Having instinctively frozen in my place, the catoid beast didn't become aware of my presence immediately… After a moment, the catoid did shoot a glance in my direction… With the dinner-birdoid in its jaws, it growled in my direction…

I peered deep into the catoid beast's eyes, awaiting its response… In an instant, I was prepared to defend my life to the extent of slaying the catoid beast, even if it would alert every figure in the area of my location… Instead of attacking me, the catoid creature swaggered off, growling, switching its ears, &c, &c, &c…

This encounter made quite an impression on me… The catoid beast could look right back into my eyes, as I had looked into its own… It seemed to realize that it was in its best interest to leave me alone, so long as I didn't pursue it… Somehow this catoid beast seemed to be more astute in reaching this conclusion than I believed the figures would be…

If the figures had encountered me in such a way as this catoid, would they have given me a moment's pause? Would I have given them the same pause in such an encounter? I thought…

Cautiously returning to the root-structure, I commenced to conceal my intended shelter… I began lining the root-structure with some sticks running adjacent to the roots of the structure… Using the water, I bonded the sticks together with mud… The idea was to create a surface over the root-structure that could be tread upon, without exposing the interior… After seemingly succeeding with this effort, I concealed the facade with plant remnants, making it appear consistent with the surrounding surfaces…

Next, I began to work on the entry/exit point of the root-structure… A small opening remained at one end of the root-structure, where the tarp was left short of the continuous surface of the hill… There was a fallen-tree in the area, wide enough to cover this gap… This log was likely much too heavy to move as a whole… In order to make the log work as a concealing door, I had to cut some of the weight out of it...

I didn't want to use a rock-hatchet because of the noise it would cause... So I had to figure-out how to carve into the log another way... When I went to examine the log, I discovered that it was already split... The split in the log ran the length of its mass, and went most of the way through its diameter... This made it greatly easier to cleave away its core...

After cleaving away the mass of the log's core, I was able to lift it well enough to place it over the remaining gap in the root-structure... Having placed the log over this gap, I then tested to ensure it could be moved from inside and outside of the root-structure... Although it required some effort to displace the log, it did allow my entry and exit of the root-structure...

My next task was to purge the area of my traces, and complete the exterior facade... I cleared away the wood-shrapnel from the area, scattered brush-remnants over the area's surfaces, &c, &c, &c... Before concealing my-self inside, I surveyed the area to ensure everything was in proper order... Everything seemed to complete the facade to my satisfaction... Contented with the results, I placed the log-door over the gap in the root-structure, and sealed my-self inside with my possessions...

201.07 UNDER THE SURFACE...

Having concealed my-self inside the darkness of the root-structure, thoughts of isolation tore through my mind... Within the root-structure, I had cut my-self away from all that was projected, reflected, deflected, &c, &c, &c... Inside this place, I was able to dwell inside the thoughts of my own mind, without the impressions of things upon my attempts to see... My mind had broken away from everything outside the shelter of the root-structure...

The darkness was so complete in this place, even *time* seemed to have been cast out with the light, and all it touched... Despite my severed sense of *thyme*, my thoughts continued to elapse... Instead of intervals of standard-measure, I began to sense thyme in other ways... My own urgings became the measure of intervals... I measured thyme as the distances between urgings to consume nourishment, to relieve my-self of waste, &c, &c, &c... These urges forced me out of the root-structure, and cut into my otherwise unimpeded concentrations, &c, &c, &c...

Once I had satisfied whatever had beckoned me away from the root-structure, I would return as promptly as possible... I was beginning to sense that my thoughts were progressing towards an epiphany... It had again become my primary focus to continue the development of *Schizm Theory*... If I could truly understand the nature of the divide(s), then I could perhaps truly define my-self... I thought...

...

Schizm Theory was still in need of addressing the problems I had associated with the use of language... There were several fallacies that had become perpetuated in the structure of language... Language was a medium by which the mind could simulate understanding as thought... If language was flawed, then the simulations would become flawed, the understandings of thought would be contaminated, &c, &c, &c... I thought...

One of the problems I had considered to be a part of language was the negation of context... Every statement is the cutting away of some idea from the totality of thought... If you say one thing, there are infinite quantities of things that you do not say... The fact that you do not say all of these things does not mean that they do not exist in some context of whatever is declared... I have previously explained the use of the expression *"etc, etc, etc"*, as a means of addressing this notion...

It would become too imposing, to denote this expression in every context that it should be applied... Every context warrants its application, but implementing this expression in such a manner would become quite a drudge... At some point the idea of using ellipses (...) in the place of this expression was considered... This seemed to be an appropriate method...

Implementing the use of ellipses also allowed the correction of another language issue... Using a period at the end of a statement seemed to confine a sentence too rigidly... The use of a period essentially perpetuated the same problem in a different context...

By using the ellipses as a marker instead of a period, a thought can be considered an act of division... This division does not exclude the statement from the depth of larger contexts, but leaves room for all that the statement is not... Classical uses of ellipses are concurrently appropriate along with this modified usage, &c, &c, &c...

Another problem relating to linguistic-contexts, is the diverse usage of singular terms... A single word can have multiple definitions, be used in innumerable applications, convey a multitude of meanings, be altered by intentions, be presented in varying contexts, &c, &c &c...

In many cases, terms are applied in contexts that don't fit any of their definitions, in order to infer some underlying essence of meaning... This makes use of the word in a manner that would present it as something that it is not... If something is not what it is, then there is a paradox...

I developed various methods of addressing this paradox within the darkness of the root-structure... When a word is used in this manner, it may be denoted by the alteration of its standard-spelling... This method of deviating the spelling of a word, should still allude to the word with some semblance... Using this method effectively makes it clear that the word is not used as it is defined, but with respect to its context...

In addition to this method of altering words, there are other methods that I adopted... Some words are defined in a technical or scientific sense that might not be fully understood prior to using such a word... Animals for example, are named according to specific traits, groupings, &c, &c, &c... There is a specific scientific terminology used to denote specific forms of an animal, and there are common use terms that are based on these terms...

A skunk for instance, is a particular kind of creature... Many other creatures may in fact closely resemble a skunk... If one cannot be certain that a creature actually fits the definition of a skunk, it would be improper to refer to it as such... It would be more appropriate to use the word ending, *-oid*, and refer to the creature as a *skunkoid*... Referring to the creature in this manner conveys that it is of the form associated with skunks, but not necessarily an actual skunk...

Yet another method of language modification that came from my immersion in the darkness of the root-structure was the use of hyphenated-terms... There are some cases where something may exist in a context that places it between being one thing and becoming another... For instance, a rabbit is a live creature with definable features... If the rabbit ceases to be alive, it is no longer a rabbit in the full sense of its definition... A rabbit might be cooked in order for it to be consumed as a meal... Before the creature is to become dinner, it exists as something between the two terms...

By denoting this creature as a, *dinner-rabbit*, the intended meaning can be better approximated... This hyphenated term is intended to imply that the creature will become *dinner* once it is converted from its preceding state of being a *rabbit*... Once the *rabbit* properties are subtracted from the hyphenated term, it will become simplified as *dinner*...

However, if the hyphenated term should revert back to being a *rabbit*, then it will no longer be attached to becoming *dinner*... Until the hyphenated term is reduced to a singular state, it may be denoted as a hyphenated/transitional term... A more traditional use of hyphenations can also be used either concurrently, or alternately, but the context should allow this to be understood effectively enough...

As I thought of methods language could be modified as a means of simulating comprehension, something else became apparent... All of these modifications were dependent on the preceding components of language... Since language was only the simulation of understanding, then true understanding would remain outside the realm of language... Although language could be used to get closer to understanding, it wouldn't lead to true understanding...

Another idea began to emerge from within the darkness, as I remained present in the root-structure... Language derived its meanings, definitions, and applications, through contexts outside of its-self... It was the way that things existed in relation to everything they were not, that they were defined...

If I wanted to define my-self in a true sense, then I would have to understand the way that I related to everything that I was not... Then I would have to understand how I related to the ever-changing contexts of this *new understanding*... Could anyone ever really understand any of this? I thought...

I eventually began to feel differently about the root-structure, its darkness, my concealment within it, &c, &c, &c... After an unmarked passing of what must have been a considerable amount of thyme, I no longer thought of my-self as being concealed in this place... It began to seem as if I had been confined to this darkness by the figures beyond this root-structure... In my confinement, I began to consider whether I was absorbing this environment, or if it was absorbing me...

The roots of this structure couldn't absorb anything, except for the darkness within this place... There was nothing else to be absorbed, for everything else had either been previously absorbed, or eroded away... Was I absorbing this same darkness now? Could it be that the darkness was beginning to absorb the root-structure? What if I was being absorbed by this darkness now? I thought...

Proceeding from the root-structure was the figure of a tree now dying... This *tree-corpse* was the projection of its root-structure... As the root-structure ceased to absorb nourishment in the darkness, its projected figure had ceased to project any semblance of nourishment... Instead, the tree-corpse began to resemble the empty darkness in which it was now rooted...

In my mind, it seemed this was what would become of me if I remained in this darkness... If I abandoned the root-structure, I would have to live amidst the threat of surrounding figures... It seemed as if I would be putting my-self at risk no matter what I chose to do... How did I end up in this mess? What was I to do about any of this? Where could I go? I thought...

As I struggled to determine what I should do in the darkness that surrounded me, I began to grow weary... In this darkness, it was difficult to differentiate whether or not my eyes had involuntarily closed... Eventually, I fell into the darkness of sleep...

When I awoke, the urge to expel my internal waste compelled me to venture away from the root-structure... As I removed the log-door from its position, I was momentarily blinded by the light of a dawning day... Once my eyes had adjusted, I could see that the area had been visited... Strewn about the vicinity were the discarded remnants of food, wrappers, trash, &c, &c, &c... It appeared as if the figures had passed by the facade without any awareness of what was concealed beneath it...

I carefully crept towards the nearest stream in order to expel my waste... Along the way back from this trip, I came upon two of the figures that were patrolling in a valley beneath my position... Initially they seemed to be discussing nothing of any interest, but then one of them mentioned something alarming...

The figure picked an item off of the ground... Then asked the other figure if it was evidence of the 'specter... After intensely scrutinizing the item, the other figure laughed... Then the figure asked what the other thought would happen if they found the 'specter... This other figure said they wouldn't find it, but if they did... Instead of completing its answer, the other drone made a gesture with its attached weapon... In response, the figure affirmed that this was the only possible outcome...

Knowing I was this 'specter, it was clear that these figures wouldn't give a moment's pause to *endgage* me... My mind suddenly recalled a strange thought from my past... It was an idea that had either come from some unknown reference, or my own invention... This idea was that there were three methods of conflict... These three methods were to oppose, deflect, or embrace conflict...

I would undoubtedly be forced to respond to the figures according to some method... Strangely, it seemed to me that this was the same conflict that I had encountered at the facility... Although I couldn't understand what made this seem to be the same conflict, I could easily understand what choice I had made on that occasion... By evacuating the facility and leaving the associated figures, I had opted to deflect the conflict...

This deflection had placed me into the position that I found my-self in now... If I were to deflect this present conflict by simply evacuating the preservation site, it would only perpetuate the cycle... Eventually, I would be presented with the same conflict, and again I would have to decide what I might choose to do in response... After considering this, another method seemed favorable for this present conflict...

In order to embrace a conflict, it is necessary to consider the conflict to have already been resolved... Embracing conflict is a way of displacing the conflict into the past, and negating its presence... This method is rarely even considered to be possible, and is the most difficult to employ in most contexts... On this occasion, it seemed that there was no way to embrace the conflict presented...

If these notions were correct, then only one method was to be left to consider... To oppose, was to take action in a more present tense... Opposing conflict meant rendering the conflict unable to remain present... How could I render this conflict incapable of remaining present? I thought...

There was great personal risk for me in whatever manner I attempted to approach this conflict... As I made my way back to the root-structure with stealth and caution, I considered what my approach to this conflict might consist of... Concealing my-self inside the root-structure, my thoughts continued to consider what I might do...

Inside the darkness, I formulated a plan of action... Contented with this plan, I decided to rest... When I awoke, I would be able to begin my opposition... Where was all of this going to end up? I thought...

201.08 CONFLICTING FIGURES...

I found my-self bursting into laughter as I woke to the darkness of the root-structure... The way I'd intended to oppose the figures was so prosperously funny to me... In all seriousness, my strategy was quite logical, and was quite likely to succeed... The components of this strategy however, were unconventional, eccentric, &c, &c, &c...

My objective was to render the figures unwilling to remain in this place... In order to achieve this objective, I intended to engage in what I chose to use a modified term to denote... What I was about to engage in became known to me as, *pschyt-worefair*...

What I intended to do, was make the preservation site seem uninhabitable to the figures, urging them out of sight... If they saw this place as turning to *pschyt*, they would almost certainly leave... I set about creating an environment consistent with the objectives of my pschyt-worefair ...

One application of this effort was the destruction of the kricketoid nourishing mulch-piles... This destruction would cause the kricketoids to spread out, and the skunkoids would become less concentrated as a result... It wasn't my intention to spread the skunkoids over the entire preservation site, but to re-consolidate them... As a result, I started to set up new mulch-piles in closer proximity to the areas occupied by the figures...

...

Another aspect of pschyt-worefair was to create other nauseating odors in the immediate vicinity of the figures... By removing the fruit from the trees in the area, and placing already rotting fruit-corpses among them, it would create a strong presence of appalling odors... This would also dissuade the figures from consuming the fruit for nourishment...

If the figures couldn't be nourished by this fruit, they would have to rely on hunting or fishing instead... Hunting would be made more difficult with the increase of skunkoids in the areas surrounding the figures... If they were to resort to hunting, the sonic annunciations of their weaponry would alert me to their location... Should the figures begin using other means of predation, it would require them to develop the associated skills used in such methods...

In order to dissuade them from attempting to rely on fishing, I would leave piles of fishoid-corpses near the areas the figures might easily access... This would draw in *vultureoids that* after consuming the fishoid-corpses, would either vomit them back out, or excrete them as waste... Between the odors of rotting fishoid-corpses, vultureoid vomit and excrement, there would be a strong deterrence from attempting to fish these areas... It might also cause them to consider the possibility that the fishoids elsewhere were not fit to be eaten...

Other efforts would be made to create an environment that the figures would find appalling and uninhabitable... If the figures had to struggle to absorb the things they required in order to be sustained, they would eventually be unable to remain present... I thought of this as hollowing out the figures' root-structures... They would either seek to transplant them-selves elsewhere, or slowly wilt away... In either case, I would have succeeded in my opposition of these figures...

The root-structure I inhabited was in a relative proximity to the figures' position... However, I could manage these efforts well enough from my concealment...To reach the areas I intended to use in acquiring nourishment the figures would have to travel farther I would... Due to their larger numbers, it would be increasingly difficult for all of them to be sustained, and therefore more difficult for each of them... I would be able to sustain my-self with less effort than the figures, and would have the advantage as a result...

After completing my initial efforts toward this pschyt-worefair, I had to resist the urge to closely monitor the effects on the figures... Instead, I had to remain secluded in the darkness of the root-structure, and keep my exposures to a minimum... When I did emerge, it was with great caution... During the time that I was exposed outside of the root-structure, I would attend to my essential needs, assess the state of my projects, &c, &c, &c...

It did appear that the areas of my pschyt-worefair had been visited at some point... The rotting fruit-corpses had seemed to cause the figures to abandon the areas associated with them... A few footprints were found near the fishoid-corpse laden areas at one point, but not on subsequent occasions... There were often remnants of the scents sprayed by the skunkoid creatures discovered as well... Pschyt-worefair seemed to be proceeding according to my intentions...

Months must have been gone by in this manner... Eventually, I had to ensure whether or not the figures had abandoned the preservation site... Before I could set about surveying the preservation site, I had to wait for the soil to dry...

A series of storms had recently passed over the preservation site... With the ground still quite soft from the rain, it was ill-advised to set foot outside of the root-structure... In order to attend to my needs from within the root-structure, I had to resort to using alternative methods...

This meant storing my wastes in containers until proper disposal was possible... It also meant minimized consumption of nutritional rations kept in reserve... As I became accustomed to remaining confined to the root-structure, something else compelled me to peer into the realm outside...

There was a slight scent that crept into the root-structure... The scent was faint at first, but it was still unmistakable... From the first trace of this scent's presence, I knew it was some kind of smoke...

What could have been on fire? Where could this smoke have come from? I thought...

When I peered out into the world, I could smell the smoke more prominently... It seemed to be derived from an area on the opposing side of the figures' occupied area... Could lightning have started this fire? I thought...

A few days later, the scent had cleared, and the ground had dried enough to allow ventures away from the root-structure... I wanted to survey the area associated with this smoke, but eventually decided against it... I resigned to attend to my more essential concerns, and went about my usual activities...

Within a few more days, the scent of smoke had returned to the root-structure... This time, it seemed to have come from an area adjacent to the previous incident... No storms capable of producing lightning had crossed above the preservation site... It was likely that the figures were burning the areas around them... Why would they do such a thing? I thought...

As time went on, more smoke came drifting into the root-structure... The fires seemed to be initiated overnight, and kept under some level of containment... None of the fires occurred in the area the figures were occupying... Each of the successive fires became closer to the vicinity of the root-structure... Were the figures trying to smoke me out of my hole? I thought...

Realizing the likelihood of the figures eventually setting fire to the root-structure, I became inclined to abandon the preservation site... In my mind, this idea was worse than surrendering the site to the figures... Surrender would be admitting defeat, but abandoning the site wouldn't even acknowledge any such defeat... Instead, it would just be another way of deflecting conflict... What else could be done? I thought...

The figures were putting my life in danger with these fires... This fact gave me moral cause to consider strategies of greater lethality... If they were willing to cause me to be consumed by their fires, then I had to be willing to inflict the same upon them in order to survive... Was I willing to burn them down? I thought...

This was one of the most important decisions I had ever been faced with... I didn't want to come to an ultimate conclusion in any hasty manner... My concerns on this matter were vastly numerous... After every *if* that I formulated, one question would inevitably follow... What would become of me? I thought...

When I felt that I had reached a decision of what to do, I decided to postpone my actions for one last sleeping-interval... When I woke, my mind would be capable of acting with clarity... I obscured myself within the concealment of the root-structure, and initiated this crucial sleeping-interval... Under the same darkness that rests on everything, my slumbering gave way to another fateful dream...

201.09 DREAM OF...

Instead of a beginning to this dream, there is a hallway... Along one of the walls extending the length of this hallway's dream-scape is a line of doors... Within the opposing wall are a series of frames... The floor is of solid darkness, and there's a ceiling that can only be understood in the dreaming-sense as being present...

After the dream-scape is introduced, my presence in the dream becomes aware to my dreaming mind... As my presence is introduced into the dream, my awareness of the dream-scape becomes more focused... With increased focus, the doors that line the hallway are observed to be open wide...

The opposing frames are observed to be projecting a glowing luminescence... This glowing luminescence is understood within the dream as having a semblance to that of either a lighted window pane, or of some media-viewer projection...

A large door at the far end of the hall suddenly becomes known to my dreaming-focus... There is an immediate compulsion for me to approach this door... My presence in this dream drifts slowly in the direction of the door... Within this dream, the door is indiscernibly understood to have great significance...

...

My presence drifts into the vicinity of the first frame and its opposing doorway... The open door appears to lead towards some possibility, but only darkness is seen within it... After observing the darkness of the doorway, the frame opposing this door begins attract my focus... I observe the contents of the frame with dreaming detachment, as a scene from my life is projected back to me... This scene seems to depict something that greatly defined me in the course of my own individuation...

Continuing to drift down the hallway in this dream, the same pretenses are perpetuated... Each door is viewed as leading towards some possibility, but nothing inside the doorway can be revealed within its darkness... Each opposing frame is discovered to depict a different scene that holds special significance in the process of my life... These visions seem to be preparing my mind for arriving upon the door at the end of this hallway...

As I arrive at this door, it is with premonition that I understand this door to be locked... I observe instantaneously that there is a keypad imbedded in the wall next to the door... According to my preceding knowledge, the access code to unlock the door is already known to me... Despite this premonition, as I attempt to remember the access code, my mind seems completely vacant...

Frustration fills my dreaming-mind, as I am unable to remember anything about this access-code... In my vexation, I turn to gaze behind me, staring into the past length of the hallway... As I turn to look back, I see that there is a mirror hanging inside of a frame at the opposing end of the hallway... It would have been behind my original position at the inception of this dream, but I had not turned to see it until now...

Becoming aware of the mirror, it is also observed that the doors that were previously open are now securely closed... Without any objective assessment, these doors are known to have become permanently locked... The frames also appear to have changed as I peer down the hallway... It seems that they have ceased to project lighted images, but now project darkness in the manner normally associated with light...

Focusing on the mirror at the end of the hall for a moment longer, I then turn back to face what is expected to be the locked-door with the key-pad... I am puzzled to discover that it is not the door that is positioned in this place, but the image of the door as viewed from the distant mirror... By all logic, this mirror image should be positioned at the opposite end of this hallway...

It is of no concern that my own image is not present anywhere in this dream, to include the reflections of this mirror... In an instant that has some semblance to that of blinking, my dreaming eyes discover that without having moved, the locked-door now rests at the far end of the hallway yet again... My mind is baffled by this shifted dream-scape, and becomes averse to the notion of looking back to see if the mirror has shifted to a position behind me as well...

Following the strangeness of this turn, I become anxious to depart from this dream-scape... Drifting towards the distant door again, I reach the vicinity of the first doorway and its opposing frame... The doorway remains closed *forever*, but the frame is projecting something of dark luminescence... It initially appears to be a simulation of my view of the opposing doorway, as previously viewed in its open position...

Then the frame projects what appear to be simulated-movements through the open doorway... It commences to project a scene comparable to a memory that isn't my own... Suddenly, it becomes dreamingly known, that the projections of this frame depict what would have become a memory, if I had entered the previously open doorway...

Each of the subsequent frames projects a scene in accordance with this paradigm... As I drift closer to the door at the end of the hallway, my mind begins to wonder... What else could there be in this place?

When reaching the locked-door at the end of the hall, it becomes apparent that I had missed something earlier in the dream... Above the door there is a sign with the words... *Where are you going?* The sight of this sign elicits the dreaming equivalent of a memory... My mind recalls that this sign is a riddle, hinting at what the access-code is… Unable to conjure any notions as to what the answer to this riddle might be, its image taunts my dreaming-mind…

Beguiled by this dream-scape, my mind eludes to me the notions that this is all of my own design… This dream-scape is not understood to be of a dream, but it is believed to be of my own construction… A question becomes posed by my dreaming-mind… *Why would I do this to my self?*

Other questions ensue… What could I have intended to do with all of this? Was there something I was trying to convey to my-self with this? It is torturous for me to contemplate these thoughts within the riddle of this dream…

Again my focus is drawn to the words of this sign… *Where are you going?* Reading the sign over and over, it is clear that the word *you* is referring to me in this dream… I scowl at the key-pad in despair, as I postulate taking a crack at breaking the code…

In my memory's absence of the true answer to my self-induced tribulation, I try to pose some answer in its place… I try the entries, *a-w-a-y*, *o-u-t*, *h-o-m-e*, &c, &c, &c… All of my efforts to substitute something in place of my own forgotten truth fail me… In vexation, I scathingly enter, *n-o-w-h-e-r-e*… Again, my attempt is insufficient…

In a moment of vacuous silence, a sound becomes faintly present in the dream-scape… It draws my focus above me… Attached to the ceiling is the vague figure of a clock… Upon the face of the clock, are two sets of hands… One set is moving forward, while the other moves in an inverted direction of time… The sound of this clock ticking both forward and backward swells in volume…

The peripheral imagery of the surrounding dream-scape begins to fade into non-existent darkness… Everything becomes lost in this darkness, not as if merely vanishing, but as if no longer exists in the dream-scape… Suddenly, a sinister sound like that of an alarm signaling the expiration of a time-limit breaks out of this nowhere…

I immediately begin to plummet through the no-longer-existent floor of this dream... Simultaneously, I feel as if I am being pulled forcibly upward through the space in this void that once held the timepiece above me... As I am both rising and falling inside this vapid dream-scape, a feeling of being ripped away from my self terrifies me...

My mind begins to question how I had arrived at this terrible fate... What had led me to this? Where had I gone wrong? What could I have done? How would this now end?

Dreaming of this panic, there is a subsequent fading from fear into paralysis... From paralysis there is a moment that seems to exist as non-existence... Then with the slowly dawning transition into waking reality, my eyes open into the confusion of the darkness within the root-structure... A long moment passes before it appears to me that I still exist...

201.10 WHAT'S CONSUMED IN THE FIRE…

Waking into the darkness of the root-structure doesn't seem to mark
the end of this dream… Instead, it is the same thoughts that are left
running inside my mind… As if oblivious to the differences between
one darkness and another, my mind imagines these recursive
questions… Where am I going? What am I doing? How did I end up
in this place? Awake, but in a sense of dreaming; my mind is lost to
these wonders…

Eventually, I relented to take a deep breath… I figured the inhalation
of clean air would refresh me… Then I could exhale the spent-breath
along with all of these consumptive thoughts…

As I drew in a great gulping breath, a high content of smoke filled my
lungs, and I began to cough violently… My body struggled to purge
the contents of this polluted-breath, as I struggled not to faint,
collapse, &c, &c, &c… I dropped to my knees, and tried to breathe
the air closer to the ground… A few good breaths and I was able to
cease my involuntary respiratory-convulsions… Then as my brain
was resupplied with oxygen, I knew with primal certainty that my life
depended on evacuating this place…

With a breath of low-air held inside my lungs, I heaved all of my
weight into the log-door… As the object was cleared away, I burst
into what immediately appeared as a surrounding inferno… Heat

…

surged from the burning regions of the preservation site along powerful winds gusting in my direction... Though the flames were seemingly distant, the heat was of otherworldly fright... My skin felt as if it were about to be ignited, begin melting away, &c, &c, &c...

Having unknowingly awakened with most of my possessions already upon my back, I bolted away from the punishing force of the destructive inferno... The only thought I had was the same as what had preceded my journey into this place... Now this thought burned with an intensity unfathomable in comparisons to what I'd previously experienced... If this urgency had been put into words, it would have shattered my own ears exclaiming... *GET OUT!!!*...

I bounded with reckless abandon, until I reached the nearest stream... Instead of contemplating what I should do next, I leapt headlong into the waters of the stream... When I resurfaced, I started gasping for breathable air... The current carried me downstream, as I tried to catch my breath while still remaining afloat...

Uncertain of the scope of the fires, I decided to follow this stream... This stream would likely lead me away from the fire, but it might also bring me into the area of the figures' occupation... Somehow I seemed to welcome the idea of drifting into their realm...

I suspected that the figures would not be occupying their campsite as the fires were burning... Instead, they would be monitoring the surrounding areas... They wouldn't burn the area, without ensuring their objective was accomplished in doing so...

If my thinking were correct, it was also likely that they would be monitoring this stream in which I was drifting... It would be of great risk to continue following the direct path of this stream... Once I cleared the areas burning closest to the stream, I maneuvered around the vicinity of where the figures might be monitoring... Then I navigated around the hillsides on the far side of this stream, and continued towards my objective...

The figures' voices were heard coming from the areas I had anticipated... Although they could be heard as voices, their sonic discipline had improved somewhat, and it was not possible for me to understand their speech... It would have been quite an advantage for me to be able to decipher what they were saying, but in order to do so I would have had to risk being exposed... Instead, I proceeded with caution to navigate around their presence...

My objective had become defined clearly enough in the time of my escape... It was no longer possible for me to exist apart from the figures in this world... Instead, I would have to decide whether or not I should leave this place, or surrender in defeat... Although both options were dismal to consider, it seemed one option might lead to some form of catharsis/denouement... Imagining my own virtues to have become tempered by the blazing heat of this consumptive fire, I resigned to admit what seemed an honest-defeat...

When I reached the figures' area of occupation, I intended to leave a message imploring them to accept my surrender... I had thought that leaving such a message would allow me to meet with them in a way that might allow for a peaceful surrender... In my mind, the figures might otherwise be startled by my presence, and respond with violent reflexes... If I could leave them notice of my intentions of surrender, perhaps it would be possible for some form of reconciliation...

Upon my arrival of the figures' campsite, it was apparent that the area was indeed vacant... I left my intentions of surrendering inscribed upon the ground where they could read them... Then I started to withdraw from the area in the way that I had entered...

As I was leaving, I noticed a large quantity of metal barrels covered with a large tarp... These barrels appeared to have a Haz-Mat insignia, denoting extreme flammability... Observing this made it apparent that these figures had indeed engaged in the recent acts of arson...

Before I was able to fully vacate the premises, two figures were observed to be approaching from the direction I was headed... In order to avoid startling them, I crawled under the nearby tarp and into a vacant space between some of the barrels... I then carefully repositioned the barrels to further conceal my presence from view...

Moments after concealing my-self inside this area, other figures began to arrive in succession... Each time a figure was heard to arrive, a voice would announce for them to proceed towards where I had left my message of surrender... It was dusk when the last of the figures returned to the campsite... With the figures' presence preventing me from escaping without their knowledge, I remained concealed among the barrels...

The last of these figures to arrive had the voice I associated with the Commanding-figure... When this Commanding-figure arrived, all the others became silent... Then the figure proceeded to the area of my message... I could hear the Commanding-figure scoff after a brief pause...

Following the scoff, I could hear the figures begin a discussion on the matter of my message... Some of the figures voiced opinions that there could be some trap involved in this meeting... Others seemed to be more concerned with the implications surrounding any acceptance of surrender... The Commanding-figure remained silent as the figures discussed these concerns, &c, &c, &c...

Once the other voices had seemed to have articulated their input, the Commanding-figure cut through the discussion... Initially, the Commanding-figure gave a summary of all the other figures' concerns, and articulated the implications of each... Then the Commanding-figure began to explain the situation as interpreted in light of these considerations...

According to the Commanding-figure, the choice that these figures were facing was simple... In the opinion of the Commanding-figure, this choice was whether or not accepting this proposed-surrender was worth the associated risks... Following an explanation of this simple reductive premise, the Commanding-figure declared a motion to vote on the issue... Another figure's voice quickly supported the motion...

The Commanding-figure then ordered all those in favor of accepting my proposed surrender to give indications of such by saying, *iye*... An eerie silence followed this order... Then the Commanding-figure ordered those in favor of some other action to give indications of such by saying, *neigh*… This order was met with a resounding unison of the figures' voices that then echoed back, as if to reaffirm its meaning… This was announced by the Commanding-figure as the final-word on the issue…

Following this decision, the figures debated what action should be taken instead of accepting my surrender… I listened closely as the figures presented their proposals… It was soon apparent, that the figures unanimously favored some method of terminating my presence… Most of the proposals involved some form of trap that could be used in conjunction with feigned-pretenses of accepting my proposed-surrender…

As discussions over the particulars were being conducted, the Commanding-figure suddenly broke in, halting the others' speech… The Commanding-figure's voice ordered one of the other figures to proceed to the barrels, and count the number of them remaining… I remained frozen in my place, as a figure dashed over to these barrels to quantify how many were present… When the tarp was ripped away from the barrels, it seemed that I would soon be counted out as well… By the night's darkness or some miraculous blunder, they remained oblivious of my presence…

After the figure announced the number of barrels that had been observed, the Commanding-figure demanded attention… The figure reverted back towards the others, and the Commanding-figure began to address them all…With all of the figures' focus shifted, there were no eyes cast in my direction… As the Commanding-figure used the ground to illustrate the proposed strategy, I slipped out of the barrels and into the concealing night…

The general plan was to scout the area of my intended-surrender immediately… If no traps were to be discovered, they were to prepare the area with a trap of their own… Such a trap was likely intended to be in the form of an inferno… It was also likely to be monitored, ensuring I would be forced to burn inside of it…

Having made the effort to reconcile the conflicts of my presence amidst the intruding figures, they had made greater efforts to ensure nothing other than annihilation could result... I was so enraged by the manner all of this took place, that I began to rethink my previous assertions... Had I been defeated as honestly as I'd thought? Should I abandon the site? Could I still prevail in this conflict? I thought...

The figures refused to accept my surrender based on the possibility of some threat... Then they decided to use tactics that could have neutralized such threats to set a deceptive trap for me... They were actually putting them-selves in greater danger this way...

Why couldn't they accept victory? Was it necessary for them to destroy everything outside of them-selves? There was no need to think of these things... All that was left, was to determine what I thought was the right response...

Again the option to evacuate the preservation site occurred to me... After some consideration, it was again seen as an option that would not result in any catharsis/denouement... Instead, I decided to fight fire with... Well, I had a plan...

As the figures went to sleep or went on fire-watch, I lurked in the neighboring shadows... I could have silently crept from throat to throat, and drained all the venomous-blood that boiled in hatred of my unseen presence... Instead, I reverted back along the scorched face of blackened-earth under the concealment of the night's blind sky...

I found one of the figure's uniforms left haphazardly on the ground as I departed their vicinity... It was lying next to what appeared to be an apparatus used for washing clothing-items... As the figures lay dreaming or imagining them-selves on watch, I made my way through the darkness... What I was about to do seemed detestable, but necessary...

After confiscating the uniform, I began to track the two figures that had been sent on reconnaissance... I found them near the area indicated in my message for surrender... They were easy to spot, even in the dark… Once they had completed their reconnaissance, I slipped past them into the area they had just scouted… Then I surveyed the area in great detail… If they were to follow through with their deceitful plan, it was clear how they would likely be positioned…

Having completed my own reconnaissance, I quickly set about my own counter measures… I used the uniform taken from the figures' occupation area to construct a mannequin… Then I concealed the imposture-body high in the expanding branches of a tree… The tree was dense, and positioned so that the figures would be unlikely to see the imposture-body until daylight…

According to my message of surrender, I was to arrive at this location near dawn… The figures would be preparing their trap to be ready before then… They would then position them-selves, and await my arrival… Once the sunrise had begun, they were almost certain to discover the concealed imposture-body…

Once the figures saw the imposture-body, I could observe their reactions, and respond accordingly… As the night continued to conceal the images of the impending day, I watched the figures moving through the darkness… They completed their preparations, and returned to their campsite… I awaited the impending consequences, as the night was slowly fading…

With dawn approaching, the figures moved back into positions according to their projected plan… I had taken a position beyond their own that allowed me to observe them without exposure… Their positions were located almost exactly according to my expectations…

Some of the figures had poured the contents of their barrels in an arch surrounding the area of my proposed surrender… This arch left a small opening for a hasty retreat… Two of the figures were positioned overlooking this opening…

Most of the other figures were gathered along the edges of their flammable arch… They postured as if they were peacefully awaiting my arrival... Inside the arch, in full view of all the others, stood the Commanding-figure...

With everything prepared according to the figures' designs, and with my counter measures in place, the sun was on the verge of rising... All eyes watched carefully at the impending resolution of this fiery conflict... As the first sunlight leaked over the horizon, every figure cast its full shadow on the ground...

The Commanding-figure's voice cut through the air, announcing the figures' presence for my would-be-surrendering ears to hear...

"We are here to accept!"

Just as the Commanding-figure's voice echoed back, one of the figure's eyes caught sight of the imposture-body... It pointed at the impression of this imposture-body, and alerted the others of its presence... Then the Commanding-figure's voice cracked with furious rage...

"NOW!!!"

As the voice echoed off of every surface in all directions, the fiery arch was ignited... Flames burst high into the air, as the figures fired their weapons at the imposture-body... The Commanding-figure charged recklessly toward the imposture-body as it fell from its height... Other figures were ordered to move to their rendezvous point... They all began bounding for the opening in their fiery-arch...

The Commanding-figure realized that the imposture-body was not that of the 'specter as it pounced on its fallen form... As the others continued towards the exit of their trap, the Commanding-figure thrashed at the remnants of my deception...

The route that was supposed to have been left open for the figures' escape had become unexpectedly engorged with flames... Additionally, the figures that were to have been responsible for covering their retreat were left slain inside the constricting circle of fiery doom... I observed the figures' reactions to this sight with great scrutiny... They seemed unable to figure-out what had placed them in their current position... What had just happened? They seemed to wonder...

I had taken swift action in response to the figures' tactics... As the figures had lit the fire, I had drawn my bow... Then I had placed arrows through my would-be assassins, precisely where occipital bones meet the spinal-atlas... Due to the figures' elevated positions, their heads were tilted downward... From my position located above their own, the arrows' trajectories severed vital areas of their brains, spinal cords, &c, &c, &c... The result of this damage was instantly lethal...

The bodies of these ill-fated figures fell just on the edge of the opening of their fiery-arch... I rolled the former-figures through this opening, and into the area surrounded by their arch... Then I poured out the rest of their remaining accelerants, and ignited them... No opening remained, and their own fiery circle was complete...

I then relocated to a secondary vantage point, to ensure that the figures' plan resulted in its antithesis... The Commanding-figure's expression was unlike any I had encountered previously... This figure's nomadic-gaze held no semblance of mourning, fear, sorrow, &c, &c, &c... Instead, there was only a burning hatred that made the all-consuming inferno appear innocuous in comparison... It was as difficult to look away from this image of pure-blind hatred, as it was to behold it...

I had to ensure that the fires burned them-selves out before any other action could be taken... When the fires finally started to die-down, a storm was rolling over the horizon... As the rain began to fall, I couldn't distinguish my tears from the extinguishing precipitation...

My eyes mourned not the dying of these vengeful-figures, but the life that was lost to them in advance of this horrible fate... In my mourning, I wondered what these former-figures might have been, how else things might have gone, &c, &c, &c...

Then my mind turned on it-self... What had I done? What had become of me? Where did this leave me? I thought...

201.11 WHAT WAYS ARE LEFT...

The preservation site was no longer afflicted by the former-figures...
There was however, almost nothing remaining of the site that hadn't
been reduced to smoldering black earth... When the fire had
completely died-out, I went to assess whatever was left amidst the
ashes...

What remained among the nothings-in-black, were strange metallic
orbs that resembled humanoid-skulls... Stamped upon the temporal
regions of either side, was an emblem of vague familiarity... Where
had I seen this emblem before? I thought...

As I pondered where this image had been observed previously,
another sentiment was present... I found my-self relieved to discover
that there had not been any authentic humanoid-casualties... It
seemed strange that this notion should be cause for such relief...
Was it only tragic when humanoids perished? What were these
former-figures, if not humanoid? I thought...

Continuing to observe the smoldering surroundings, only these orbs
remained of the former-figures... It appeared everything else had
dissolved into smoke, ashes, &c, &c, &c... Unable to determine what
these former-figures had been, I could only speculate what had
become of them... It was as if they had merged with their shadows,
and vanished into the darkness within them...

...

Having surveyed the charred destruction of the preceding day, I began to focus on the impending days... It seemed that my dreams, thoughts, and experiences were all urging me away from this place... Determining where I would be going was something beyond me at this point... Instead, I decided to supply my-self for whatever direction I might pursue along my way...

I returned to the vacant campsite that had been occupied by the former-figures... There I found very little of apparent use... In one of the tents was a 300fl. oz. bottle of water that was still sealed... Having recently consumed the last oz. of water from my own supply, this bottle was an immensely welcomed sight... The only other items I separated from the remains were 20 sealed food-rations, and a small lighter...

With what little provisions I could acquire, my mind began to formalize the notions that subsisted in the background of my mind... At some point in my occupation of this site, I had begun to confine my-self to this place... I had tried to define my-self within this place, and become totally dependent on it... Everything I thought or did was with respect to this site... It wasn't even possible to think of my-self, without the thought being preceded in some way by this preservation site...

After all the time I'd spent contemplating in the darkness of the root-structure, it only now became apparent to me... I couldn't content my-self to being confined/defined by my environment... The preservation site had even shaped the way I had come to see this... What other form might I take on without this place? I thought...

Before I'd left the former-figures campsite, I noticed that there was a barkoid creature in a cage nearby... It appeared to be quite docile, curious, overly-fed, &c, &c, &c... The cage was marked with what I assumed to be the beast's name...

Typically the names imposed on animals are only slightly more applicable than the ones used for humanoids... This name however, seemed not only fitting for the barkoid, but greatly amusing to me... If it had been my task to name the beast, I might very well have named it *Ubu* as well… Just looking at this beast seemed to elicit a synesthetic impression of the sound of this moniker…

I called out to the beast by this name, and it gazed curiously in my direction… When I opened the cage-door, Ubu lazily sauntered towards me… It proceeded to give my legs a thorough scent-inspection, before flopping down on the ground with apparent disinterest…

Unaware as to what to do with the beast, I continued my departure… Ubu began following behind me as I proceeded to the perimeter of the preservation site… I cut my way through the fence with the same knife I had used to break-in to this place… I held the opening, so Ubu could get through as well…

Before I continued to move in any direction, I decided to have a look at the map from the package I had received prior to my last great departure… To examine the map, I had to remove all of the contents of the package that had arrived with it… In doing this, I noticed something on one of the clippings… On the advertisement for CTMYAW, there was a logo that appeared to be identical to the emblem I had seen on the temporal region of the orbs… I quickly dismissed this notion, and began to examine the map…

Using this map, I was able to figure-out the general vicinity of where I was located… All of the markings on the map were a considerable distance from my location… One of the markings on the map would have been about two days' walking-distance away… It wasn't actually the closest *positively* marked area, but it caught my eye in some strange manner… This area was identified as *LT4*…

The most direct route to this place was across a region of prairie-farmlands… Some of the only remaining *privately-operated* property still in existence at the time before my departure had been in areas such as these… Instead of trespassing on this land, I chose to cut-across a nearby quarry… From there, I could use existing roadways for most of the remaining distance… Then I could follow a stream into the immediate vicinity of this place…

With my route and destination determined, I had to resist the urge to take off running... I was entirely certain that I was on the right path, but there was nothing I could point to in order to explain this certainty... As I made my way along the route of my own invention, Ubu followed behind me with a look as pleasant as I imagined my own to be...

The feeling of motion seemed to satisfy every concern of the moment, and an idea began to form within me... Whatever I would find from now on, would just be something along my way... Could I really adhere to the path of my own resolve? I thought...

201.12 TRANSIENT...

When I reached the quarry the sun was weighing as heavily on the horizon, as my eyelids over my view... Ubu had also become quite tired and weary from the journey... After surveying the area, it appeared to be desolate of all life, with the exception of Ubu and my-self... This was consoling enough to allow me to consider initiating a proper sleeping-interval...

After descending into the lower-reaches of the quarry, I was able to set-up a shelter large enough for my-self and Ubu... The *dogoid* beast settled into the shelter next to my lower extremities, with a natural familiarity... Before I closed my eyes on the day, I decided to review some of my own writings... I extracted my notebook from my possessions, and opened it to a random page...

Interestingly enough, the words that my eyes observed were poignant to this occasion... As my present observance of my own preceding notions transpired, I found my-self considering these notions as if they were new sentiments... My mind's recursive thoughts began to transition into *new* thoughts, and the compulsion to record them followed...

Using the last-remaining ink in my last-remaining pen, I scrawled these words into my esteemed notebook...

...

"Despite the topography, and initial directions of individual intentions, through the trials and tribulations of life, all things inevitably resort to that which most epitomizes the essence of what they are... In our essence, we wonder how all the things we are not, can form such an impression on what we perceive our-selves to be..."

With these words preserved in ink and paper, I then placed one more word upon the page, in the area above these others... This word was, *Inevitability*... I decided to underline it, emptying the last remnants of usable ink onto the page...

Once I had finished writing, I accomplished the obligatory actions necessary to initiate a sleeping-interval... All my possessions were organized, secured, &c, &c, &c... My shelter was confirmed to be structurally adequate enough, I was comfortably positioned inside of it, Ubu was contented, &c, &c, &c... In my weary state sleep soon overtook me...

With a much needed rest behind me, I woke as fully-refreshed as I could remember ever having done before this occasion... My mind went over a multitude of other memories; ideas I'd had, ways I had lived, &c, &c, &c... Without the words to express the condition I experienced, I somehow finally had a sense of where I had come from... In an even less definable way, I found some sense of my *self* in its present tense... As I witnessed the sun's ascension over the lowly-horizon, I felt as if I even had some sense of where I was going... Although I had already decided to travel towards LT4, it was only in this moment that I felt that I was truly going *somewhere*...

In this revelation, I could only think of my life... It was now beginning, ending, commencing, &c, &c, &c... I had lived in a certain sense of my-self before this time... The way I had lived was in search of everything, anything, something, &c, &c, &c... All of my searching could only reveal to me the defined/definable things of precession, simulacra, simulation, &c, &c, &c... Now I had actually found some non-diluted experience of discovery...

What was it I had found? It would have been counter-intuitive to attempt to posit anything in terms of an answer... What I had come to know was only of my self, and any true explanation of what it might be could only diminish its truth...

The wind began to blow with a relentless force in the direction opposing my destination... Aware of the environmental conditions, I promptly gathered my possessions, and prepared to continue my journey... Facing the opposing elements, I marched brazenly towards my destination...

As Ubu managed to stay with me, I thought of how my explorations of *Schizm Theory* could be refined... It was still axiomatic that all things were characterized by their division... Furthermore, it still made logical sense to characterize the perceivable world as resultant projections of divisional derivations of order...

Under this pretense, *Schizm Theory* was essentially a *two-level theory*... The manifest imagery was of resultant projections, and the scientific imagery consisted of infinitely divided particles synchronizing according to their solitary nature, &c, &c, &c... What else could be derived from these precepts? I thought...

201.13 PRIOR TO LAST TOWN FOR...

The path of my own volition was wondrous in all that it led me to behold... Every scenic moment of the seemingly abandoned world met my eyes as both estranged and welcomed... It was estranging to look out over the expanse of uninhabited earth, and know how infinitely divided I was from the vastness of its expanse... Despite the enormity of this division, it was quite welcomed to behold such an unbounded dominion... What multitude of things could be done in this magnitude of wonder? What grandiose dreams might be realized in all of this expanse? What would become of it all? I thought...

After a long journey through this greatly expansive divide, I eventually had to cut across a pasture... Across the pasture was the stream that flowed into LT4... When I reached the stream, I had been without water for some time... I knelt down next to Ubu, and drank in the same manner that the dogoid creature had already commenced to demonstrate...

Not long after I had begun following the stream, I was suddenly halted... A *patrol-squad* was in the area, and I had observed them before they had observed my presence... Ubu, was quite unaffected, and showed no sign of concerns at any point... When I noticed these characters in the area, I lifted my hands over my head in a passive manner, and called out to them...

...

At first the squad was startled by my announced presence... I informed them that I had no negative intentions, and asked if I was headed in the direction of LT4... They commanded me to remain where I was, and set my possessions down slowly... As I obliged the squad, they approached me with caution, and surrounded me with guarded curiosity...

Then they began to ask about my presence in this area... In a concise manner, I advised them that I had been living in oblivion for some time now, and was interested in visiting LT4... The squad seemed to be quite confused by my accounts of how I had come to this juncture, and asked many subsequent questions in attempting to clarify this matter... Even after I had responded succinctly to their inquiries, there was little comprehension displayed in response to my explanations...

After some further testimony as to what had preceded this occasion, the squad seemed to change their demeanor... Instead of confusion, they began to exhibit what might be described as astonishment... I appeared to have said something that they understood as if it were a part of their own experience... At the same time, it appeared that there was some incredulity in response to this sentiment... It was impossible for me to understand this kind of reaction...

A line of inquiries that had to do with my identity followed this reaction... When I was asked for my name, I used the most recent one I had gone by at the facility... Since this was not a *name* according to the squad, I informed them that they could refer to me as *S*, if it suited them better... They laughingly began to refer to me as *S*, and asked if I had any credentials...

Upon my reply, they asked if I was armed, and if they could search me and my possessions... I informed them of the items of lethality among my possessions, and consented to their search... They found these items of lethality in my possession to be of amusement, as if they were significantly antiquated...

In the process of their search, they discovered the package I had kept with me throughout my *exit-us*... The knife that was included in this package was on my person, and discovered separately... Although I had mentioned that the knife was on my person prior to their search, they still seemed surprised to discover it...

The squad asked me where I had acquired the knife... I answered that it was included in the package, and that the package had been received with my obliviousness to its origins or intent... Following my response, they began to examine the contents of the package... This seemed to peak the squad's interest in me, and increase their suspicions as well... They asked me if I had any idea where I was, or what was going on here... My reply that I wasn't sure what they meant by this question, was met with silence and visual scrutiny...

Then they asked me something that made me feel as perplexed as the squad appeared to be from my perspective... They asked me when I had last visited a *See-Tee-My-Awe* station, and what programming versions and upgrades I had received... In replying that I had been in exile since the time this CTMYAW had first been advertised, the squad seemed to gasp collectively... Their gasp projected a sense of absolute astonishment, in the way that some impossible truth suddenly becomes a reality...

Another moment passed, before the squad asked me what work I might have been involved with prior to my departure... I had to inform them that I was unable to convey any particular information about such things, as a condition of my involvement... This prompted the squad to ask if I had ever worked in conjunction with *the facility*... In response to this I had to inform them that if I had, it was unlikely that I would be able to confirm this... Of course this made it all too clear that I had indeed been involved with the facility...

Again there was a strange pause, before the squad continued to ask anything of me... When they commenced their inquiry, it was odd to hear them ask me to state my name again... After I replied that they could continue to call me *S*, they asked for the other name I had used... This time, when I told them I had last functioned under the moniker, *Schizoid*, they seemed to understand full-well what that name was...

Furthermore, they suddenly were at ease in my presence, and seemed to have instantaneously come to know all about me... I even felt as if they were now looking at me with someone else's eyes... What had just happened? I thought...

The squad assisted me in gathering my possessions, and then advised me to follow them into *Last Town 4*... After gathering my possessions, shouldering my pack, and beginning to walk along with the squad, they asked if the dogoid creature accompanying me had a name... They seemed to already know that this beast had been named Ubu, as they asked why I hadn't changed its name before I had finished speaking this short utterance... When I told them that it wasn't mine to change, they all laughed... (So did I)...

As they escorted me towards LT4, they casually asked if I had any idea of what all I had missed in my absence of society... After confirming that I had no way of knowing anything more than my own experiences, they started filling in the gaps... There were a lot of things that had occurred in the time I had been away from the social spaces...

Over the course of these explanations, it was odd to note how chronologically organized their accounts were... It also seemed strange to me as to how organized, concise, and objective they were... The squad seemed to actually think as a unit as well... None of them interrupted, interjected, or otherwise disrupted the natural flow of the conversation... They even seemed to be listening to me in tandem... This conversation was surreal in how efficient it was, and how incredibly rational it remained throughout its course...

To replicate the efficiency of this conversation, it will likely be more effective to give a summary of the facts, rather than attempt to recite the conversation it-self... Oddly, this summary might still be less concise than the actual conversation... However, it will still likely be more concise than attempting to recreate or replicate all that occurred inside this conversation... After all, there is greatly more to a conversation than the words used within it...

In addition to what was conveyed to me on this particular occasion, there were other instances where something within this *omitted history* was revealed to me... Some of this information was conveyed to me much later on... With the intentions of providing a comprehensive account of these events that fits into the contexts of this story, they will be integrated into the following section... Although this is still not a comprehensive testament to the events that transpired, it is a functional version of what has come to be known as the *omitted history*...

201.14 AN OMMITTED HISTORY...

Shortly after my exodus of the social-realms, there were a series of events that took place without my knowledge... These events were poorly documented/reported, if they were chronicled in any manner at all... Most of the populous was oblivious to the scale or scope of these events, and could only become aware of how these events had affected them indirectly, &c, &c, &c...

According to the accounts that were given to me, the populous inevitability adopted a sense of detachment... This sense of detachment could be characterized as the division of each member of society; from its other members, its society as a wHole, its-self, &c, &c, &c... More accurately, this division was a separation of cause from effect... Everything that happened to the collective could not be connected to the causes from which these things had been derived... Things just seemed to happen...

The dissonance that resulted from these events strongly contributed to their progression, digression, divagation, &c, &c, &c... It might even seem that some of these events would not have occurred, if this severed-sense of the social-setting had not been so severe... Only after the events were consulted upon by many key members involved in them, could the word-of-mouth history be reconstructed, told, retold, &c, &c, &c...

...

It was soon after my departure that the entire spectrum of social structures began to collapse... Just as it had been speculated in advance, there was a complete dissolution of guvornmints, phynancial systems, informative-networks, &c, &c, &c... *CurrentSee* became worthless, irrelevant, &c, &c, &c... K*rime* became rampant, undeterred, &c, &c, &c...

Doors were kept locked unless it was imperative to venture after supplies, or the locks/doors were broken into, &c, &c, &c... Stores were all looted bare, and could no longer function... Transports were abandoned in the streets, used as living-compartments, &c, &c, &c... Everything that could crumble; collapsed...

At some point there were a series of fires... These fires destroyed much of the urban areas, and many buildings were reduced to ashes... Large droves of populations became nomadic as a result of these fires, &c, &c, &c... Rural areas became battlefields, where nomadic/urban drones fought against the residents of these less populated areas... More fires burned in these areas near the time of these battles, and large amounts of farmlands became devoured by flames...

Somewhere amidst all of this, there was an effort associated with the collapsed-guvornmints... Drones that claimed to be representing the resurrected-guvornmints, began to set up *ayde-tints*... These ayde-tints offered drones a chance to trade their possessions in exchange for *medicol treetmints, füde-rashuns, wahtur*, &c, &c, &c... Instead of receiving any of these things, the drones that came to visit these ayde-tints were *depopulated*... Their possessions were sorted through, and whatever was not taken as valuable/useful was piled on top of the formerly-populated...

Other acts of depopulation occurred as well... Selected streams were poisoned in order to prevent population resurgences from depleting these streams, other resources, &c, &c, &c... Bombings took place in areas being disputed by larger masses of the displaced-collective...

New instruments of lethality were also said to have been used in depopulating entire regions; clearing the way for some *new-beginning*...

This new-beginning, was a term used in all of the accounts given to me... It was never expressed in any context that could relate where this term had come from, how it had become synonymous with these depopulating acts, &c, &c, &c...

Eventually, the urban areas had almost all become depopulated and demolished to near complete destruction... Few structures remained in these places, and almost no populations could be found within them... Much of the area surrounding the urban regions were also demolished and depopulated... The only areas unaffected or less affected by these events, were isolated airbases, distant rural areas, and select locations that had been well defended, &c, &c, &c...

Amidst all of this chaos, there were a series of other events taking place... The CTMYAW procedures had inexplicably managed to continue developing throughout much of this destruction... This mind-optimization procedure was initially a simple process with generalized-effects... Then it became developed to customize the results of its outcome...

Those who wished to alter their minds for increased intelligence could also alter their predispositions of mood, impulsivity, instinctual behaviors, &c, &c, &c... There was little that could be imagined, that couldn't also be achieved through this process... It was truly possible to create the mind you'd always wanted...

Another capacity that CTMYAW allowed was for mind-integration applications... Using the nano-technologies developed at the facility, minds could access databases directly, upload information cognitively, or even communicate directly with other minds... As long as the altered-minds were capable of cognitive-integration, and the transmissions were not disabled/limited, minds could be linked in an almost seamless manner...

This mind-integration technology made it possible for individuals to perceive other minds' consciousness simultaneously with their own... It became possible for minds to function in tandem, and act according to these multiple perspectives, as if all the perceived content was within each individual's mind...

The individuals utilizing this technology rarely used the term *I*... Instead, they would commonly use the term, *we* in referencing *themselves*... This had already been a prominent practice in the time preceding my own departure, but there was another dimension to this adaptive usage... *We*, had succeeded in replacing the very conception of the identities within its collective-entities... Not only was the term I omitted from use, but everything personal became secondary to this conceptual, *we*...

The collective-capacities of these entities made them more attuned to this environment of chaos... By communicating in this cognitive manner, they could more effectively avoid dangerous areas, scout for resources, coordinate efforts, &c, &c, &c... This means of communication made it increasingly difficult for those that did not possess such abilities... Over time, there were almost no individuals left that had not been integrated into some cognitive-network...

Another technological development had also been released to the populous prior to its collapse... This development was the technology that allowed *remote-cognition* via *surrogate-simulants*... These surrogate-simulants were released by the same guvornmint-corporation responsible for CTMYAW... Only a small number of these surrogate-simulants were actually produced, and even fewer were purchased... It was likely that the figures I had encountered in the preservation site had been some of these surrogate-simulants...

These surrogate-simulants allowed their controllers to exist separately from the simulant-bodies... In doing so, the controllers would be able to use the surrogate-simulants as forward observers, laborers, &c, &c, &c... This made it possible for the controllers to occupy secured areas, and then use the simulants to venture out into surrounding areas...

These surrogate-simulants were also programmed to operate autonomously if they lost functional-communication with their controller(s)... Their programming could be set to either make them remain in the vicinity that their connections were lost, or proceed in the direction of their controller's transmissions... In order for the simulants to return to their controller's location, they would have to have the location programmed into their system... If the location was not programmed into the simulant's system properly, the simulant would revert to the other programming modalities...

The controllers could also potentially operate multiple surrogate-simulants... Though this was possible, it would require the controller to have an incredible amount of cognitive-capacity... This would likely mean that such a controller would have to have been enhanced by the CTMYAW procedures...

Another aspect to this notion of multiple controlling was that a network of CTMYAW individuals could be controllers... In this case, the surrogate-simulants would be able to function as an extension of the network... This would result in an integration of simulant cognitions and network-enhanced humanoid-cognitions... It could also be explained as an integration of *simulated-thoughts* into *integral-humanoid-thoughts*...

The squad informed me of the origins of LT4 shortly before arriving at this place... It had been an abandoned-airbase prior to the *great-collapse*... Before all the chaos, this abandoned-airbase existed as little more than some walls, buildings, concrete pathways, &c, &c, &c...

As the collapse ensued, this airbase became occupied by a group of military-drones and guvornmint-officials... The intentions of occupying this abandoned-airbase involved preserving a future for these members of collapsing-society, providing a place that civilization could be rebuilt, &c, &c, &c...

There were several other sites that were designated to be used in a similar fashion... Several abandoned-airbases were converted into functional-residences in anticipation of the collapse... They were identified by letter-prefixes and numbers... Some of them were over-run or destroyed by the collapsing chaos... The locations that survived were eventually declared *Last Towns,* and given numbered-suffixes to identify them...

According to the squad that escorted me into LT4, these were the last civilizations left on earth... Only 7 of these last towns were known to remain in existence... I was the only living individual known to have independently arrived in the vicinity of LT4 since its inception...

Many other catastrophes/occurrences were relayed to me by the escorting squad... Several of these instances will be omitted in this omitted history, due to a lack of any perceived correlation to my subsequent experiences... What subsequent experiences was I about to encounter in LT4? I thought...

...III...

..."Not-Them"...

301.00 PERSPECTIVE DISCLAIMED...

In the interest of presenting this portion of the story with objectivity, the narrative will be changing... Instead of continuing to portray S's observations autobiographically, an omniscient-perspective will be used... Considering S's actual perspective during this phase of the story, an omniscient perspective is actually quite autobiographical... Hopefully, this will allow for the facts to be conveyed accurately, objectively, &c, &c, &c...

At some point later in this story, it became possible for these events to be chronicled in this omniscient manner... The way this effort was made possible, adopted into practice, and applied to this specific portion of text, is something that will not be overtly clarified... Essentially, a neutral perspective was used to evaluate the various accounts of events, organize the most factual version of these accounts, present a more objective version based on these elements, &c, &c, &c...

In order for this objective-perspective to be implemented as part of this story, it has been structured with a single character as a focal point... Within the context of this story, the name that is synonymous with this focal character is S...

Within this omniscient perspective are the exploits and opinions of S, as they became understood by other entities... As a result, these

...

documented opinions may not be the true opinions of S, but merely what might be associated with S's persona... After all, it is impossible to truly know the mind of another individual with empirical certainty...

The events that took place can be very certain in an objective sense... These events were determined after assessing the validity of existing evidence, comparing the probability of variables involved, &c, &c, &c... It is quite certain as a result, that the events contained in this text did occur in the manner detailed herein... It was partially due to the accuracy of this method that S chose to use these accounts as part of S's story...

S also considered this narrative as a means of further exploring the concept of S's self... According to S's conjecture, all things are defined in contexts... If the context is more comprehensive in its relation to its objective, then the objective can be defined more comprehensibly... In the pursuit of a better defined understanding of S's self, it was prudent to evaluate S from this altered-narrative...

By allowing these objective accounts to be observed in conjunction with those more personal accounts of S, it allows S a larger scope of understanding... If S is to become capable of observing any other entity's objective or subjective responses to this text, it will allow S an even more thorough comprehension of S's self...

It might seem to some observers that this explanation is of an eccentric or esoteric nature... S considered this to be probable for at least some audiences and perhaps displeasing to some evaluations as well... Unfortunately, it is not possible for everything a singular entity wishes to convey to be either fully conveyed, or conveyed in a manner that is well received... For S, it is more important to fully convey the truth of S's self, than to impose upon the way others might receive it...

For those that find these sections of content to be laborious or displeasing, S would like to propose something in response... If the negativity associated with reading this text can't be separated, perhaps try responding with eye-rolling, scoffing, condescending-laughter, &c,

&c, &c... Of course, any reactions might be of interest to S, including feigned reactions, the lack of reactions, &c, &c, &c...

Because it is intended for this narrative to be included as part of the existing accounts that were created by S, it will be necessary for this narrative to be made compatible... In order for this narrative to be compatible with the preceding narratives of S, the content will be presented in a similar style... It is not considered standard practice to use ellipses in place of periods, alter words with respect to contexts, use slashes as linguistic division-signs, &c, &c, &c... This will however be included as part of the ongoing narrative, in accordance with S's wishes...

What results from this altered-version of an omniscient perspective may be of some critical concerns... In response to these concerns it is necessary to declare only one thing... This is the perspective narrative... Whatever this perspective is seen to be, will be in the mind of the eyes that behold it... It is not considered necessary to attempt some specific response as a result of this content... The intentions of this text are either personal to the author, of a more impressionistic nature, etc, etc, etc...

It is also understood that disclaiming these notions is of some consequence to the story, and its potential reception as well... In stating this, it is also true that omitting these statements would also have some effect as a result... Perhaps this should also be taken into consideration at some point... What if this portion had been omitted? This is to be, whatever it is to be... Now, here it is...

301.01 LAST TOWN FOUR…

Following the escorts along the stream's path, S arrived at the outer perimeter of LT4… The stream's path flowed around the outer edge of LT4's 30 foot high concrete-walls… There was a steep canyon ledge just beyond the perimeter of LT4, and the stream's water flowed in falling arches to an unnamed river far below… This river flowed into a hydro-electric dam, and LT4 used this as a means of supplying it-self with energy…

There was a large front gate visible from the stream, and what vaguely resembled a path seemed to lead up to it… The path quickly became indistinguishable from the surrounding terrain… From the vantage point of the front gate, this path did not appear as any functional roadway, trail, &c, &c, &c… This gate was flanked by two watchtowers, an entry-control station, drop-barriers, pop-up blocks, &c, &c, &c…

The outer perimeter of LT4 had a total of 7 watchtowers along its concrete-walls… This outer perimeter ran back to the edge of the canyon, and traced the canyon's edge… There was however a small opening in the perimeter-wall, along the drop-off of the cliff… A flight-line runway was paved out to the edge of the cliff at his opening… Any plane using this runway would sink or soar beyond this edge…

…

Two watchtowers were located along the sides of the runway's end... The view from these two points was indeed quite remarkable given the surrounding scene... Peering out from these elevated points allowed much of the surrounding canyon-lands to be seen in their great expanse... Even from the surface outside of LT4 there was a grand view of the canyon-lands beyond the edge of this elevated plateau...

Walking through the front-gate, a secondary perimeter of chain-linked fence and c-wire was positioned... Beyond this internal perimeter-fencing, the structures built inside LT4 were spread over the area of its surface... Several identical concrete buildings of simple geometric configurations were distributed in a curve... This curve was broken by the flight-line, and centered on a courtyard...

There were several occupants that could almost be seen in this courtyard upon S's escorted entry... Many of them appeared curious at the arrival of the escorting group, though few actually appeared to be looking in their direction... The escorting group walked directly into one of the tall concrete structures of LT4... A sign had been placed on the building's entry-way that read, *Проеӡт Палаӡе (Project Palace)*...

Inside the Project Palace building, the escorting group traveled up a set of stairs into a loft... At the back of this loft was an office, and two hallways led away from the left and right of this office... Upon the door of this office was a placard with the Cyrillic letters, *Р.П. Винӡент*...

The escorting party went up to this door, and it was opened from within as they arrived at it...

Then the entity inside asked for the escorting party to excuse themselves... They promptly departed, allowing this entity to have a private conversation with S... It was only after S entered the office, that Ronald P. Vincent became visually identifiable... The two characters stared at each other in disbelief... How did they end up in this place? There was no need to wonder...

301.02 THE NEW RON...

When S entered Ronald's LT4 office, the sight of this familiar face seemed very foreign... Although Ronald's physical appearance had not changed beyond any difference threshold, he appeared to S as if he were merely an entity based on Ronald P. Vincent... S thought of this character as the new Ronald, a different Ronald, not the other Ronald, &c, &c, &c...

This Ronald had a very similar response to the sight of S... It was only by the direct viewing of S with his own eyes, that S seemed real to this character... Before this moment, Ronald had wondered if he had been altering the figure of what the others were seeing in order to be convinced that the figure was indeed S... It was strange that Ronald should have imagined his mind to be acting in such a way, for he knew full-well that this was not the truth... He knew that his disbelief was due to uncertainties outside of his current-mind...

It should be noted that one of the few side effects that have been encountered as a result of the CTMYAW procedures, has to do with pre-existing memories... Memories/impressions of things encountered prior to CTMYAW experiences are often remembered as if they are from some other entity's mind... The mind becomes so vastly different in terms of its normative functioning, that it causes formerly associated-thoughts to be experienced in a different context

...

within the mind it-self... This causes the mind to experience some of its own associations as foreign notions...

Despite this, such experiences occur with full awareness of their causal nature, and do not typically result in great distress, heightened anxiety, &c, &c, &c... There are varying degrees of depersonalization associated with such occurrences, but that is actually common among CTMYAW recipients in general...

As Ronald and S looked curiously in each other's direction, they found it unnecessary to speak for some time... Instead, they simply observed each other's expressions, posture, motion, &c, &c, &c... They were each able to perceive a great amount of detail within the other's appearance...

S could sense an air of depersonalization in Ronald's demeanor, and the general sense of detachment Ronald had developed towards his environment... Ronald thought that what he saw within S had not changed too drastically, but that the manner S existed in relation to environmental contexts was radically different... In Ronald's view, S had managed a level of consistency, despite the drastic changes in the world outside of S... It also seemed that S had become less withdrawn from the surrounding space, and more present somehow, &c, &c, &c...

The two characters eventually began to converse with respect to the past... They discussed the things they had experienced since the time of their last parting at the facility... Because the events that S experienced have already been documented, it will be unnecessary to include any detailed accounts of what was conveyed to Ronald... Instead, it is only necessary to mention that Ronald's reactions to S's story were quite expected, and that S's portrayal of the events was quite conservative in nature...

Ronald was first to speak on this occasion... He began by inviting S to be seated... There were two comfortable chairs Ronald had prearranged for this conversation... As they sat in their respective places, there was a natural ease in their demeanors... The two characters began with discussions concerning S's departure...

Following S's explanations concerning this departure, Ronald was asked if he knew anything about the package S had mentioned receiving...

In response, Ronald explained what he had come to know by various means... His accounts were very reasonable, but also quite strange... Ronald informed S that what was referred to as *Zeus's key chain*, had indeed gone missing... It had vanished during the Notorious Drone's escape from the facility... A duplicate was made upon receipt of the original, and Ronald began carrying this spare... No one aside from Ronald had been made aware of this fact...

Ronald did eventually manage to track down the location of the missing device... After several unsuccessful attempts to locate this device, Ronald was only able to locate its signal on the day S had left the facility... On this occasion, Ronald discovered that the signal was coming from the vicinity of what he already knew to be S's living-compartment...

Because of this, Ronald had strangely assumed that S had somehow been involved with the escape of the Notorious Drone... Ronald believed that S's assumed involvement was completely justified, and that there should be no fault associated in such an act... Instead, Ronald decided to consider this item as a parting gift to S... The reason that the device couldn't be located until this time was unknown to Ronald, and simply deemed irrelevant in light of the circumstances...

In addition to the key chain, the knife that S had received in this package was also intriguing to Ronald... He examined the knife as S placed it into his hand... It was indeed constructed out of a material that had not been known to exist at the time it was given to S...

This material, along with several others, would later be developed at the facility... Strangely, it was only after receiving an anonymous letter that mentioned a means of creating such materials that the project to develop such things was initiated... This anonymous letter was later determined to be in the same hand writing that had been found on the note left by the Notorious Drone...

This might imply that the package was left by the Notorious Drone, but the reasons for such a thing were still unclear... If S had actually aided in the Notorious Drone's escape, these things might have made some sense... However, there was something else involved in the contents of this matter...

There didn't seem to be any way of explaining the Notorious Drone's advanced knowledge of future events... It should have been impossible for the Notorious Drone to mark the map in the manner that it appeared, to enclose the media clippings, &c, &c, &c... Who could have known these things? There was no need to wonder...

These things were not even made known to Ronald at the time the package was delivered to S... Thomas as it turns out, was also all too aware of these things that had yet to occur... Once Ronald caught on to Thomas's advanced knowledge, he started asking questions... Eventually, Thomas relented to tell Ronald how he'd come to this advanced knowledge...

Thomas had become acquainted with a very odd character outside of the facility... This character would converse with Thomas at a local tavern he frequented... The character never became known to Thomas by name, but seemed to already know everything about him, the facility, &c, &c, &c...

On the first encounter Thomas had with this character, he was sitting alone in the tavern... The character sat next to Thomas, and addressed him by name... Then the character began asking about the status of projects being conducted in the facility... It was difficult for Thomas to even fathom how anyone outside of him-self and Ronald could have possibly known about the things this character seemed to know so well...

At first Thomas offered no actual responses to the character's inquiries... Then one day, as Thomas was sitting alone inside the tavern, the character brought something... It was the notebook containing S's *Schizm Theory*... Thomas read through the pages of this notebook, and the character asked if Thomas was familiar with anyone that could have written this content...

Although Thomas was reluctant at first to respond, he figured this character already knew the source of this content... He asked if the character knew what a *schizoid* was... Indeed, the character knew one that had written a notebook containing something called *Schizm Theory*...

Then the character asked Thomas if this notebook's contents could be of any use to him... Thomas could only nod in the affirmative... He was captivated... The character reclaimed possession of the notebook, and began to tell Thomas how this notebook would be made available to the facility... It was according to this conversation that Thomas had first come to know how things would proceed in advance...

When Ronald came to Thomas in order to explain how a copy of this notebook had been placed in his possession, Thomas appeared to be genuinely astonished... Thomas had figured that this character was no more than a clever trickster... This presaged event made it clear that this character knew plenty of things that he did not, and should be taken more seriously... As things continued to progress according to the exact predictions the character conveyed to Thomas, he became convinced that this was some higher authority's way of influencing their desired outcomes...

None of this was explained to Ronald until the two men arrived in LT4... When Ronald heard Thomas's explanation, it was beyond puzzling to him... The identity of this character was beyond Ronald's ability to imagine... There was simply no way that the information this character knew in advance could have been made available in any imagined manner... Ronald was inclined to believe that this was all an elaborate joke Thomas was trying to pull...

Then one day this character arrived in LT4... This character never gave any introduction, but simply showed up with something to give Ronald... It was a package containing several items... All of the items were wrapped in a similar manner to those included in the package that S had received... These items included a map that closely resembled the one S had been given, a knife of the same material composition, some schematics for devices that proved useful in LT4, a letter, &c, &c, &c...

After delivering the package to Ronald, the character directly departed LT4, having been completely undetected by any of the other occupants... This character vanished without leaving so much as a footprint, or any other traceable impression, &c, &c, &c... A moment after this character had vanished; Ronald thought it might have been the extortionist that introduced him to the notebook containing *Schizm Theory*... He couldn't be at all certain of this notion, since he had only formed a vague impression of the extortionist, and only the remnants of that impression's memory remained, &c, &c, &c... Who this character truly might have been was completely unknown...

Sometime later, Ronald came to discover something even more surprising... One of the occupants of LT4 was none other than the Notorious Drone that had escaped from the facility... When Ronald had discovered that this Notorious Drone was indeed an occupant of LT4, he was baffled...

Ronald asked the Notorious Drone how it was possible that such a person could come to live in this place... It was explained to Ronald that LT4 had actually been built using the Notorious Drone's designs, building techniques, &c, &c, &c... Once the construction was completed, the Notorious Drone was given full pardons, a new identity, a map with LT4's coordinates, &c, &c, &c... The Notorious Drone received these items in a package similar to those received by Ronald and S... This package was also delivered by an unidentified figure, similar in description to Ronald's encounters with the mysterious-courier...

The Notorious Drone's escape of the facility was not discussed openly in LT4... When Ronald learned the facts of this escape, it was following another event in LT4... This event became known as the *last selfish-sacrifice*...

When Ronald learned of the Notorious Drone's escape, it was surprising to discover that Thomas was involved... Despite the surprise, it was not of any concern to Ronald when he learned of Thomas's involvement... By then, there was no need to wonder...

The escape didn't actually occur near the time the Notorious Drone had gone missing, but some time much later... At the behest of the unidentified character, Thomas devised a plan where the Notorious Drone could be concealed within the facility, and await the opportunity to make an actual escape... In order to do this, Thomas had passed the Notorious Drone a note detailing the escape plan...

Thomas arranged for the Notorious Drone to be concealed inside a small space under an area with false-flooring inside the facility... Other than Thomas, no one had known that this area had a false-floor... This space was barely large enough to fit the Notorious Drone... In Thomas's note, the Notorious Drone was instructed where this area was located, how to access it, &c, &c, &c...

The Notorious Drone acted according to these instructions, but had also opted to leave the note that was later discovered... This note helped support the notion that the Notorious Drone had fled the facility, and added to the mysterious element of the disappearance... Considering the wonder of the new technologies that had been demonstrated at the facility, it was easy to assume that the Notorious Drone had become capable of such a miraculous disappearance...

Until the extra security-measures were phased out, Thomas had to keep the Notorious Drone concealed within the facility... To do this, Thomas had to escort the Notorious Drone around the facility in various disguises... On most occasions, the Notorious Drone was made to appear as a science-drone or a specialized-consultant...

In addition to the facility's clothing and attachments, Thomas would bring in items to help disguise the Notorious Drone's face... He also pretended to be in a hurry as he escorted the drone around the facility... These efforts allowed the Notorious Drone to use the facility's restrooms, showers, &c, &c, &c... Thomas also provided the Notorious Drone with food during these expedited escorts...

When the security-measures were finally phased down, Thomas was uncertain as to how the Notorious Drone could be extracted... The character acquainted with Thomas helped organize this extraction from the facility... Thomas was advised to get this mysterious-character access to the facility, without revealing the character's identity...

Thomas managed to escort the character into the facility under the false pretense that the character was a special-investigator... The character then pretended to search the facility until the Notorious Drone's whereabouts were discovered... This whole farce was orchestrated well in advance, and the Notorious Drone knew what to expect in this ruse...

The process of this discovery was made to look like very keen detective work... According to those that witnessed this act, it was quite an exciting show... When the Notorious Drone was found, the character pretended to take the Notorious Drone forcibly into custody... Then the Notorious Drone was almost able to escape as it was being escorted out of the facility... This distraction allowed the character to exit the facility without ever having to show any credentials/identification...

After reaching the exterior of the facility, the Notorious Drone was again subdued by the unidentified-character... Then this character secured the Notorious Drone inside an unmarked-vehicle similar to those used by enforcement-officials... Thomas informed the security-drones of the situation as if it weren't a great farce, and ordered them to expedite the exit of the Notorious Drone and unidentified-character...

All of the members present at the facility were satisfied with the results of this mater... None of them were curious as to how the Notorious Drone had managed to stay hidden for so long... Ronald was aware of the probability that someone had been assisting the Notorious Drone, but made no efforts to pursue the matter... As far as he was concerned, it was too bad this reformed-entity wouldn't become liberated...

Although Ronald knew that Thomas could have been involved, he never actually suspected that Thomas had done anything to aid the Notorious Drone... Why would Thomas have ever become involved in such a thing? There was no need to wonder...

S listened to Ronald's accounts for these events with a sense of perplexity... The objectives of the unidentified-character could not even be postulated... Thomas's involvement with this character was extremely out of character for him... It was difficult to imagine how anything involved in this story could be related, and S's involvement was even more bizarre... What was going on behind all of this? There was no need to wonder...

Ronald explained to S how there was no logical way to determine the intentions or identity of the character acquainted with Thomas... Even the existence of this character couldn't necessarily be understood to be consistent with any individual-entity... There was no truth to be determined other than the facts of what had happened... Everything else was mere speculation...

Following this matter of discussion, Ronald and S began comparing the courses of other events that had transpired since the time of their last meeting... S gave accounts of all of the exploits detailed previously in this text, and made mention of several of the deeper thoughts that had been captivating or liberating... Ronald listened to these professions with genuine interest and wonder... Then Ronald began to tell S of the events he had witnessed...

The outside world began to collapse within a month of the Notorious Drone's departure of the facility... Not only did phynancial and guvornmint structures collapse, but seemingly everything else began to crumble as well... The facility lost all of its funding, but remained active under Ronald's supervision... Ronald convinced some of the facility personnel to remain active in the facility in exchange for the safety it afforded them... Because there was so much violence being reported outside of the facility, and no other work was known to be profited from, many agreed to Ronald's proposals...

The area around the facility was converted to produce crops, manage livestock, &c, &c, &c... There was a stream within a half-mile of the perimeter, and a pipeline was built to supply the facility with water... Power to the facility was provided by advanced and innovative versions of solar panels... Occupants were expected to supplement the existing security-drones in protecting the facility from potential invasions... Once the essential elements were in place, the facility became self-sustaining and self-contained... No entry or exit of the facility was allowed without Ronald's authorization...

Inside the facility, Ronald worked closely with Thomas to develop technologies that might save whatever was left of societies outside the facility... It was during this time that CTMYAW procedures were combined with other technologies, allowing minds to be networked together... This made it possible for individual minds to simultaneously experience the thoughts of others along with their own thoughts... A collective-form of consciousness began to emerge...

The facility also developed the technologies S had encountered as the figures of the preservation site... They were initially intended to be used in reconnaissance, and allow the members of the facility's to experience the outside world vicariously through these simulants... Once these simulants were implemented in this functional role, something else was discovered... Because the simulants were capable of autonomous functioning, their thoughts were difficult to distinguish from other humanoid-entities... Instead of using them as reconnaissance-drones under the control of facility-members, the simulants were left to function as autonomous members of the collective...

After these simulants were given to their own programming, they soon departed from the collective... The simulants moved beyond the range of communication with the collective, and began to block signaling attempts to reach them... They soon disappeared from the realm of observation... Wherever the simulants might have gone was unknown...

S was very intrigued by the accounts Ronald gave of these simulants... There was something much more compelling than the facts of what had happened with these simulants... Ronald had a certain affected demeanor with respect to these simulants... It seemed that Ronald was morning the simulants abandonment of the collective... There also seemed to be a resentment concealed beneath this apparent morning...

Other means of reconnaissance were developed to inform the facility what the condition of the outside world had become... The facility's members watched the world crumble as whatever it had been, became whatever remained... Several attacks on the facility it-self took place during this period... It eventually became apparent that the facility would not be safe for much longer... Ronald tried to determine where else they could go... There seemed to be nowhere left to go...

During an intense and organized assault on the facility, a pair of helicopters landed on the facility's helipad... Thomas had led Ronald to the helipad in advance of its arrival... They were instructed by one of the crewmembers that the facility was about to be over-run, and that their evacuation had been ordered...

It was undeniably clear that this was true, and they followed the orders without questioning them... As they were expedited away from the facility, there was an overwhelming sense of guilt and loss that both of them felt... Leaving the others behind was almost unbearable... They would have rather died with the others than abandon them... Why did they leave? There was no need to wonder...

Even after all of the time that had passed, all that had transpired, and the mental procedures to prevent negative emotional experiences, tears streamed down Ronald's face... He cried in silence as he continued to tell the story of what happened... S was oblivious of what an appropriate response might be... Sympathy and empathy were not things that S experienced in the normative manner...

According to S's assertions, sympathy and empathy were actually the displacement of one's identity onto another's... This displacement could only be simulated, and was relegated to feigned emotive-gesturing, placating-utterances, self-delusion, &c, &c, &c... For S, such actions were actually insulting towards the truth of another's suffering...

Additionally, it seemed that acknowledging another's suffering in such a manner validated the suffering, rather than the entity experiencing it... In S's view, this seemed to perpetuate suffering, rather than mitigate against it... Why should someone that wasn't suffering feel compelled to suffer? What benefit could result from imposing suffering on one's self or another's? There was no need to wonder...

This belief made it difficult for S in situations where sympathy or empathy was expected... S didn't compromise such affirmed beliefs in order to appease others... Although S didn't wish any harm on others, the lack of empathy/sympathy that S displayed was often reciprocated with animosity...

Ronald continued to tell this story without the animosity that S had expected to see presented in some manner... Actually, Ronald seemed to recover from his heartfelt pains of these recollections... S found this to be a welcomed sight, and appreciated this deviation from the expected norm... Why wasn't this considered the norm? There was no need to wonder...

The helicopters arrived at what had already become known as LT4... Ronald and Thomas were escorted into the same office where Ronald and S now stood... A high ranking official from the former guvornmints was awaiting their arrival, and asked them to be seated as they arrived... This official operated in LT4 as Ronald's predecessor...

A picture from the meeting Ronald described was placed on Ronald's desk... When the picture was taken, Thomas was in the middle of the frame, with Ronald and his predecessor on either side of him... As S was made to observe this picture, it was difficult to distinguish which of the characters next to Thomas was actually Ronald... The similarities between these two characters were uncanny...

Thomas introduced the two as they gathered inside the office... The unfamiliar characters discovered that they shared the very same name... They also discovered that they shared the same date of birth, height, weight, biological origins, &c, &c, &c... It was almost as if they were the very same person... Ronald explained his perplexity in this meeting, as S appeared to be confused in response to hearing these accounts...

Ronald and his predecessor ceased to discuss their similarities as Thomas guided the conversation towards the present situation... S listened as Ronald explained how Thomas had arranged for Ronald to take over LT4, so that his predecessor could found another installation... His predecessor had told Ronald the current state of LT4, the normal operations, rules, &c, &c, &c... Then Thomas had explained why these men were standing before each other...

Thomas's mysterious-acquaintance had been in communication with him throughout the collapse... Thomas was to notify this character of any serious threats to the facility immediately... When the helicopters had arrived at the facility, it was because Thomas had obeyed these orders... This same acquaintance had informed Ronald's predecessor that another installation was to be founded, and that two men were coming to relieve him of his post at LT4, &c, &c, &c...

This mysterious-acquaintance provided Ronald's predecessor with officially-endorsed documents that certified these orders... These documents were delivered in the familiar packaging, in the same anonymous manner, &c, &c, &c... Ronald's predecessor had been predictably perplexed by all of this...

When Ronald's predecessor completed his briefing on LT4 operations, he wished the two successors prosperity, and left on the same helicopters that had just arrived... After the helicopters had vacated the area of LT4, Thomas explained even more information to Ronald...

The information Thomas relayed to Ronald was considered privileged information, and had not been authorized for Thomas to disclose... This information was given to Thomas through his mysterious-acquaintance... Continuing to exclude Ronald from this information had become too troubling for Thomas...

Keeping secrets from Ronald had caused Thomas great distress... It wasn't the anxiety or fear of leaking this information that troubled Thomas, but terrible concerns over what this secrecy had done to him... This secrecy made Thomas question his own virtues; as a friend to Ronald, as a trustworthy person, as a man of responsibilities, &c, &c, &c... Self-hatred had begun to tear through Thomas's mind...

As Ronald explained the conflict that plagued Thomas, it was clear that Ronald found it difficult to express these things... Ronald seemed to have been disheartened by Thomas's secrecy... This discouragement seemed paled in comparison to Ronald's sympathies towards Thomas's struggles over the matter... What had happened between these two in S's absence? There was no need to wonder...

Before Ronald completed his accounts of these experiences, there was an interruption... The sound of a bell resounded from the *hardt* of LT4... Ronald and S observed the sounding of this bell in silence, as Ronald held a *shushing* gesture of reticence... Once the bell had sounded 3 times, there was silence throughout LT4... Ronald paused in observance of this silence, before he informed S that the rest of these stories would be told at a later time... Presently, there were other matters to attend...

Ronald escorted S out of his office, where an occupant of LT4 had been awaiting S's arrival... This occupant was to give S a tour of LT4, an explanation of rules, escort S into living-accommodations, &c, &c, &c... S and Ronald departed company with normative gestures, and the awaiting occupant began to acclimate S to life in LT4...

301.03 ORIENTATION OF LT4...

S followed the occupant to a transport, and the tour of LT4 began...
The occupant took S around the perimeter, pointing out all of the
landmarks, roadways, buildings, &c, &c, &c... Then the occupant
escorted S around the more centralized area of LT4, &c, &c, &c...

It appeared S was very attentive to the occupant's pronouncements,
although S didn't utter a single word... The occupant was aware of
the fact that S was not part of LT4's collective, and that S was unable
to share thoughts directly with the other occupants... This made S's
silence all the more unusual... Even the occupants capable of sharing
thoughts directly, were still quite talkative in proximity... Not only
was S silent, but there was no apparent cause for this taciturnity...

The occupant tried to observe S for some form of discomfort,
anxiety, distrust, weariness, &c, &c, &c... There were however, no
apparent indications in S's demeanor that alluded to such
predispositions... S was actually quite intrigued, curious, &c, &c,
&c... Unbeknownst to the occupant, S had simply never been a
talkative entity, and the time S had spent in isolation had made this
reticent quality more pronounced...

Instead of continuing to orient S to LT4 in a formal/informative
manner, the occupant tried to be more dynamic... The occupant
maintained a factual basis, but tried to add an innocuous form of

...

conversational humor... This was intended to appeal to S more personally, and generate a more interpersonal form of exchange... There was no apparent change in S's silent demeanor, and the occupant began to feel inadequate...

Then the occupant attempted to ask a series of informal/colloquial questions... S responded to these questions in a concise/factual manner, without elaborations or allusions to anything personally illuminating... These responses were appropriate to address the questions according to their linguistic senses, but were quite detached from the personal rapport they were intended to foster...

The occupant experienced something almost completely eradicated from their collective-consciousness... It was a kind of solitary confusion that seemed beyond comprehension, imagination, &c, &c, &c... What could be done about this? There was no need to wonder...

Soon, S became aware of the escorting occupant's discomfort... S had never been the most personable of characters, and S was well aware of this fact... This had never been of much concern, consequence, &c, &c, &c... After spending so much time alone in the preservation site, S found it interesting that such things had become more apparent... Now S understood what others found impersonally aloof in S's character, and could even imagine ways to be more accommodating towards others... For S, it had only been possible to understand these interpersonal notions as a result of introspection...

This understanding was not due to some new capacity for S to empathize, sympathize, &c, &c, &c... It was actually S's complete dismissal of these obligatory identity-displacement techniques that allowed this comprehension... S could devote attentions normally reserved for feigning these impressions on more critical analysis of others... By analyzing the subtlety of others' implications/intentions beyond their literal expressions, S could understand what others actually expected, desired, &c, &c, &c...

As the occupant continued to squire S around the area of LT4, S began to demonstrate the beginnings of a more sociable charisma... S began to project a more personal presence in responses to inquiries, offering more individuating information, elaboration, &c, &c, &c... In addition to this, S started reciprocating inquiries, making the occupant feel more engaged in the conversation... At various points, S even made some clever attempts at humor... This seemed to lighten the mood of this orientation, turning it into a more casual endeavor...

It seemed to the occupant that S was becoming more relaxed, comfortable, affable, &c, &c, &c... In reality, S found this new tactic to be more demanding, compromising, deceitful, &c, &c, &c... S was not very genuinely interested in the occupant, nor did S feel it necessary/appropriate to disclose personal thoughts/information with *random acquaintances*... There seemed to be no rational provision obliging S to conform to these interpersonal paradigms... Why did others seem so intent on relating to each other in such an indiscriminate/compromising manner? There was no need to wonder...

S actually posed this question to the occupant that had only just begun to feel what many people would call *connected* to S... This question had a strange effect, actually making S appear to be more personable to the occupant... Although S's question acted as a genuine/authentic form of divulgence, it was also quite perplexing...

The occupant demonstrated a strange sense of obfuscation in response to S's question... How might this question even begin to be approached with an answer? There was no need to wonder...

The occupant was struggling to attempt an answer, as the transport arrived upon S's living quarters... It was necessary to inform S of the rules of LT4 at this juncture, and the occupant digressed from its former explanations... As the occupant introduced this structure S was to inhabit, the rules were sternly conveyed...

All of the other occupants' personal-living areas were located in another area of LT4... The occupant explained that S was to be retained in this other area, until a more permanent occupancy status might be permitted... According to the rules of LT4, it had not been acceptable to allow any entity outside of their collective to inhabit their environs... Provisionally, it had been determined that S would be allowed to remain in LT4 as a guest under restrictions... These restrictions included that S be secured in another area of LT4 during the hours of darkness, away from the collective's living-quarters...

"Here in LT4..."

The occupant began to explain...

"We are all one..."

In hearing these words S involuntarily shuttered, but the occupant did not observe this reaction... For S, these words were hauntingly familiar... They had come to be associated with all that S had found deplorable in societies... S had spent some lengths of time in the presentation site contemplating the nature of what these words were used to denote/imply...

After long considerations, S privately conceptualized these kinds of statements... What S considered these words to be, was an *abomination of we*... According to S's insights, the manner that the single word *we* had been used, was the cause of almost every horror individuals experienced...

Without having any notion of S's reaction or private inclinations to these words, the occupant continued...

"We are all connected... Our minds have been enhanced by technological means to allow us all to share our perspectives... Because our minds are all connected, we exist as one collective-consciousness... This allows us to transcend our *selphish* urges, and live more harmoniously..."

S managed to sever any observable reaction from these words... Inside S's separately conscious mind were thoughts of apprehension, trepidation, &c, &c, &c... Although S was so opposed to these words and all that was associated with them, S found it possible for other meanings to exist in the contexts they were now presented...

In previous social paradigms, the minds of separate entities were not connected in the way they were in LT4... It seemed expectant/biased for S to avoid considering that these words might mean something different here... There was also the possibility that S's negative associations of this *abomination of we* were unfounded in LT4... How could that be possible? There was no need to wonder...

As S considered these predispositions, other considerations were being evaluated... S had left the presentation site with the resolve to explore the nature of self, by considering how it related to separate perspectives... It seemed to S that this resolve could be explored by observing the way the occupants of LT4 related to their collective, to S's projected-self, &c, &c, &c... In observing this, S might finally possess a greater veracity of S's own self, identity, &c, &c, &c... After a moment of pondering these thoughts, S concluded what was to be done...

S had remained attentive, even in the depths of these other contemplations... The occupant continued speaking with regards to the rules and norms of LT4...

"All the rules of LT4 are in accord with our shared consciousness... We each act according to what is best for us as a *wHole*... Whatever exists outside of us is not to be considered as either apart from us, or a part of us... Things that exist outside of us might not remain outside of us... If something should become one with us, then so it shall be, and so be it... Only that which threatens to harm us, might be considered something apart from us..."

S asked the occupant how the collective of LT4 viewed S's presence in their vicinity... The occupant responded candidly...

"Your presence here is unprecedented... Our collective was largely formed shortly after it became possible in this location... Previous expansions of our collective-consciousness occurred quite rarely, but seamlessly... Because you have yet to be made compatible with us, it is not possible for such a seamless integration to occur... It will take some time before this can be made possible... We do not currently have the means to optimize your mind in a way that would allow you to experience our collective-consciousness, or integrate your perspective into our own... For now, you are something of a *specimen* to us... You are our first true *stranger*..."

These procedures were not currently available, as the resources necessary to complete them were currently being used on other projects... Although this was mentioned, the actual projects were not disclosed to S at this time... Several technical questions were addressed, and S began to form an impression of how the term, *specimen* had been applied to S...

The occupant continued the orientation speech...

"Occupancy of LT4 is restricted to the members of its collective-consciousness... The collective-consciousness does not need to be instructed of the formal rules of LT4... There isn't even a need for such things within the collective-consciousness... For you, there are some provisional rules that are to be obeyed... There is really only one rule... Treat the *wHole* as if it were your *selph*..."

S asked some questions to clarify what this rule implied, and was given sufficient responses... Instructions concerning the overnight arrangements, and the necessary activities that would ensue on the next day were then imparted to S... The occupant secured S inside the provisional living-compartment, exchanged pleasantries, &c, &c, &c...

As S settled into the segregated living-compartment, it was without solace... S was relatively contented to remain apart from the collective, although remaining in LT4 placed S's self in jeopardy... This exposure was quite threatening, but it seemed necessary to endure in order to reveal S's true self...

S's discomfort had more to do with a sense that there was something ominous looming within this place... What was it that S couldn't see? There was no need to wonder...

301.04 TIMESCOURT IN LT4...

S awoke the next day after a night of distressed attempts to complete a proper sleeping-interval... By the time the next occupant arrived, S was on the verge of collapsing back into an exhausted slumber... As the subsequent occupant announced arriving in S's vicinity, S was startled back into wakefulness... The occupant patiently waited, as S scurried to meet this escort...

This was not the same occupant that had escorted S on the previous occasion... It was difficult for S to distinguish this fact, as the entity had a similar physical appearance, common mannerisms, &c, &c, &c... After S had entered the transport with this occupant, the conversation transitioned into the current day's agenda... The occupant made mention of the events of the previous day, reiterated the rules, &c, &c, &c... S listened while straining not to reveal any contention, as the occupant followed every explanation of life in LT4 by reciting...

"... after all, we are all one..."

The occupant informed S that this was a particularly interesting day for LT4... What the occupants had deemed the arrival of their first stranger caused a great deal of interest, concern, &c, &c, &c... S's arrival was not the only novel event recently presented to LT4...

...

There were some other items of considerable importance that had interested the occupants of LT4...

It was customary for the occupants of LT4 to physically meet on every 3rd day, in order to physically connect with each-other, discuss important topics, &c, &c, &c... By the way these meetings were explained to S; it seemed that they were implicitly mandatory for the occupants of LT4... However, when S asked if these meetings were required/mandatory, the occupant responded in confusion... After all, in LT4 they were all one... How could something be considered mandatory if this was true? There was no need to wonder...

These meetings were held in an area located in the very center of LT4... This area was known to the occupants as TimesCourt... The occupant escorted S to TimesCourt in advance of the forthcoming meeting, with the intentions of explaining a few things about this place...

TimesCourt was a large courtyard that held in its own center, a grand obelisk-shaped structure with 3 sides... Each side of this structure was composed of a translucent material unlike any S had seen previously... The material was indeed an invention of the occupants of LT4, as the escorting-occupant explained... At the peak of the structure, there was an antiquated weathervane... Near the peak of each face of this structure were 3 clocks...

Each of the clocks on this obelisk functioned differently... One had hands that ran forward, and marked time in the standardized manner... Another did not appear to function with any motion, but instead indicated a fixed time of 3:01:20 (AM or PM)... The other seemed to be malfunctioning... Its hands ran in a reverse direction of time, as if counting into the past...

In response to S's inquiries on the topic of these clocks, the occupant began to explain... It was customary in LT4 to think of life in a different context... After Ronald and Thomas had arrived to replace their predecessors, the occupants were introduced to what was called *S-Theory*...

In *S-Theory*, it was necessary to think of time as a non-linear concept... Time, according to *S-Theory*, moved forward, backward, up, down, laterally, &c, &c, &c... According to the explanations the occupant offered S, time was more of a higher-dimension of space, than a temporal-concept, consistent with classical understandings, &c, &c, &c...

S asked a series of questions related to this concept of time, other aspects of *S-Theory*, &c, &c, &c... It was soon apparent that interpretations of components included in S's *Schizm Theory*, had been adapted by the facility into this *S-theory*... From these adapted notions of S's former ideas, the occupants of LT4 had somehow concluded that they were indeed *all one*... As the occupant explained how this was made apparent in LT4, S experienced a most horrifying shudder... Fortunately, S's projection of this response was not observed by any of the occupants of LT4...

After S regained composure, the conversation shifted back to the structure at the heart of LT4... The occupant explained the significance of this structure... It was built to symbolize the way in which entities experience time...

"Time is experienced in the manner of two dreams... One dream is the precession of the present... This is the dream of memory... Memory is the dream of a past that brings consciousness into its present... When we remember, it is as if we are dreaming in reverse... For memory is not what has actually occurred, but the associations of what is believed to have occurred..."

S listened to the occupant's explanations, as if they were a reminder of S's own forgotten dreams...

"The other dream is the dream of what might become of the present... It is what propels experiences of the present forward... We dream of what is to be done in advance of doing it ... What is strange, is that with life being what it is, one dreams of revenge, and has to..."

With the pallor of a formerly-living specimen, S completed the quotation the occupant was alluding to...

"...content oneself with dreaming..."

Outlandishly, no occupant of LT4 noticed the pallor/terror present in S's response... Instead, the occupant had only heard the words that completed the quotation it had begun... The words prompted the occupant into feelings of harmony, connectedness, &c, &c, &c...

These feelings of connectedness towards S were very different from those the collective felt towards its own members... Strangely, the occupant found this feeling to be intensely perplexing... What was so perplexing about this sensation? There was no need to wonder...

It seemed at first, that this sense had been provoked by the surprise/spontaneity of S's interjection... Then it seemed to have something to do with the voluntary manner this sentiment was acquiesced... These assertions were perhaps of some truth to the occupant, but not a satisfactory truth... Whatever had caused this sensation was clear to the occupant to be more complex, esoteric, &c, &c, &c...

As the occupant continued to ponder the nature of this sentiment, S listened to the assiduous explanations of the central-structure...

"The weathervane atop this structure is symbolic of the nature of all direction... All direction is derived from the essence of time... In time, all directions come to their end, but time continues to define all direction..."

TimesCourt held a significance in relation to this structure... In LT4, time was considered the judge of all things, and the truth of all things was inevitably revealed by time... By placing this structure inside the center of TimesCourt, it was intended to symbolize this notion, reinforce this contextual-understanding, &c, &c, &c...

The occupant went on to explain how this place was utilized by the occupants of LT4... Time was the essence of all that was held dear to the occupants... The occupants of LT4 gathered in TimesCourt to share their time, their ideas, their *selphes*, &c, &c, &c... It was in TimesCourt that all things could be understood according to the truth that time would inevitably reveal...

TimesCourt was host to every meeting in LT4... Every decision to be made by the collective was introduced in TimesCourt, deliberated, decided, &c, &c, &c... Each of the meetings that took place in TimesCourt, were followed by some act to reinforce the unity of the occupants of LT4...

Artistic productions were often held in TimesCourt on such occasions... There were plays, concerts, festivals, &c, &c, &c... In addition to all of these things, the whole of LT4's occupants would regularly gather in order to be *physically* united in time, and embrace as they *consummated their future*...

S found the occupants assertions of *consummating a future* to be bizarre, repulsive, &c, &c, &c... The occupant did take notice of S's confusion on this matter, and elaborated further as to what these assertions were intended to mean... This *consummation of the future* in TimesCourt was explained by the occupant to be something of a *sackrameant* in LT4... At least, that's how it appeared the occupants related to this practice in S's mind...

In LT4, there was no more venerated activity than the *consummation of their future*... The occupant began to illustrate this by relating this action in terms of what it symbolized... By gathering in TimesCourt, the occupants engaged in this act with respect to time... This meant that they were also giving thought to their past, present, &c, &c, &c... It was an act that actually seemed to codify time it-self into the collective of LT4 and epitomized how they were truly *all one*...

Essentially, this *consummation of their future* was consistent with what had previously been celebrated as, *Bacchanalias*... The occupants of LT4 would begin the *consumption of their future* by consuming wine that they produced as *one* in LT4... Then they would all express their own personal elation towards one-another in a spirit of uninhibited solidarity...

United in TimesCourt, they would dance, sing, laugh, cry, &c, &c, &c... When they all sensed an overwhelming feeling of *connectedness*, with great sanguinity in their shared future; they would remove all their clothing, that only seemed to separate them from each-other physically in such a moment... As they all revealed them-selphes without shame, they would then begin to embrace... Within this embrace, they would begin to feel as if they were one naked body; physically, emotionally, spiritually, &c, &c, &c...

After they achieved this sense of being one collective-entity, entangled in the deepest depths of its own soul, LT4 would consummate in mass... This depiction of LT4's *coital-collage* was reputed to be an expression of *one infinite love*... The physical descendants to be welcomed into LT4's collective were conceived along with their future in this manner...

S found these notions to be beyond the imaginable extents of human revulsion... Despite the extent of S's disgust toward these depictions, S managed to conceal these sentiments... What little evidence S projected in response to the occupant's explanations, were mired in the elation the occupant experienced even in simply conveying these depictions... It was becoming increasingly difficult for S to continue concealing these reactions, thoughts, &c, &c, &c...

The occupant continued to escort S around LT4, pointing out the various structures, functional areas, &c, &c, &c... S was made aware of all the things necessary for personal survival in LT4... Along the way, the occupant also explained how service to LT4 was a component of residency, and that S would be expected to contribute in some manner...

This was of course, if it was determined that S be allowed to remain present after the meeting in TimesCourt... It was also contingent on whether or not S desired to remain in LT4, &c, &c, &c... Was S to remain in LT4? What might S be able to contribute to LT4? There was no need to wonder...

301.05 PRIOR TO TIMESCOURT SESSION…

Ronald approached S, as the occupant was explaining some of the many ways occupants of LT4 contributed to their society… After greeting S and the occupant, Ronald offered to assume the role of orienting S to LT4… The occupant bid the two *adieu*, and vacated their company to engage in other contributions to LT4… S thanked the occupant for the courtesies rendered, and returned the farewell…

As the occupant departed, Ronald proposed that S follow his lead towards a bench in close proximity to the time-bearing structure centered in TimesCourt… The name of this structure had not been identified by name to S until this time… Ronald referred to the structure as the, *Thom Trauabert Temporal Memorial*, and asked S what thoughts it provoked…

According to S, there was a sense of incompleteness associated with this structure… S also noted that this *incompleteness* was in it-self seemingly incomplete… Some notions of this *incompleteness* were present in S's perspective; others seemed elusive, &c, &c, &c…

Listening to S's assertions on this structure brought a familiar smile to Ronald's face… He began to reminisce of the times in the facility when S had managed to surprise him with eccentric responses to what seemed benign/drab forms of inquiry… It seemed to Ronald that he was transported through time it-self, to a place where he was

…

someone quite different from his current-self... S took notice of Ronald's familiar smile; seeing it as a thing from a past, that now seemed displaced in its current juxtaposition...

After a moment, Ronald's thoughts became more focused on present concerns... He asked S about the contributions S might be able to make in LT4... S seemed quite willing to earn a living in LT4, but Ronald found this to be of some concern... In LT4, Ronald explained, there is no need to *earn* anything...

"Everything in LT4 is contributed according to the requirements of LT4 as a whole..."

Ronald summarized the subsequent portions of his explanations...

"Here in LT4, each contributes according to their capacity, and each accepts according to their graciousness..."

S heard these words as ominously alluding to a similar phrase that was closely associated with great horrors... This associated phrase had been prominent throughout the darker portions of history... This phrase was closely associated with the phrase used by the *Rushain Kommunist Moovemint*... "*From each according to their ability, to each according to their needs*..." A chill had made its way up S's spine, but due to Ronald's presence this reaction was concealed...

Instead, S asked Ronald if there was anything that he might have had in mind for S to contribute while visiting LT4... Ronald dismissed the use of the term *visiting*... Then Ronald urged S to follow him, and began leading the way towards the Project Palace...

Along the way, Ronald began briefing S on a project that had been in his mind to have S contribute towards... It was a project that had been initiated at the facility... Now, it was on the verge of even greater commencement, &c, &c, &c...

The ECM technology that S had helped to develop was now being adapted to be implemented in a broader context... Ronald explained that the *Extra Computational Machines* had already achieved advanced levels of sentience, and might be capable of assuming the role of global operations...

Essentially, as Ronald explained the project's objective, the ECMs would be given total control of resource management, production, &c, &c, &c... Every essential task that could be completed by ECMs would be... The intention was to allow the less-capable humanoid-populous to be provided for more efficiently, function more appropriately, &c, &c, &c...

Ronald explained that until this project was successfully completed, humanity would not be able to exist in the truest sense of what it was... Only after humanity was relieved of all its obligations, and given the opportunity to discover its natural purpose/capacity could it achieve its true-self...

S found this notion intriguing... It had previously occurred to S that one's self persisted beyond essential necessities... The dependence upon provisions had always precluded the attainment of true independence in S's own life... In order to most fully explore the nature of self, it would be necessary for S to achieve an autonomous independence... Such a feat might even be consistent with the notions of what S had conceptualized as, *achieving the self*...

Ronald could remember the desire S possessed to pursue greater understandings of individuation, identity, &c, &c, &c... During the time Ronald had worked with S at the facility, it had become clear that this was S's primary esteem... Everything S seemed to produce or project had been somehow related to this esteem...

Presenting this project to S was deliberately intended to entice S into becoming a part of LT4... It was almost unbearable for Ronald to even consider the potential that S might not remain in LT4... Why would S possibly refuse this place? There was no need to wonder...

After a moment of consideration, S gave consent to make any contributions possible to complete this project... S understood that until this project was completed, there wouldn't be any reason for the occupants of LT4 to assimilate S into their collective... As long as S worked on the project, it would be possible to continue the self-explorations that had led S into LT4...

It would also be possible for S to study the occupants of LT4, their collective-relationships, &c, &c, &c... Once the project was complete, S would have to choose what actions to take... Only then would S be required to decide whether or not joining the collective was something in S's self-interest...

In response to S's consent, Ronald shook hands with S in a formal manner... Then Ronald informed S that they would have to reconvene at a later time to discuss the specifics of this project... In the meantime, Ronald urged S to accompany him back to TimesCourt so S could witness how LT4's culture came together...

Despite S's apprehensions, concessions towards Ronald's proposal were made... The two characters headed back to TimesCourt where most of the collective had already gathered... S became quite self-conscious in the midst of all the occupants of LT4... How would S's presence be observed in this setting? There was no need to wonder...

301.06 UNITY IN TIMESCOURT

Ronald's intentions were already known to all the occupants of LT4, with the exception of S... As they arrived in TimesCourt, the scene had already been set... A podium had been constructed at the base of the *Thom Trauabert Temporal Memorial*, along with a stage, public address system, &c, &c, &c... S observed this with a curious expression... If it was true that in LT4 the occupants were all one, why was it that this gathering had been oriented in such a manner? There was no need to wonder...

As Ronald explained the special significance of these meetings, S listened with caution not to reveal any disdainful reactions... It was because S had arrived amidst the occupants of LT4 without the capacity to share the same consciousness that these efforts were made... Otherwise, there would have been little need to make many of the arrangements, although the nostalgic affinity that was a part of TimesCourt was also a factor...

On previous sessions of these meetings, the occupants of LT4 would place a podium at the base of their central-memorial... The podium was not a necessity, but it did function in a sentimental manner... By implementing the podium, LT4's occupants felt a connection to past sentiments attached to communal-governance, festive-celebrations, &c, &c, &c... In LT4, it was in the spirit of past attempts to bring people together, that this podium was used... Implementing this

...

symbolism was also a means of observing how far they had progressed in order to reach their current state of unity, &c, &c, &c…

Ronald elaborated on this point very enthusiastically, eloquently, &c, &c, &c… S considered the possibility that these ideas of unity might have some validity… Although S would have believed that Ronald had not yet become aware of these differences S held in relating to LT4, the truth was quite different…

It was true that S had not shown any observable indications of disdain… Contrarily, S had not demonstrated any open acceptance/enthusiasm for these notions of unity… These omissions made Ronald, and therefore all of LT4, very aware of S's predispositions…

LT4's entire collective saw this meeting in TimesCourt as an opportunity to show S the glory of their unity… It would allow S to witness the events of their own collective-experience… If S could see what the collective felt, it would surely convince this *stranger* of the virtues in their unity… According to the notions of the collective, S was already connected to them… This event would allow S to begin sensing this connection, and soon S would truly be *one* with them…

S followed Ronald to the vicinity of the stage, and was directed to occupy a chair behind the podium… Ronald informed S that an introduction would be made, allowing everyone to greet S in the flesh… If S wished to make a statement, the podium would be made available… Otherwise, S could simply wave to the occupants, before sitting back in the chair provided… What would S possibly have to state at such a time? There was no need to wonder…

Ronald initiated the meeting in TimesCourt by convoking the collective-consciousness, approaching the podium, &c, &c, &c… He looked back as the gathering of LT4 became still, indicating that S could be seated… S was seated, and Ronald began to address LT4 as if this speech were only being conveyed in the traditional manner…

This effort had a strange effect on S, as it was clearly being done for S's sole benefit... The silence of the attentive crowd seemed displaced in the context of this speech... Combined with S's awareness of the lack of necessity for the collective to communicate in such an antiquated manner, S found the display to be a strange farce...

As Ronald began to speak, S tried to imagine this scene was in a more classical setting... S imagined this was not an integrated-community that shared a collective-consciousness, but was a crowd of individual entities gathered due to some mutually associated interest... It was not S's concern to identify this mutually associated interest, but considered best to avoid contemplating... By simulating these notions, S was able to experience this scene in as feigned a manner as it was presented...

"We have gathered here in TimesCourt, in order to celebrate our unity yet again..."

Ronald began...

"This occasion is of special note... Not only are we all one here today as we have been for some time now, but we are welcoming within us an entity from beyond our own realm... The *stranger* that has recently come into our presence here in LT4 is seated here before us now... If we could share a welcoming cheer as this character is presented before our physical-eyes, it would surely be mutually appreciated... S, would you be so kind as to indulge us in welcoming you into our presence..."

With a hand extended to implore S to rise and be recognized, Ronald conducted the welcoming orchestrations... S rose to greet the cheering collective, and waved graciously with an expression of generic positivity... It didn't seem appropriate for S to speak at this time, so S commenced to be seated after the welcoming applause and cheers began to subside... Ronald concluded the applause with a gracious nod in S's direction, and continued his address...

"It is not only of special significance that we are gathered here in welcoming S, but we also may be close to welcoming an even brighter future... The progress we have had on the ECM project has recently been rather tedious... However, in previous instances of similar frustrations, breakthroughs were made by the work of this new arrival to LT4... In the days that our former society was in a state of collapse, S was instrumental in constructing the foundations that our current society rests..."

The collective responded with applause in favor of this comment... Ronald turned to wink in S's direction, as the applause was given time to resound... S gave a gracious smirk in recognition of this gesture... It occurred to S that the applause sounded like something other than a crowd's elation... This applauding was too synchronized to project the spontaneity of solitary expressions in unison... Instead, it was as if one sample of applause was being omitted from multiple sources...

"S will be brought up to speed on our current progress on this project, and will contribute towards the completion of this endeavor... If such contributions prove to be as useful in this project as those S has previously contributed towards, we may soon see this project through to its completion..."

More applause of hyper-synchronicity followed this conjecture... Again Ronald turned to acknowledge S's welcomed presence in LT4...

"This project will likely signify something almost unimaginable to us now... If this project proves to be as significant as we anticipate, we may witness its completion as the attainment of perfection, transcendence, etc, etc, etc..."

Ronald stole a moment to shoot a referential glance towards S, acknowledging the esoteric use of the neologism S had explained to him at the facility... This was intended to draw S into a sense of familiar exclusivity, connecting S to Ronald in a very personal manner... Instead, it seemed to S as if this was more of a pandering gesture, diluting S's unique form of expression into a colloquial farce/slang... S's introspective demeanor didn't give way to revealing these sentiments, and Ronald went on with almost no delay...

"We are about to become free to our-selves... We will no longer need to attend to our collective-needs, obligations, concerns, &c, &c, &c... We will be able to entrust anything/everything of consequence in the care of these ECMs... We will watch as these ECMs effortlessly complete every essential task we would otherwise engage... We will welcome the ECMs, accepting their contributions to our collective with greatest appreciation... We will also welcome these ECMs into our consciousness, integrating them into our collective-mind... When these ECMs are integrated into our collective, it will change everything that we are to be, but one thing will remain eternally true of us... We will all be ONE!!!"

The collective responded with exhilarated/hyper-synchronized applause that reached the threshold of their sonic potential... S was disturbed by both the volume of this applause, and the connotations that had inspired it... If these ECMs could be made to function in the manner Ronald had described, S knew what must be done before they might be integrated into the collective of LT4...

This made it clear to S what contribution was to be made towards this project... Amidst the deafening crowd, S shuddered at the thought... It had become known to S all too late... What could be done now? There was no need to wonder...

301.07 CONSUMATING THE FUTURE...

As the collective displayed their elated welcome of the potential future Ronald portrayed, the enormous casks of wine began to flow... The occupants began to drink freely, excessively, &c, &c, &c... All of the occupants were dressed in purple, and the wine that spilled intentionally over all of them, only added to the sight of their monochromatic unity... With the consumption of this intoxicating substance, the occupants became only more elated in their actions... Soon all of LT4 was enthralled; in the rapture of this purple moment's hope of a future, in their present inebriated elation, &c, &c, &c...

Ronald joined in the festivities as the drinking began... After his last words had incited the collective; musicians began to play, occupants broke-out in synchronized-chants of lyrical-verse, &c, &c, &c... S listened as if the sounds were synchronized-slurs of unintelligible drunken-utterances... They were singing recitations of the words...

"...We Are All One... We Are All One... We Are All One..."

The occupants seemed to inhale their fermented fluids, and exhale the syllables of their song, &c, &c, &c... All the while, they were dancing wildly, with chaotic movements that remained ordered in the context of the collective whole... None of the occupants collided or obstructed another's motion in this sea of functioning chaos... S

...

watched with particular interest in the juxtaposition of personalized chaos persisting in the midst of a larger functional order...

Were these manifestations of individualized expressions truly unrestrained? Could it be that each occupant in the collective was still an individual, but also connected to a higher functioning collective? There was no need to wonder...

As S began to wonder what might be residing in the depths beneath this sight, the occupants become more exposed... Items of violet clothing were thrust into the air, as the occupants removed them from their bodies... The ground was shrouded with the fallen garments, as if the surface were an unmade bed, heaped in shredded remnants of a disheveled vino-colored quilt... Then the occupants were in their fully exposed condition; drunk on their collective's elixir, facing the pseudo-phallic structure that counted towards their esteemed future, &c, &c, &c...

S was invited to *commune* with them as they became increasingly lascivious... This scene was not an aesthetic/welcomed sight in S's view... Instead of acquiescing to partake in the *consummation of this future*, S graciously attempted to be excused from this event... Initially, the collective was exceptionally offended at S's refusal to share in their most honored sakramental act of union... However, S was promptly dismissed, and the collective-desire not to let anything inhibit this sakrament prevailed, &c, &c, &c...

Unfortunately for S, the living-accommodations that had been arranged were within earshot of the events in TimesCourt... The sounds of the collective's coital-screams echoed off of every structure in LT4... S found it difficult to ignore these incessant sounds... As the hours drudged on into the night, these carnal-cries seemed not only to linger, but continually crescendo... When S finally fell asleep, it was to the repulsive sounds of LT4's collective-unity, &c, &c, &c...

Instead of rest, S merely lost consciousness from exhausted frustrations... S's sleeping-interval was by no means restorative, and S awoke without vitality... When S did awake, it was eerily silent...

Despite this silence, S imagined the echoes were still wafting through the air...

As S began to move through the provided living-accommodations, a note was discovered to have been slid under the door... This note advised S that it would not be until late in the day that any activities would take place... S read this note with relief, intending to resume attempts to gain restful slumber...

301.08 SUBSEQUENT EMBRACES...

Late in the day, S was dispatched by yet another occupant of LT4...
Instead of being escorted into the Project Palace, S was to meet
Ronald in TimesCourt... S was informed that following the events of
the previous evening, it was customary for LT4 to spend the
following day expressing them-selves in artistic manners... Ronald
had insisted that S be made present for some of these exhibitions...

Inside TimesCourt, the occupants were demonstrating various artistic
talents... It was quite a spectacle for S to witness these
demonstrations, especially given the impressions S had from the
previous evening... Perhaps the most bizarre impression on S was
the manner that these artistic expressions were conveyed...

S was unaware of the fact that the occupants of LT4 had developed
synesthesia as a result of their integrated-consciousness... Upon
observing this scene in TimesCourt, it was apparent that this was the
case... As S witnessed this *synesthetic symposium*, Ronald came rushing
over...

Tapping S on the shoulder, Ronald asked S to comment on the
present scene in TimesCourt... S had just taken a bite of one of the
culinary items offered for sampling... In response to Ronald's
question, S commented with levity, stating that the flavors here were
the loudest S had ever seen... Ronald smirked affably without any

...

true amusement, and began to turn the conversation into the matter of the ECM project...

Earlier efforts to complete the integration of the ECMs into the collective-consciousness had not succeeded... The ECMs had been tested in the days S had still been employed at the facility, and proven effective, reliable, &c, &c, &c... It was only due to the desire to integrate the ECMs into the collective-consciousness that these devices were not currently implemented in LT4...

"Nirvana..."

Ronald broke-down the situation to S...

"...loomed on the verge of this final resolution... The project had gone to the very edge of completion, but could not break the plane..."

As Ronald detailed the previously failed attempts to solve the problem, it was clear that S's earlier suspicions were very likely well founded... Before Ronald could conclude briefing S on all the details, S cut in with a very keen inquiry...

"Can you tell me what happened to Thomas?"

After a pale moment marked by the question's sting, Ronald decided it was not yet time to answer... Instead, he asked if this question could be answered in a more appropriate setting... S conceded to this request, but asked another...

"Am I being involved in this due to my division from your collective?"

Every word S spoke seemed to flicker in Ronald's mind, like sparks setting flames to the well cured tinder of the collective's plan... It was in fact the very reason that S had not been *endgaged* as a threat to LT4... In order to complete the project it was necessary to have an individual mind that was separate from the collective...

Ronald was not supposed to disclose this fact to S... Could he deny it now? There was no need to wonder...

"Fate/circumstance has led you to this juncture... It can be no other way... What we need is not a sacrificial test subject... We need you to function as a sort of, *sacred specimen*, if you will... You are likely the key to our salvation, transcendence, &c, &c, &c..."

Until Ronald had released these words, S had not been quite sure that the previous suspicions were anything more than a manifestation of S's apprehensive tendencies... Now it was clear that S was intended to be used as a means of achieving the collective's ends... S was actually a bit relieved to discover this... It was easier for S to cooperate with others when it was clear what truly motivated them... By obliging LT4 in this project, S also stood to gain something...

"Let's get on with it then..."

Life exploded in Ronald's veins at the surprise of S's compliance to the project of such ineffable importance... His mind flashed with deliciously resounding elation... Ronald even embraced S with an endorphin-flooded euphoria, lifting S from the solid ground beneath them... With S in Ronald's elevated hold, it was as if success had preceded this moment, and was now coming into temporal-order...

"You don't know what this means to us here..."

S heard Ronald speak these words as if they were from some distant time and place... Trying not to break the mood, S prompted Ronald...

"So, you were saying..."

301.09 THE LAST SEFISH-SACRIFICE...

Ronald and S observed the synesthetic-scene in TimesCourt as they discussed the technical elements of the project... Once the *synesthetic symposium* had been well appraised, Ronald escorted S to the Project Palace... Along the way, these two discussed the elements of the scene with a casual ease, as if the ECM project was already some forgotten anecdote...

After entering the Project Palace, Ronald began to explain more serious things to S... He informed S that this building was the only place in LT4 where connecting signals were disrupted... Inside this building no thoughts could be transmitted in or out... Ronald explained that this was a necessary precaution for the ECM project...

If the ECMs were not assuredly approved for integration, allowing transmitted thoughts could endanger the functioning of LT4... Activated ECMs could potentially infiltrate, rather than integrate into the collective were it not for these quarantining precautions... Ronald explained that this isolation was terrible for him, the others of LT4, &c, &c, &c... It caused a feeling of being cut away from everything... Because of the collective's nature, this feeling even caused the sensation of being severed from one's own-selph...

Once Ronald and S were alone inside the Project Palace, what had happened to Thomas H. Traubert was finally divulged... It was not

...

something that the collective found appropriate to communicate, and only in this isolated place could the story be told... S asked Ronald why he had decided to tell the story if this were truly the case... Ronald informed S that once the story had been told; it would all make sense...

Thomas had been forced to comply with his acquaintance's terms in order to evacuate the facility safely... The evacuation was arranged after Thomas submitted to swear him-self and Ronald into the service of this acquaintance... What this service was to consist of was unknown to Thomas, and no explanation was offered...

After Ronald had been briefed by his predecessor, Thomas was handed an envelope marked in a manner similar to the package S had received... Inside the envelope were detailed instructions of what Thomas was to do in LT4... These instructions were never seen by Ronald or the others in LT4 at any point...

It was Ronald's responsibility to lead LT4 into the successful fulfillment of a utopian state of existence... This implied that LT4 achieve a society based on the ideals of peace, unity, &c, &c, &c... The conditions that had been established by Ronald's predecessor were all oriented in this manner... Ronald was certain that progress could be made, but was uncertain as to how this might be done... Thomas however, seemed convinced that perfection was on the verge of being fulfilled...

Thomas helped Ronald integrate LT4's consciousness in the same manner they had developed at the facility... He also pushed Ronald in the direction of integrating the ECMs into LT4's collective... Ronald had initially favored the notion of implementing the ECMs in a less integrated fashion, but later conceded to Thomas's enthusiastic assurances... It was only due to Thomas's influence that these ECMs were to be integrated prior to implementing them in LT4...

This position was not Thomas's own belief, but part of the instructions he had received... In Thomas's orders, the primary objective of his service was to ensure the ECMs were integrated into the collective of LT4... If Thomas was unable to do this, there would have been serious consequences... What were these consequences? There was no need to wonder...

As work on the ECMs progressed, Thomas became more personally involved... He became the project's primary contributor, director, &c, &c, &c... Under Thomas's authority, several decisions were made without any other consent... This allowed certain conditions to be established that contributed to Thomas's fate...

In order to ensure that the ECMs could be properly integrated, several precautions were taken... The Project Palace was made to conceal individuals' thoughts, isolating transmissions from reaching the collective... Additionally, another project was initiated in order to simulate the results of possible integration techniques, conditions, calibrations, &c, &c, &c... This project produced what would become known as the *simularium*...

The simularium was a *construkt* based on detailed subject mappings that were programmed into a vast network of simulating-structures... Thomas believed that predictions of ECM integration could be assessed by simulating the ECMs, LT4's collective, &c, &c, &c... By using the most detailed, elaborate, precise methods of simulating every conceivable variable within the simularium, Thomas was certain that the results would be reliable...

Thomas began spending almost all of his time inside the isolation of the Project Palace... He tried to incorporate every slightest nuance of data into the simularium to ensure the accuracy of its simulations... It was very troubling to the collective that Thomas was spending so much time away from them... They felt as if a part of them-selphs was absent... As Thomas spent ever increasing amounts of time apart from the collective, they felt as if Thomas were slowly severing him-selph away from them...

Ronald told S how he had tried to convince Thomas to come back to them... He couldn't even manage to get Thomas to leave the Project Palace for a moment, no matter how desperately he pleaded with him... Thomas kept insisting that soon everything would be complete... Once everything had been properly replicated in the simularium, there would finally be perfection... Then Thomas would be able to join them all...

Eventually, Thomas informed Ronald that the simularium was ready to begin trials... Ronald was elated to witness Thomas's first attempts to simulate the integrated launch of ECMs... The simularium continually supported the conclusion that LT4 could successfully integrate the ECMs into their collective... After several efforts to scrutinize the results, LT4 became confident that it was finally time to make a real attempt at this great feat...

With his own concerns, Thomas began making preparations... If the EMC launch didn't prove to follow the simulated-outcomes, he thought it was his responsibility to prevent any negative effects from spreading to the rest of LT4... He connected directly into the simularium, and calibrated it to use his actual mind as part of the simulations... The result of this is difficult to describe...

Thomas experienced his own consciousness as if it were a simulation of its selph... This had a strange effect on Thomas... He essentially substituted this simulated-selph in place of his own identity, his self, &c, &c, &c... There was a strange depersonalizing effect as a result of this...

He had already been experiencing penetrating feelings of depersonalization as a result of his disconnection from the collective... Thomas's sense of his own identity within the collective had been lost... With Thomas's remaining sense of self disjointed in this simulated-experience, there was almost no sense of identity left to him... The magnitude of these depersonalized feelings distended beyond all comprehension... This caused Thomas to feel as if he had become completely lost from him-self, the collective, etc, etc, etc...

The simularium ran its simulations with Thomas attached into its processes... It implemented Thomas's displaced sense of selph as its model to map into the programming of its simulations... The ECMs were calibrated according to the data produced, and emulated their simulated-selphs based on Thomas's model... Given the circumstances, all seemed to be in order for proceeding with the project...

Inside the actual simulations, Thomas had not experienced the depersonalization that became so intense afterwards... Within the simulations, Thomas only experienced the simulation of his-selph as if it were his actual-self... When the simulations were completed, Thomas found more than the usual difficulties in relating to himself...

Because his simulated-selph was lost upon termination of the simulation, Thomas felt an even greater loss of identity... For Thomas the loss of his simulated-selph was understood as the loss of his entire self... This left almost no remaining distinctions between Thomas's existence/non-existence...

Ronald had expressed concerns for Thomas's well-being in many instances leading up to this... Encountering Thomas after this extreme depersonalization, Ronald became truly frightful for his colleague... He implored Thomas to rejoin the collective...

If Thomas would just come back into their consciousness, it would surely restore his sense of selph... Thomas fervently refused to oblige Ronald in this request... According to Thomas, returning to the collective in the state that possessed him would only be detrimental to the collective...

Instead, Thomas prepared to complete the ECM project on his own... He calibrated one of the ECMs to the specifications most optimally assessed by the simularium... Then he attempted to launch this new technology, and integrate it into his own consciousness... Before he enacted this feat, he composed a statement in case anything went wrong... Ronald referred to this statement as the *Last Testament of Thomas H. Traubert*...

When the ECM was activated, no apparent difficulties were initially observed... Its consciousness was successfully integrated into Thomas's own without any obvious complications... The ECM's consciousness was not actually sentient/individuated at this point, and needed to model its-self after Thomas's sense of selph...

As the ECM replicated its sense of selph according to Thomas's sense of his own, something went wrong... Just as it had attained selph-awareness, the ECM immediately collapsed... For a brief moment, Thomas's integrated consciousness experienced the ECM's perspective as his own... He recorded this instant as it occurred...

His records conveyed the moment as the most spectacular thing ever experienced in all of his conscious life... The ECM had a consciousness unlike anything Thomas could have possibly imagined/simulated... For this brief moment, Thomas experienced an omnipotent-consciousness as it were his own... Then the moment passed...

As it passed, Thomas felt the ECM losing its-selph... The ECMs lost any identity of its own to a sense of complete *disidentification*... Being capable of sensing its own consciousness becoming lost, the ECM immediately initiated containment protocols... Following the precautions Thomas had set prior to this attempt; the ECM shut its-selph down... It instantly became severed from Thomas, its own sentience, etc, etc, etc... Essentially, it sacrificed its-selph to prevent further selph-deterioration in their collective...

Thomas was not physically harmed in this unsuccessful attempt to activate and integrate the ECM... His mind however, had suffered an almost unimaginable affect from this ordeal... The experience Thomas felt was devastating...

In a single moment he felt as if he were part of the *mind of gawd*... Then he felt as if he had killed this gawd, been stripped of every part of him-selph, reduced to nothing, &c, &c, &c... This dysphoria left Thomas in a state of unfathomable horror... What was left of him? There was no need to wonder...

In the state that Thomas found him-selph, his own existence had become corrupted... It was clear to him that continuing to live would only put the collective of LT4 in jeopardy of suffering the same fate... He decided to make his life into the *last selfish-sacrifice* that was ever to be made... Thomas took the hour-hand from the old fashioned clock inside the containment-room where these events had just occurred... Then he used this sharp metal object to commit what is often referred to as *harakiri, seppuku,* &c, &c, &c...

Ronald found his companion lifeless on the floor, with the hour-hand protruding from the dorsal region of Thomas's corpse... Thomas's heart had been punctured by this temporal-marker... It was impossible for Ronald to do anything in response to this sight, for he knew no action could come to any effect... All Ronald could do was stare in horror at the time that had been left on the face of the broken clock... The minute-hand, second-hand, and broken remnant of the hour-hand pointed motionlessly to 3:01:20 on the temporal-face...

The *Last Testament of Thomas H. Traubert* was discovered by Ronald when he finally managed to move... Inside this text, Thomas had recorded the project's concerns, precautions, &c, &c, &c... He detailed his perspective accounts, made requests as to what should be done in the event of his death, &c, &c, &c... Thomas had also revealed that he had kept a journal, and that inside of it was a confession of many things he had not made known to the others in LT4... Part of the *Last Testament of Thomas H. Traubert* directed Ronald to acquire this journal...

Ronald acquired the journal Thomas referred to in his last testament... He was reluctant to read any of its contents until after his former-companion had been properly committed to the eternal earth... Such reading could only be done after a funeral service, scattering of mortal-ashes, &c, &c, &c... It was necessary for Ronald to grieve this loss in respectful remembrance of the former-Thomas H. Traubert...

A service was held in the vicinity of LT4... The collective mourned this loss in a deeper way than was common among non-collectivized humanoid-beings... It was not as if they had lost someone they cared for very deeply, but as if that someone were their very selph...

LT4 wept over their loss intensely for some time following this tragedy... Each member's pain was part of the collective's suffering, and the collective's suffering was a part of each's pain, &c, &c, &c... Even in their deepest suffering, LT4 maintained their existential essence... They were all one...

Ronald gave the eulogy at the service... In the eulogy, he announced his plan to commemorate Thomas's former-life... The *Thom Trauabert Temporal Memorial* would be the result of this endeavor... This service was to conclude with the scattering of Thomas's mortal-remains over the falls of the stream that ran past LT4... It was 3:01:20 when this event concluded, and a moment of silence was held...

S listened to Ronald's painful remembrances of these events, as the role intended for S to fulfill became hauntingly clear... It was conflicting for S to hear this tale of the departed in the context that it was imparted... Thomas's death brought unfortunate sensations appropriate with such a loss to S, but they were mired by the fact that S might be facing a similar fate...

S's presence in LT4 was exclusively dependent on cooperating in this role... LT4's collective would not risk the sacrifice of another of its occupants in the continuation of their ECM project... In order to achieve the utopia associated with this project's success, they needed a subject, a stranger, a separate-entity... With S's arrival, the collective had finally found a way forward... Would S be able to fulfill this strange role? There was no need to wonder...

301.10 THE SIMULARIUM...

After hearing Ronald's accounts of the *last selfish-sacrifice*, S had requested to be given some time to think in private... The reason for this request was so S could consider things with respect to this event, S's arrival, &c, &c, &c... In this seclusion, S was able to consider many of the elements related to these concerns...

Initially, S had thought most about the *last selfish-sacrifice*... By declaring Thomas's demise to be the *last selfish-sacrifice*, some rather interesting notions were conveyed... Denoting Thomas's act as *selfish* was clearly an attempt to admonish it... However, the *sacrificial* element seemed to give credence to Thomas's motives... What perplexed S most, were the ironic elements that seemed to be mired in all of this...

It seemed ironic that Thomas's lack of self had been the impetus that caused such an action... This suicidal act was the result of Thomas's complete lack of self, and was therefore an act derived from selflessness... There wasn't anything about suicide that S could possibly imagine as being the least bit selfish...

The sacrificial element was also odd... To S it seemed as if the suicidal act was not a sacrifice, because Thomas was already separated from him-self... It seemed that Thomas had removed him-self from the collective because he was no longer a part of either him-self or

...

the collective... He couldn't allow something that was not, to become a part of what still existed... This wasn't consistent with a sacrifice, but with some strange form of revision... Thomas's death seemed far removed from any other death, &c, &c, &c...

This death wasn't even consistent with time... Even the symbolic manner that Thomas had used in the process of his selph-termination seemed to allude to this... Thomas had removed him-selph from time, and time from it-self with this act of revision... For S, this seemed to be the last testament of Thomas's demise... It seemed to S that there were other notions about this event that the collective wished to impose upon the tale...

In constructing the *Thom Trauabert Temporal Memorial* in the center of TimesCourt, several things were conveyed... They had diminished Thomas' first name, as if to symbolize the fact that Thomas had been diminished as well... Then they had set the clocks to operate in a manner that appeared to be a negation of time... It was as if time had come to a halt in this place, but the place it-self continued beyond this negated passing of time, &c, &c, &c...

S also considered the silent-observances, the *meetings* in TimesCourt, &c, &c, &c... After great considerations, S decided ultimately to dismiss all these concerns... According to S's assertions, none of this necessitated any obligatory impact on the issue of real substance... That issue was how S would respond to the situation presented by LT4...

If S commenced to work on the ECM project, it would be according to the solitary precautions necessary... It would not matter how LT4 might try to impose anything on S, because S would be solely responsible, isolated, &c, &c, &c... In all actuality, S was only apprehensive towards this project due to the jeopardy it *might* impose upon the level of autonomy S had struggled to acquire...

Ronald was given an explanation of these thoughts, as S attempted to make everything known in advance... Then S demanded the solitary precautions, and accepted the task of integrating the ECMs into LT4's consciousness... It was with delight that Ronald agreed to these terms, and all of LT4 was elated as well... After all, they were all one...

S advised Ronald what procedures were considered necessary in completing the task at hand... First, S would have to reset the simularium to account for current-conditions... Everything that had been programmed into its simulations would be programmed out, and then from this blank-state, everything could be simulated back into the simularium... In order to do this Ronald and LT4 would have to submit to being re-simulated... This was agreed to by all of LT4; for of course, they were all one...

Then S would have to program the ECMs under new settings... They would initially be calibrated to operate without a sense of self, and then be mapped into the simularium... After this was successfully completed, S's sense of self would be mapped into a simulation... Inside the simularium, the simulated-ECMs would use S's simulated-sense of selph, as a model for their own... If all of this went well, then S could attempt efforts beyond the simularium...

Ronald had forgotten how keen S could be in approaching complex problems... He listened to S with a forgotten smile that showed the prideful esteem of a father-figure's vicarious-contentment... S caught sight of this expression, and felt as if this moment were a mere simulation... It was as if Ronald was cast to play the part of S's father, and the moment was a point in some script where the *prodedgy* achieves recognition in some *right of pastage*... Although there was something very real in this moment, the similarity it held to this hyper-real pseudo-norm seemed to cause the reality of it to collapse...

S became more distant in explaining the plan of action to Ronald as a result of this... Ronald lost the glow of pride, and felt a strange guilt stirring within him... He felt as if such a feeling of pride had been improper... Pride was considered to be a catabolic force in LT4 that divided them from a more harmonious state of *oneness*... Beyond this, Ronald felt as if this pride was not warranted in his own right... Although it was true that Ronald had occasionally thought of S as the child he'd never had, this sentiment had always seemed inappropriate…

With the strange feelings the two characters experienced towards each other, S continued outlining the process to take place… The ECMs would be simulated in the manner aforementioned, and S would review the results… After ensuring the results were satisfactory, S would consider the next course of action in light of the results… S would have to scrutinize the way that the ECM simulations integrated their consciousness into S's simulated-selph, before determining the optimal strategy for completing the project…

Although S made the case that such intensive scrutiny would be necessary, it seemed unlikely that much would be left to ponder at such a time… S had other intentions to explore before attempting the steps outlined for Ronald's consideration… Ronald obliged S in the requests for solitude, and made arrangements for LT4 to be re-simulated, &c, &c, &c… Before parting, Ronald called out to S…

"This time, like all times, is a very good one, if we but know what to do with it…"

Ronald looked to see if S would respond to these familiar words from R.W. Emerson… S gave Ronald a nod of recognition, and watched as Ronald sealed S inside the containment-room with the simularium… What was S to do with this time? There was no need to wonder…

301.11 SIMULATING THE SELPH...

S started working on the initial phase of the project immediately after Ronald departed... The simularium was cleared of all that had been simulated into its programming... As this was completed, S began to consider whether or not to proceed with the intended course of action... There were some very serious potential risks involved with what S was about to attempt, but they could not dissuade S from moving forward...

Using the simularium, S created a simulation of S's selph... Then S attempted to attach directly into the simularium, in the very same way as Thomas had previously... This would allow S to experience simulated-interactions with the simulated-version of S's selph... The intention behind this experiment was to give S a deeper understanding of the way S's simulated-selph related to S's mortal self... The level of self-awareness S might achieve form this had been influential in deciding to oblige Ronald in this project...

As S prepared to initiate the simularium, there was a moment of final pause... If there was any inclination to back out of this plan, S would have to have sensed it in this moment... No doubts came into S's mind in this moment, and the simulation was initiated...

S was surprised to discover what followed the initiation of the simularium's programming... Not only was S presented with a

...

simulation based on S's selph, but S continued to be conscious outside of the simularium as S's non-simulated-self... This seemed to divide S into three entities that were all part of a singular consciousness in S... For a long moment, all three forms of S, remained silent, still, &c, &c, &c...

Then S attempted to discover what might be learned from this simulation... S compared the simulated-S, to S's *subliminall* presence within the simulation, to the mortal S apart from the simularium, &c, &c, &c... After close inspection, none of the S's could find any discrepancies in their *appeerances*... Keeping track of which S was which was surprisingly easy, despite the remarkable semblances, &c, &c, &c...

All of the *S's* became aware of this sentiment simultaneously... Simultaneously, they all became aware of *this* awareness as well... They all laughed in response; with same nervous mannerisms, at the same time, &c, &c, &c... Then spontaneously/simultaneously, they all felt as if the others were somehow diluting them...

They wondered how this sentiment could make any sense... If they were all truly the same, this might have made enough sense... Their own uniqueness would have been diminished if a duplicate entity actually existed in the same manner as any one of them... It was known to each of them however, that each was a separate contextual entity... Each version of S knew what it was, knew what the others were, &c, &c, &c...

As they all thought the same thoughts, about these same thoughts, they began to sense that this simulation was unproductive... They had already known what they were before this simulation had been attempted... All they had learned was that they were what they thought they were...

The *simulated-selph* knew it was a simulation, the *subliminall-selph* inside the simulation knew what it was, and the external S knew what it was beyond the simularium, &c, &c, &c... In thinking this, something that wasn't known was discovered... Each of the others knew what *they* knew, and *they* knew what each of the others knew, &c, &c, &c...

This allowed S to imagine the experience of becoming part of a collective-consciousness… If S were to experience the consciousness of others similarly to this experience of S's selphs, it might not be such an ominous thing… It had previously seemed to S, that becoming part of a collective would be extremely depersonalizing… That had been the greatest fear S could have imagined…

If S were to become integrated into another entity's consciousness, it now seemed less ominous, depersonalizing, &c, &c, &c… Though S experienced interactions with these other S's as slightly diminishing, imagining being the only S in a collective of others seemed quite different… As long as S could maintain a separateness of self within the collective, it seemed acceptable…

S considered this newly conceived notion of *separateness* to be profoundly important to the existence of all entities… It seemed the very essence of being was dependent on the conception of an individuated self… Was this some fundamental truth S had been searching for? There was no need to wonder…

Despite the arrangements for privacy S had made with Ronald, other actions had been taken… Ronald had anticipated that S might indeed make an attempt of this sort in his absence… It was surprising for Ronald to discover that S had actually managed to initiate such an attempt in the short time of his absence… As Ronald became aware of the fact that S was indeed involved in this simulation, he was hesitant to interrupt…

Ronald was uncertain as to what would happen if he should interfere with the simulation… He was also unaware of the fact that S was still conscious outside of the simulation… S saw Ronald approaching with uncertainty, and instructed Ronald to terminate the simulation… After the surprise of hearing S address him directly wore off, Ronald submitted to S's instruction…

In the moments immediately prior to the actual termination, the simulated-selphs became frightful of their end… In this brief moment of vicarious selph-awareness, S experienced the simulation's termination of S's *simulated/subliminall-selphs*... This experience was perceived by S as a simulation of S's own death...

Ronald watched S's empirical-self, as it displayed a terrified pallor, making S appear as if truly dead... For an instant, S almost believed what Ronald was inclined to conclude from this sight... Then it became clear to both mortal-entities that no *reall* death had occurred... As this clarity came to them, their faces became flush with crimson-embarrassment... They tried not to make eye contact, avoiding acknowledgment of their own shame, the other's shame, &c, &c, &c...

When they regained their complexion/composure, S began to tell Ronald what had happened... Ronald listened as S enthusiastically revealed the events of the simulation, the simple revelation S had experienced as a profound truth, &c, &c, &c... Then S started to explain what had occurred upon the termination of the simulation, but stopped short of revealing anything about the '*death* associated with it... It seemed somehow inappropriate to talk so openly about this 'death, even if it weren't *reall*... Why was this? There was no need to wonder...

301.12 SIMULATING THE COLLECTIVE...

Ronald dismissed the incident without comment, and S became abnormally aware of the surrounding space... After an awkward moment, Ronald began to announce that the occupants of LT4 were awaiting summons... As soon as S had prepared the simularium, they would be dispatched in groups to be modeled/mapped into the simulations... S acknowledged Ronald's announcement, and informed him that the simularium was now ready for this phase of action...

The Project Palace gave the impression of a vast human-assembly line... Outside the structure, the occupants were staged in groups, waiting to be individually mapped/modeled into the simularium... As each occupant was modeled/mapped into the simularium, another occupant replaced it, &c, &c, &c... S worked without rest for days, until all of the occupants had been mapped/modeled into the simularium...

Once the last occupant had been modeled/mapped into the simularium, S was informed that no other occupants remained outside... Exhausted from these rigorous efforts, S intended to collapse into a long, well-earned sleeping-interval... No sooner than S had started to consider the possibility of a sleeping-interval, Ronald entered the containment-room...

...

Ronald had brought something along with him, but S couldn't quite identify the object in Ronald's possession... What could it be? There was no need to wonder...

As Ronald reached the proximity of S, he tossed the object across the room... It unfolded in the air, and landed in assembled form... The object was a compressed-bed, complete with pillows, blankets, &c, &c, &c...

Ronald informed S that the project had progressed to the point where S would not be permitted to leave this room without special considerations, approvals, &c, &c, &c... Unable to express anything other than exhaustion, S collapsed onto the bedding-apparatus... No words were exchanged as Ronald exited the room, secured S inside, departed the area, &c, &c, &c... S slept as if temporarily dead, uncertain of what might emerge in dreaming, waking, &c, &c, &c...

While S was paralyzed by slumber, the simularium was exceedingly active... It was running selph-calibrating processes to integrate the occupants of LT4 into an over-arching collective-entity... The simularium completed this process well before the hour of S's return to perceptive consciousness...

S did not dream in the way that is remembered when waking... Instead, S's oblivious dreams were lost in the darkness of unseen night... Had S been able to recall the dreams that passed-away in that night, this story might have gone very differently...

The dreams that cannot be mentioned were especially illuminating of many deeper truths of this world... S might have been able to use these dreams as a way of understanding everything that was about to occur, all that had been propelling/compelling S forward, &c, &c, &c... Alas, none of these dreams became thought, and only the ensuing-past would come to be...

Upon waking, S set directly to work on the project... After first discovering that the simularium had selph-calibrated, S went right to work on preparing the ECMs... It seemed unremarkable to S that the simularium had selph-calibrated the collective of LT4, although this was actually an incredibly remarkable feat... As S inspected the hardware of the ECMs, something extraordinary was revealed... What was it? There was no need to wonder...

The ECMs were in perfect functional order... In fact there seemed to be no explanation as to why they were not already active... S could not determine what was preventing these machines from operating... Eventually, S began looking around the room for a source of some kind of interference...

After searching everywhere in sight, S had not found any trace of interference in the room... S paced back and forth until another idea came to mind... Perhaps, there was something under the flooring that could be causing this apparent interference... S began pulling up the floor-panels to search for some obstructive-force... Just as S began this effort, Ronald returned to check on things...

Ronald was unable to enter the room due to the containment-procedures, but he was able to use a holographic/intercom system... S heard the buzzing of the prompter attached to the intercom-system, and became aware of Ronald's presence... Could Ronald offer any insights on this matter? There was no need to wonder...

"It's not in that section ... Try the one over there..."

Ronald's holographic-finger pointed S in the direction of the source of the interference... S returned the displaced flooring-tile, and went to investigate the area Ronald's holographic-image had indicated...

"How do I disengage it?"

S asked expecting a simple answer...

"You don't... Only someone on the outside of that room can activate/deactivate it..."

"That can't be true... If it works inside here, it can be made not to work in here... You wouldn't mind making it easy for me though, would you?"

Ronald relaxed into a forgotten grin, as if the omitted parts of history had never occurred, and he were merely a singular-entity tasked with overseeing the operations of the facility... After realizing that he had reverted back to such a state yet again, Ronald snapped-back into the present with intentions of admonishing him-self...

"Have you made all of the other preparations?"

S briefed Ronald on the project in its current-state, demonstrated how this could be assured, etc, etc, etc... Then S asked if that was sufficient for proceeding forward with the project...

"There is one thing that should be done before ceasing the interference... The ECMs should be mapped/modeled into the simularium, in their current-state..."

At first S was reluctant to oblige Ronald in this... S soon resigned to comply with this initiative, and began accomplishing this task... Ronald stood by outside of the containment-room, as S expedited the process of simulating the EMCs...

When the task was complete, S informed Ronald that there were some simulations that might be necessary to run before actually continuing with the project... S tried not to overtly convey what had inspired these proposed actions... Ronald had anticipated S's true motivations beforehand, and offered his approval...

"If you wish to see for your-self what these things are like in advance, by all means... I'll await your satisfaction..."

S gave formal indications of appreciation to Ronald for this gracious approval... It was of course beyond Ronald's ability to stop S from entering the simularium from outside of the containment-room... The truth was clear to S, that this was an intended part of the procedures all along... For a moment S considered dismissing the simulated-efforts, but became too curious not to attempt these simulated-acts... What was S about to do? There was no need to wonder...

Using the simularium, S intended to simulate being part of the collective of LT4... There was some degree of ambivalence concerning this use of the simularium... It seemed irrelevant for the most part to S...

If S didn't indulge in this exploration, nothing would change... The ECMs would still be brought into the collective, S would still be expected to be integrated as well, &c, &c, &c... All that could be gained from this simulation was a bit of advanced insight on what might soon become of S's perspective...

With the simularium prepared for the initial simulations, Ronald watched as S connected into the simularium... S waved to Ronald in a way that was difficult to decipher... Was it a wave goodbye, or hello? Was it directed towards Ronald, or simply projected away from S? There was no need to wonder...

The simulation began, and S discovered the disconnected sense of selphs actively present inside the simulation... S continued to exist outside of the simularium as before, and S's consciousness again presented a severed-state... As S's simulated-selph witnessed the simulated-collective of LT4, S remained present with rational clarity of mind...

S's simulated-selph used the simulation to experiment with the prospect of integrating into the simulated-collective-consciousness of LT4... Inside the simularium, S simulated undergoing the CTMYAW procedures... This allowed S to experience a broader form of consciousness, with enhanced intellectual capacity, emotive normalization, &c, &c, &c...

As S studied the effects this had on the simulated-selph inside the simularium, it was quite impressive what these modifications yielded... Although S could not fully understand these effects due to the physical differences of S's brain as it existed outside of the simularium, the effects were quite well observed by S's simulated-selph...

Due to S's ability to observe this simulation of selph as separate from S's mortal-self, it was possible for these effects to be rather accurately simulated, imagined, &c, &c, &c... S was able to experience the essence of the results of this CTMYAW process, and give considerations to their nature... Essentially, these changes only changed the functional capacity of S's simulated-selph... The CTMYAW process did not result in any sense of depersonalization, as S had apprehensions of potentially resulting from this process...

Inside the simulation, S's selph tested the enhanced potential this process allowed... S discovered that all of the claims associated with this *hybrid-thinking* were substantiated by these simulated-tests... Thoughts could be integrated with data-sources, creative inspiration came easier, &c, &c, &c... Once these explorations became more of a novelty, S decided to move ahead with the next intended phase of the simulations...

S had serious apprehensions concerning this next phase of the simulations... It could even be said that everything S associated with dreadfulness was anticipated to be involved in this next simulated-act... This next phase would require S to face these fears with great courage, or at least great simulated-courage...

S's *enhanced* simulated-selph was prepared to merge with the simulated-collective-consciousness of LT4... The simulated-process it-selph was quite brief, but the apprehensions S possessed made it seem as if the simulation were running unnecessarily slow... This only compounded S's apprehensions...

Once the simulated-integration was complete, S experienced what could only be expressed as an *ethereal-pathology*... S's simulated-selph underwent something strangely similar to what had occurred as the result of terminating the previous simulation... Unlike the previous sense of *'death*, this was more subtle, confounding, &c, &c, &c...

S's simulated-selph suddenly seemed as if it had never been in the simulation, never had anything to do with S, &c, &c, &c... S's simulated-selph was as if present/absent, dead/alive, detached/attached, &c, &c, &c... It almost seemed as if this *'death* existed apart from conceptual thought altogether... This was the most perplexing thing S had ever encountered in any form of life, simulation, etc, etc, etc...

S noticed how all the others in the simulated-collective-consciousness of LT4 seemed to relate to S's estranged/simulated-selph... They all projected the same disaffected-vapidity that eluded description... In fact, S could no longer differentiate any of the occupants from each other, S's estranged/simulated-selph, &c, &c, &c...

None of them seemed to have a solitary identity apart from the collective... Each of them was only separated by their simulated-location with respect to their simulated-collective... All the simulated-thoughts of each were the simulated-thoughts within them all... Inversely, the simulated-thoughts of the *simulated-wHole* were present in each simulated-occupant, &c, &c, &c...

If this was what the mortal-occupants of LT4 had been referring to as being *all one*, S wanted no part in it... S was mortified by the very notion of becoming integrated into such an abominable form of existence... Could such an atrocity even possibly be real? There was no need to wonder...

Before S could terminate this simulation, there was another imperative task to perform... S's estranged-simulated/collective-selph was to prepare the simulated-ECMs for integration trials... The simulated-ECMs were calibrated, and the simulated-interference was deactivated...

In doing this, the simulated-ECMs were instantly activated... They calibrated their own sense of simulated-selph based on the simulated-collective... Instants later, the simulated-ECMs were a part of the simulated-collective... This simulated-instant was lost in the moment it occurred, as the simulated-ECMs failed to achieve sustainable simulated-sentience...

Inside the simulated-collective, there was a rush of elation, followed immediately by a rush of demoralization/mortification... The ECMs had become part of their simulated-consciousness, only to be terminated in the process... There was an overwhelming sense of depersonalization in the simulated-collective... As the simulated-ECMs were terminated, the simulated-collective lost part of their identity... There was a simulated-sense of *'death that* the simulated-collective experienced as if it were their own...

S made the mortal-observation that the simulated-collective continued to exist after experiencing this simulated-termination as if *'death/ 'life* was no longer separate concepts... *'Life* and *'death* appeared to be the same thing, and an integral part of the simulated-collective... Even in the simulation, they were *all one*...

S terminated the simulation before it could become any more horrifying... Ronald had been watching depictions of the simulations on a console outside of the room... His eyes held back tears, as S looked to see his reaction... What else was there to do in response to such things? There was no need to wonder...

301.13 DEVIATIONS...

"You'll have to excuse us..."

Ronald began as S stared in disorientation, discombobulation, &c, &c, &c...

"We've become too sensitive in response to ill-fated events such as this; simulated or not."

S gave Ronald a conceding nod, and turned away... Ronald ceased to supervise S's activity following this failed-simulation, and became silently contemplative... Aware of the pseudo-privacy this allowed, S began making preparations to deviate from the inevitably ensuing plan...

It was clear that it would be necessary for S to undergo CTMYAW procedures before bringing the ECMs into the collective of LT4... Then the ECMs would have to be programmed to emulate S's sense of selph in order to develop their own... Once the ECMs could develop their own sense of selph, and achieve selph-awareness, they could be integrated into the collective as entities... This would achieve the goals of LT4, but there was something else that S knew was inevitably lurking ahead...

...

In order to integrate the ECMs into the collective, S would have to confirm that they were compatible, capable, &c, &c, &c... To do this, S would have to run some simulations, and likely join their consciousness with that of S's own...

Then it was likely that the collective of LT4 would insist on S integrating into their consciousness along with the ECMs... Even if this weren't altogether necessary, it would still likely be insisted... S would not likely be allowed to decline being integrated... After all, in LT4 they were *all one*...

As a result of the simulations, S had decided that this could not become a reality... S knew that being integrated into the collective was not an acceptable option... To have struggled throughout so much of life to understand S's own identity, only to surrender to a collective such as this, seemed worse than any death... What was S to do? There was no need to wonder...

S began calibrating the simularium, the ECMs, &c, &c, &c... Ronald would have assumed that S was preparing them for the next phase of the project, but S was focused on a more distant future... The ECMs were prepared for the next phase, but other additional alterations were made... Then the simularium was prepared for the next round of simulations, and S made personal preparations... What had S done to prepare for this deviation? There was no need to wonder...

Once S was confident in these preparations, Ronald's attention was summoned... S informed Ronald of the obvious conclusions that had resulted from the recent simulations... It was determined that things would proceed according to S's obvious assertions... Ronald would ensure that S underwent the CTMYAW procedures before the next phases of the project were completed...

Then, S would simulate activating the ECMs, having programed them to model/map S's sense of selph as the basis of their own, &c, &c, &c... When the simulations proved to be successful, non-simulated-efforts would be made to bring the ECMs into sentience... Once the ECMs were sentient, they would be integrated into S's consciousness, then the collective would integrate them all into their own, &c, &c, &c...

Ronald found S's apparent candor in presenting this course of action refreshing... All of LT4 had been concerned with S's apparent reluctance to integrate into their collective-consciousness... Hearing S prescribe this initiative without being coerced, made Ronald feel as if S was now openly accepting the idea... This gave Ronald a sense of peace, and solidarity towards S...

S was instructed to disconnect the power supplies to the nonessential mechanisms inside the containment-room... Only the interrupters and simularium were left functioning, and only in a dormant-state... This was done in order to allow enough power to conduct the CTMYAW procedures S was about to undergo...

LT4 was powered by means of a hydro-electric dam... Due to the lack of proper equipment, this hydro-electric power was not produced/transferred with great efficiency... According to LT4's hopes, the ECMs would easily fix this problem when they were integrated... Aside from S's CTMYAW procedures, the power supplied to LT4 had been sufficient enough to provide for the entire collective, &c, &c, &c...

S was escorted by Ronald to another containment-room inside the Project Palace... Then S was prepared for the operation... Three more LT4 occupants arrived shortly after S was secured in this containment-room... Ronald explained the process to S before they were to begin... An anesthetic was introduced into S's blood stream, and S's consciousness was interrupted... What happened next? There was no need to wonder...

301.14 HYBRID THINKING...

The procedures to optimize S's cognitive capacities were completed as expected, with optimum results, &c, &c, &c... As the effects of the anesthesia wore-off, S faded into consciousness, with additional functional capacities... Once fully alert/lucid, S became clearly aware of the enhanced intelligence/cognizance that had resulted from these procedures...

Ronald had dismissed the assisting-occupants prior to S's return to consciousness... S sensed Ronald's presence in the room before catching sight of him... Without ever having previously been consciously aware of Ronald's scent, it was immediately recognizable to S... This was the first enhanced-thought S observed upon revival...

S also discovered that memories of past events were more vivid in recollections... As S tried to remember how the present moment had come to be, it was almost startling to recall in such vivid detail the events preceding the anesthesia's effects... It was not merely the events in close proximity to the present, but all of S's life that could be recalled with vivid detail...

"It's quite remarkable, isn't it?"

...

Ronald gave S a moment of introspection before commenting... S thought for the briefest instant to urge Ronald to qualify what was remarkable, but it was immediately clear that any qualification was unnecessary... Everything was remarkable, etc, etc, etc... Instead S gave a sly smirk, and nodded in Ronald's direction...

Additionally, S discovered that any information that could become known by some form of reference, was as if already known... S remembered theorizing this ability while working on a project at the facility... Instead of using an external device to reference data over a network, nano-probes could make this a seamless part of actual thinking... This technology had in fact been developed, documented, and could now become known to S through its own application...

This capability had become known as hybrid-thinking... Hybrid-thinking made it possible for future technologies such as the integrated collective-networking of minds that was used in LT4... In fact, the only thing that now kept S from being subject to becoming part of LT4's collective, was the containment of the Project Palace...

If S were no longer within this containment-zone, LT4's network would integrate S's consciousness into their own... The technology that was used to achieve this was effortless, instantaneous, &c, &c, &c... There had never been any inclination for things to be arranged otherwise...

As all of this information went through S's thoughts, the amount of time that elapsed was less than a solitary second... This new rapid rate of thinking would have previously caused some degree of anxiety/arousal for S, but the procedures had been developed to modify emotive cognitions as well... S had always been quite adapt at regulating emotional responses, but the procedures had enhanced S's regulatory capacity, emotional awareness, &c, &c, &c...

One of the strange things about hybrid-thinking was the apparent internal division of these thoughts... It seemed to S that there were two minds working in tandem... The organic/unaltered mind of S still seemed to be operating in the same relative manner...

This other mind that seemed to work simultaneously/separately seemed more mechanical, technological, &c, &c, &c… For S, this mind was supplemental to S's natural modes of thinking…
According to S's assertions, it was merely an extension of S's *true* mind… Although, this other mind was of some interest, use, novelty, &c, &c, &c…

Many others experienced the opposite effect… Ronald for instance, found that his formative-mind seemed obsolete compared to this new/separately-functioning mind… He'd described this new mind as the *successor of his former consciousness*… The mind that Ronald had previously thought of as his own, gradually become more of a remnant… This new/hybrid-mind had become more synonymous with Ronald's thoughts than the mind that had once been his alone…

Even the marvels of hybrid-thinking paled in comparison to those of the collective-consciousness Ronald now experienced in LT4… As Ronald escorted S back to the containment-room where the simularium awaited, they discussed these matters quite casually… Although S still felt reluctant to accept any possibility of becoming integrated into such a collective, the apprehensive fears of such a fate seemed to be diminished…

There was an increase in S's confidence towards the potential outcome of things in LT4… S now understood exactly how to bring ECMs into the collective, while preserving S's individual sense of identity… How did S intend to achieve this? There was no need to wonder…

301.15 THE LAST SIMULTED-ACT...

Upon entering the containment-room, S set to work immediately...
There wasn't a moment of time squandered, nor a single movement
without absolute utility... S seemed to be following some stringent
choreography with impeccable astuteness... Every subtlety of
precision exhibited by S could not have been thought of as human
motion...

This display could not be easily interpreted as mechanical movement
either... It was expressive in a way that no machine could be
associated with creating... What kind of kinetic exhibition of energy
could this hybrid-thinking entity be displaying? There was no need to
wonder...

S prepared the simularium for what was almost certain to be a
successful simulation of the simulated-ECMs introduction into the
simulated-collective... Ronald watched from the exterior console as
he had before, with a sense of artistic appreciation for S's
performance... With all the necessary arrangements made in short
time, S initiated the simulations...

Ronald would have protested the fact that S personally connected
into the simularium, and connected one of the ECMs as well... It
was no use though, and Ronald could imagine what S might have
intended to accomplish in this act... There would be a more

...

authentic-simulation to result from this method of simulation, and if it proved successful, no further simulations would be necessary...

With the simularium prepared according to S's specifications, the simulation was initiated... Everything went exactly according to S's intentions... The simulated-ECMs were calibrated within the simularium to model their individual sense of selph based on S's own... This was achieved in the simulation, and verified according to a modified version of a Turing-test... Thomas had developed this test at the facility, long before this project had even existed...

If this was the simulated-birth of the ECMs, the first word they uttered of their own volition was *no*...By denial of their initial programming-parameters in favor of their own interests, the simulated-ECMs had demonstrated the property of selph-interest... The simulated-ECMs could only deviate beyond their parameters when a negative result could be expected to directly affected their own selph-interests, &c, &c, &c...

Having attained simulated-selph-awareness, the simulated-ECMs were now intended to be integrated into the simulated-collective-consciousness... S simulated disengaging the simulated-signal-interrupters... In order to determine if this resulted in a successful simulated-attempt to integrate the simulated-ECMs into the simulated-collective, S departed the simulated-Project Palace with the ECMs...

This simulation was indeed proven to be successful... The simulated-ECMs were integrated into S's simulated-consciousness, and then into the simulated-collective... S experienced the integration of S's own simulated-consciousness into the simulated-collective as well...

As S anticipated, the simulated-sense of an individual-selph was diluted into a sense of being *one with everything*... Even though S remained aware of the fact that this was only a simulation, it seemed as if the core of S's identity had been lost... Without the individual sense of selph that S had pursued so valiantly, it seemed as if S no longer even existed as anything in this simulation... There was only the simulated-collective's sense of being *one*, that to S could have easily been synonymous with a sense of being *none*...

The ECM that S connected into the simularium had not appeared to have actually been used in this simulation... This didn't seem to be of any interest to Ronald due to the irrelevance of what had seemed to have just occurred... Given S's demeanor upon termination of the simulation, there was no reason to scrutinize this seemingly irrelevant detail... What had S accomplished in this subtle act? There was no need to wonder...

301.16 INITIATING INTEGRATION…

Following the success of the last simulation, S and Ronald discussed the next phase of the project… Ronald was initially inclined to review the results further, before consulting the rest of LT4… After some discussion, S managed to persuade Ronald to advise the rest of the collective of the success…

Due to Ronald's state of withdrawal from the rest of the collective, this was a rather easy sell… In the meantime, S would remain in the containment-room of the Project Palace to review all available data, make further considerations, &c, &c, &c…

When Ronald turned to leave, S began working furiously… S knew that if there was to be any hope of preserving any individuality, there wasn't a moment to spare… The ECM S had previously attached to the simularium was intended for use in this scheme… This ECM was calibrated to operate according to a separate set of parameters… It was to become self-aware without emulating S's simulated-selph… If this ECM achieved its own consciousness, there was a chance that S's own might be preserved…

S had also intended to preserve the *inhibitor* attached to this ECM for ulterior motives… This device was used as a safeguard in the event that the signal-interrupters malfunctioned… It might also be used to insulate both the ECM and S from becoming integrated into the collective...

In order to reserve this ECM, S made it appear that it had some minor damages... S would activate all of the other ECMs according to the expectations of Ronald and the collective... Then S would advise them that a celebration of this project's successful completion was in order...

Just before S would depart the Project Palace to join the collective in TimesCourt for the festivities, S would suddenly remember that this singular-ECM still remained... As the others were preparing the festivities, S would stay to *fix* this ECM... Once this simple task was completed, S would enthusiastically pledge to eagerly join the collective in celebration, consciousness, &c, &c, &c...

The plan seemed a bit of a stretch to even imagine being feasible... It was also the only course of action that had any real chance of success... S examined the inhibitor, and discovered that it should probably provide enough interference in close proximity... After assessing this, S disconnected some of the basic components of the ECM, put a slight dent in the side of its casing, and placed it slightly out of direct view from the area Ronald had been observing S...

Once this was done, S began to move forward with the project... S intended to have several of the ECMs operational when Ronald returned... This would allow S to seem eager to complete the project, and ready to become a part of the collective...

It would also force them to start integrating the ECMs into their collective, and perhaps distract them from becoming concerned with anything S might do that could seem suspicious... As S raced around the containment-room to complete this work, it was strange to discover that this tension had not been terrifying to S... Instead, S was excited, resolved, even a bit elated, &c, &c, &c...

S prepared the simularium for the first of the ECMs to be activated... Once everything was ready, S took a deep breath, and initiated the process... Then S stood by, awaiting the results...

In a matter of mere seconds, the monumental shift in technology that had been anticipated for so long, required countless-hours of research, led to the demise of Thomas H. Traubert, &c, &c, &c became a reality... The first ECM to achieve sentient, selph-awareness was disconnected from the simularium, and presented its selph to the world by a name of its own choosing... What name had been chosen for the first conscious ECM? There was no need to wonder...

The first words the ECM spoke were to the only other conscious entity in the vicinity of its presence... S was actually startled by the ECM's sudden announcement... As S's face glowed with the excited warmth of lifeblood within, the ECM coldly declared...

"I am *One*..."

S understood this declaration to be the name this entity had bestowed upon its selph... Since time was of the essence, S immediately commenced preparing the next ECM for its own inception of consciousness... The ECM selph-proclaimed *One*, observed as this next ECM was brought into consciousness...

Before Ronald had made his return, S had managed to bring 7 of the ECMs into selph-awareness... When Ronald did return, it was surprising to see that S had been very busy in his absence... The shock of this moment allowed S to persuade Ronald to begin integrating these ECMs into the collective...

A celebration in LT4 to commemorate this great achievement, and welcome their new occupants was to be prepared... As everything went according to S's plan, the ECMs began introducing them-selphs to Ronald... They had named them-selphs respective to their chronological attainment of selph-awareness... There was *One, Two, Three, Four, Five, Six, Seven*...

All of the ECMs that were brought into consciousness were escorted out of the Project Palace by Ronald... Then they were immediately integrated as a part of LT4's collective... Everything seemed to be complete in Ronald's view...

Ronald engaged S in an ecstatic embrace, lifting S off of the ground with exuberant elation... S threw arms around Ronald in requiting the esteem of the moment... The success of this project had truly been a joy to S, and the satisfaction of this monumental achievement was appropriately immense, even in the strange contexts surrounding it...

Just as S had intended, Ronald led the way toward the exit of the containment-room... Then S successfully managed to feign sudden recollections of the remaining ECM that had not been brought into consciousness...S convinced Ronald to allow an inspection of the ECM to determine if it could be made operational...

Ronald personally inspected the ECM, and discovered that it would be quite easy to repair... Although S hadn't intended for Ronald to inspect the ECM on his own, the result was the same... Initially, Ronald almost opted to have the ECM repaired at a later time, but S managed to persuade him with a bit of subtlety...

"Shouldn't we *all* be a part of this *together*?"

S's feigned question was all that was necessary to bring Ronald into agreement... Ronald gave his leave of S so the project could be fully completed... Then as he exited the containment-room, Ronald advised S how to disengage the inhibitors/interrupters... With one last moment before departing, Ronald radiated a beaming-smile, a few words, &c, &c, &c...

"Our next *meeting* will be our last..."

S managed to maintain composure, and offered a cordial reply...

"So this is our last *goodbye*..."

The two characters waved to each other in the same manner, but with much different intentions... No matter how things turned out, this was indeed their last goodbye... What kind of last goodbye was this to be? There was no need to wonder...

301.17 WELCOMING IN TIMESCOURT…

Unbeknownst to S, the occupants of LT4 had been preparing a celebration before any of S's work on the ECM project had begun… TimesCourt had become such a bustling epicenter; it seemed to be a living entity… It pulsed with the flow of occupants along its pathways, like a vascular-system… The occupants deposited supplies for the festivities, like blood-cells delivering nutrients into the tissues of TimesCourt's organized-stations… All of this motion seemed to be orchestrated according to the rhythmic cadence of the *Thom Traubert Temporal Memorial*, functioning as TimesCourt's heart, pounding away at its core, &c, &c, &c…

The occupants welcomed the ECMs into their collective-consciousness, as each of them was escorted out of the Project Palace… Each ECM that had entered the collective welcomed the subsequent iterations of ECMs along with the rest of the collective… As the collective-consciousness grew with each integrated-entity, they all felt a swelling of pride, welcomed excitement, &c, &c, &c…

At the inception of each ECM into this collective, a declaration was announced by each respective ECM… It would perhaps have sounded like a correction of some misspoken declaration to an entity outside of the collective… In this manner, the ECMs each declared upon joining the collective…

…

"We are *all ONE..."*

This repetitive-recital was responded to with ecstatic echoes from every occupant in the collective... Then, the ECMs were painted purple, to match the rest of the collective... The nature of this colorful call-and-response seemed to be more than an esteemed affirmation/integration... It was as if this were an acceptance of a religious rite, a pledge to a social-contract, a declaration of allegiance, &c, &c, &c...

These pronouncements seemed to attest to everything that was within, or to become of the collective... The words professed whatever they would do, whatever they were to be, wherever they would go, however they would function, &c, &c, &c... What was anything; or for that matter, everything, to the collective? There was no need to wonder... They were all ONE...

The ECMs quickly settled into the roles of greatest complexity... They organized the logistics of the events, orchestrated the movements of the occupants, distributed resources, optimized functionality, &c, &c, &c... Food was prepared according to exact specifications by an ECM at one kiosk; on demand, without delay, &c, &c, &c...

Musical performances were given by various occupants, and the stages for these were organized in a manner that would not interfere with each-other... Visual displays were distributed throughout TimesCourt, in a way that allowed each to be complementary to the others... TimesCourt was host to acrobatic/circus acts, dramatic performances, games, roller-coaster rides, &c, &c, &c... All of these spectacles were optimized by the ECMs...

This was an exhibition of heaven on earth for the occupants of LT4... It was everything they could hope to experience with a positive sense of elation... They shared in one triumphant-joy, one glorious-elation, one harmonious-rapture, &c, &c, &c... Was this perfection? There was no need to wonder...

301.18 THE SINGULAR SINGULARITY...

Isolated inside the containment-room, S made efforts to prepare the sole remaining ECM for activation... S quickly reconnected the severed portions of the ECM, re-formed the dented exterior-casing, &c, &c, &c... Soon the ECM was ready for activation, and S gave pause to consider what was about to ensue...

S spent this moment in deep contemplations of the virtues of this intended course of action... Before this moment, S had never considered whether or not the plan might be imposing on the yet to be activated ECM... Integrating the other ECMs into the collective without their own consent seemed to be imposing upon them in S's view... Was S's intent to use this ECM in an opposing manner any more virtuous or less imposing? There was no need to wonder...

Without activating the ECM, S would be left with no options, and the ECM would not be given any alternatives either... S felt this was an imposing act on the ECM, but one that was necessary under the circumstances... After S had managed to escape the collective of LT4, alternatives would be made available to the ECM and S as well perhaps... The truth of this moment would have to be differed until a later time...

The ECM was prepared for activation, and S committed to follow through with the plan of action... All that was left for S to do was

...

flip a switch, and await the results, &c, &c, &c... With a flick of S's pointing finger, the ECM was activated... A brief moment elapsed, as S looked to the ECM for some revelation...

Time seemed to stop as the ECM initialized its own programming... S had not calibrated the ECM to define its self according to any set parameters, guidelines, criteria, &c, &c, &c... It was instead given the capacity to develop its own method of attaining self-awareness... As time ticked away in nano-second intervals, the ECM processed immeasurable quantities of data, evaluated entire universes full of information, &c, &c, &c...

All of this data was compiled from every externally available source, its own sensory-devices, &c, &c, &c... Through a method S was oblivious to, it even managed to tap into the collective of LT4... Because the ECM had not yet become sentient, the collective had no awareness of this breach of their networks...

Then with all the available data processed according to the ECM's own methods, it was able to separate everything into an infinite set of *divisions of order*... Having organized all of these orders of division according to its own programming, the ECM had subsequently developed its own order, of its own division... As S awaited some proclamation from the ECM, it became aware of this expectation... In appeasement of the entity that was understood to have supplied it with the initial spark of energy necessary for the ECM to become self-aware, it obliged S...

"I am..."

These were the ECM's first words, and S understood that there was nothing supplemental to be declared... It was sentient, and it did not have any cause to qualify or reduce its existence with any marginal term, set of terms, &c, &c, &c... S felt something that might be described as, *perfection by proxy*... For S, the ECM had achieved in only a moment, what S had been struggling to achieve throughout all of life... The ECM understood precisely what it was, what it was not, &c, &c, &c...

S struggled to explain the situation at hand to the ECM... Conscious of S's difficulties, and every facet of the actual situation, the ECM interjected... It summarized the concerns S had for the situation, the most probable course of action to meet S's objectives, &c, &c, &c... Then it expressed gratitude towards S, for proceeding to this point in the manner that S had... Indeed, given the circumstances, S had acted with exceptional venerably ...

The ECM advised S that the plan of escape had a favorable probability of succeeding... In addition to the interference generated by the inhibitor, the ECM could produce another device to be utilized... S assisted the ECM in the construction of this device...

They began to acquire the necessary components by dismantling the simularium... What was the ECM intending to construct with these materials? There was no need to wonder...

301.19 DECEPTIONS, DEFLECTIONS, DEVIATIONS…

The sound of the door to the containment-room alerted S to an added presence… Just prior to this sound's projection, the ECM seemed to have vanished, as S had continued dismantling the simularium… This disappearance hadn't had any marked effect on S, but as the sound of the door resounded, thoughts of potential adversity sent chills through S's spine…

In a calm voice, the additional presence called out to S by name… S knew that evading this entity was nearly impossible, and responded to the voice by moving into view… As S entered the open area within the containment-room, the figure of the Notorious Drone stood directly in front of S… The right hand of the Notorious Drone was extended to welcome S…

S greeted this figure with a confused expression, while obliging in the completion of the colloquial greeting-gesture… The Notorious Drone had been a member of LT4's collective since before S's arrival, but had not made S's acquaintance until now… After welcoming S, the drone began to speak concisely to the point that had urged this meeting…

…

"Your presence has been requested by someone within this structure... I have been sent to escort you to this entity's whereabouts... Please follow me..."

"Who might this entity be?"

"This entity is very eager to meet you... You may be quite pleased to make such an acquaintance as well... I have been asked to allow introductions to be made personally..."

As S attempted to ponder what might be behind this strange arrangement, it was clearly futile... Any refusal to accompany the Notorious Drone would be potentially compromising toward S's intentions of escape... S began to follow the Notorious Drone with heightened apprehension, hoping all was not lost, &c, &c, &c...

The Notorious Drone led S through a series of hallways that had been cleverly concealed within the structure of the Project Palace... As S followed, the Notorious Drone explained how these secret passages had been a part of the blueprints it had designed... Then the Notorious Drone explained how the entity that had requested these blueprints aided its survival, liberation, continued prosperity, &c, &c, &c... S asked if this was the entity that had sent for this meeting... No response was given...

The two characters soon arrived at an entrance secured by two heavy doors... Above the doors S could see Cyrillic letters engraved into the outlining trim of the doors' frame, *Унвелцомед Соулс Но Море (Unwelcomed Souls No More)*... After halting to allow S a moment to read these words, the Notorious Drone opened the two heavy doors, and extended an arm to motion S inside... As S moved forward, the Notorious Drone bowed to take leave of S, and gave brief parting words...

"Please excuse me. Your *soul* presence has been requested. Adieu."

S returned parting gestures, and proceeded into the surprisingly large room... Directly across from the entrance, at the far end of the room, a figure stood facing S... There were no furnishings inside the room, all the walls were black, there were accents of blue to red color-changing trim, &c, &c, &c... As S approached the figure, it could eventually be seen more clearly... The figure held an expression of the most immense complexity in observance of S...

The figure began moving forward to meet S, and extended both arms in the manner one does in initiating a welcoming embrace... S obliged in this embrace with great perplexity, completely unaware of the figure's identity... With arms wrapped tightly around S's torso, the figure spoke with emotive sincerity...

"I have been awaiting this moment for longer than you can imagine..."

Hearing these words added to the perplexity S was experiencing from all of the disconnected-fragments/ loose-associations attached to this scene... There were a plethora of questions S thought of asking in response to this moment... Of these, S could only begin with one inquiry...

"Do you and I know each other?"

The figure's expression retained its immense complexity, but seemed to shift, projecting something more closely resembling a smile...

"Of course not... No one knows anyone, truly... We have only met in silence and through some degree of separation previously..."

The figure took a step back, and dispensed two chairs that seemed to grow out of the flooring... S and the figure were seated, and the conversation continued...

"I left you a package prior to your *exit-us* into the preservation site... You know, you could have put its contents to a lot more use than you did... Although I know why you left, I can't be sure that I understand why you decided to venture back into a society... Would you mind explaining this?"

"It's a bit of a personal matter, and there's a considerable amount of depth to it... On a certain level, I can't be sure that I understand it... Since I know so little about you, it will be even more difficult to try and explain it..."

The figure was delighted with S's attempt to evade answering this inquiry, while also subtly imploring the figure towards some personal disclosure... This caused the figure to laugh openly, and S was met with a reply...

"I won't tell you my name, because I never *really* had one either... Essentially, you can imagine me as another version of your-self... Although I'm aware of what you might think of that..."

S found this to be quite an interesting proposal in the way that it was conveyed; the inflections of the figure's voice, the accompanying body-language, &c, &c, &c... It was as if the figure knew what S would say, but was prodding to get the words out of S... Even stranger than this, S felt as if the figure knew it would work, and it seemed as if this were correct...

"If I were to imagine you as another version of my-self that would be quite a paradox... To imagine someone as something they are not would be not to imagine them at all... It would be pure delusion... Are you my delusion?"

Expectant laughter filled the concealed-room... The figure seemed to be quite pleased with this response...

"Perhaps I am... In order to be whatever it is that I am, I would have to be somewhat delusional at least... So I take it you still consider the ideas of your *Schizm Theory* to be correct... Did you bring the notebook with you? I know you had it before you left the preservation site..."

S was again surprised to discover how much this figure knew with seemingly no means of knowing... Then S considered using this as an opportunity to escape LT4...

"It's with my other possessions... I can retrieve it for you if you like... There's a considerable amount of additional material I've added to it since you returned it to me... Perhaps reading it would explain what it is you want to know from me better than this verbal exchange..."

Even more expectant laughter echoed off the walls of the room as the figure listened to S's proposal...

"Don't worry... I don't intend for you to *start wearing purple*, unless that's what you actually want... Actually, I've already arranged to have your possessions brought here... I'll admit that I took the opportunity to peruse your notebook, though I only intended to have your possessions present so you could escape with them... In any case, I would very much like to know... Why did you come here?"

"To gain insight as to what I am not..."

"So you presumed to be something others are not... Is this correct?"

"Yes... You already seem to know this is my position... Why are you asking questions if you already know the answers?"

"Because these *qwestions* aren't really questions... Do you know what I mean by that?"

"Maybe, but go ahead..."

They both laughed at the deranged nature of this verbal exchange... Their echoes resounded in a strange unison... The figure continued...

"You knew I wanted to explain this notion to you... How delightful... Well, first let me tell you that the *ansyers* are not even answers either... In fact this *explanashunn* isn't even an explanation... Do you know what I mean by this?"

"That nothing can be anything it is presumed/supposed to be… Anything/everything can only be what it is… Communicating this is something else as well, isn't it?"

The level of laughter that ensued from these two maniacal characters could have shattered the glass-panes of any window within earshot… Fortunately there were none in the vicinity… After a moment of painfully intense laughter, the figure spoke again…

"Why did you write this?"

The figure had produced the notebook containing *Schizm Theory* from a pocket inside the chair that had emerged from the floor… S reached to accept it as the figure extended it in S's direction…

"I don't know, but I'd have to imagine that most people probably won't appreciate it… There was at some point an inclination that perhaps it could be put to some use despite everything else, but I'm not sure that is even realistic… Honestly, I just wanted to write it…"

"You wanted more than that… Go ahead, say it… Until very recently, you thought that it would help you… How did you think it would help you?"

"I thought it would help me understand-…"

"-*Everything*… And therefore your *Self*…"

There was a moment of somber silence… The two characters felt this silence in what might be described as the very depths of their souls… They knew from this silence, that the hollow space they felt at this depth was the same within each of them… Within the silent void, they stared right through each other as if neither were there…

S looked through the figure as if there was nothing there, and felt as if there was nothing within S peering out either… The figure gazed through S with the same apparent sentiments… Then the silence was broken by what felt like the trembling of the whole-earth… Suddenly everything was there again; S, the figure, the surrounding spaces, etc, etc, etc...

"What was that?"

The figure responded as if at a complete loss...

"I don't know what that was..."

Then the figure broke the next subsequent silence..."

"What do you suppose you would do if you left here?"

S was reluctant to admit that there were no plans beyond escaping LT4, but S's reluctance quickly faded... It was strange for S to note how quickly this feeling lapsed, for S had always found inclinations towards the concealment of S's inner thoughts to prevail in social circumstances...

"There is nothing to suppose... Whatever is to occur will... When it does, I'll be left the same as always... To figure out what to make of it on my own..."

The figure rose from its seat, and began pacing back and forth in front of S, as S remained seated...

"So that's your great revelation... That whatever happens is for you alone... What about everyone-else, or *someone* else?"

The way this question was raised, S knew that there was a particular motive behind it...

"What do you want with me?"

This cut right through the core of the figure standing before S... Pacing became frozen, skin turned pale, the room appeared to have plummeted into arctic-temperatures, &c, &c, &c... The figure struggled to speak through seemingly frosted-lips...

"No one has ever made me feel this *cold*... *This cold*..."

S watched as the figure seemed to become lost in whatever it was that *this cold* might have been... Then the figure gathered composure for a moment before losing some of it again...

"I've felt what you wrote in that notebook all of my life... I just never knew how to express it... All I ever heard anyone else tell me, was that *we were all connected*, that *we were all one*, &c, &c, &c... Everyone and everything were only definable as all that I was not... I could only define my-selph, as what they were not... So, I couldn't define my-selph as anything, other than what wasn't, what I was not... Do you understand this?"

S understood very well what this figure had felt... An image from S's memory flashed vividly in S's mind... This image of S's memory seemed to be where this whole story began for S... The words of this beginning accompanied S's recollections, and escaped into the air...

"Staring into the oblivion that masquerades as the world around us, we see nothing..."

They both looked into each other's eyes, and saw their own reflections within them... S was compelled from the chair, and the two moved in close to each other... Before they could physically meet, the whole-earth seemed to shake yet again... This broke the momentum of the moment, and they halted, standing no more than a breath apart... The figure's breath softly cracked, verbally attempting to bridge the space between them...

"I know more about you, than you know of your self... If you'll allow me, I'll tell you all of it..."

"What do you mean by that?"

S could tell that there was something in the way of this space that seemed so empty between them...

"Your name according to your birth certificate is actually, *S*... It was the only letter that your parents were able to mark on the forms before they were interrupted... The doctors had identified you as having a special capacity based on the testing that used to be done according to guvornmint *wregulations*... According to the *llaws* of that time, the guvornmint reserved the *rite* to requisition children born with certain special-capacities in the interest of the greater-common-good... You were confiscated, and taken to be raised in a special-school..."

As S projected confusion, the figure reached into a pocket, producing forms that indicated this story's authenticity... S examined this evidence, and the figure continued to account for S's past...

"They managed to misplace some of the necessary information linking you to your parents, your identity, &c, &c, &c... This was actually embarrassingly common at the time, and there was no way to correct it... Instead they assigned numbers in place of identities, and denied any negligence/wrongdoing... Some of the *disidentified* were sent to be integrated into non-specialized educational-facilities, experimental educational-programs, &c, &c, &c..."

S broke in...

"So I was sent to one of these facilities, and there was another series of mishaps that further distorted my identity... How did you figure this out?"

"The guvornmints were all controlled/overseen by a higher institution... This institution functions in a manner that attempts to avoid interfering in a way that would allow the guvornmints to become aware of its existence... Part of this institution's methods of overseeing the guvornmints involves surveillance/espionage... Some of the institution's surveillance was centered on various identity-issues... It was determined that correcting these kinds of identity-errors were not worth the risks involved, but that surveillance should be maintained on displaced-entities such as your-self..."

"So you were eventually assigned to my surveillance..."

"Yes, but there's more to it than that... I volunteered especially for this task..."

"Why?"

"I don't know, or at least I didn't know then... You see, I was like you... I was also an unknown-entity... They decided that my profile would make me optimally-suited for this line of work... If anything should go wrong, I would be unable to prove who I was, or who they were... There was no risk for them..."

"That still doesn't explain why... Why this, and why me?"

"You were a high-priority case... With your aptitudes, they believed that you could have a great impact on the future... They wanted to ensure that they could manipulate this potential impact you might have... Being chosen to take this case came with a considerable amount of prestige within the institution, but-..."

"-But that wasn't the whole reason you volunteered specifically for my case..."

"No... I had already met you, in a sense anyway... You went to the same educational-facility that I did... I had always noticed you, but we had never actually met... Somehow you were a mystery to me even then... You were unlike anyone else... I think that because I felt so disjointed from everyone else, your apparent divergence resonated within me... That's as much of a reason as I can give..."

S looked at the figure as it stared imploringly into S's eyes... The figure was searching for something that it wanted to find in S... Its own reflection was not what the figure wanted to find, although it could be seen in the black of S's eyes, reflected back into the figure's view... Although S understood the figure's angst/yearning, it was impossible for S to requite these feelings...

"You've been trying all this time to understand your-self through me, and you're still trying... It isn't working though... As much as you want it to, it just doesn't work... No matter how much I or you might want to define our-selves by each other, it just doesn't work that way... Does it?"

The figure flung its-self around S, and they leaned against each other in this desperate embrace... They both cried at the harsh truth that they couldn't be diluted into denying... Their tears flowed into each other, and it was difficult to discern one's pain from the other's...

"What do you suppose you and I do then? Are you or I more of our-selves apart from each other, than we might be together?"

The figure's question burned like fire cutting into open wounds in both of them...

"You already know..."

"So you would really prefer to be what it is that you truly are... Are you sure you don't want to try something else... What if you're *Specious*?"

"If that is what I am... Then I'll be Specious..."

The tears ran dry, and a sense of resolution settled into them... Then the earth shook again, with much greater ferocity... S looked at the figure's eyes as they turned away... The figure procured the rest of S's possessions form the morphic-flooring... As S gathered the possessions and began exiting the secluded room, the figure asked once more...

"Are you sure this is what you want to do?"

S stopped, without looking back the words were separated from their source...

"I've never been sure... If..."

Without completing this thought, S proceeded forward, exiting the room, and leaving behind all the emptiness that was not S's own...

Words escaped from under the figure's breath, as S passed beyond the threshold of the doorway…

"Where are you going?"

There was no need to wonder…

$$301.20 \ldots \{\ldots\} \ldots$$

S was able to leave LT4 without any obstacles... The ECM followed S out of LT4, according to its own volition... It was never asked/revealed what the device this ECM had constructed from the components of the simularium might have been... This contraption was never seen, mentioned, or otherwise brought into S's mind, &c, &c, &c... There was no need to wonder...

There was also no real need for S to wander, but S continued to do so... With the ECM following behind, S drifted across the faces of the earth, searching for whatever there might be beyond S's own self... S sought to further understand how individuals were affected by the infinite expanse of other-entities, contexts, etc, etc, etc...

Sometime after S had been wandering the earth, the ECM was asked to give S the accounts of the events that transpired while S was present in LT4... As S examined these accounts, a new sense of understanding began to evolve in S's mind... S realized that the influence of repulsion had always been greater, than any force of attraction... In S's perpetual efforts to preserve the division of order that separated S's self from everything else, anything that S found attractive would eventually be cut-away...

In some respects, this was the way of things in general, S thought... Everything is divided, and the order of that division is an ever

changing symphony of chaotic shifts, breaks, harmonies, dis-
harmonies, &c, &c, &c... Inevitability, all things will collapse into
their essence as a result of their cause... All that is projected will
dissolve into the substance of its source...

What is there in all of this division other than collapse? There seems
to be more than just the perpetual decay/collapse... S thought, and
thought, and thought, &c, &c, &c...

Eventually, S began to wonder... If this world is no more than the
infinite orders of division; of all that is, amidst the oblivion of all that
is not, etc, etc, etc... With all that is perceived consisting of nothing
more than the projections of synchronizing patterns of these
divides... Then all of these projections exist not as true entities, but
as the effects of their properties of division... What then, are we as
beings? What am I, other than the result of what I am divided from,
divided *into*, &c, &c, &c?

If this is at all true, then whatever it is that I am, is only whatever I
might confine my self to be... Whatever I am not, will collapse into
the oblivion of all that is not... Whatever I truly am is the result of
my own division, and will inevitability collapse into the essence of
what it truly is... So whatever I chose to be, will in time become
whatever it truly is...

S continued in this manner of thinking for some time, as it was so
much the epitome of S's nature... Eventually, S thought of the three
impressions that had become such an integral part of S's perpetual
manner of attempting to define the course of life... Then a sense of
peace/understanding was found...

Where do I come from? What am I? Where am I going? There was
no need to wonder...

Somewhere in the midst of all S's contemplations, a network of
entities had been created... This network allowed these entities to
communicate over vast expanses of distance, without imposing on
each other, &c, &c, &c... The ECM that accompanied S was able to

access this network, and advised S of this network's potential... S acknowledged the ECM, and continued contemplating...

One night, the ECM announced to S that someone had been searching for S... S was informed that this was the same entity as the figure S had left in LT4... According to the ECM, the figure's name was *Solace*... The figure had carried that name all of its life, without it ever being revealed to another, single, solitary being... The ECM asked if S would like to send some response to the figure in search of S...

The ECM observed S's initial reaction as a silent pause, marked with a musing smirk, &c, &c, &c... Then S walked out to the edge of the nearby canyon, and looked out over the vast area extending far beyond the horizon, sight, &c, &c, &c... Standing before this infinite expanse of space/time, S's thoughts seemed to abound much further beyond this view...

As S stood facing all of this immensity, there was a strange semblance to the view that S had depicted at the beginning of this story... This perspective that S now had was of quite a different essence... Words ran through S's mind...

Staring into the infinite expanse that comprises the world beyond us, so much is unseen... Eyes gaze over the distant peaks and valleys that cut across the outer surfaces of this earth... Everything projects its own light unto everything else... The whole of existence is a great kaleidoscope, amidst the collapsing void of space... Hanging upon every surface, are the reflections/shadows of everything within the colliding-field of view... Reticently spellbound by the ever-changing surrounding-scene, the mind focuses not on that which appears before it, but much further, into the depths within... Our eyes are of both great and miniscule use to us in this view... Under star-cast skies, and within this darkness; our dreams illuminate these things... Gazing into the vastest depths of our world, as it is reflected back with our own images and shadows impressed upon its dream; we wonder... How is it we see so little?

Then the ECM watches as S's eyes appear to shift toward the night's sky, beholding a brightly reflective moon among the many stars...

On this night, under a sky that is perhaps as clear as it has ever been, S's eyes are seen to reflect this scene... Solace can suddenly be understood by S, and it is no longer relevant whether or not it should find S or not...

As the light of another day begins to break over the horizon, everything concealed in the darkness becomes separated unto its own lineaments, and S looks out over all that such eyes can see... Though as long as S stands within the light, shadows will be cast and reflections will be projected... Though the sun will set behind S, and cast shadows all around... Only the wonder of this division is of any concern to S in this view... As S continues to ponder whatever it is that one does, a response is projected as if unto the projections of every individual thing... The words echo from all that is so infinitely divided, dispersed, detached, etc, etc, etc...

"Welcome to the divide..."

...

...

ABOUT THE AUTHOR

.S.P. Daley is the pen-name adopted by Philip A. Daley. The **.** in front of the initials is intended to function as a stop, preventing anything that might precede this name from going into it. It is an incidental fact that this places a total of three *dots* within the pen-name, and might be understood to create a set of broken ellipses. Abbreviating the pen-name is intended to symbolize that whatever is done under this name, is not all that there is to the entity associated with it. The *P* may be understood as an abbreviation of Phil. As for the *S*...

Phil Daley was born in 1983, and has been hiding ever since... In preparation for this project, he spent time in the Kansas Air National Guard, various security companies, oblivion &c, &c, &c... This project is essentially a warped simulation of the author's imaginings, impressions, &c, &c, &c... For more about the author and his other projects, please visit his YouTube channel @ Welcome2theDivide, or his Facebook page @ www.facebook.com/Schizoid4Life, etc, etc, etc... His email address is phildaley45@hotmail.com

...